MW01234431

THE SILENT
FRATERNITY

CODE OF SILENCE

...but not a card-carrying member

A NOVEL

TRISTEN A. TAYLOR

PAGE PUBLISHING, INC.
Conneaut Lake, PA

First originally published by Page Publishing 2021

All scripture quotations, unless indicated, are taken from *The Holy Bible, Authorized King James Version – Dictionary and Study Helps.* Copyright 1989 by World Bible Publishers, Inc. Printed in the United States of America.

Cover Image, Coat of Arms (copyright) by Tristen A. Taylor. All rights reserved.

ISBN 978-1-6624-5161-4 (pbk)
ISBN 978-1-6624-5175-1 (hc)
ISBN 978-1-6624-5162-1 (digital)

Printed in the United States of America

Dear Friends,

GOD is Love.
GOD loves you and HE always will.
HE loved you yesterday. HE loves you today.
And HE will love you tomorrow and forevermore.
No matter your situation,
No matter what you have done in the past,
No matter what others might think of you or say about you,
Don't ever allow anyone to tell you otherwise.
Depend on HIM daily for everything.
And pray daily.
Praying to GOD is just like having a conversation with HIM.
Just talk to HIM.
HE is always listening, even when you think HE is not.

CONTENTS

ACKNOWLEDGMENTS

SPECIAL THANKS TO those people who have supported me throughout this journey.

And to those who provided me with the inspiration to continue this body of work.

I must also thank all of you who have taken the time to read this book whether you bought this book, received it as a gift, borrowed it, or checked it out at the library. It means so much to me.

Sometimes I wonder if I had a chance to repeat my childhood, would I change much. I am sure that I would change some things about my circumstances, but I know for sure I would not change my relationship with my family. My challenging childhood created character.

AUTHOR'S NOTE

THIS IS A work of fiction. Any references to real people, living or dead, actual events, or real locales are intended only to give the novel a sense of reality and authenticity. Other names, characters, businesses, organizations, places, events, and incidents are either the product of the author's imagination or are used fictitiously, and their resemblance, if any, to real-life counterparts, is entirely coincidental. (Some of the issues in this book are real, but the people and organizations are not.)

PROLOGUE

TIME MAKES TIME for everything. Everyone has his time. Men only respond to three main things: pain, consequence, and reward. Many have had their rewards for many years. Now it's time to experience the other two.

We must live and act within a framework of time. We cannot always understand why things happen when they do or the way they fail to happen when we think they should. It is not very important that we know the place and time of such a happening, but in most cases that it is possible.

A Time for Everything

To everything there is a season,
A time for every purpose under heaven:
A time to be born,
    And a time to die;
A time to plant,
    And a time to pluck what is planted;
A time to kill,
    And a time to heal;
A time to break down,
    And a time to build up;
A time to weep,
    And a time to laugh;
A time to mourn,
    And a time to dance;
A time to cast away stones,
    And a time to gather stones;
A time to embrace,
    And a time to refrain from embracing;
A time to gain,
    And a time to lose;

A time to keep,
And a time to throw away;
A time to tear,
And a time to sew;
A time to keep silence,
And a time to speak;
A time to love,
And a time to hate;
A time of war,
And a time of peace.

—Ecclesiastes 3:1–8,
THE HOLY BIBLE
The New King James Version

A SECRET FRATERNITY

The Members Of The Silent Fraternity

We share a secret, the unmentionable, the unspeakable...

The Silent Fraternity, a secret fraternity. It has a double meaning. The life but not the lifestyle. We are "of the life but not in the life." We share an unbreakable bond; we are closer than most biological brothers. Closer than most fraternal brothers, but we are not card-carrying members. We share a brotherhood of brotherly love. A bromance. We share codes of silence and secrets. Although we have thick skin, we suffer a grave internal void, being ostracized by the place in which all should find comfort. We play major roles in sustaining the Black Church. We dedicate our lives to the church and not just in the choir. We hold highly visible positions as board members, church officers, and administrators. We are elders, deacons, fund-raisers, grant writers, program organizers, and committee leaders. The contemporary Black Christian Church would fall apart without us, guys like us. So why do so many of them reject us, chastise us, and try to change us.?

THE "G" MEN
DEXTER B. CAVANAUGH III
LISBORN TAYLOR
EMERSON CARTWRIGHT III
CHANDLER "CHANCE" JAMESON
PARKER DUNWOODY
PATRICK McINTYRE

Our constant struggle with self-identity.
Understand me.
Respect me.
Accept me.
Don't limit me.

THE SILENT FRATERNITY

Coat Of Arms

THE COAT OF Arms is a symbol that represents our unbreakable bond, the love of brotherhood. It masks the very essence of who we are as we cope with our seemingly endless internal struggle with self-identity. Although not visible for all to see, we wear it daily in the midst of our yearning for unconditional love from those we care about. It is a beacon of hope that one day we will no longer be ostracized by those we love—the most.

Our Creed

Love of man and humanity, friendship and brotherhood, faith, justice, loyalty, and uncompromising secrecy. We have learned from the past. We live in the present. We thrive on the hope of the future.

A Description of the Coat of Arms

Colors

Black signifies the internal long-suffering and the grief that is invisibly seen.

Gold signifies the unyielding faith and the search for wisdom.

White signifies the search for truth and peace.

Red signifies strength and magnanimity (noble in mind, high-souled, rising above pettiness or meanness, generous in overlooking insults, although occasionally bouts occur in which we fall from grace and allow the carnal self to personally defend and attack those who initiate a threat to us).

Purple signifies justice and temperance (moderation in one's actions; self-restraint in conduct; regardless of the situation, we try to act and react with class).

Parts of the Coat of Arms

Top banner—floating above the crest, it bears our unspoken mantra: *Code of Silence.*

Crest—affixed (but not actually attached) at the apex of the helmet, the fleur-de-lis is the golden heraldic figure that symbolizes our belief that there is a higher power, a celestial entity that is something above us, something greater than us, something outside of us that truly controls our destiny. Although we are given the right of choice.

Top mantle—the ornate plumage cloaks the top and the sides of the helmet, adding another layer of protection allowing us to wear a *false face* without easy detection.

Helmet—attached to the top mantle is the helmet, the rigid protective headgear that covers and protects the most fragile and the most important part of *the body envelope.* The helmet is also adorned with three additional accented plumes—purple, gold, and red, which signify *justice, faith, and strength* respectively.

Shield—the abstract heart-shaped centerpiece of our treasured symbol is commonly used to guard, protect, defend, and provide solace, thus allowing us to express the essence of that in which we embody, *love.*

Shield supporter—although a subordinate component to the shield, which connects to the top mantle, this sturdy viable appendage stands on either side of the shield. The supporting structure is designed to support as well as strengthen the shield. The elaborate decorative pair of components symbolizes *confidence and courage.*

Shield layout (charges on the shield)—the crown is the source of our unwavering *faith* that *the Prince of Peace* loves us in spite of ourselves; our continued growth in *strength* and our never-ending journey to seek the *truth* of HIS will for our lives. The cross is also a reminder of the ultimate sacrifice that HE made for us. Yet the double swords signify that if we allow HIM, GOD assigns guardian angels to each of us to fight our battles. The symbols in the shield layout represent our daily morning mantra: "Nothing is going to happen to me today that GOD and I cannot handle together."

Bottom banner—the underside pennant below the shield displays our most valued character traits—*justice, faith, and strength* respectively. The same as the mentioned accented plumes on the helmet.

No one should ever die feeling that he is not or was not loved. And one of the worst things in life is to experience the sudden death of someone and not have the opportunity to say goodbye, always wondering if they knew how much you cared about them, how much you valued their friendship, and how much you truly loved them. That feeling leaves a large hole in the heart of those left behind.

CHAPTER 1

The Broken Circle

Why do we take the sun's warmth for granted and why do we take THE SON'S warmth for granted?

FRIENDS AND FAMILY had just left the cemetery. However, several of Patrick's closest friends desperately wanted to say their own private and final goodbyes to him before they lowered his body into the ground. Without hesitation, the family graciously agreed, allowing his long-time buddies to have a brief but separate farewell moment.

Patrick was one who lived his life to the fullest. He was a young man who passed away with so many unfulfilled dreams. It might be true what they say about the cemetery being the richest place on earth. The soil is so rich. It is filled with so many wonderful talents, unused talents. It is filled with so many priceless and valuable dreams. Dreams that will never be fulfilled. Wishes that will never see the light of day. Goals that will never be realized.

About ten minutes after the last family member had left, a slow procession of all black vehicles with dark tinted windows drove up: three stretch limos, a convertible Bentley, a Maserati, a convertible SL 650 Mercedes, a Porsche Panorama Sedan, a Limited Edition BMW 870 Sedan, and a black custom-designed Range Rover. The scene seemed choreographed in slow motion as each car opened at the exact same moment. Twelve well-dressed young African-American men exited the vehicles. Immediately, the men greeted each other with handshakes and heartfelt hugs.

The men were dressed in black custom suits and high-end designer shoes. As the ole saying goes, these guys were "dressed to kill." Each man's monochromatic ensemble was accented with a black-and-white paisley silk ascot, black fitted silk gloves, and black armbands on their right arms. Together, these bruthas were fitted with enough understated bling-bling to fund two four-year degrees at Harvard. It was obvious that these guys were successful. They looked like they either came from money or undoubtedly had their own. These bruthas definitely had major swag.

Soon after the small assembly of guys welcomed each other, they began to slowly walk in a single-file line toward the final resting place of their departed friend. The posture, the stance and the stride of each young man exuded a sense of self-confidence. They eventually approached the carpeted tent. However, no one wanted to sit. They stood in a circle around the mahogany and gold-plated casket. There was absolute silence for several minutes. One could only hear the tweeting of the birds in the nearby distance. No one said anything. Seemingly staring in space, their facial expressions barely changed.

As the cemetery workers walked toward the tent to begin the process of lowering the casket, one of the men said in a loud voice, "Wait! Wait! Please wait a few more minutes!" The workers looked at the minister for approval. The minister nodded, signifying yes. Then the workers walked away.

Not sure if he was really needed, the minister took a step back and continued to observe them a few more minutes. He eventually took another step backward and slowly turned to walk away. Only a few steps from the tent, the minister looked over his shoulder and took one last glimpse at the solemn group of mourners. Of course, the twelve sorrowful young men were still standing there, saying nothing, still staring in space.

The minister soon returned. "I know that you are grieving, but can I help. Is there anything I can do to help?"

Suddenly, one man called out to the minister. "Please read Psalm 23. I got up this morning needing to hear Psalm 23. I thought they always read that chapter at funerals. Would you please read it now?"

The minister obliged the young mourner. He began to read, "The LORD is my shepherd; I shall not want..." As the minister continued to read, the blank stares of all the young men gradually turned into smiles. Cold expressions grew warm. Indifferent hostility turned into friendly nods.

The minister continued, "Yeah, though I walk through the valley of the shadow of death; I will fear no evil; for thou are with me…"

No sooner than the minister finished, somebody else said, "Please! Please read Psalm 27."

The minister continued to read, "The LORD is my light and my salvation, whom shall I fear…" The guys continued nodding.

The minister continued to read further, "The LORD is the strength of my life; of whom shall I be afraid."

Someone asked, "How about verse 10?"

"When my father and mother forsake me, then the LORD will take me up?"

Then another yelled, "How about Psalm 34?"

As soon as the minister finished that one, someone wanted Psalm 27. Then another wanted Psalm 46. Then 51.

These men appeared to have it all together, on the outside, that is. But at that moment, these men were hungry for the love and acceptance for the Word of GOD and the love of GOD. And most of them knew that they could not get that love at most churches, especially in the traditional conservative Black Churches. And most of the contemporary Black Christian Churches were not much different. These young men definitely couldn't get it from most of their family members or from the majority of their friends either. Most churches, families, and friends are too busy being *culturally holy* to be Christ-like-loving and Christ-like-helpful.

Then someone wanted Psalm 90. Someone else requested Psalm 91. This went on for almost an hour. They stayed there *having church* around that gravesite, at their close friend's final resting place. Well at their friend's final resting place on earth, that is. What irony. It took a sad occasion like this for these young men to experience something that they had been yearning for most of their lives.

Then one of the men asked specifically for a verse from Romans. He said, "I have to hear it, I desperately need to hear it. It's about GOD's love; a love greater than your love or my love." He reiterated, "Please read Romans chapter 11, verses 35 through 39."

Just picture it, these men, ostracized by the Black Christian Church, put down by the saints, put out by those holier-than-thou church members, and put up with by their insensitive family members.

These men had fine homes, expensive clothes and jewelry, exotic cars, promising and successful careers, and bright futures. Some had even traveled internationally. They were on top of the world. But those things really didn't matter as much as trying to fill the void in their lives, the love and acceptance from the Black Church. This obviously visible feeling of yearning left a huge hole in their hearts.

See them standing there; in this isolated cemetery feeling the love of GOD. That someone loved them in spite of themselves, for themselves. Again, what overwhelming irony.

The minister noticed that the tone of the service had suddenly changed. As he continued, one of the young men interrupted.

> Who shall separate us from the love of Christ?
> Church folk.
> Saved folk.
> Narrow-minded folk.
> Closed-minded folk.
> Homophobes.
> Ho-mongers.
> Hoe-hoppers.
> Who?

Another continued,

> Who or what shall separate us from the love of
> Christ?
> Shall tribulation,
> or distress,
> or persecution,
> or famine,
> or nakedness,
> or peril,

or sword?

Then another continued,

> For I am persuaded that nothing shall separate
> me.
> Neither death
> nor life,
> nor angels,
> nor principalities,
> nor powers,
> nor things,
> nor things to come,
> nor height,
> nor depth,
> nor any other creature—NOTHING or NO
> ONE!

The minister felt increasing aggression and frustration coming from these young proud yet scorned African-American men. An attitude much different from when they originally approached the gravesite. The aggression and frustration soon grew into a subtle level of anger.

Then another man continued,

> Not who I am, not who they say I am.
> Not their opinion of me or my impression of
> myself.
> NOTHING!
> NOTHING!
> NOTHING!
> Nothing shall separate me from the love of Jesus
> Christ!

Another continued,

They don't sit high enough to see low enough.
To dare.
To pressure.
Or to judge another one of GOD's children.
Aren't we GOD's children too?

Another continued,

Why! Why! Why!
But why do they judge us so harshly.
Most of us have dedicated our lives to the church.

In all his years as a pastor, the minister had never seen anything like this. He stepped forward. "Young men, I feel your pain. Those who have judged you. Those who have ostracized you. And those who have defamed you need to examine themselves and throw themselves on the mercy of heaven's court and ask GOD to have mercy on their souls."

The minister left a few moments later. The cemetery workers approached again and stopped for a moment just outside the tent.

The twelve young men gathered closer around the casket and bowed their heads. As a group, they all said in unison, "Goodbye, my brutha. We will miss you. We will never forget you. We will always cherish the good times and great memories. You will always be in our hearts. We will meet again. We love you. Take care. May peace be with you."

Then one of the most visibly heartbroken young men walked closer to the casket, leaned over, placed his hands at the top end where the deceased's head would be, kissed it, and said in a low mournful voice, "My friend, my dear brother. I don't understand how this happened. I will find out who did this. I won't rest until I find out why this happened. You didn't deserve this. I love you, man. This is not goodbye but until I see you again."

Just before the committal service was performed, the funeral director stepped under the tent, carrying a large white box filled with long-stemmed white roses. Each flower was individually tied with a black silk ribbon and gold tassel. He approached each mourner and handed each one of them their special token of their brotherly love. Then each man took a step forward in unison, placed the white rose on the casket, and stepped back. Before the funeral director left the tent, he said in a low voice, "I hope that as every year passes, your grief will weaken."

As the workers placed the casket in the vault and securely attached the vault cover, each of the twelve men threw a handful of white rose petals on top of the vault. This passionate display by these men had a much deeper and intense meaning that it had appeared. Even the cemetery workers were crying, an action rarely seen.

As the casket was lowered, the men began to sob vigorously. Then each man turned and gave each other another warm embrace. They slowly walked to their respective vehicles and resumed the slow procession until they left the cemetery.

These men had a secret, and from their reactions and overt display of emotions, the minister soon knew what it was.

The minister returned to the cemetery an hour later as the workers had just finished arranging the flowers over the covered grave. Because he was a close friend of the family, he wanted to make sure that all was okay after the twelve young men had left. He pulled up behind a black limo. The driver was leaning on the front passenger door with his arms crossed, noticeably in deep thought. He got out and approached the tall muscular man dressed in a black suit and tie with black sunglasses. The minister noticed another gentleman standing at Patrick's gravesite, holding a single red rose in hand.

"Hello," said the minister. The man did not respond. "Excuse me."

"Oh! Hello, Pastor."

"Hello, again. I guess you were in deep thought. But are you with the gentleman over there?"

"Forgive me. I was not intentionally ignoring you. And yes, I am. He is my employer. He did not want to attend the funeral because he would have caused too much unnecessary attention."

"He looks very familiar. Who is he?"

"I would rather not say. And I would really appreciate it if you would just allow him to have his last few moments with the newly departed by himself."

"Are you sure he wants to be alone? In times like this, people say that however, they really need a shoulder or support."

"No disrespect, Pastor, but yes, I am sure. That's why he waited until everyone left. We tried to be inconspicuous and watched you and the twelve men a little over an hour ago. That was something else. It really touched my heart. But again, he really wants to be alone. For personal reasons, he really needs this."

"Okay, I guess I can respect his wishes."

"And, Pastor, please don't mention to anyone not even the family that we were here. Can you promise that?

"Well, I really don't promise such things. But in this case, I will keep my word that I will keep this information confidential."

The minister turned and walked back to his car. As soon as he started his car, he glanced one last time at the last mourner. The mysterious man suddenly fell to his knees, crying uncontrollably. Knowing how the minister would probably react, the driver quickly walked toward the minister's car and waved signaling the minister not to get out. "He is okay. He will be fine." The minister wasn't sure if he should leave. He paused for a moment and eventually drove off.

CHAPTER 2

Shaking My Faith

A buddy is like always having a dollar in my pocket. A good friend is like having a million dollars in the bank. True friendship is priceless.

BURYING ONE OF my best friends was one of the most difficult, stressful, and most painful things I have ever done. My name is Dexter B. Cavanaugh III and Patrick McIntyre was my brother in Christ; my confidant and a major part of my support system.

I met Patrick over ten years ago, a few months after I moved to Atlanta. Shortly after we met, my grandmother transitioned. He was always there for moral support. Three months later, Patrick took me out to dinner for my birthday. The next day my great-grandmother transitioned. She was like a second mother to me. Once again, Patrick was right by my side. Ten days after that, my godmother transitioned. As always, Patrick was there for emotional support. It seemed as though for the next several months, we were joined at the hip. He became my sounding board. I could have never repaid him for the love and support he gave me during those mournful times. His laid-back persona allowed me to be free to express various moments of unbearable grief during those tumultuous months. His nurturing spirit, accompanied by a few months of grief therapy, eventually changed my feelings from despair to hope and acceptance. One of his most valued qualities I treasured the most was the fact that he quickly learned how to deal with my quirks and anal-retentive idiosyncrasies. I was well aware that I had one hundred and one issues. I often compared our friendship to that like Jonathan and David in the Bible. It was based on five simple principles: our mutual belief in and love of GOD, humility toward one another, mutual respect, selfless love, and a genuine commitment to support one another when needed. Several months later, after we had unintentionally begun to form the building blocks of a lasting brotherly relationship, he became my part-time admin assistant, my right-hand man. It was actually a win-win situation for the both of us. He needed a job and I desperately needed someone like him. We had a great rapport. He was actually partially responsible for the current success of my career.

Before we met, I had a serious attitude problem. Being a self-centered egomaniac, I was a typical angry Black man who was married to his career, one who was diligently trying to climb the corporate ladder but met various obstacles. But my supportive friendship with Patrick completely changed my perspective. He knew how to handle me. He taught me to be more patient, to slow down, to learn to relax, to reduce stress, to balance work and play, and to enjoy time with family and friends. Regarding the way I resolved my issues, his mantra emphasized that I review it then relax, relate, and release. It included taking the emotion out of the situation, then simply trying to take a step back and review it. It also included relaxing my mind and body as well as taking my mind off the problem for a while. And lastly, it included releasing the negative energy in order to begin to rationalize and think clearly. He also persuaded me to focus on choosing my battles carefully. Most importantly, my close friendship taught me how to walk away from unhealthy situations and negative people.

Patrick was my ray of sunshine and the godsend that surrounded me. He definitely changed my life, for the better. From the first day that we met, our spirits had seemed to connect. A few years later when I finished law school, I moved to Chicago. I accepted a position with a prominent firm as a corporate attorney. Five years later, I moved back to Atlanta to start my private practice. My buddy assisted me in building a successful legal practice. Patrick served as my office manager for the next year. As my practice quickly prospered, Patrick became motivated to prepare and apply to law school. He eventually left my firm with my blessing. I even helped him prepare for the state bar exam.

Over the next few years, our careers and our hectic schedules began to dominate our lives. After Patrick joined the legal department of a large bank in Atlanta, we did not talk or see each other very often. And although I was not a member of his immediate circle of friends, there were numerous occasions in which we would think of each other and one of us would call the other. He often called us kindred spirits. One day shortly before he became ill, I was home watching TV. A scene on a TV show reminded me of him. A few hours later, he called. He stated that he was watching a story on TV, a study that Koreans have found a simple way to reduce stress. We chatted briefly. I asked him jokingly how he knew that I was allowing work and family problems to stress me out. He replied, "I just knew. You have been on my mind the last few days. I just felt it. My spirit felt your spirit. We are connected. You are my brother in Christ."

A few days later, I received an urgent call that Patrick was in the intensive care unit at Peachtree Memorial Hospital. I wasn't given any details, but I was told that his condition was critical. My heart felt heavy. I could not focus. I could not work. I immediately cancelled all my appointments for the rest of the day and prepared to go to the hospital. I was on a mission, a mission to see my best buddy. When I arrived at the ICU waiting room, I noticed that the visiting hours had ended over twenty minutes ago. But surprisingly, I was met with no opposition. The LORD was on my side. I picked up the phone anyway and told the nurse that I needed to see Patrick McIntyre. She came to the door and pointed to the sign that stated the visiting hours. Then she asked me my name. Of course, I was not a family member. I desperately wanted to lie and tell her that I was his brother, but he was the only child. Noticing the obvious extreme pain on my face, she paused for a moment, smiled, then opened the door and led me to his room. What a relief. I was not aware that Patrick's mother had ordered strict and limited visitation only to the immediate family. I didn't care. Time was of the essence. I desperately needed to see him. I had recently learned and often expressed over the last few years that one of the worst feelings in the world is when you never get a chance to tell someone how much they mean to you, and then they die. Or you never get a chance to say goodbye before they take their last breath and close their eyes.

When I walked into his room, I was in shock. I couldn't believe my eyes. This was not my energetic buddy who lived life to the fullest. He was just lying there, lifeless, motionless, eyes closed as though he was asleep. But there were so many beeping machines and monitors. He also had breathing tubes and a feeding tube.

I came over to the right side of the bed and held his hand.

"Hey, buddy, I am here," I told him.

"I am not sure if you can hear me, but I want you to know that I love you and I want you to fight."

After that, I did not know what else to say. So, I just began to reminisce about our friendship over the last several years. Some of the memories made me smile and some of them made me cry. I told him how much I loved him over and over again and how much he meant to me over the years. Then all of a sudden, he twitched. Then I thought I saw him kick his foot. I thought I was seeing things. I continued to share more of our heartfelt past memories. Then I saw his foot move again. Was this a sign? I told him that I was sorry that I did not tell him more often what he meant to me. Then to my amazement, he appeared to rise up although he was still unconscious. Was he trying to communicate with me? Was he trying to tell me something? I kinda thought that it might be just muscle spasms or probably reflexes. When the nurse came in to check his vitals and read the monitors, I asked her if he could hear me. She replied that he was in an induced coma. There was little brain activity and she was not sure. She also stated that it would not hurt to talk to him. The continued reminiscing was good for me too. So, I did, for an hour and a half.

 I visited him every day for the next three days, at 8:30 p.m. sharp. Each time I was met with absolutely no opposition. His condition was still the same. As usual, I stood beside his bed holding his hand, sometimes tightly, sometimes gently. I continued to tell him how much I loved him. I pleaded with him to fight, to hold on. I didn't want him to let go. I didn't want him to give up. Maybe I was selfish; I didn't care. I needed him. I wanted him to fight for life. My buddy had so many dreams unfulfilled. He had so much to live for, so much more to contribute to the world.

On the morning of the fifth day, I decided not to go to the office, because my heart felt much heavier than it had the last several days. The sadness increased to periodic moments of severe crying. This was not like me. I was always in control of my emotions. At first, I was not sure what I was really feeling. Then it hit me. I knew our spirits were connecting. I called our mutual friend David and my sister. I told them, that somehow, I knew that either he was fighting for life or that he was slipping away. That evening I received the news that he was not improving. Then I knew he was slipping away and that GOD was calling him home. I rushed to the hospital. The ICU waiting room was full of his friends. We patiently waited for an update. Finally, his mother gave the doctor permission to give us a status.

"We have done all we can do." The doctor stated that his condition had not changed and there was a 95 percent probability that it would not change. The doctor also stated that his mother had given the approval to disconnect the life-support systems. Everyone burst into tears.

"LORD, give me strength," I said in a low murmur and dropped in my seat. "LORD, LORD, help me, please help me."

About two hours later, the doctor came back to the waiting room. He shook his head and said, "I'm sorry, I'm truly sorry, but he is gone."

But I didn't get a chance to say goodbye. I wondered if he heard me during my visits over the past four days. After I calmed down, I waited a few minutes then I went to the rear exit of the hospital. I waited outside for over two hours until the funeral director came to pick up the body. A hearse finally pulled up, and I asked the driver if he was there to pick up Patrick McIntyre. He stated that he could not give me that information. Thirty minutes later, he returned and Patrick's mother followed. I waited by the rear of the hearse and touched him one last time before they closed the door. I was still determined to say my goodbye.

"Goodbye, my dear brutha. May you be at peace. I love you."

As the vehicle drove off, I stood there in a daze. I don't even remember driving home but somehow, I got there safely.

I took off a few days off and took advantage of a few of my bereavement days. Although bereavement days are usually only granted to the immediate family members, it was my company so I allotted myself that privilege. I needed some quiet time, some quiet time with just me and the LORD. I prayed and prayed the first night. I asked the LORD to help me. But of course, praying didn't help right away. I wasn't just sad; I was in excruciating emotional pain. I hadn't felt that way since my great-grandmother passed away. And I didn't want to think about what I had learned in church about what happen to someone when he dies. I didn't want to be rational. I wanted to mourn in my own way.

After a few days, reality was beginning to set in. My buddy was gone. I finally had to accept that GOD heals in various ways, sometimes through doctors, nurses, and modern medicine and sometimes through an unexplained healing, a miracle. But HE chose the third option for Patrick. HE decided to take away all the pain by calling him "home." As hard as it was to accept, I had to trust my GOD and HIS decision. I decided to give myself an indefinite amount of time to deal with my pain and cope with my loss. I learned later that sometimes GOD allows things to happen to shed light on a bigger picture.

Patrick had a heart of gold. I supported him in so many ways; his hopes, his dreams, his business endeavors, and his adventures. I truly wanted him to be happy, and I wanted the best for him. But there was one issue regarding his personal life, one thing that bothered me. I felt that he was cheating himself. He was involved with someone, someone that I didn't approve of, a relationship that caused him so much pain. He was trapped. Patrick was involved with a prominent local minister, a married but separated man who was almost twice his age.

Although Patrick was closer than a brother, I just could not accept that torrid, heartbreaking one-sided relationship. That man would never be able to give all himself to Patrick. That was not fair. That relationship even cost him his position as a leader in his church. But because I wanted to support my buddy and because he was an adult, I tried not to judge him, criticize him, or chastise him. He really thought he was happy in that three-year relationship. He knew how I felt, but he also knew that my love for him allowed me to respect his decisions regarding his personal life.

Within the African-American community, Black men have been falsely stereotyped as having one or more of several dysfunctional characteristics, personal flaws that stigmatize them, sometimes preventing their financial, emotional and spiritual growth. They are often accused of suffering from one or more of *the seven sins of the Black man*.

- He is a mama's boy; he can't develop or sustain a long-term relationship because of his codependent relationship with his mother. And he constantly compares others to her.
- He is afraid of relationship commitment; it would require diligence and a grave level of responsibility.
- He is a bad father and a dead-beat dad. He doesn't financially support his children. In many instances, he deliberately avoids paying child support if he does not have a healthy relationship with the child's mother.
- He can't keep a job, and he is lazy.
- He has bad credit, and he has no money.
- He has been arrested or has a prison record.
- He is a homosexual, bisexual, or on the down low.

And my best buddy dealt with two of these issues. Being a mama's boy was fine. But I had a problem with how he handled one of the other issues. It was destructive. It resulted in bouts of drinking and caused severe levels of depression. The depression of course, was an indirect result of how he dealt with *the seventh sin.*

The seventh sin has the worst stigma attached to it. Yeah, it looks like things are changing. Just look at some of the recent TV shows and movies. But that's not real. His family members, his friends and much of the Black Church will accept and deal with all of the other bad habits and negative behavior but not if it involves an alternative sexual lifestyle.

There is a difference between being gay and being homosexual or bisexual. One is a lifestyle and the other is an internal psyche. Not all homosexuals or bisexuals live a gay lifestyle. Most African-American homosexual men hide their homosexuality. They don't wear their sexuality on their sleeve. Whether they are fake hardcore gangsta rappers, hip-hop moguls, sports stars, athletes with multimillion-dollar endorsements, celebrities, teachers, executives, blue-collar workers, politicians, or prominent ministers. They have too much to lose. And it's not about the money, not even close. It's all about protecting their level of status in their careers, their reputations, their public images. They care too much about what others think.

Patrick was involved in an underworld in which many African-American ministers live a life of hypocrisy and deception. In many cases, many of these men of GOD don't practice what they preach. They preach that homosexuality is a sin, the worst kind of sin. An abomination. Many who emphasize the demonic spiritual behavior regarding the practice of homosexuality; actually, live secret bisexual or homosexual lifestyles themselves. And unfortunately, sometimes the best-kept secrets are disguised in open view, but the secrets are often camouflaged to appear as something else as mentoring relationships or as assistants to the pastor. Clever idea, isn't it. And no one questions it. This type of façade has been perpetrated in the Black Church for decades. It's so ironic how some of the ministers have even pressured gay and bisexual members to seek counseling while others have created homosexual deliverance ministries in their churches in hope to cast out the so-called evil spirits. Others have pressured gay and bisexual parishioners to get married and have children, hoping it will change them.

All the while, they are living the same lives in which they preach is wrong, cruising areas of town widely known for gay prostitutes, soliciting male prostitutes and hustlers who advertise themselves as models and private masseurs. They frequent the gay chat lines and mobile apps for sex hookups. But of course, they don't disclose who they are or their position in the community.

So why are they not questioned? And why are they allowed to continue this devious behavior. Apparently, most people only see what they want to see. Or is it that these men and their lifestyles are not detected because most are married with children?

CHAPTER 3

The Unmentionable

Adoption is a conscious decision to make some-one a part of a family. It creates a new relationship that entitles the adopted person to all the rights and privileges that belongs to a biological child. Jesus Christ is the Son of the Almighty GOD, Jehovah. When Jesus died on the cross, HE reestablished our relationship with the heavenly Father. As believers, we have been adopted into GOD's family. From GOD's perspective, adoption mean we are chosen, accepted, valued, loved, justified, made righteous, and above all, saved through faith in Jesus Christ.

GOD doesn't have any stepchildren. HE doesn't have any favorites either. Although like most parents, when a child is in crisis, HE gives that child a little more attention. But that doesn't mean HE loves the others any less.

GOD definitely didn't make any mistakes.

My GOD is a respecter of the soul.

MEMORIAL DAY WEEKEND is a little different this year. My heart is heavy. I buried my best friend today. He simply slipped away. I wasn't ready for that. This melancholy holiday celebration has brought together so many loved ones and close friends, bruthas that I have not seen in a while. Reminiscing about the good times with the recent passing of my closest cohort only helped a little. Although the sun shined brightly, huge dark clouds hovered above us. And I am sure that a nebulous cloak will linger over us for several more weeks; if not several more months.

The repast was held in the family life center at Temple of Faith Christian Center, his mother's church. My buddy was truly loved. The funeral service had standing room only. The main sanctuary seats about five thousand, and that's not including the balcony. And it looks like over a thousand people showed up to fellowship after the burial. Shortly after I arrived and spoke to the family and got something to drink, I overheard Minister Calloway and Deacon McKenzie talking about Patrick. His body was barely cold and yet the gossip had already started. The audacity of them.

Patrick McIntyre was my ace boon coon. Yes, I respected their ministerial positions in the church, but hell no. I just could not and would not be silent and allow this scrutiny, the defamation of a good man, a faithful parishioner who devoted much of his life to the Black Church, specifically to the parent church of this church. It was bad enough that Patrick, the former Director of Finance of his former church, could not be eulogized at the house of worship in which he spent seven years as a dedicated and loyal member. Well, until he was pressured and forced to leave. Uh-uh! Hell no!

So, I did what any loyal best friend would do in that situation. I interrupted the two men. I tapped one of them on the shoulder and asked to speak with them. Like Job, I am not at rest. And I will not be quiet.

"Wait a minute, just wait a cotton-pickin' minute! Patrick just died! But who else died and made you judges! Damn hypocrites!"

"Watch your mouth! Young man, who do you think you are talking to."

"Who the hell do think I am talking to? Maybe I am talking to the old white lady across the room wearing the big white hat. No, I am talking to you."

"Well, I guess you were eavesdropping on our conversation. Didn't your mama teach you better? And who are you anyway? Oh, I assume, you knew the deceased."

"Don't worry about who I am, but I definitely am well aware who you two are. The real issue is why you are judging my dear friend. We just buried him a few hours ago. What gives you that right?"

"Control yourself, little boy. Don't let this preacher collar fool you. Now I know that you are upset and that is understandable. But don't get stupid up in here."

"Minister Calloway."

"Apparently, you know of me."

"Something like that. But it's your reputation that precedes you. You are a married man with four children. And don't you have not one but two illegitimate children by the same married parishioner who was also an administrative staff employee of the church? And once it was publicly disclosed a few months ago that you were the father, she left this church. It was also rumored that she had recently left because she had filed a sexual harassment suit against you and the church.

"And as for you, Deacon McKenzie, you are married too. It is a documented fact that you have been arrested and convicted of drunk driving not only once but twice. And what about your recent arrest and conviction of soliciting a prostitute. And the prostitute was dis-covered to be a transvestite.

"So, it's obvious that you two don't walk on water. So why are you throwing stones when you two obviously don't live in glass houses? What gives you two the right to judge anyone? Hypocrites! You sound like the holier-than-thou, judgmental pharisees. And why have you been able to keep your positions in this church? Does GOD still love you? Has HE forgiven you? Or are you going to hell for your sins?"

"Don't be blasphemous. And don't forget where you are."

"Oh, believe me. I am well aware of where I am."

"Then show some respect and calm down."

"News flash, gentlemen. Jesus loves Patrick. Jesus loves me. But why does this church as well as his former church have such issues accepting us, embracing and loving us or even a part of us? Why does this church have such problems with us? Growing up, I always thought that the church was the safest place on earth. Why is this church, like so many others, not a place of total acceptance and of unconditional love, especially regarding the *unmentionable*?

"When we examine the issues of our families and relationships, in most instances we do not mention the unmentionable. But today is the day and now is the time to discuss this unmentionable. We should launch out into the deep and address the issue head on as to whether or not the *Good News of Jesus Christ* has anything to say to or about persons who are homosexual or bisexual and to family members of persons who are homosexual or bisexual. Or does the Word of GOD only limit itself to those persons who are heterosexual."

"Are you planning to preach to me, little man? Huh?"

"If you and people like you continue to pressure us or kick us out, the Black Church simply wouldn't be the same. We know it and you know it too. We have been and always will be valuable assets to the growth and stability of the Black Church. On any given Sunday, I wish that I had the power to snap my fingers to make all the unmentionables in the church disappear for a month. By that I mean men who are homosexual or bisexual as well as those who are in denial. Many leaders, including a few in the pulpit, would be gone. The administration and the finance office wouldn't be the same. The choir and the music department definitely wouldn't be the same either. And there would be much backlash from others who would be deterred by the disappearance of so many who really run this church. In turn, the dramatic decrease in attendance would considerably affect the tithes, general offerings, pastor's love offerings, and special donations. And we all know how important money is to this church. So, this church should seriously think about not biting the hand that feeds it.

"I overheard you two gossiping about Patrick. My best buddy is gone now. He is not here to defend himself, so I will. You two sound like Satan when Jesus was in the wilderness for forty days when Satan tried to twist *the Word* to validate his argument. You are taking the scripture out of context. It's really incredible how after over two thousand years that some of the same like-minded self-righteous, holier-than-thou, sacrilegious saints are still twisting the Bible to fit their own needs and to pass judgment on others. Typical self-righteous judgmental saints are always going there. Well, not today. Not in my presence."

"Oh, okay. I thought you were about to preach. Now it sounds like you wanna play the dozen. Again, watch it, little boy. Big mistake."

"GOD created all things, didn't HE?"

No response.

"GOD created man."

Still, no response.

"It is only man who constantly goes around and decides which things are HIS mistakes. I thought GOD was perfect. I didn't know that GOD made mistakes. Hmmm."

"This is going to be good. Boy, you need to stay in your place. Stay in your lane before you have an accident and become seriously hurt."

The deacon added, "Little boy. Be careful. You are playing with fire."

"I am not a little boy. I am a grown ass man. And, I am warning you. Don't let my age fool you. I am not one of those young naive babes-in-Christ who allow those like you to spew out anything and expect me to accept it and believe it. You two need to be taught a lesson."

"And you are going to do that, teach us a lesson. And what lesson is that? Okay. Go for what you know. Bring it on. I am so sick and tired of those like you who try to force us to accept boys and men like you."

"I agree brother," said the deacon.

"Well, young man, the truth is the truth and the truth is sometimes painful. Man is not supposed to lay with man. Adam and Eve, not Adam and Steve. I'm sure you have heard that before."

"Amen."

"It is an abomination."

"Amen, again."

"When a man finds a wife, it is a good thing."

"Preach, Brother."

"Here we go again. May I respond now? Because you are bringing up the same ole typical self-supporting, weak-ass arguments that most *fake* Christians do. Like so many others, the judgmental hypocrites are picking and choosing specific verses from the Old Testament in order to defend their beliefs and to justify their actions. You are quoting that part of the scripture out of context and twisting the meanings of "the old law" to fit your argument. Scriptures like Leviticus 20:13, referred to as one of the penalties of lawbreaking. You and your kind love to throw around that infamous word "abomination." You try to give that word so much power in order to generate fear and hatred in others. But what about verse ten in the same chapter? You two committed adultery: "the adulterer...shall surely be put to death.""

No response from either of them.

Yes, I believe that the Bible is the Word of GOD. I believe that the Bible is GOD's written revelation of HIS will for man. HIS thought and revelation are divine, but the expression of the communication is human. There were between thirty-seven and forty authors who actually wrote the Bible. Although much is historical, man wrote his interpretation of the Word of GOD. Yes, I believe in the Old Testament as well as the New Testament. However, what happened in the New Testament? What happened when JESUS died? Why did HE die? What happened to man's relationship with GOD after JESUS died? And what happened after HE went back to heaven and left us with the HOLY SPIRIT. In the Old Testament, we have the covenant of the law. In the New Testament, we have the covenant of grace through Jesus Christ.

Minister Calloway responded, "Oh okay. This boy seems to know a little bit about the Bible. But he seems like one of those who thinks that the Old Testament doesn't apply anymore."

I didn't say that. Don't put words in my mouth.

Minister Calloway continued. "So since you want to focus on the New Testament, let's do it. The apostle Paul is credited with have written nearly half of the New Testament. Of course, the Old Testament was the only Bible that he used because it was the only part that was written at the time. In 2 Timothy, which of course is in the New Testament, he writes that 'All Scripture is inspired by GOD and is useful to teach us what is true and to make us realize what is wrong in our lives.' Also, in the New Testament, four words sum of what the apostle Paul had to say about homosexuality and those like your friend. Such words include shameful, unnatural, indecent, and perverted. He states in Romans 1:27, 'Men committed indecent acts with other men, and received in themselves the due penalty for their perversion.' In other words, they are perverts."

"Okay, sir. So you are calling my best friend a pervert. And at his repast of all places. And you didn't even know him. Did you? Hmmm. That was the ultimate level of disrespect. How should I respond to that? Hmmm."

That really hurt. My heart dropped. However, I couldn't let them see how much it hurt me. I had to stay composed. I had to suck it up. I was determined not to show any weakness. *Hell no*! I said to myself. *Hell no*! While looking both of them straight in the eyes, I took a step back and folded my arms in a defensive mode. I took two big deep breaths.

Then I took two steps forward and responded, "What if someone called you a trifling *hoe* who disrespected the sanctity of marriage and made his wife look like a damn fool? And not once but twice. What do you think her family and friends are saying about her? And not to mention the church members. She should have left your trifling whorish ass. And what about your four daughters?" Then I turned to Deacon McKenzie. "What if someone called you a nasty, despicable drunken *hoe* who could have given his wife an STD and a few other diseases that have no cures? And what about the ridicule and bullying that your children will experience? When your children are older, they will see all of the ugly and vicious online stories written about their dear ole dad. They won't look at you the same either.

"Now regarding that speech that you just gave. It needs a little dissecting. So let me clarify a few things for the both of you. Many Bible scholars, as well as some Bible experts, argue that the apostle Paul isn't saying what it sounds like he is saying. Their interpretation of the referenced scriptures includes two major theories. Paul is condemning heterosexuals who try to go against their nature and experiment with homosexuality. And he is also condemning homosexuals who don't lovingly commit themselves to their homosexual relationships. Instead, they are always on the hunt for sex. Some Bible scholars also infer that the apostle Paul is also referring to an ancient collection of Jewish oracles. The writer says that Jewish men should honor their marriage vows and should not engage in sexual intercourse with boys as did many Phoenicians, Egyptians, and Romans. And some historians even say that all but one of the first fifteen Roman emperors had homosexual affairs, with one exception, Claudius.

"Kings, emperors, and other persons of royalty were above the law of the people, as well as exempt from Jewish and Christian biblical law. Most did not have to obey any type of law even if they had written it themselves. And in those days, one wouldn't dare criticize or chastise a king or a Roman emperor without the risk of grave punishment or execution. Even most judgmental pharisees praised most kings and emperors.

"Whether documented facts or embellished historical facts passed down through generations, those stories are rarely told to the current mainstream. You and your kind would never preach or teach those theories from your pulpits.

"Well, you didn't expect that comeback, did you? I'm sure that little tidbit of information is news to you two. This is not my first rodeo. So as you can see, I don't mind going toe-to-toe with false prophets.

"Question for the both of you. Is a married man supposed to lay with a woman that is not his wife? Or is a married man allowed to lay with any woman, whether she is single or married?"

"Your friend was a sinner."

"Give it to him, brother!"

"All of us are sinners. We were born into sin."

"Yes, but he was the worst kind of sinner."

"A sin is a sin is a sin. There is no such thing as a greater sin. Hmmm. You tell me. Which sins are more important or more serious in GOD's eyes? Huh, which one? Only man prioritizes sins. You think it's okay to hide behind the Old Testament and judge. In that case since you want to quote the Old Testament, how many of the big ten have you broken? What is your response to that? And not over your lifetime, just this past month. When was the last time you two coveted anything of your neighbor's, including his sixteen-year-old daughters?

"Isn't adultery one of the big ten? You have repeated that act numerous times. Or did you just have a series of bad luck and got her pregnant the only two times that you happen to have sex. I'm sure that you didn't have sex with her only twice, and by chance, you produced those two children. And I'm sure she wasn't the only other woman besides your wife.

"And what about you? Was that the first and only time you stepped out on your wife with a prostitute? Although it was foolish and you are full of double standards, you seem relatively smart. But I am just wondering if you really knew if that prostitute was really a man. Or did you know and just didn't care.

"Do you two eat shellfish? Do you work on the Sabbath? When was the last time you told a supposedly little white lie?"

No response. Their facial expression changed.

"What's wrong? Cat got your tongue? I am not the one, gentlemen. Not today, anyway. But if you want me too, I can do this all day."

"The wages of sin is death."

"True. Very true. But have you ever wondered what the babies who die before their time or what innocent bystanders who are murdered have done to deserve such violent deaths? So, is The LORD going to banish me to hell because I have to work on Sunday?"

No response.

"Okay, you are right. The Bible says that the wages of sin is death. You allowed a transvestite to perform oral sex on you and who knows whatever else you did to him. Statistics still show that the largest group of new HIV/AIDS cases are African-American women. Who do you think they are getting it from? Toilet seats, other women, transfusions, kissing, or casual touching? Don't insult my intelligence."

They just smirked.

"They are getting it from cheaters and fornicators like you. And do you use condoms with these transvestites and other women outside of your marriages? You could be bringing home diseases."

They still didn't respond.

"You don't have to answer. Your facial expressions give me the answer I need. In GOD I trust. But in man I check. In GOD I trust. But in man I monitor. I am always aware of your presence, observing your ways, observing and correcting you when you step out of line in my presence. Because if someone like me does not check you, hypocrites with double standards will continue to spread your deadly venom, all the while poisoning the minds of so many others, especially young people.

"Now that you have finished your poor attempt to twist the *Word* to fit your own way of living, let me give it to you straight, with no chaser. Now that it seems as though I have your full attention and you realize that I am not playing a game, I have a few more things I need to say. And don't interrupt me when I am talking. This is not a dialogue. I owe you nothing. I respect the LORD'S House, but I owe this church nothing. You don't know me. So, you don't know what I am capable of. And yes, you don't have to stand here and listen to what I have to say. But you will. I seriously advise you too. And if you decide that you don't want to listen and try to dismiss me and walk away, I promise you that I will embarrass you in front of everyone. Are we clear?"

No response. They knew I was serious.

"People like you two misinterpret the Bible and twist the meaning of what the Bible states to fit your own self-centered beliefs. I refuse to believe that my GOD only loves some of HIS world. My Bible does not say that for GOD so loved *some* of the world or *most* of the world that HE gave HIS only begotten Son. That any heterosexual that believes in HIM. My Bible says, *all* the world. And WHOSOEVER. Not just those I like or those who you like. WHOSOEVER. Not just those who are like me or those who are like you.

"I refuse to limit my GOD and lock HIM into your biblical interpretation or your cultural understanding because culture is fickle. As you two are aware, history tells us that culture is often wrong about many important life-changing issues.

- Culture was wrong about the advanced civilizations of the Indians and the Africans.
- Culture was wrong about slavery.
- Culture was wrong about Jim Crow laws.
- Culture was wrong about women's roles and women's rights.
- Culture was wrong about civil rights.
- Culture was wrong about the possibility of electing the first African-American president so soon after the ending of slavery.
- And most of all, culture was wrong about Christ.

"I refuse to limit GOD and lock HIM into a tiny cultural presence, no matter how uncomfortable you and other self-righteous parishioners may feel. I have become a pariah and an outcast of many because I won't join them in their homophobic bashing.

"Many, like you two, have a problem with those homosexuals or bisexuals and their sexual activities. Yeah! But I wonder why many of you don't seem to have a problem dating married women and sleeping with women other than your wives. And it seems like most homo-bashers are banging more *hoes* than the law will allow. In addition, anybody's wife, sister, or daughter is fair game for them. As long as she is giving it up, you and others like you are willing to try to get it. And you don't seem to care whose wedding finger says they are committed too. I know that I am walking through a field of land mines right now because I know what an emotional subject this is. But you two need to hear this. And you are going to listen. This issue has even divided many Black Churches for decades. It amazes me that how unreasonable people become when you start talking about things and actions that make them uncomfortable.

"I compare this to being at a KKK rally and discussing the dignity and worthiness of African-Americans. The Klan does not want to hear that mess. Just like many of you don't want to hear anything positive about anyone who is not like you.

"I think you are well aware of what I am saying, Minister Calloway. From the expression on your face, Deacon, you get my point too, don't you?

"It is definitely a great thing that GOD doesn't get caught up in all your hang-ups! GOD doesn't make any junk! GOD doesn't make mistakes!

"And as surprising as that may sound, people still have these antiquated views of homosexuality:

- Homosexuality is an illness.
- Homosexuality is caused by family configuration.
- Homosexuality is a result of how a child responds to his environment.
- Homosexuality is a deliberate or physical choice.
- Homosexuality is a demon possession.

"But it's strange how straight society or church folk in particular, will tolerate or forgive almost anything heterosexual:

- Adultery
- Fornication
- Divorce
- Promiscuity
- Prostitution
- Sadomasochism
- Rape
- Incest
- Child molestation
- Sexual harassment

"A man in the Black Church could be a previously convicted drunk driver charged with a hit-and-run and beg for forgiveness and he would probably get it. The same man could admit to fathering three unrelated children outside his own marriage and he would be forgiven. That same man could even steal money from his own church and the Black Church will forgive him. But if it is discovered that he has had an encounter or an affair with another man, all bets are off. The large majority of Black Churches would crucify him without question.

"If you really want to be *so-called* holy, what about all the other sinners, like the ones I just mentioned? Don't just pick and choose. Are you going to kick out the adulterers, rapists, fornicators, child molesters, thieves, and liars? If so, then the two of you should be kicked out. What the hell are you still doing here?

"Just look at the news any given day or read the newspaper. Scandals are being uncovered weekly, some in the churches. And there are a few in this church.

"As long as it's with somebody of the opposite sex, many of you will tolerate it or forgive it. But some people especially those in the Black Church become livid or downright rabid when same-sex issues are discovered. You will tolerate a man beating his wife or cheating on his wife much quicker than you will tolerate two people of the same sex who are committed to loving each other. And those same-sex couples who don't dishonor their partners with either violence or infidelity. I guess that some people are just funny that way.

"Why are they that way? I really don't know if there is one answer to that question. But I can tell you two that it's simply not about sex between two men. It's much more complicated than that. In the controversial theory of psychosexual differentiation, the argument still exists by explaining a series of opposites as to how a person's sexuality is developed.

- Is it Nature versus Nurture?
- The Genetic versus The Environmental
- The Innate versus The Acquired
- The Biological versus The Psychological
- The Instinctive versus The Learned

"The basic proposition should not be any of the above referenced series of opposites but their interaction. I believe it's not an either-or reality but a combination of several or all the theories. Are they born that way? Who really knows?

"The causes, but what does it really matter. Who are they really hurting? They just want to be. Did you really think someone would choose to be ostracized, criticized, demoralized, chastised, or ridiculed? Or verbally abused and physically beaten? Because of how they are and how they feel. Especially when they are not hurting anyone. They are just living their lives like everyone else.

"Even if homosexuality or bisexuality is wrong, even if they are sins, is that sin any worse than the sins that you two have committed? Also, your sins are considered unlawful but being homosexual or bisexual is not breaking the law. Well, at least, not in this country.

"I truly don't believe that my GOD does not love me any less than HE loves you. HE will forgive me of my sins as He will forgive you of your sins.

"Patrick was important and GOD loved him. HE loved him in spite of me, in spite of you, in spite of everyone. Patrick didn't pick this life, it picked him. He didn't choose this life; this life chose him.

"Gentlemen, I think I have given you some serious food for thought. Think about it. Let it marinate for a while. Then chew on it some more for a few minutes. I am done, for now anyway. See you at church on tomorrow morning. Oh, and by the way, although it took some considerable arm-twisting, both services on tomorrow will be dedicated in Patrick's memory. And he will be honored with the respect that he deserves. I will make sure of that.

"And, gentlemen, one last thing, I seriously advise you to take heed to the serious tongue-lashing that I just gave you. You haven't seen the last of me. Watch me because I will be watching you and those like you. Small minds are never in short supply, especially in this church. Now you two have a good evening."

I turned and walked away. Yeah, I know that I was vicious. But they deserved it. And little did they know that when I am finished with them and others like them, they are going to get a lot more of the same. And what others don't know is that they have not seen anything yet. My wrath. My vengeance. Just wait. Yeah, yeah, I know. Vengeance is mine, saith the LORD. But, LORD, please forgive me. I desperately want to help YOU. I know that YOU don't need my help. But I am offering. I am at YOUR disposal.

CHAPTER 4

The Ultimate Denial

The definition of narcissism—when he won't allow his pride to be denied.

"GOOD AFTERNOON, BISHOP Short. My name is Dexter B. Cavanaugh III. I am an attorney. Do you know who I am?"

He stared as though he was a little confused but he didn't respond. His reaction was if I looked familiar, but he wasn't sure.

"Well, I will just get to the point. Three young gentlemen have retained my legal services. Two others are also being counseled by my firm, and I will probably be representing them as well to file additional claims. I'm sure that you know Ethan Griffin, Colan Richardson, and Brandon Cooper, as well as Nicholas and Jonathan Devereaux, who are brothers. My clients and I have had serious conversations regarding your relationship with each of them. Yes, this visit is quite unorthodox, but with the approval of my clients, I have come to you to discuss the matter before any further legal action is taken."

"Relationships! What relationships!"

"C'mon, Bishop. Let's not take it there. Let's not play games. And don't play me for stupid. I was there that Sunday three years ago. I was visiting your church on that infamous Sunday morning when you made your defiant declaration against a particular group of men in your church. This was during the time that you were actively campaigning to become a bishop in the contemporary Black Church. You needed a platform to promote, and the platform you chose, of course, was homosexual deliverance. You said you were tired of all *those* young men in your church including the elders, the leaders, the choir members, and others in your congregation and the behavior in which you supposedly did not approve. You stated that many of these men had nice cars, fine homes, and promising careers, men who were financially stable. You mentioned that they drove around town with two men in the front seat of the cars and two men in the back seat, but they did not have any women in their lives, women with whom they should be romantically involved. You went as far as to say that they were wasting seed. You demanded that they put some women between themselves, in the midst of all those male cliques. You stated that you were not going to tolerate that type of behavior in your church. You reiterated that *the Cathedral of Grace Christian Church* was your church. Don't deny it. You knew exactly what you were doing. The main purpose of that performance was to advance your career. I thought that being a minister was supposed to be a calling on your life not a continuously, ever-advancing competitive career. More importantly, I suspect that you made that speech publicly only to hide your indiscretions. You pressured and coerced so many young men—homosexual men, bisexual men, and men with homosexual tendencies—in your church to get married. The ceremony of a marriage, the bond of being married to a woman could not change these men. Has your marriage changed you? You have been married for over twenty years. Have you changed? Many of those men that you targeted were destined to destroy the lives of so many women and children."

"What is this really about? Where are these ridiculous accusations coming from? Who put you up to this?"

"I see you are not taking me seriously. You think this is a joke. You think that I am bluffing?"

"You are smarter that I thought. Actually, yes, I am not taking you seriously. Yes, I think you are a joke. And yes, I think you are bluffing."

"You damn hypocrite! You are in denial. No, I take that back. I don't think you are in denial. I think that for some warped reason, you have somehow learned to rationalize your behavior. You believe that some of the things that you preach about don't apply to you. You proclaimed a declared mission against an entire group of men who had homosexual tendencies. All the while you were having sex with younger men."

"You are getting on my nerves. Again, what is this really about?"

"You have a mission. Now, I have a mission too. It is going to be my pleasure, my personal mission to expose you to be the narcissistic, fake-ass preacher that you are. Your ass is grass! No pun intended. Yes, you have done a lot for the community and the city. Big damn deal!"

"Young man, attorney or no attorney, you better respect who you are talking to. This is a stupid move on your part. Why would you come to warn me? Real attorneys don't do that. They don't operate using preemptive strikes. Real attorneys file their claims in court and wait for a response. Then they proceed and prepare to go to court. They don't warn the other side regarding their intentions. So why are you here warning me about something you might do? Just do it, if you think you have such a great case."

"See, that is exactly what I mean. That's your damn problem. That damn superior attitude. You think you are beyond reproach. You can perpetrate around your church and around this city all you want. You flaunt these precarious relationships, disguising them as mentorships, assistants, and spiritual sons. Others can buy it, but I don't."

"Young man, you are really trying my patience. I am busy. I really don't have time for this foolishness. Who are you to judge me?"

"Hell yeah! You are right. I am judging you. Well, how does it feel, Mr. Almighty One? Not a very good feeling is it, huh. My great-grandmother used to say, I can say what I want, when I want to, to whom I want. Well, as long as what I say is the truth."

"Do you know who I am? I don't think you really do?"

"Oh! Oh! I know! You think you're a god! You think you can walk on water! You enjoy standing with boisterous pride on the pedestal that so many people put you on. Look at you. From the look on your face, I actually believe that you think you have a right to be on a pedestal!"

"Be careful, young man. I'm not afraid of you. But you should be afraid of me, very afraid."

"That is your second biggest mistake."

"So, what are you saying is my first?"

"It's not even the fact that you like to have sex with young men half your age or the fact that you have been cheating on your wife by desecrating your vows. Your biggest mistake was not just preaching against homosexuality and bisexuality in the pulpit but openly campaigning against them. All the while you were having sex with those young men. Well from my understanding, two of them were actually climbing on your back. That's the ultimate level of hypocrisy. And one of my main goals is to expose your true colors so the world can see who you really are. Well, at least you were smart enough to choose boys over the legal age. Otherwise you would be looking at some serious federal prison time. How would you feel if your son was having an affair with one of your colleagues or one of the senior ministers in your church? That was a rhetorical question. I don't expect you to answer. You never expected this to happen in a thousand years, huh?"

"Young man, young naive and apparently stupid young man, you are about to make a serious mistake. You are a young attorney. So, you have been practicing only a few years. Attacking me publicly and losing would destroy your career. I seriously advise you to rethink this."

"Is that a threat?"

"Take it as you like."

"Well, old man, don't let the young face fool you. I don't think you want to take it there. You might want to Google me."

"You are pissing me off! How dare you! Who the hell do you think you are? Coming in my office with this *bullshit*! I am going to say it again. Watch your damn mouth, little punk-ass boy! Yeah, I said it, *boy*!"

While giving me a stern stare, he took two steps toward me and paused. Then he unbuckled and unzipped his pants and turned with his back to me.

"Mr. Short, what are you doing?"

"Waiting for you to kiss my black sanctified ass."

"All right, sir. This is the arrogant asshole that I have heard so much about.

"Okay, I see that you really do want to take it there. Now this is what I wanted to see, the real you. This is the reaction for which I was hoping. I needed something to fuel my motivation to win these cases. And you just gave it to me.

"Have you forgotten that you are a man of GOD? I could have easily handled this much differently, as most attorneys would have. I could have easily just filed the claims and went straight to the media. And we both know that the local media does not care for you and your lavish, nontaxable lifestyle. They would have a field day. I would be delivering their Christmas gifts five months early."

"Now is that a threat. Are you actually threatening me? I don't take kindly to idle threats. Don't let my title fool you. I have battled and defeated many people as well as numerous negative and evil forces much powerful than you. I didn't get to where I am by being weak. Or as the young folks call it, being a punk-ass bitch!"

"Sir, I don't make idle threats. I know better. I don't write checks my ass can't cash. But to answer your original question. Who the hell do I think I am? I am a litigator with a personal mission: a vengeance to stop the perpetuation of negative behavior. One who believes in practicing what you preach.

- I believe in preaching love and acceptance.
- I believe in exposing hypocrisy.
- I stand for defending those who feel like they have been hurt and wronged.
- I stand for making those who have done wrong; repent and then pay. And if they don't want to repent then they will just have to pay. And I mean pay big time.
- And I stand for justice.

"Men like you only respond to three main things. Pain, consequences, and reward. You have been reaping rewards for many years. Now it's time for you to experience the other two. Everyone has his time, and this is your time. I am about to flip the script. This is my duty. You stand in your pulpit on Sundays and Wednesdays and judge. Well, this is the time for change. The judge will soon be judged.

"This case was brought to me for a particular reason, a reason that you will find out later. Please don't underestimate me. And please don't insult my intelligence. That would be a huge mistake. I have been interviewing these men for several weeks and my team has been verifying their stories for the past few weeks since the break-in."

"The break-in?"

"It is public knowledge that the safe in your downtown condo was burglarized two months ago during one of your exclusive, high-security private men's fellowship and mentoring 'parties.' The perpetrators took four iPads, three iPhones, three passports, some jewelry, several personal greeting cards, several intimate handwritten letters, some incriminating photos, and some cash."

"How do you know what the specific contents that were taken? That information was not public knowledge. And it was not disclosed to the media."

"Hmmm. Good question, but I can't disclose that information. I know who took the stolen items and so do you. The person or persons knew the location to your panic room behind your master bedroom walk-in closet. Access could only be given by the use of the fingerprint biometric system. Who gave them access? And they obviously knew the location of the safe and someone obviously had programmed their fingerprints in the system. The authorities suspect that it was an inside job because there was no evidence of forced entry and there was no mess. Suspicions were also raised because you weren't even aware that the items were missing until three days later. We both know why they took those specific items. Someone obviously took those specific items because they needed evidence."

"Evidence? What evidence?"

"One of my inside sources verified that you contacted two of your church members, the assistant DA, and the chief of police and asked them to drop the investigation regarding the break-in and not to pursue the case. You wanted this incident to go away, but because of the constant daily media attention over the past week, it's obvious that is not going to happen. Even as loyal as they may be, they are not going to put their careers on the line. Not even for you. Again, you know what I am alleging. I can just see Pandora's box trying to open itself. And once it's open, it can never be closed again.

"Now, I am coming to you before the media gets wind of the details and the incriminating material that I have examined. Because when news and innuendoes like this becomes viral, we will not be able to control the potential snowballing effect of the negative, malicious publicity. Your reputation precedes you. The benevolent work that you do and the churches in your organization are well-known internationally. You have contributed much to the community. You have been a very generous benefactor to various charities and worthwhile causes. All of that is very commendable. However, that won't matter much to the media. As I mentioned earlier, the local media has been after you for years. This potential scandal is just the fuel they need to build a huge roaring fire."

"Young man, you really don't know what you have gotten yourself into. I am the Reverend Dr. Bishop William H. Short! That's S-H-O-R-T, period, exclamation point. Apparently, you really don't know what that name means. And obviously you really don't know who I am. I am well connected in this community, in this city, in this state, in the South and in the contemporary African-American Christian world. I lead one of the largest churches in this country. My parishioners love me. They worship me. They are loyal to me. And I am very well acquainted and well connected with influential and powerful people. And soon all will even know of my next venture. A small group of my associates and I are in the process of breaking away from the county services and campaigning to form another city. And I am going to be the mayor. So, I don't know what type of case you think you have, but I am going to shut this down. This is *bullshit*. I have helped these young men financially and spiritually for years. I have mentored them. I have been the father that they have never had. And this is how they repay me. I don't believe this. This is betrayal. Someone else put them up to this. This is a setup."

"How could it be a setup if the allegations are true? I have absolutely no proof or evidence that this is a setup. Well, anyway, even if they were coerced, the evidence does not dispute the facts.

"Okay, I see where this is going. The charges among others will be coercion, abuse of power, sexual seduction, sexual misconduct, and inappropriate sexual relationships with several young men from your church. My clients accuse you of using biblical scripture and your authority as well as church money to sexually seduce them. Yes, they were of legal age, but they stated that they felt that they were coerced. You told them that it was their Christian duty to serve you literally as well as figuratively.

"You are a licensed professional. And you are upheld by certain professional standards, ethics, and codes of conduct. And if you misuse your power or violate the trust of your parishioners especially those who you counsel, you are held accountable. You are in violation of your license. But it's up to the state if it takes additional actions against you. Off the record, there have been rumors that you have been doing this sort of thing for many years. I am truly surprised that no one has brought charges against you before now.

"Not to mention you are a married man. You have pressured homosexuals and bisexual men in your church especially those in leadership positions to get married. Your actions have been ruining lives in so many ways. And we all know that during your aggressive mission and rise to become a bishop, you chose to openly preach and campaign against the most controversial issue in the Black Church. You have constantly preached about homosexual deliverance for several years, and you have openly campaigned against gay marriage and civil unions. Is that the utmost level of hypocrisy or what?

"I have so much scandalous dirt on you that I feel dirty sometimes. And you know how messy Georgia clay is. It won't wash out. And as my great-grandmother used to say, I can smell the rain.

"Once again, I am not at rest. Nor can I be quiet. I am here to tell you that I'm here to cause your demise. Sir, a storm is a-comin'. The type of storm that can bring down large buildings. And his name is Hurricane Dexter. He is a category 7 hurricane. Katrina has nothing on him. He will have no mercy. Your constant narcissistic and hypocritical behavior over the last twenty plus years has made it so easy. I am going to completely shatter the glass house in which you live, not to mention the glass cathedral that you have built. Shatter it into a billion pieces.

"The chickens have come home to roost. This scandal will rock the foundation of the church. And not just your church but the African-American Christian Church. Not to mention, this scandal will probably spark many more claims or cases like this. Because we all know that you are not the only perpetrator. Too many of your colleagues have been doing the same thing for years as well. Practice what you preach, yeah right! Your entire world is about to change. Your empire is about to collapse. Your reputation is about to be diminished beyond repair. You are about to fall from grace.

"After all I have said, I still don't think you realize how serious this is. I hope you realize what is going to happen very soon. I truly hope for the sake of your wife, family and church that you don't take this too lightly. Your ambivalence could cost you more than you realize."

"Huh! Boy. What do you want? What do they want?"

I didn't respond, just a long stare and a smirk on my face. "My clients want justice. They feel emotionally broken and they want to be made whole again. They want to turn back the clock and erase the last several years."

"Is that what you want too? This impromptu meeting is not the norm for most attorneys. Intuition tells me that you want something else."

"What do I want? Good question but this is not about me. The politically correct answer should be that my ultimate goal is to seek justice for my clients. I usually try to take the high road, but in this case, I am not. I just can't. What do I really want? You are asking me what I want. I will tell you what I want. I want the damn head of the snake."

"What the hell does that mean?"

"Many of the hypocritical doctrines that you spew from the pulpit on Sundays and Wednesdays are considered poisonous venom. And it is well-known that the quickest way to kill a snake is to cut off the head. Quickly, in one swoop."

"So, you want to kill me! You want me dead. Huh, boy! All those lazy trifling illegitimate bastards have sold you alleged ridiculous claims and this fabricated evidence. Have you lost your damn mind?"

"No, I don't want you dead. Not literally. That would be taking the easy way out. Naw, I want you alive and kickin'. But I do want you to suffer as you have made so many others suffer. You have inflicted so many wounds on so many people. Deep painful wounds that might never completely heal. Wounds that have left permanent scars. Naw, I want you well and sober so you can get the opportunity to reap what you have sowed.

"I suggest you contact your attorney immediately and settle out of court. Let's put this thing to bed and quickly. It's not going away. Actually, you have already fallen from grace, just by the accusations. Save what you can. You could lose your corporate and collegiate board memberships, your ministerial empire, your reputation in the upper echelon of national ministers. And most importantly, you could lose your wife and family. But on the other hand, your wife is not stupid, I'm sure she has heard the rumors over the years. She might stand by you.

"Man, how could you be so narcissistic? Damn, man, raw black diamonds and four Rolex watches in your safe. Yeah, I know about those too. Although they were not taken. And twenty-five thousand in cash? What was that? Emergency money. Petty cash. IRS is going to have a field day. And you definitely don't want the internal revenue service to start an investigation regarding comingling of personal and church funds. And the lavish gifts you bought these young men. Buying one of them a BMW. Many of your parishioners don't even have cars. Just wait until the word gets out. Not to mention to your loyal congregation."

I could see the anger in his face steadily growing; but I wasn't afraid.

"And I want to leave you with this. Call it a direct warning if you like. Mr. Short, I need to emphasize again that I am not bluffing. I must tell you that I have a particular set of very valuable talents and skills. I have a nonyielding, relentless diligence and unwavering persistence, bold characteristics required to win my cases. When I strike, I strike with precision. So many people are going to be affected by these cases, including innocent people in your circle. Please don't let your pride and arrogance cloud your judgment. You are a smart man. You can minimize the fallout and settle out of court. And if you don't, and I am sure that you won't, it will be my personal and professional agenda to make an example of you and your actions. I am so glad that we had this little impromptu meeting. Now I know how I will proceed. Yes, you have a lot of clout in this town. Fear will not break my mission. Fear will not break me down. I will come after you with the wrath of everything in me. And no, that is not a threat. That would be unprofessional. So, I am going to be straight up with you because you need realness. This is personal. Oh, and by the way, tell Stephanie Richardson, the coordinator of one of your brain-child ministries, homosexual deliverance, that I said hello."

"What?"

"And boom goes the dynamite. I see that I have finally gotten your attention. As I stated in the beginning, this visit is extremely unorthodox. I just came to give you heads up. Your reaction, your response, and especially your self-indulgent delusion only confirm the information that I have already obtained. Your behavior is so predictable. I am not surprised. But I do think that you finally realize that I am serious and that my clients are serious too. I have said enough for now. But before we continue, with any future conversation, you might want to call your attorney. Here is my card."

Of course, he didn't take it, so I laid it on his desk. The expression on his face said that this man really wanted to hit me. It was actually funny.

"Get out of my office! Get the hell out of my damn office, now!"

"I am determined to overthrow the king. I will end your reign of narcissism. I will end your reign of manipulation. And most importantly, I will end your reign of the utmost level of hypocrisy."

"For the last time, get the hell out of my damn office!"

"The ball is in your court. No! No! Actually, your balls are in my fist! And I am about to squeeze much harder."

His admin assistant suddenly burst into the room. Obviously, she heard him yelling.

"My attorney will be contacting you! Get out before I have you thrown out!"

"I will be in touch. And until then, I will see you in court soon. Mr. Short, again, I am not bluffing. I know that you think that my words are only threats. But please believe me when I say that my bite is ten times worse than my bark. If you go against me, you will lose. Settle this and settle this quickly or else."

I walked out with a smile. Man, that felt really good. Wow! I loved my career. Sometimes I really couldn't believe that I was actually earning large paychecks to do this. To do what I loved to do, defending the underdogs, promoting justice and most importantly, exposing the truth. It's also a huge thrill to knock someone off his high horse. And it's even much sweeter when it was a pompous, egomaniac.

CHAPTER 5

Me, Myself, And I... And Him

How did I become the person I am? Where did
these feelings, these deep emotions come from.
You know me and you don't. The person you see
is not me. I am not the person you think I am.
Who am I? I am me. But it depends on who I
am with.

A MAN IS the sum of what is put into him. Me, myself, and I...
and him. That is the best way to describe it, to describe myself.
There are four sides to who I am. By that I mean there are four sides
of my personality. I know it might sound strange. And no, I am not
bipolar. It is just a way that I prefer to psychoanalyze myself, the
manner in which I have learned to deal with my one hundred and
one issues.

First there is *me*. I refer to him as Dex. Dex is the laid-back,
easygoing, fun-loving guy that everyone likes. He thinks life is good
and that the world is a great place.

Then there is *myself*. I refer to him as Dee. Dee is the childlike,
little boy in me. He is the boy from the hood who still likes to dream.
The simple things in life please him the most.

And there is *I*. He is referred to as Dexter B. Cavanaugh III,
the articulate, educated, successful, anal-retentive professional perfectionist. Borderline obsessive-compulsive, even in his sleep. He values his career and making money, constantly focusing on improving
his self-image. It takes a lot of work and preparation to be Dexter

B. Cavanaugh III. Most of the time it can be an extremely stressful daily task performing the role as an aggressive, complex, self-driven workaholic. He has to win. He has to be the best, or at least the best at everything he attempts. Failure is not an option. He can't return to the life of poverty and despair in the projects.

And lastly there is *him*. I refer to him as Dexterio, the quiet, spiritual, "professorial" introvert who gives advice and helps the other three parts of my personality to solve my life's problems. He is the wise one who often gets their attention when they least expect it; usually offering enlightenment or sound judgment to a situation. He lives or exists in the subconscious although he is always aware of the actions, behavior, decisions, thoughts, and emotions of the other three cohorts. He appears during quiet moments throughout the day, when they are alone. He also comes to them in their dreams; to provide them with comfort and security during the storms of life; both brief brutal storms and seemingly endless tumultuous storms. Dexterio is always patiently waiting in the silence.

Until a few years ago, there was always conflict between Dexter B. Cavanaugh III and Dee. The sometimes snobbish, arrogant elitist constantly in battle with the immature, poor ghetto boy from the hood. Dexter B. Cavanaugh III often felt ashamed of the uncouth, underprivileged outcast who constantly reminded him of his humble beginnings in the inner-city projects. Dexter's obvious disdain for Dee was so severe that he desperately wanted to keep Dee locked in a trunk, hidden in a closet in a basement, where no one would ever find him. He meant that figuratively, of course. Dexter often went to great lengths to hide his past. Actually, he was quite successful for many years. And Dee's reaction to the loathing embarrassment caused the blatant affliction which resulted in his either internalizing the emotional pain or by expressing angry outbursts; much as a child would do. This in turn embarrassed Dexter, creating a vicious cycle. But thanks to Dex, currently they are somewhat at peace with one another. They have learned to respect, accept, and appreciate each other's minor idiosyncrasies. Dex also brings harmony and balance between the two other internal rivals.

I have loved my profession ever since I could remember. I had wanted to be a champion legal gladiator. My passion of becoming a successful defense attorney had stemmed from the numerous cases of injustice that I had seen on the news as a child. I had possessed an unyielding yearning to defend the underdog and the downtrodden as well as the weak and the less fortunate. Someone needed to stand up to the arrogant, overconfident DAs and prosecuting attorneys. They taught me time and time again that there was a huge distinct difference between being innocent and not guilty. Too many are unjustly accused. Too many are wrongfully convicted. Too many are sentenced too harshly. And unfortunately, too many are represented by overworked and underpaid and in most cases inexperienced public defenders.

I was determined to break the cycle of poverty, the curse that had plagued my dysfunctional family for generations. A single mother at sixteen years old and a seventeen-year-old absentee father who was a semiprofessional criminal, only perpetuated that vicious cycle. My love for my young mother grew more and more every day as she did the best she could by sacrificing everything for me. She was a child raising a child. While serving as a housekeeper for many years, she always made her children her first priority. My father went to prison when I was two years old and he was released when I was thirteen. He missed the most important formative years of my childhood. I grew up very poor. I lived in public housing and my family received welfare, Medicaid, and food stamps. We also had access to free dental care. We never abused the system like so many others. Although living in the ghetto was not easy, I was raised to be very disciplined, obedient, and respectful as well as to have respect for myself. We probably had the best-kept apartment in our housing projects. One could literally eat off my mother's bleached white floors. It was very difficult to maintain a positive attitude and continue to be motivated while living in the projects, constantly being exposed to crime and destitute living conditions. I felt that most of the people around me were not motivated to improve their lives. If there was such a thing as the American dream, most of them had absolutely no idea what it was not mention whether or not it could be achieved. They were just living from day to day, existing without any since of direction or purpose to elevate themselves. They had lost the drive of living life to the fullest. That is, if they ever had it. Unfortunately, most of them continued to live in their small little worlds, never leaving their destitute secluded environment. Sometimes I wonder if I had a chance to repeat my childhood, would I change much? I am sure that I would change some things about my circumstances, but I know for sure I would not change my relationship with or the qualities in my mother. My challenging childhood created character.

I had always felt that I was different from other guys, having strange feelings about guys. I thought it was because my father was missing in action and I was subconsciously yearning for male bonding. I also thought it might be because I was a mama's boy, being pampered by my mother and great-grandmother. Although I was not effeminate, I did not play much with other guys in the neighborhood. And I had very few close friends. I was somewhat of an antisocial introvert. Performing very well in school was the most important thing to me. I focused on attaining the best grades in hope of an academic scholarship to one of the top-notch schools. My Black classmates as well as the other kids in the neighborhood used to tease me and call me a sissy, a punk, a mama's boy, and a wannabe bourgeois nigga. They also labeled me as king of the Oreos—Black on the outside and white on the inside. When I attended a predominantly white school, the white kids thought I was an "uppity" nigga. Although I often felt isolated and rejected, hiding the emotional pain and camouflaging the deep-rooted scars were skills that I seemed to master well. I would not be deterred from my goals. I would be the first in my family to attend college. I eventually got the last laugh the evening of my high school graduation when I received several full academic scholarships to several Ivy League schools. While sitting on the stage as student government president, I stood as the school administrator called my name. As she announced over twenty other scholarships, awards, and accolades, the applauses and cheers from my family drowned out the faint but noticeable sound of groans. But I did not care. Those snarls of jealousy and envy and the loathsome stares did not bother me in the least. Eventually much of the audience mostly Blacks jumped to their feet in applause after she had announced the fifth award. Graduation night was my night to finally shine. I finally left the old neighborhood and my white racist classmates to begin my journey of higher education, the key to breaking the cycle of poverty. My dreams were out there, and I was determined to go and get them. Get them all. Yes, I wanted to be successful. But it wasn't just about me. Most kids feel like their parents owe them because they didn't ask to be born. Not me. I owed my mother big time. For all the sacrifices that she made for me.

Contrary to my somewhat successful academic life, my personal life definitely needed some work. Although I was a clean-cut somewhat attractive guy, most girls treated me like the nice guy next door or just wanted me as a friend. I was never considered the sexy, popular jock who dated all the popular girls. I think a healthy self-confidence had a lot to do with it, which was something that I lacked. Unfortunately, I didn't develop that trait until several years later. I was considered the guy that girls would come too after their boyfriends had broken their hearts. I was the consoling male friend, the nice guy. Like a few other guys that I knew, my first sexual experience with a guy was in college. I was sexually attracted to men although I had sex with women, one woman in particular. The "messing around" with guys that I had done was off-campus. If word had gotten out, I would've transferred to another school. And if I had transferred, I would have lost by scholarship. Besides, that sort of lifestyle was not a part of my plan. My plan was to complete my undergraduate degree. Start my career and after two years, complete my MBA or any masters, and eventually acquire my JD. Then get married and have two kids. And don't forget the five-thousand-foot-square house in the suburbs and his-and-hers Mercedes Benz 500 series sedans.

Studying higher statistics sharpened my natural analytical skills while the psychology fueled my passion for understanding human behavior. A unique dichotomy that would eventually become one of my best assets. Shortly after I graduated summa cum laude from Northwestern University with a double major in mathematics and psychology, I accepted a position as a senior statistician in the actuarial department at a large insurance company in Atlanta. I took a brief detour because I wanted to work a year before I continued any post-graduate work in business and political science and eventually in law.

Within two years of my relocating to Atlanta, my career was diverted back to its original course plan. I was drawn to aggressively pursue my once distant but always yearning career goal in the legal profession. I won my first legal case a year before I even started law school. Although it happened by accident, the result was a rewarding experience. It was supposed to be a simple small claims case against a short-term roommate who borrowed money and wrote several personal bad checks to me. But he decided to hire a local prominent attorney. It was a big mistake on his part to unfairly attack an alpha male with a type-A personality. It was not easy to intimidate me, to say the least. His owing me the money and his blatant disrespect changed the friendship. But the lies, deception, and disturbing obsession exposed before and after that simple case made it a thousand times worse. It also made it personal, very personal.

CHAPTER 6

Twisted Minds, Twisted Hearts

I will never understand how I ever allowed myself to get in this predicament. I could not see the forest for the trees.

AS SOON AS I relocated to the ATL, I hit the ground running. My new employer paid for my moving expenses and gave me a considerable signing bonus. In addition, I received a lucrative compensation package that included stock options. I leased a two-bedroom condo in a high-rise building on the north side with a spectacular view of downtown Atlanta. I wanted to be close to work, and I didn't want to deal with the hustle and bustle of downtown. I also became a regular attendee of an inspirational, spirit-filled Christian Church on the north side, although most of the congregation consisted of too many superficial materialistic yuppies and buppies. However, I still received a much-needed spirit-felt message whenever I attended a service. The pastor was not only an incisive teacher but he was also an intuitive and inspirational preacher as well. And the choir practically raised the roof off the sanctuary every Sunday. My demanding new job prevented me from socializing often. But when I had some free time, I tried to balance work and play. I eventually met a friend who became a close buddy. Unfortunately, soon after we met, he turned out to be a codependent friend with a jealous and controlling wife. Then it became worse. Then he became the financially irresponsible friend, then a jealous friend, an ex-friend, and finally, an obsessive suicidal stalker who became a defendant in a lawsuit. All in that order. However, against my better judgement, I didn't completely cut-off the relationship.

I met Marcellus at a coworker's Christmas party. At first, I thought he was a pompous, pretentious, spoiled immature kid in a grown man's body. After I really got to know him and overlooked his flaws, I soon learned that we had several mutual interests. He was an educated, fashion-conscious mama's boy. I couldn't fault him for that. And the more time we spent together, the more I noticed that he was becoming somewhat attached to me. Marcellus, a low-level office manager, had been married only three years to a corporate attorney. At a distance, it seemed like he had the good life. But he didn't seem to be truly happy. I knew that money couldn't buy happiness, but I always thought it could get you pretty close to it. As I learned more about him, it appeared as though his marriage was a marriage of convenience.

Marcellus seemed to revere our newfound friendship. And so did I; well, at first I did. He viewed me as an independent, ambitious, goal-oriented, educated brutha with a healthy self-confidence. He also saw me as a warm-hearted, nurturing and generous Christian who often influenced him to go to church. He often called me his faithful buddy; his loyal brother; his stable and reliable ace boon coon, and his nonjudgmental cousin. All rolled up into one. He said that I always seem to have his back, accepting him without judging. Although there was only a three-year age difference. He even referred to me as kinda fatherlike. I thought it was creepy until he explained. I was his secure, strong-willed, straightforward confidant who possessed strong moral values while giving him sound yet stern advice. I was one of the few people that he could depend on to tell him the complete truth without sugarcoating it, as most fathers or father figures would. He once said that most guys especially bruthas had relationship-oriented voids in their lives, and the qualities that I offered, fulfilled all those empty spaces. And that was something special and should be treasured. And if you found that one person with all of those distinctive traits, you better hold on to him because he is extremely rare. He often said that I was real and genuine. A quality he did not find in many people in his immediate circle of friends. He said that some day; I was going to make a really good boyfriend and a great husband. But I later discovered that what he really meant was that I would make a great lover or partner.

Over the next few months as our friendship grew, Marcellus invited me into their social circle. He also included me in many of their weekly and monthly social activities. Although I fit in very well, my constant presence eventually created problems. The more time we spent together, the more his wife, Ramona, noticed his admiration for me. She also noticed subtle changes in him, which ironically were some of the same qualities that he saw in me. I learned later that he wanted to emulate me. She picked up on that too. For that main reason, I assumed his wife did not like me. I was not sure whether or not she thought I was consciously or unconsciously influencing him, but either way, I was not going to change my behavior because of her insecurities. Those were her issues. My response was "Get over it."

Although she spoiled him financially, the unattractive, bitter, paranoid nag controlled every aspect of his life. He was the opposite of a trophy wife; he was a trophy husband. At first, I thought it was my imagination, but sly, subtle hints of sarcasm grew into noticeable jealousy. For the most part, I tried to ignore her little verbal jabs at me because I didn't want to offend my new friend by insulting his wife. It became quite obvious that she was extremely jealous of anyone who came too close to her precious "kept" man, especially me. And I was right. He confirmed it. He told me that his wife did not want me around as often because she thought I was influencing her husband in a way that she did not like. He was becoming too independent. But as she called it, he seemed to be straying away and drifting away from her and their marriage. As her insecurity increased, their marital problems seem to multiply. I soon learned that I was indirectly responsible for many of their problems. Of course, my influence was not intentional. Yes, I may have had a few of those tendencies, but they were definitely buried. And they definitely were not directed toward him. I was not a threat to her or their relationship. Or at least, that was not my intention. So, I did the noble thing; I put distance between the three of us. But I tried not to be too obvious. I simply began to decline the majority of the invitations that included her.

On several occasions when Marcellus wanted to get out of the house, he would visit me. He considered my home to be his safe haven, free from worries, problems and arguments, and constant nagging. I understood Marcellus and accepted him for who he was. But periodically, I would make comments regarding his self-centered attitude and his excessive spending on frivolous things that he really couldn't afford. But I never voiced my opinion regarding his toxic codependent relationship with his wife.

But the drama still did not end there. The soap opera continued. Their arguments regarding their marriage became more frequent, all because of the recent changes in his behavior. His wife was losing the stronghold that she once had, and she couldn't deal with it. The verbal confrontations escalated to physical altercations. He tried to leave, and of course, she tried to stop him, clawing at him and ripping his clothes. And although I was never present during the arguments or the scuffles, they were still totally my fault. I was to blame. When I was not available to hang out, he would go to bars and clubs; but of course, she assumed that he was with me, but he wasn't. As usual, he would eventually return home between three and four in the morning. And of course, his wife was furious, always waiting to confront him. To prevent the heated arguments from escalating to violence, he would pack a bag and leave. On several occasions, he ran away to a friend's house for a few days, but he eventually returned. But while he was gone, I caught hell from his wife.

She called me at least three times a day, but I rarely answered her calls. She wanted me to use my influence to persuade him to stop staying out late. Although she still loathed my very existence, she accused me of not being a responsible friend. If I was a true friend, I would try to convince him to stop running the streets and spend more quality with that evil, bitter dominating wench. She wanted me to try to force a grown man to do what his wife couldn't. But I reiterated that he was an adult. It was obvious to me that her dislike for me grew into borderline hatred. One day she actually told me that I was to blame for her marital problems and that I should fix them. She stated that they were fine until I came along. I gave her a pitiful look, laughed to myself, quickly turned, and walked away.

I refused to allow Marcellus to stay with me; and I desperately tried to stay out of their problems. Finally, after a week of constant fighting, with great hesitation, I finally allowed him to stay at my place for two days. But I had to ask him to go back home and try to work things out because he constantly tried to include me in their rollercoaster of a marriage. His personal problems became too stressful for me. He was so disappointed by my request that he didn't call me for over two weeks.

When he finally called, he told me that he had been staying at a hotel for over a week. He had moved out again. He confided in me as always, but I just listened without a response. Three weeks later, he called again, and against my better judgment, I gave in. I finally let my guard down and allowed him to move in for a few months. Once he told his wife where he was staying, she made it very clear that because they were still legally married; she had the right to visit her husband as often as she pleased. As irrational as her thought process was, to my surprise, I didn't say a word. I was taught to never argue with a fool. And she did; she visited my home whenever she pleased. And I just let it slide for a while. I usually went to my bedroom or left the condo. The first time that she dropped by, she started crying and screaming going from room to room ranting and raving because she saw a few of her things that he had taken in his bedroom, bathroom, the kitchen and his office space. He had lied earlier and told her that his belongings were in storage.

During that time his wife came to my condo several more times, always causing a scene with him. My patience was wearing quite thin. So, I requested that she not come to my residence again. They would have to go elsewhere to discuss their problems. Of course, my comments infuriated her.

A few days later after returning home from work one evening, she stormed in the sports facility. I assumed the concierge told her where I was. I could tell from the expression on her face that she was very angry.

"Dexter, are you having an affair with my husband?"

Of course, I didn't respond.

"Dexter!"

Still no response.

"Damn it, Dexter! I know that you hear me!"

I turned and looked at her but still I didn't respond.

Then she yelled, "Are you having sex with Marcellus!"

I was too embarrassed to say anything. I was so glad that no one overheard her. Still dumbfounded, I just walked into the men's locker room and left her standing there. When I came out, she was gone. She had visited my house several more times, always unannounced, uninvited, and in a rage. Enough was enough. I would not continue to be disrespected in my own home. I immediately contacted the concierge, office management, and the security officer regarding banning her from the building. I also filed a temporary restraining order against her. That evening I told Marcellus about the incident. I told him that was the last straw, and before I had allowed that psycho paranoid bitch to push me to my limit, I thought that it would be in everyone's best interest that he leave. Besides, I could no longer deal with his financial irresponsibility. I also thought that he expected a free ride.

A few days later, when he returned from out of town, I told him that he had to leave. I guess the visit with his mother did some good because he didn't argue with me. Actually, he started moving the next day. By the weekend, he had moved everything out of my place. I felt a sigh of relief. No more drama. He had moved back home, and they started seeing a marriage counselor. Not a licensed practitioner who had gone to medical school but a counselor at a church, the Cathedral of Grace Christian Church. Marcellus was also seeing another counselor in the same church regarding another issue. The *homosexual deliverance ministry* was a church counseling ministry that healed those with homosexual tendencies by exorcising or healing them from spiritual demons. Their philosophy was that bisexuality was an evil spirit that could be cast out of a person. Stephanie Richardson, the ministry coordinator, ordered Marcellus to immediately cease all contact with me at once. That was the first step in healing the mind, body, and spirit of such a spiritual abomination. She instructed him to banish Satan, referring to me, from his marriage and from his life. But of course, that did not happen. He had a hidden agenda. He told the coordinator what she wanted to hear, that the LORD was punishing him for breaking his marriage covenant. He decided to play along. His intention was to pacify his wife because she confiscated all the credit cards and placed him on a strict budget. He wanted financial security. I supported his decision. Actually, I was happy that he was gone. But the real issue was clear. How could I have been so naive? It wasn't me. I finally saw the real issue. The wife was trying to gain more control over him. Once again, she allowed her suspicions to get the best of her.

CHAPTER 7

Guilty Pleasures

Be careful in what you ask for; you just might get it. Make sure you are really ready and can you really handle it. Chances are, that it will not turn out the way you expect.

GUESS WHO WAS waiting for me in the lobby one evening after arriving home from the office? Ramona.

"Good evening, Mr. Cavanaugh," said the concierge.

I only responded by rolling my eyes at the concierge. It was obvious that I was not happy.

"Mr. Cavanaugh, I tried to reach you on your cell, but it went straight to your voicemail."

"Why didn't you leave a message or text me? I don't like surprises, especially unexpected or unwanted guests. It would have been nice if I had advance notice that I had a visitor."

"I apologize, sir."

Then I turned to her.

"You know that the restraining order is still in effect, right?"

"Yes," she replied.

"Mr. Cavanaugh, should I escort her out?"

"I will handle this. Well, I guess you are looking for you know who. I don't know where he is? I haven't seen him since I asked him to leave."

"I know where he is. He went to visit his mother for a few days.

"Then why are you here?"

"I need to speak with you."

"Does your husband know that you are here?"

"No, of course not. And he won't know either. Not unless you tell him."

"Okay. I will give you five minutes. Make it quick, I have had a long day."

She followed me into the business center to the right of the main lobby.

"Now, what is it?"

No response. She just stared at me. It was like, she was searching for something inside of me.

"What is it, Ramona? I'm tired. I just told you that I have had a long day."

"He is faking it."

"What are you talking about?"

"Marcellus is faking."

"Faking what?"

"He is just going through the motions regarding the counseling."

"What does that have to do with me?"

"What did you do to my husband?"

"Oh, here we go again. Ramona, what are you talking about?"

"Marcellus has changed. He is not the man I married. I am not stupid. I know that he married me for convenience. He married a financially secure lifestyle. But ever since he met you, he has slowly changed into someone that I don't recognize anymore."

"Don't you mean that he is evolving into someone whom you can't control anymore? Maybe he is growing a backbone."

"It's more than that. It's something that you did."

"Something that I did? Yeah, right. I don't know what you are talking about."

"Dexter, what did you do to my husband?"

"Ramona, be careful. Be very careful. Don't even start. If you dare begin to spew this BS about my controlling or manipulating or brainwashing Marcellus, you will be portraying yourself not only as the bitter and jealous wife, but you will look like a raving lunatic. Keep it up. This is nonsense. You are becoming your own worst enemy. He has shown you time after time his respect for you. Or the lack thereof. And from what I was told and what I see now, he left you and your loveless so-called marriage years ago. You need to move on. Find happiness within yourself. Then find someone else."

"He will never leave me. And I am not leaving either. Well, not until I am ready. Not until I am tired of being sick and tired of dealing with that immature, superficial, weak little mama's boy. Yes, we have a dysfunctional, codependent relationship. He needs me and I need and want him. But it works for us. Besides I really do love him."

"Huh. Control your pride, little girl. I see that you are still living in your fantasy world. Life is short. And you are constantly wasting precious moments every second of every day when you refuse to wake up and accept reality."

"I don't need a lecture from you. And you continue to evade my question. What did you do to my husband?"

"Ramona, your five minutes are up. You need to leave."

I walked out and headed toward the elevators. I asked the concierge to escort her out.

What a stressful day. I really didn't need that today of all days, wrong day, wrong time, wrong person. Immediately, I went upstairs, I stripped down and took a long hot shower. Before I got out, I changed the shower setting to steam sauna, sat down on the shower bench, and relaxed for a few more minutes. That really helped but I needed something more. As soon as I stepped out, I slipped into my favorite silk lounging pants and a black wife beater. I fixed a drink, a double Jack Daniels, straight, no chaser. Boy, I needed that. I turned on my iPod, tuned to my preprogrammed light jazz favorites. I dimmed the lights and lit a few scented candles. I eventually made my way out to my favorite spot, my wraparound terrace. I loved the spectacular view of the city skyline, especially at night. Although it was seasonally warm for that time of the year, the early night air somehow conjured up a well-desired light crisp breeze. With my hectic schedule, it wasn't very often that I got a chance to really enjoy it. I truly valued my quiet relaxing moments alone. That's one of the main reasons I chose the forty-sixth floor of a highly secure building to isolate myself and unwind.

It was too good to be true. My perfect evening was soon to be interrupted. The drama was about to continue. An hour later, my doorbell rang. It was Ramona, again.

Damn! I was sick of this woman!

I guess she really didn't care about the consequences of violating the temporary restraining order. I opened the door, shaking my head in disgust.

"What the hell are you doing here? How did you get past security? This is blatant harassment. Why are you constantly disrespecting my home? Why are you willing to risk going to jail? This could become public. What about your miss goodie-two-shoes professional reputation? Your colleagues and clients could find out that just how deranged you are. And what about your friends and family?"

Without a response, she pushed me to the side and headed toward the balcony.

"Ramona, wait! What are you doing?"

Then she turned, just staring at me. With a slight smirk on her face, she said, "Huh, if by chance you were thinking what I think you were thinking, I would not give you that satisfaction. I'm not suicidal."

"I am warning you, Ramona. You need to leave. Now! I had a long day and I really don't feel like the drama this evening."

She didn't move. She just continued to stare at me, but this time it was different. Surprisingly she was calm, no yelling this time. Very strange. I didn't know what to think. But of course, I still didn't trust her. I knew she was up to something. She was definitely on a mission. I just didn't know what it was yet. But I was sure that I was about to find out and very soon. She just kept staring.

"Since you are not staying, I won't offer you a drink. But I think I am going to need another one, a strong one." I turned, and she was still staring.

"What? What do you want from me? Why in hell are you still blaming me for your marital problems? Marcellus is a grown man.

You can't control a grown-ass man, especially a grown-ass man who is on a mission. Besides, this is not new to you. I am well aware that you have had suspicions long before you met me. You knew about his affair with that guy in college."

"How did you find out about that?"

"That's not important."

"So apparently you two had serious discussions about his tendencies and his repressed issues. Did he tell you that he was molested as a child?"

"Ramona, you got what you wanted. Your man is home now. Aren't you two in marriage counseling working on your relationship? Oh, I forgot. You said he is faking. Still, I don't quite understand what does that have to do with me. I have intentionally distanced myself from him so that he can focus. Ramona, what else do you want from me?"

"May I ask you a question?"

"Do I have a choice? What if I said no?"

"Do you hate women? What did your mother do to you to make you hate women so much?"

"You crazy insecure bitch! Don't try to psychoanalyze me! That's enough, now get out!"

She didn't move.

"Did she run your father away? Now, what is this? A subliminal or unconscious payback for women that you come into contact with?"

"Aight! Don't go there? And keep my mother out of this!"

"Were you abused as a little boy? Were you molested and now it has manifested itself in the manner in which you treat women? Or is it just me? What have I done to you? What?"

"You are pitiful."

"I feel so much hatred toward you!"

"Huh. Wow, like I don't know that already."

"When Marcellus met you, you did something to him. You destroyed my marriage. You took my husband from me. I hate you! I hate you with every fiber of my being. You changed him into someone I don't recognize. Or is it just me? I have good reason to hate you,

Dexter, but why do you hate me so much? Why couldn't you just leave him alone? Leave us alone?"

I didn't respond.

"Dexter! Look at me. Don't you feel guilty? Do you have any remorse for what you have done?"

"I am not the problem. Don't blame me. You two had problems and issues long before you met me."

"That may be true but nothing like this. He is different. Completely different. And I can only attribute the drastic change to something that you have done. I have seen how my girlfriends look at you and flirt with you. And you just play the game right along with them. You are a tease."

"That's funny. I hope that you don't think I am having sex with any of your friends."

"No. I know that you are not. They would have told me. Although at least five of them want to and three of them are married."

"Not going to happen."

"I am not stupid. Over this past year, since we have included you in our social circle of friends, I also have noticed how even some men gawk at you. While others, especially those in the company of other women, give you a sly, subtle glance while trying not to be conspicuous. You might not be aware of it, but I am. And if you don't see it, I think that it is because you don't want to see it. But I actually believe you are aware of it. You exude a sexual aura that is hard to ignore."

"Wow. So, I am being scoped. But believe it or not, I really wasn't aware that I was getting so much attention. Hmmm and why are you watching who is watching me. I find it interesting that the watchers were being watched. Okay, so what?"

"Dexter, are you having sex with Marcellus!"

Almost spilling my drink, I said, "Here we go again."

"I really need to know."

Her tone changed. Solemn. Almost submissive.

"What does my husband see in you? I give him everything. What can you possibly give him that I can't?"

I didn't respond. That did not work, so the other Ramona resurfaced.

"You have some type of power over him that I can only attribute it to that possibility. Again, are you having sex with my husband?"

I laughed. "Girl, you give me too much credit. You really need help."

"Mainly because of you, he has not touched me in over a year. I don't feel like a woman anymore."

"Are you saying that is my fault?"

I finished the last big gulp of my drink. Shaking my head, I chuckled again.

"Do you love Marcellus? Did you make love to him?"

Again, I didn't respond. I walked over to the buffet to fix another drink.

"Answer me, damn it!"

"I know you have your pride. And you don't want to deal with the disgrace of all the *I told you so's* who knew that your marriage was doomed to fail. You should leave before he hurts you even more."

"I want the truth."

"The truth? What truth?"

"Yes, the truth! You do know what that is, don't you?"

"Are you sure? I don't think you really know what you are asking me, Ramona? Once you open Pandora's box and hurtful things are released, you might not ever recover from them. You can't just simply place them back in the box and close it as if it never happened. You won't be able to unhear it."

"Damn it! Tell me, Dexter! Please!"

"C'mon, girl, you are a corporate attorney. Why are you playing stupid? You know that you are not one of my favorite people, but I don't want to intentionally hurt you. Why do you want me to tell you something you already know? Ramona, you are walking around in a minefield, but you are sadly mistaking them for daisies. You actually think that this truth that you are searching for will give you solace. You think it will help you deal with your issues. It won't. I promise you, it won't. You really feel that hearing from me the so-called truth is going to set you free, to set your mind free. You think that someone actually telling you something you already know is going to make you feel better. Not this time. I guarantee it won't."

"You don't care about my damn feelings. You are avoiding the damn question."

Then she grabbed my drink and threw it in my face.

"Just tell me. Damn it! Are you fucking Marcellus?"

"Oh, okay! That did it! You want the truth! You want to hear it! Okay! HELL YES! YES! Yes, I was fucking your husband! Well, I was until he started trippin'. And acting like a jealous possessive little bitch! And that's all it was, just sex. I am not trying to take your husband from you. I don't love your husband, and I am not in love with him. Yes, I care about him despite his immature, selfish behavior. But it's not the way you think. I care about him just as a friend. If it makes you feel any better, he came on to me. He seduced me!"

I paused a moment. She just stood there. No response. Just a blank look on her face.

"See, I told you. Now, are you satisfied?

I paused again.

"It started a month or so after he moved in to my place. One night, I went to a party and he asked if he could tag along. I was fine with that. By the time we left I was extremely tipsy. I don't even remember leaving the party or driving home. So, I assumed that it was him that had driven us home. I fell asleep on the sofa, still in my clothes. Sometime later, I woke up in complete darkness to someone sucking my piece. Still inebriated, it was not clear to me where I was or who was giving me such an incredible head-job. I found my cell phone that was right next to me. I turned it on for a source of light. When I saw who it was, I immediately pushed him back. I guess I pushed him so hard that he fell back, and he hit his head on the coffee table. I jumped up and flicked on the light and ran over to pick him up. He was okay. He said that I was moaning in my sleep and massaging my crotch. It must have been a combination of all the strong top-shelf liquor that I had consumed and the overt flirtation from several women. And a few subtle passes from a few sexy-ass bruthas also probably caused what appeared to be an erotic dream.

Although I didn't actually see Marcellus for most of the night, apparently, he was watching my every move the entire time.

"Then after I helped him up and sat him in the chair, I went to get a glass of water. He seemed okay, so I went to my room. I quickly stripped down to nothing but my boxer briefs, then I flopped down on the bed and fell into another deep coma. But it was obvious that he was on a mission. I woke up again to his slurping and gulping down on my piece again. Once the initial shock wore off, this time I allowed it to continue. I laid back and let him do his thing. Then one thing led to another. Naw, I am not blaming it on the alcohol. I knew what I was doing.

"Over the next few months, I gave it to him every time he wanted it, which was often. It's like he was becoming addicted to me. Then he began to show signs of being possessive. When he started trippin' and acting a fool, I had to shock him back into reality. He started acting jealous when other friends would come by to visit me or would stop by to pick me up. He was even jealous of the women. So, I told him that he had to leave. I told him to go home, get counseling, and work on the marriage. He didn't like it, but he really didn't have a choice. I was tired of his drama.

"He caught me at a weak moment and I let it happen. Now what? Huh? You got the answer you wanted, now what? Are you satisfied? From the look on your face, I don't think so. I told you. I told you about Pandora's box. Now you can't close it. Marcellus has been hiding behind your so-called marriage for years, probably from day one."

She slapped me.

"Okay, now you know. You finally got your answer. Now, please leave."

She slapped me again.

"He loves me," she said.

"I have no doubt that he cares for you and he probably loves you in his own way."

She slapped me again.

"I had no intentions of telling you, ever. And I definitely didn't want to tell you this way. I really didn't want to go there. Now you know. I said it. Just leave."

"Dexter, make love to me? Make me feel like a woman? Or just make me feel like you made him feel?"

I dropped my glass.

"Dexter?"

I didn't respond.

"Dexter, please."

Again, I didn't respond.

She slapped me again. Much harder this time.

"Then fuck me. Fuck me like you fucked him!"

"What? Girl, you are not just delusional. You are really messed up! You really need help."

Shaking my head, I laughed again. I had to stay calm. Laughing was the safest response. Although that's not how I felt inside. I probably shouldn't care, but I really didn't want to hurt that girl anymore.

"That's enough. Ramona, I think you better go home."

She didn't move.

"Now! Ramona, now! Leave now! I am warning you. One of the worst things you can do is get what you ask for. You just think you want that because you are hurting right now. Now, leave!"

"Now, you are rejecting me too. You probably have never even had sex with a woman! You are a perpetrator!"

She attempted to strike me again, but this time I grabbed her hand.

"I said that's enough!"

"Then fuck me like you hate me!"

"Leave, Ramona!"

She attempted to slap me again, but this time I caught her hand with a firm grip before she actually struck me. I grabbed her other arm and gave her a mean grimace. I shook her. She froze, obviously in shock.

I pushed her down on the sofa. Then I leaned over and straddled her. Breathing heavily and shaking a little. It was obvious that she was scared. Well, she had reason to be. She really didn't know what I was going to do. How would she be able to explain her being here? There was an active restraining order against her. And this time she was not just sitting in the lobby; she deliberately bypassed the security officer and the concierge to get to my condo. I slowly stood up while continuing to give her a firm stare. Although she was not sure what I was about to do, she definitely knew I was not playing and that I had enough of her foolishness.

I picked up her petite frame and slowly placed her upright on the couch. Then I kneeled on the floor right in front of her, lifted her skirt slightly, and spread her legs apart. I told her to close her eyes and not to open them until I told her too.

Without popping a single button, I ripped open her designer silk blouse. For such a small frame, she was quite well endowed. I guess I never paid any attention to her in that way. And I really didn't care if they were real or not; I had a job to do. And regarding any major task, I always strived to do my best. And this chore was no exception.

I snatched off her provocative black lace wonder bra and immediately nestled my face between her breasts. Then I sat her up and began to massage each of them in a circular motion to the rhythm of the music. She gasped and moaned. Then for the next few minutes, I went straight for the nipples. Only tongue action. I kissed and licked each nipple, alternating back and forth, left and right, right to left. The gasps and moans began to grow louder and louder. Then I suddenly stopped.

"Be quiet. I don't want to hear that right now."

Still alternating the singular circular tongue action, I reached around her waist with one arm to elevate her a bit. And with the other hand, I reached under her skirt, maneuvered her panties to the side, and slid my forefinger inside her. I rotated my finger and stroked her a few times. I slowly pulled my finger out and put it in my mouth, sucking it like a Tootsie Roll lollipop.

"I expected nothing less from you, the essence of peaches and cream. Hmmm. And I taste sweetness. Whatever you are doing down there, it's really working for me right now."

She swooned and arched her back.

"Stop it. Be still!"

Her breathing gradually slowed down to a low moan. I could tell that the erotic foreplay was getting to her. She was now relaxed. I think she realized now that I was not going to hurt her. My plan was working. Obviously, she was not aware of my "skills." But I still wasn't sure how far I was going to go with this.

Now that she was completely relaxed, I was determined to find the special spot—her G-spot. I began to stroke her again, scraping and massaging the walls with two fingers. Found it. I anticipated that she would arch her back again, and of course, she did not let me down. But of course, I was not going to let her know that. But to my surprise, she screamed louder than I had expected.

"Yes, I know. I found the spot, but be still. I am going to play with it for a minute unless you want me to stop, I will."

She froze again.

"Good girl."

I repeated the tantalizing sensation two more times using two fingers then with three fingers, each time continuing to lick them individually. I intentionally intensified my animated yet erotic antics by continuing the loud sucking and slurping of my fingers. I wanted her to hear what I was doing because I would not allow her to watch me perform.

All the while never allowing her to look at me directly in the face. Never allowing her to speak to me. And never allowing her to kiss me. Kissing was too personal, too intimate. I wouldn't even allow her to touch me. There was to be no emotional connection here. I was well aware that I had already snatched the lid off another one of Pandora's boxes. But now I was about to with grave aggression, flip the top off, and fling it across the room. Ironically, it would be opened in a controlled environment with limits and restrictions, but such limits and restrictions would not apply to me. I also had placed no limitations or restrictions on what I could do or say. I was determined to teach her a lesson. She asked for it and now I was about to oblige.

I leaned forward, lifting her up gently just enough to raise her skirt above her tiny waist. I ripped off her matching black lace panties and threw them in the corner.

"You are not going to need those."

Then I lifted her legs up and placed them on my shoulders.

"A Brazilian wax, I see. Nice. Real nice."

I blew on her hole and kissed it. She moaned louder and louder. Then she locked her legs around my head.

"Damn, Ramona! Let go! And be still!"

I blew on her hole again and then kissed it again and again. Then I licked it up and down several more times. Treating her hole not like it was an inanimate object but as though it had a mind and that it understood what I was saying; I began to talk to it.

Hey little friend, I'm Dex. How are you doing right now. How do you feel? Umm. You taste good. I want to spend a little quality time this evening getting to know you. That is if you let me. Is that okay? Okay, now just relax. I am not going to hurt you. I promise I will be good. Naw, let me change that. I am going to treat you better than good. I am going to take you on a trip, to a special place to which you probably have never been. I promise that you will not only enjoy the journey of getting there but also the final destination. In fact, you just might enjoy the journey a little more than reaching the final destination.

Then I refocused my attention directly to her. With her legs still on my shoulders, I raised my head up and told her to listen.

"Listen. And listen carefully. We are going to play a game. And there are several more rules. And you are going to obey these rules or you get nothing. As I stated before, don't look directly at me. Don't talk. Even if I ask you a question, don't respond. I don't even want to hear a moan or a groan. Don't move. If you squirm or start wiggling, the game is over. If you break the rules, I will stop. If you scream, it's over."

This unusual tryst was an extreme twist even for my somewhat freaky bedside manner. This was the first of many firsts. Usually I preferred that the other person express themselves. It was definitely a turn-on. And mainly because I wanted them to visualize and recall the intensity of the details during the next day and thereafter.

Expressing oneself by using more than one of the senses simultaneously while having sex only intensifies or magnifies the level of the passion. I often tell the other person to watch me while I am on top of them or doing the oral thing. And I look down at them as well. It's all part of taking them to that special place. A place that I call *La La Land*.

I picked her up and wrapped her legs around me and carried her to my bedroom. I gently laid her on her back; opened her legs to a V. As I began to lick, slide, and wiggle my tongue inside her spot, she grabbed the back of my head with both hands and pushed it in further. I immediately smacked her hands away.

"Stop that. What did I tell you? Don't move. And stop the moaning. I know it's difficult. I know it feels good, but I really haven't done anything yet to cause all this unnecessary and exaggerated moaning, squirming, and wiggling. So be still."

I leaned back and flipped her over. Doggie style. What a tempting site.

"Ramona? Why are you moving? Do you want me to stop? I have no problem stopping."

Suddenly she froze. She remained completely still for a least a minute. Now she was ready. I flipped her back over on her back and stood up. Then I finished undressing her.

"Don't move."

I soon returned. I took her right hand and guided it to the tip of my magic stick.

"Feel that. Yes, I am wearing a condom. And don't worry, it won't break. It's an XL Magnum. But just in case, you are still okay because the second one won't."

She didn't seem to want to let go, so I had to smack her hand away again.

"Okay. That's enough. Now, move your hand back to where it was. Now try to relax and let me do my job. I am on a mission."

I spread her legs, forming the infamous V position again and placed them on my shoulders. I parted her lips with two fingers and allowed the head of my piece to lightly tap the opening.

"Be still. Stop squirming. I got this."

I rubbed the head of my piece up and down her hole. I repeated it twice more. Up and down. Up and down. I slowly slid inside her with just the mushroom head. Then I suddenly froze for several seconds. Teasing her even more, I pulled out quickly. I slid back in but this time I pushed all the way in. As soon as I felt what I thought was the bottom, I slowly pulled out. She gasped and jerked. I repeated the slow action a few more times. She started squirming again, all the while matching the rhythm of my long deep strokes. I guess she didn't believe me. I immediately pulled out and stood up.

"Damn! You know why I pulled out, don't you? Why are you continuing to break the rules? Get up, get dressed, get out, and take your ass home."

"Okay! Okay! I'm sorry! Don't' stop! Please don't stop!" she yelled.

"Why are you talking? See what I mean, another rule broken."

"Please! Please!"

"I told you what the rules were. You think I am playing with you. I meant what I said. I told you to get up and go home!"

She didn't move. I left the room and returned to her lying in the same position.

"Get up! I'm not playing!"

She didn't move. I stood there for a moment.

"Aight. Let's try this again."

I spread her legs forming the infamous V position again and placed them on my shoulders again. I began to rub the mushroom head causing her lips to open slightly. Then I began the tapping the mushroom head up and down, up and down. Trying to control herself, this time she only flinched a little bit. I guess that was okay.

"Now we are going to play another game. It's called six hundred strokes. And yes, I will be counting the numbers with the speed and intensity of each stroke. Sometimes silently and sometimes, so you can hear me. Yeah, I know. Kinda different, but I think you will like it. Naw, I know that you are going to love it. It's the freak in me."

Extremely vocal, I described each exercise in detail while initially demonstrating them, I continued counting. All the while, giving her an additional one hundred strokes. I'm sure that she didn't mind. Well, she said that it had been over a year since her husband had touched her.

I call it my *Erotic Horizontal* workout. All the while not using my hands, first, I massage the hole by sliding all the way in and holding it. I allow my piece to pulsate at the bottom then I pull all the way out. Next, I slide in the hole again but this time from the left side, then repeat from the right side. Then I suddenly stopped. She flinched and jerked a little hinting that she wanted more.

"Yeah, I know. I know. You didn't want me to stop. Just relax. I got this. Well, surprisingly, overall, you followed the rules quite well, although you had a little trouble adjusting in the beginning. You have been a good girl, so in lieu of your extreme discipline, I have another surprise for you. There is one more exercise. And the surprise is that none of the previous rules apply but one. No kissing on the mouth. And I think you know why. And the final exercise is called 'grind and scrape the walls of the hole with a vengeance.' So, I am about to work your hole with a vengeance. And you can decide which position you want to start." She stood on the end of the bed and motioned me to come toward her.

She wrapped her arms around my shoulders and followed by wrapping her legs around me. I guess my piece was in for a real treat. She slowly slid down on me. She arched her back, screamed, and began to bounce up and down. I grabbed her from behind and palmed each cheek with each hand. I began thrusting upward attempting to synchronize her bouncing with my thrusting. We were in rhythm together.

"Okay, that's enough. You did your thing, but that's not what I had in mind."

So, I laid her on the bed on her back. I jumped up again.

"Give me a second. Don't move. I will be right back."

I quickly went in the bathroom to wipe off the sweat, spray a little cologne, and slip on fresh condoms. Then I returned to work.

"My break is over. Now relax."

Still on her back, I gently bent her legs to her chest. I told her to look at me.

"After this, you will never look at me the same again. Now pay attention to what I am about to do."

I slid in her and froze.

"Look at me. Focus. Focus on what I am doing."

I started thrusting with deep long strokes. She continued moaning and screaming.

"Yeah, I know. I know it feels really good. No one has ever done you this way. So just relax and look at me. I got you."

I opened her legs in the V position and immediately started thrusting again. Then I leaned on top of her and motioned her to wrap her legs around me. Then I whispered.

"Do you remember what you originally asked me to do the last time you slapped me?"

She didn't respond.

"You said, 'Fuck me like you hate me!' Well, it's time."

So, I did. Still on top of her, I reached her from behind firmly gripping her ass. Pushing myself deeper inside her, I now realized that I had her locked in. She wasn't going anywhere, even if she tried. All the while I was pounding her profusely, alternating slow deep strokes with fast choppy thrusts, constantly pushing myself deeper and deeper inside her and steadily holding that position for several seconds. After another thirty minutes of nonstop earth-shattering thrusting, she exploded a third time. She beat me by one. Oh well, that part was not a contest. They say that most young viral Black men, whether gay or straight, are young, dumb, and full of cum. Young and full of cum I might be, but dumb I was not. I didn't have to brag, but I knew what the hell I was doing. And I was doing the damn thang. And I was doing it well.

Then I gave her an additional bonus. I escalated the erotic frolicking by combining a few of my other erotic games. I leaned over, pulled her close to me and whispered in her ear.

"Lick it, then stick it. Glide on it, then slide in it. And lastly, jump in it and pump it. And no rules but the one: kissing. Still too personal." And that was enough. After a few minutes, she reached another climax as did I. While still in her, I lifted her chin up and tilted it in my direction.

"Hey, look at me. Did that make up for all the abstinence over the last year? Well, hopefully it helped, a little."

She didn't answer. She closed her eyes and slowly turned her head away. I leaned over and couldn't believe what I saw. A slight tear rolled down her face.

"I know you are curious. I hear you thinking. There is one question that you are too proud to ask. I think that you realize now and after all that I have told you. And the wrong answer would hurt you even more. It could be devastating. Not to mention your insecurity regarding your sex appeal and your ability to please a man."

She still didn't respond. She turned her head the other way. So, I leaned over to the other side so I could see her face.

"Well, to answer your question. The answer is no. No, he didn't get the same treatment as I gave you. Yeah, you have your issues and you can be a real bitch, but you have nothing to worry about. I guess that goes part with being a smart, successful, self-made Black woman. Yeah, I did all the work but I definitely got mine too."

Then I pulled out. I stood up and returned with a robe. I motioned her to follow me. I led her to the bathroom, preheated the shower, and laid out a set of fresh towels. For obvious reasons, I deliberately gave her the nonscented Neutrogena body wash. She stepped in the oversized floor to ceiling glass shower to experience one of my favorite adult toys—the alternating, oscillating showerheads. I gave her a few minutes alone. As I passed by the mirror, I noticed all the scratches on my chest and back. Well, there is nothing I can do about that now. Although my shift was over, I intended to work a little overtime. So I returned to work.

I wasn't quite finished just yet. A few minutes later, I returned. I dimmed the lights and turned on the speakers in the bathroom. I opened the shower door, reached over, and changed the setting to rain shower. Then I stepped in behind her and gently glided my hands across her shoulders and motioned her to straddle the wall. I reached around and gently grabbed her breasts, massaging them a few minutes. Then I kneeled down on the floor behind her, gently grabbed her cheeks, and once again went to work. I gave her another grueling round of tongue action. When she seemed to have had enough, I stood up and whispered in her ear.

"Well, they say that the tongue is the cleanest organ that is until it is exposed to air. Did I wash it good? I was hoping to clean it, but from the cream on my face, it looks like I got it dirty again. I made a real mess. Oh well, I am not sorry. I guess I will leave it up to you to clean it up."

I rinsed off, stepped out, and allowed her to finish. It took a minute to blow-dry her hair straight. Soon after, she reappeared and started to get dressed.

"Looking for these?" I asked, holding her panties between my teeth. "They are staying."

She took a step toward me, reaching for them.

"No."

I snatched them back and placed them in my boxer briefs.

"I am keeping the panties. Not as a souvenir although they smell like one of my favorite perfumes, Boucheron. I want evidence, just in case you continue the drama. But I really don't think you want anyone to find out about this. Although I am sure that the security cameras caught you coming in and will catch you leaving. And of course, remember the restraining order is still in force. How will you explain to Marcellus and to the authorities about your being here?"

She seemed to be in a daze. I guess she was still feeling euphoria although I was absolutely positive that she was sexually satisfied. I wasn't quite sure if she was somewhat happy with ending tonight's little escapade. She seemed melancholy. I guess while she was getting ready in the bathroom, she spent a little time thinking about what she had come here for, what she had asked for and what she had actually received. She finished getting dressed, checked herself in the mirror, reached for her purse, and headed for the door.

"Wait!"

She stopped, but she didn't turn around.

"Again, I am not worried about you telling anyone about this little encounter. Well, maybe no one but GOD. As far as we are concerned, this never happened. You were never here. No one must ever find out about this. As much as I care about your husband as a friend,

I won't hesitate to hurt him if he finds out and comes after me. Kill him if I am provoked. I am serious, Ramona. You know how he is. If he gets stupid, I won't hesitate to hurt him. And with our recent history, self-defense won't be hard to prove." I expected her not to respond to such a threat. And of course, she didn't.

"You can leave, now."

She left. It's a good thing he was out of town. Damn! It's 2:00 a.m. What about security and the concierge? What are they going to say about this? And because of all the drama over the past year, all three shifts were very familiar with who she was. I was not worried. Besides, I was sure that those guys had seen a lot of secret encounters and many other private things that they really weren't supposed to see. They seemed discreet. But to be on the safe side, I will stop by the ATM tomorrow and give each of them an incentive to forget anything that they might have seen. I dropped off three sealed envelopes with each concierge's name on it.

I knew exactly what I had done. Yes, it was wrong on so many levels. Not to mention that she was a married woman and the fact that I had sex with her husband several times in the recent past. Although I had no remorse for what I had done, I still asked the LORD to forgive me. I could've said that she asked for what she got, but that would be a cop-out. I knew what I was doing. I am a grown man. And I am far from stupid, innocent, or naive. She didn't pressure me. And her slaps really didn't provoke me either. To be honest, I was drunk on power and not the liquor and I liked it—a lot.

Over the next few days, I received several anonymous calls from a restricted number. The person just held the phone. Then I heard breathing. I knew it was Ramona. When I called out her name—"Ramona, I know that it is you"—the caller hung up.

My suspicions were eventually confirmed. She appeared at my door a week later.

"So, that was you calling me?"

She didn't respond.

"So are you coming in or not?"

"No."

"Okay, why are you here?"

"Dexter, I hate you. I slept with the enemy."

Chuckling with a smirk on my face, I said, "You still hate me? Okay, but you must admit that your body feels much differently than it did before. I am well aware of the special place that I took you to over a week ago. Rarely does a person get a chance to visit *La La Land*."

"I hate you, but we are inextricably linked. My husband and me, my husband and you, and now, you and me. Now you have touched a part of my inner being, I can't get you out of my head. That special place, as you called it, is very dangerous. We are connected in ways that are wrong. This complicated triangle that has been created has only made the situation worse. I feel possessed and I can't control it. When I see you, I still see Satan?"

"Are you serious? The way that I had you moaning and groaning and screaming and squirming, all you can say is that I am the devil? Did you see the scratch marks that you left all over my body? I have been called a lot of things, some good and some not so good. But this one is real mind-boggling."

"The devil made me do it."

"The devil made you do it? That's a good one."

"Yes, the devil made me do it. I was stressed, depressed, and confused, and I fell into a place of grave darkness. And while I lost focus and I became distracted, the devil slid in my mind and made me do it."

"So, I slid in. So, do you mean that I slid in literally or figuratively? Ramona, baby, you really are crazy."

"Baby? I am not your baby."

"I guess you are going around telling others that you were spawned by the devil. Do you know how ridiculous that sounds? Do you want to be committed? Do you want to flush your career down the toilet?"

She just looked at me.

"Ramona, baby. Oops. Sorry. Okay, I can't believe I am saying this, but I don't think you are crazy. Your suspicions were on point. It's just the way that you found out and what happened afterward. I just think you need professional help. You need to talk to someone,

someone who can be objective. With someone who is board certified and has acquired a PhD or MD."

She turned and left.

Just enough time for me to make a drink, the doorbell rang again. I knew it. She was back.

"Huh. How did I guess? I'm not surprised. So, I, being the devil, made you come back."

She didn't respond.

"I know why you came back, back to the den of iniquity. That little speech that you made a few minutes ago was just your way of trying to rationalize your behavior. Remember one very important thing, I never asked you to come over the first time or any other time. And I didn't force myself on you. And now I see that it will be up to me to stop it. This is not going to become a habit. This can't happen again."

She acted like she didn't hear a word that I just said. She walked past me and went straight to my bedroom.

I grabbed her by the arm.

"Look at me."

"No."

"Look at me!"

She slowly turned and looked up at me.

"Ramona, as you can see, I can easily practice dissociative behavior. I can be very intimate with you and not feel a thing."

"I don't care."

"Oh, okay. You don't care? You are a lying liar. *You do care!* I think what the real truth is that you realize that you have gotten yourself in a situation that you had not planned on. Oh, you love *it*! That's why you are back. You crave it. I think you really hate yourself for what you have done, the role that you have played in this and for how your so-called enemy makes you feel. Well, you think that you hate me now. Just wait until tomorrow and the next day and the day after that. When you have had some time to think about what happened, your hatred for me will become a thousand times worse. Just wait and see."

Over the next three weeks, she just showed up at my place five more times for some more. And for some reason, I obliged her; I gave her fantasies that most women only dreamed of. But was I controlling her or was she now manipulating me? I played with her. I played her game. Or had she flipped the script. It was not ending the way that I am sure that she was expecting. Who was I fooling? What had I done? How long could I allow myself to do this? This situation had become much more complicated than I ever could have imagined. This time, this mess was entirely my fault. I knew that I was totally responsible. I had to stop this and I did. I told her no more. Of course, she didn't agree with my decision, but she eventually got the message. Besides, what could she do? We never spoke of the encounters, again.

CHAPTER 8

Secret Obsession

Stop the world, I want to get off. Or at least, slow it down a little bit.

THE SAGA CONTINUED even farther but with another interesting twist. When Marcellus moved out of my place and back home to work on his marriage, he left with an unpaid balance of living expenses and several personal loans. Initially he made what I thought was a good faith effort to make good on his financial responsibility. However, the situation with Ramona seemed to be less tense. At last a little peace.

Well, it was good while it lasted. A month after he moved out, I received a notice in the mail from my bank. Seven checks that Marcellus had recently written to me before he left had been returned as NSFs. I should have gone with my first thought, which was to cash all the checks at his bank. Big mistake. Although all my online payments and ATM transactions had cleared, the large dollar amount of the combined bounced checks and NSF fees had caused a major dent in that account. I tried to contact Marcellus several times that afternoon at work and on his cell. My calls were ignored. And he did not respond to any of my messages. The next morning, I contacted the bank to transfer the necessary amount from my savings to checking. Later that day I received another NSF check written by him in the mail. I called him again several times that day at work and on his cell. Of course, I desperately needed to resolve this issue, so I called his home, which was a big mistake. Ramona finally answered. When she realized it was me, she hung up? I wasn't sure if she was upset because I cut off the sex with her or if I was calling to speak with him. I called again; she hung up again. I called a third time and left a detail message. Since I did not receive a return call after one hour, I went to their residence to discuss the matter. And yes, I was highly pissed. Ramona came to the door. She yelled, "Go away, Satan. When I see you, I see Satan," and slammed the door. I saw red. After the sixth or seventh kick, the door completely fell off the hinges. Her insults and actions and reaction led to an argument and an altercation between Marcellus and me. The police were called and charges were filed against me. I had just given his wife and their marriage counselor the ammunition they needed to discredit me.

Yes, my temper got the best of me but I had absolutely no remorse for my actions that night. A few days later, even though I initiated the incident, Marcellus tried to apologize for allowing his wife to interfere and cause the situation to escalate as it did. But I really didn't want to hear anything he had to say. How could I allow myself to stoop so low? But I had bigger issues. Was I going to fight those bogus charges? He also tried to remedy the situation by meeting with the assistant DA on several occasions to drop the charges. After a few unsuccessful attempts, he also contacted the judge to reduce some of the charges. Obviously, he didn't know that a judge does not have the authority to reduce charges. However, he was desperate. He would try anything.

His wife supposedly felt threatened by me, but she continued to harass me. I eventually filed another restraining order against her. How ironic. And when much of my evidence was presented in court, the judge realized the wife's motives and intentions. His wife was determined to get revenge by using her clout. She tried to use her influence as an attorney, and she continued her efforts to manipulate the legal system to cause much more harm to me.

Marcellus pleaded with the court again and again but to no avail. He petitioned the court to modify the mutual no-contact order against the both of them. However, I learned my lesson. I decided that it was in my best interest not to communicate at all.

They were two mentally unstable peas in a pod. They were meant for each other.

Initially completely oblivious of his scheme, I began to see his secret plan unravel. Although I was provoked, I kicked in his door and assaulted him. Now Marcellus actually wanted a relationship with me. He explained that he was in love with me. Of course, I reiterated that the feelings would never be reciprocated. The next week when I arrived home from a business trip, I found a letter from him in my mailbox.

> *Dear Dexter,*
>   *Man, I need you. I trust you. I will always want you in my life. We can work this out where both of us can benefit and be happy. Not to mention we will have a stronger focus on God's purpose for our lives.*
>   *Always and forever,*
>   *I will never stop loving you,*
>   *You are my man!*
>   *Love,*
>   *M*

This guy was delusional. He needed serious help. Marcellus could not separate the friendship from his fantasy. I was bombarded with letters, cards, emails, text messages, and calls for the next five days. In the letters, he shared his plans of finally divorcing his wife to pursue a long-term relationship with me. I had replied numerous times that I did not see him that way. I told him several times that the type of relationship he envisioned would never happen. Never.

I learned a few weeks later that he shared his plan with my long-time female friend, before he shared it with me. He told her that he loved his wife but he wasn't in love with her and their marriage was stifling his growth. He wanted to be with me and that he would not settle for just a friendship. He told my friend that he wanted a relationship or nothing at all. If he only knew what I had done to his wife not to mention the manner in which I slowly took her to a special place. He would definitely feel and react much differently.

I couldn't believe that my girl was aware of his secret all along and that she did not disclose it to me. She was supposed to be my friend, one of my closest friends. I thought she had my back. I was furious at her for not telling me. Her secret changed our friendship forever.

Over the next few weeks, I tried to distance myself, but as usual, Marcellus made it extremely difficult with lies, acts of manipulation, and threats of suicide. When I rejected his advances, I noticed even more destructive behavior than I had seen before. When I ignored his calls and refused to see him, he went on drinking binges and he smoked marijuana. One time he supposedly took a half bottle of sleeping pills, but fortunately, his friend arrived there in time and called 911. The ambulance rushed him to the hospital and they pumped his stomach. He was forced to stay for several more days for psychiatric care. Although I assumed he pulled that stunt to get my attention, it only confirmed that he needed long-term psychiatric care.

I supported his recovery until he was released from the hospital. But shortly after that the jealousy, irrational behavior, and possessiveness continued when he was upset and depressed. As long as I was receptive to him and appeared to respond the way that he wanted, there was peace between us. I continued to reiterate to Marcellus that I only wanted a platonic "friendship." But his irrational behavior continued.

After Marcellus admitted his true feelings and his hope for the future with me and I steadily rejected his advances; he still didn't give up. He ignored the court-ordered restraining order. His actions escalated to borderline obsession. I continued to receive numerous daily phone calls from him mostly on my cell but also at work and at home. Every day for another week, he continued to leave cards and gifts for me with the concierge. I didn't want them, so I sent them all back or told the concierge to get rid of them.

The next week while Marcellus was on a business trip in Chicago, he called me several times. He left me a detail message that he was coming home early and that he wanted to meet with me and maybe have dinner. I did not return the call. I learned later that in hopes that I would meet him, he lied to his wife and told her that he had to stay in Chicago for an extra day. When I arrived home, he was parked across the street from my building. I passed by without stopping and drove into the underground parking. He called me several more times, but I did not answer. The concierge called me and told me that he was in the lobby. I told the concierge to tell him that I was not receiving guests. He eventually left the building.

The stalking continued for several more days. I assumed Ramona became suspicious of his routine because on a few occasions she followed him and discovered that he was parked in front of my building in one of the visitor's parking spaces. I guess she assumed he was waiting for me. On another occasion, I saw them in his car arguing in front of my building, but once again, I passed by the both of them without stopping and drove into the underground parking. They eventually left after they realized I was not coming back out. On the way home, he called me several more times, but again, I did not answer.

The most disturbing incident was after a business trip with Ramona to Florida. When Marcellus returned from that trip, he planned one of his many fake last-minute business trips, this time pretending to leave town to go to Savannah, GA, all the while staying in town in an effort to get away from his wife. The evening Marcellus returned, he could not locate me. Angry that he could not find me, he began driving around.

That evening my friend Ernest called.

"Hey, dude, how is it going?"

"I'm cool. What's up?"

"Well, have you seen Marcellus lately?"

"No, not really. He has been calling a lot and he comes by and parks downstairs, but I haven't seen or talked to him. Why, what's up?"

"Well, Marcellus came to my house looking for you and he was mad as hell. He had a strange look in his eyes. I could tell the first time that I met him that he was very jealous and possessive."

"What do you mean?"

"Dude, wake up! That dude has it really bad for you."

"Was it really that obvious?"

"Really. Dude, really. Just be careful. And leave that crazy dude alone."

"Yeah, dude, and thanks for the heads up."

Later that night, Marcellus and I passed by each other on one of the side streets near my condo. He turned around and followed me. I stopped at the next block. He jumped out of the car, yelling and screaming.

"Where the fuck have you been? I've been driving all over Atlanta looking for you. I went to your job and to your friend Ernest's house. Where in hell were you? I left you several voicemail messages. You knew that I was returning today. You have been missing for six hours. Why are you ignoring me?"

Once again, I had finally allowed this deranged idiot to push me to my limit.

"Nigga, you are just as crazy as your crazy-ass wife. What the fuck is wrong with you, involving my friends in your drama. Have you lost your mind? You better lower your damn voice and calm down. Behavior like this is the main reason I cut you loose."

Realizing that I had enough, he finally settled down.

"Now I'm going home, and if you follow me, I will call the police."

"But, Dex, I love you! I want to be with you. Dex! Please, please, Dex. Please!"

"Man, go home! Go home to your wife."

Then I turned and walked to my car and drove off. I left without any further incident that evening.

Ramona still blamed me for all their problems. She forged a mission to destroy me, my life, and my livelihood. However, Marcellus went to extreme measures to try to minimize the damages. But the final outcome of his efforts would only benefit him. Marcellus sent the judge in the case a detailed letter. The judge was a nonsympathetic, biased, stereotypical angry Black female who had a reputation of dishing out harsher sentences to Black men. It was rumored that her ex-husband left her for a white man. If Marcellus had known about what her ex had done, he might not have written the letter. He expressed more details regarding his imaginary relationship in hope to persuade her to change her mind and rescind the mutual restraining order.

> *Your Honor,*
>
> *I would like to take this opportunity to address the court and to convey my feelings regarding this case. I realize that the court ordered a "total stay away, no contact" be placed on Mr. Cavanaugh. And that Mr. Cavanaugh has demanded that mutual restraining orders be placed on the both of us. In no way am I condoning his actions regarding the incident that occurred on that tragic night. But just to let you know, I am not concerned about my safety with him. Consequently, I have violated your ruling. I have voluntarily contacted Mr. Cavanaugh. I have spoken to him on several occasions after the incident to inform him that I want to start a relationship with him. And hopefully when this case is over, and I have divorced my wife, he will consider planning a future with me. The incident was not totally his fault; I must take much of the responsibility for the mentioned incident. Mr. Cavanaugh has never been violent toward me in*

the entire year and a half that I have known him. It was a surprise to me to see that side of him. To me it was a normal reaction that escalated and got out of hand. He became very angry when my wife disrespected him by slamming the door in his face when he came to discuss the unpaid living expenses, loans, and bounced checks. She never approved of our friendship. Maybe subconsciously she knew or suspected that this would happen. At the time, I did not want to continue my cycle of being selfish. And I could not deal with the guilt. But I now regret even coming back home to help her get through this.

Your Honor, I am in love with Mr. Cavanaugh. My behavior was very unfair and very deceitful. I tried numerous times to explain to her that I was dealing with my sexuality, and I felt we needed to get a divorce. She was in denial. I have seen therapists ever since I was a child. I have also tried marital counseling. I even tried spiritual counseling at a church because I felt that I did not leave the right way. I realize that this was a big blow to my wife's ego. I honestly did not want her to get hurt anymore. I have tried to set aside my feelings and help her get through this. I knew it would be difficult for her to phantom how this could happen. So, it was important for me to help her understand. That was the only reason I came back home after moving in with Mr. Cavanaugh for those six months. Actually, Mr. Cavanaugh supported my decision to move back. I am hoping he will wait until I dissolve this charade of a marriage. This became very difficult, so after about six weeks, I just gave up and filed for divorce. I exposed all of my feelings for Mr. Cavanaugh to my wife. I shared with her all my deep, dark secrets, and I participated in the spiritual counseling to show her that I was willing to try to work through it just so she could understand things better. My feelings did not change for him. So, I decided to end my marriage. I have retained an attorney and I have started taking affirmative steps toward ending the marriage. I have not slept with my wife in over a year and a half. We sleep in separate rooms and we have not conducted ourselves as husband and wife for a very long time. I realized that I married for the wrong reasons and that I should have married for love and not convenience. I love my wife, but I am not in love with her. I am sure this sounds like a soap opera, but this is the story of my life.

Being a victim of sexual abuse as a child is a very traumatic experience. In the aftermath, you want to live according to the norm or what society feels is normal but sometimes your feelings and emotions get caught up into things and you have to follow your heart. That is what finally happened to me; I met a man who I felt comfortable with and not ashamed of what we were together. This man, in spite of the violent act, has given me so much self-confidence and his buddy-ship has been a blessing in my life despite the wrong that has happened. To know that I can't even talk to him and plan the future with someone that I really love hurts really badly. Especially after all the trouble I went through to protect all parties involved. I have contacted the assistant district attorney and asked if he could initiate the process to amend the stay-away order from no contact to nonviolent contact. At least this would enable me to maintain our friendship. Mr. Cavanaugh is not a bad person; he just did a bad thing. The outcome of the altercation could have been a lot worse. I feel that I am being punished for being true to myself and fair to others. Believe it or not, I was trying to free Ramona from all my mess.

> *I want a relationship with Mr. Cavanaugh*
> *and I think he wants the same with me. I request*
> *that the "no contact" section of your ruling be recon-*
> *sidered. I just want everyone to be happy. Right now,*
> *I am so miserable! If there is any more information*
> *you need from me to help you make your decision,*
> *please contact me.*
>
> *Thank you for your consideration regarding*
> *this matter.*

I can just imagine what she thought when she read a three-and-a-half-page handwritten letter from a husband who allowed another man to barge into his house and assault him in front of his wife.

"Now he wants me to reduce the charges. And he wants me to amend the restraining order so he can leave his wife, and start a relationship with the perpetrator. That arrogant asshole had absolutely no remorse for his actions. How could this man do this to another 'sista,' one of my colleagues? First of all, I can't reduce the charges. But if I could, I wouldn't. That's up to the DA. I wish I could contact her and persuade her to divorce him. And I wish I could have thrown the book at him too."

The judge did not respond to the letter. I didn't think she would.

Over the next few months, I continued to shy away from him. Although he still called me daily, he eventually stopped the other antics and irrational behavior. I assumed reality was kinda setting in for him and that he was trying to move on with his life. Soon after when I heard that he eventually started dating someone, a doctor, I felt relieved. Although I rarely answered his calls, with much hesitation, every once in a while, I would occasionally accept one. He always rambled about how much he missed me and that he thought about me all the time. He constantly talked about his new boyfriend's many annoying habits and about the bad sex, subjects that I really didn't want to hear. He also mentioned that they frequently argued about me; he constantly compared him to me. I guess insecurity got the best of his friend; the guy called me one day and left a voicemail message, demanding that I should not talk to Marcellus. Of course, I deleted the message and I did not respond.

The very next week, Marcellus's new boyfriend called me and told me that Marcellus was admitted the hospital. He tried to commit suicide. He came home from work that day and found him crying in the corner with a gun in his hand. He said that he wasn't over our friendship and that no matter how hard he tried, he could not get over me. He still loved me so much and that he didn't want to live without me.

He persuaded Marcellus to give him the gun. He tried to console him and drove him to one of the private psychiatric hospitals on the north side of Atlanta. Marcellus's psychiatrist called me one day and we had a brief conversation. He mentioned that he had several sessions with Marcellus, but he was making very little progress. To my surprise, the doctor inferred that he wanted me to consider sitting in on one or two of his sessions. He mentioned that Marcellus was in a deep depression and that the medication and the sessions were not producing the result that he had intended. I replied that I did not want to get involved, but I hoped that his condition would improve. I heard that he was in the hospital for sixty days. I also heard that the relationship between Marcellus and his friend ended one week after he was discharged.

CHAPTER 9

Payback

Inside me there are two dogs: one good and one bad. These two dogs are always fighting. The question is which dog will win this fight.

MY ATTORNEY BELIEVED that the letter that Marcellus wrote to the judge might have added fuel to the fire. Marcellus was not aware of her past regarding her ex-husband. Hence, she will be quite insulted by receiving such a request. My attorney also believed that she will feel that the letter was an indirect personal attack against Ramona, another Black woman being abused by her cheating husband. If Ramona was an older White woman or a man, she might have felt differently.

Every Black man knows that lady justice is not blind. And the scales that she holds are not balanced. In most cases, the scales weigh heavily against us. My attorney and I also agreed that Marcellus's feeble attempt to sway the judge only infuriated her even more. There was no way that judge could check her biases and personal views at the door before she entered the courtroom. I was in trouble—big trouble. We believed that she was going to throw the book at me because I needed to be taught a lesson—a big lesson. She needed to make an example out of me.

However, somehow, the weight on the scales were about to change considerably in my favor. The cousin of my attorney's wife was a senior clerk in the superior court division. A few weeks ago, several local sororities had a fundraising event at the Hyatt downtown. She took a few photos on her phone and posted them on her local sorority chapter's Facebook and Instagram pages. A few days later, she dropped by my attorney's home to celebrate recently passing the state bar exam. Later that evening, when my attorney arrived home, he crashed the informal impromptu girl's night for a quick snack and two strong drinks. While my attorney was skimming through the pics on her iPad, at first, he thought he was hallucinating. He couldn't believe what he was seeing. After the initial shock wore off, his facial expression changed to a huge smile then eventually to uncontrollable laughter. He saw a photo of the presiding judge in the background chatting with Ramona. Apparently, both of them were members of the same sorority but not the same chapter. They appeared to be in deep conversation.

Christmas came much earlier for my attorney and me that year. Two days before my next appearance in her court, my attorney filed a motion with the chief superior court judge, siting ex parte communication between Ramona and the presiding judge on my case. My attorney couldn't prove what they were chatting about, but the appearance of impropriety and a copy of the letter were enough. The chief judge reviewed the evidence, and the motion was granted. Of course, the presiding judge did not fight the issue. I don't believe in coincidences. Everything happens for a reason. But I definitely dodged the bullet on that one.

After everything that had happened, Ramona was still determined to get even with me. The fleeting yet misdirected passion that she once had for me took a back seat to the once again deep-rooted hatred toward me. Still completely delusional, she actually convinced herself that I influenced her husband and persuaded him to leave. Of course, I was not responsible for the problems in her marriage, but her growing paranoia told her otherwise. Another determined, scorned Black woman with an attitude, and her vengeance continued. And I needed to be taught another lesson.

Once again, Ramona truly surprised me. Any other scorned woman would have used the big secret to her advantage or at least destroy her husband's allusion of me. I admit that I was on guard and on edge for a few days. Any day now, I truly expected one of us to be lying in the intensive care unit at the county hospital or dead and the other in jail. But surprisingly, she kept quiet. I was glad that she thought that was best.

However, several months after the altercation, I received a letter from her insurance company requesting subrogation. They requested that I forward a check to them for $15,961.75; supposedly the cost of the damages caused as a result of the disturbance. The letter stated that I was responsible, and I was found guilty in a court of law. Once again, I had to defend myself against the powerful and the influential. And I did.

> *Dear Mr. Jamison:*
>
> *This letter is in response to the demand for payment regarding a loss that occurred on the above date.*
>
> *The facts of this case are much more complicated than you are aware, as they were to the assistant DA. You stated that your firm investigated this claim. You may want to review this case in more detail.*
>
> *The original charges were two counts of terroristic threats, burglary, and criminal damage to property and two counts of assault and battery. During the court hearing, it was obvious that the claimant, a corporate attorney, attempted to "manipulate" the system to cause irreparable damage to me.*
>
> *The results: The charge of terroristic threats was dropped. The claimant supposedly felt threatened, but continued to harass me via several unwelcomed and unwarranted phone calls and visits to my residence. It was disclosed that I did not assault the claimant or intentionally cause bodily harm to her. It was also discovered that the legal definition of "burglary, breaking in and entering with the intent to steal or harm" was not the case. The intent was to discuss bounced checks that the husband had written to me, but as usual, the claimant interfered.*
>
> *After the defense presented its case, the remaining charges were reduced to "criminal trespassing."*

It was discovered that the claimant attempted to receive "double payment" (payment from me and payment from you, the insurer) for the supposed damages. The court ordered me to pay a much-reduced amount ($500) in restitution to the court, which will be forwarded to the insured. A twelve-month payment plan (with an option at my discretion of early completion) was accepted. The claimant's soon-to-be ex-husband refused any restitution. (Although the claimant included a claim of $1,000 in medical damages for her husband's dislocated thumb. The court dismissed his medical claim.)

Settlement Offer: In addition to the restitution ordered by the court, I am willing to increase the court ordered payment by one dollar for the damages, provided that your client(s) agree to a "claim release," which will prevent any future legal action in re this case.

I have known the claimant for over two years. At that time, I was extremely familiar with the décor of every room in the claimant's residence as well as the general cost of their personal property. I have an extensive background in the property and casualty insurance industry in the areas of claims, underwriting, and risk management, and I am fully aware of what it would cost to indemnify the insured. I was also aware of their marital problems and volatile history. If further legal action is taken, the following evidence will be submitted by me.

- *The court records of the hearing.*
- *Several hours of recorded conversations to my residence by the claimant's husband in which he admits that I was provoked. He admits that he was partially responsible for the events*

that evening. He also admits that there were discrepancies in his version of the events, the claimant's version of the events, and the police reports. He also admitted to biased interference and malicious coercion from their counselor.

- *Sworn testimony from the claimant's husband as to the actual damages that occurred that evening. He is willing to disclose in detail that the amount of the claim is extremely exorbitant and as to why the claim is such.*
- *Some damages occurred to the residence as a result previous altercations and assaults between the claimant and her husband. Damages included broken glasses, dishes, and holes in walls by the claimant's husband and "split lips" as well as others. The husband will testify if necessary.*
- *Previously documented 911 calls from the claimant's residence will also be submitted as well as sworn statements from their neighbors.*

As did the assistant DA and the claimant, please do not assume evidence presumably not related to that evening and information undisclosed to the insurer and your firm, will not be admitted in court. I look forward to hearing from you with a response within thirty days.

I did not receive a response. I guess they got the message. So, in turn, her feeble attempt to cause harm to me, once again, failed.

Now it was finally my turn. I still had some unfinished business with Ramona. I filed a formal complaint with the Georgia Bar Association, citing blatant abuse and deliberate misuse of power by an officer of the court. I forwarded the statements from the previous court hearing in which the chief judge stated that it was obvious that she had attempted to "manipulate and abuse" the legal system to cause irreparable damage to me. Because her actions were in response of a personal matter, the judge insisted that action must be taken. I guess there was no worse enemy than a scorned woman. The chief judge's written statement in conjunction with my complaint and an eleven-page account of the details of her antics over the past two years, could have led to her possible disbarment. Following two years after the melodramatic chain of events, she was eventually sanctioned by the Georgia Bar Association. I filed a civil suit and was awarded monetary punitive damages in the amount of $100,000.

CHAPTER 10

Against All Odds

Never underestimate the power of an educated Black man—a determined, educated Black man who feels like he has been cheated regarding his money—especially when it's more than about the money, when he is on a mission to prove a point. It's the principle.

THE SAGA CONTINUED. After all that drama, I was still determined to get my money regarding the numerous past due bad debts owed to me. I admit that I had a major part in the altercation at his house, but he was partially responsible too. As was his wife. He knew me well enough that I would come over to discuss the money, especially after I called and his wife hung up the phone on me. He should have behaved like a real man and either called me back or came outside to discuss the matter. But instead, he hid behind a woman. He got what he deserved—a ghetto ass-whipping. Yes, I was stupid. Very stupid. I risked everything I had built so far. I had too much to lose. Actually, I thought the angry, violent side of me had died. I thought I had buried that negative spirit long ago, but apparently that incident resurrected him. Nevertheless, the altercation was a completely separate issue. He still owed me money and I wanted it. I waited awhile until the dust kinda settled. So, after two years, I sent him one final letter. I emailed it and I sent a certified copy of the letter to him at his home.

Marcellus,
*   I hope that all is well with you, but enough of the small talk. The reason I am writing this let-*

ter is that I still want the money that you owe me. Yes, you read it correctly. I want my money! *And I plan to collect it one way or another. I am sure that you could have made some effort to make small payments over the last two years.*

I have been extremely patient, waiting for a response regarding the mentioned past due loans. I completely understood that you were having financial difficulties a few years ago after your cousin passed away and left you custody of her two sons. After all that has happened, I am still very disappointed at how this has affected our friendship. When you needed me and asked me for help, I was there for you, assisting and supporting you. Your disloyalty and your cowardice have placed you in this situation.

Per the most recent of the emails of those listed below, you stated that you would contact me (date: Tuesday, March 9, 2:01 p.m.: "Dex... I received your emails. I will respond to them shortly.")

But as of today, two years later you have not responded.

When I spoke to you over two years this month, I assumed that you were getting some type of additional assistance for your receiving custody of the kids. In addition, you mentioned that your sister filed the two boys on her taxes. I'm sure that you benefited in that agreement. Again, I assumed that you would have made some effort to start making payments.

You are on official notice. If I have not heard from you within three business days with a concrete plan that includes your efforts to start making payments, I will have no choice but to file a small claims suit against you. (In addition to the emails, please remember that I still have two handwritten

IOUs that you insisted that I accept as a guarantee that I would receive repayment.)

When I receive the judgment (and I definitely will), I will immediately file a FIFA against you, which will place a lien on your home (if you still own it). I will garnish your wages for the full amount (that is if you are still working). The FIFA will also monitor all bank accounts and credit union accounts. And lastly, I will request that the FIFA monitor and investigate your present, future, and past three years of your IRS filings and refunds as well as the social security numbers of the two boys. In turn, this will lead to an investigation of possible tax fraud and I'm sure that your sister and others do not want that. Again, I have been more than patient.

To prevent further action, please respond immediately.

Yeah, I know that I was harsh. I was being a total asshole. But I didn't care. I was wronged. And I wanted my money. This was personal.

He didn't respond. Apparently, he didn't take me seriously. I guess he thought that just because property damage was caused during the altercation a few years ago that he no longer owed me the money. He assumed we were even. Wrong answer. Or maybe he thought that a judge would not award me a cent after he introduced the details of the altercation. But wrong again.

I guess he thought I was bluffing. I said what I meant, and I meant what I said. So, I filed a lawsuit in small claims court. I know that I should've handled that situation in small claims court a little differently, but I thought we were close enough as friends once upon a time that we could have handled this matter without legal intervention. But the three Jack Daniels that I had after work that day probably did not help me think clearly about the consequences of filing the claim. So instead of trying to resolve this potentially simple legal matter in a timely manner, his intentions were to complicate the situation because I finally ended the friendship. Once again, he tried to hide behind another woman. He hired a local attorney, Vivian Blackwell. She filed motion after motion for a continuance. I guess she thought that the typical legal strategy of delay after delay would eventually persuade me to give up and go away. It didn't work. The judge finally ordered both sides to mediate. During the mediation session, Marcellus blatantly lied and stated that all the loans were gifts and that he didn't have to pay any rent or household expenses. Anyone who knows me knows that I would not financially support any adult person, excluding my mother. And this was a man, and he wasn't even family. And he also stated the he was not responsible for the NSF checks. They were supposedly the result of several bank errors.

After the mediation session failed, Ms. Blackwell filed a motion to disclose—another stall tactic. Also, she wanted to see my hand, my evidence. So, the court ordered me to forward my evidence to her within thirty days. But I didn't make it easy for her. I wasn't going to just lay my entire case in her lap so she could deceptively counter each piece of my supporting documentation. So, I complied with the judge's request. It was now time to play hardball. So, I gave her what she wanted plus a whole lot more of what she probably didn't expect. I sent her a letter; the letter that was the straw that broke the proverbial camel's back.

> *Dear Ms. Blackwell:*
>
> *Per the judge's request on September 6, please find the enclosed documents regarding the mentioned case in which your client may not have access or does not currently have in his possession.*
>
> *Enclosed documents: living expenses, copies of utility bills, copies of checks written to your client, and copies of checks for expenses for your client (loans); a check from the insurance company (auto accident that occurred during the mentioned period); a letter to your client requesting repayment*

for balance of living expenses and loans; a few NSF checks (other payments/NSF checks are listed on the bank statements); a spread sheet outlining some of the loans (transfers from account to account); a plane ticket receipt and the receipt for flowers for your client's mother. Please note that some originals could not be copied (e.g., the grocery bills). I will present the originals in court.

Since your client and I have accounts at the same bank, please have him submit copies of his bank statements to you or request copies from the bank dated during the mentioned period. The statements will show transactions from his account to my account and vice versa. Also, please have your client forward to you any documentation of repayments to me and any other evidence that will assist you in his defense such as any correspondence sent to me (e.g., emails, letters, and notes). Please be aware I may submit other evidence in which your client has access or additional documents that is currently in his possession.

As I stated to you after the judge left the courtroom on September 6, I completely understand your position regarding this case and your responsibility to your client. You referred to me as being "stubbornly litigious and operating in bad faith." I think you realize that my case is not frivolous and that I am not bluffing. From the comments made during the mediation process, it is my opinion that your client has voluntarily chosen to suffer from selective amnesia.

Hopefully, this case will be settled on October 7. Please be aware that you are on notice. If for some reason you request another continuous or if you or your client requests another appeal, I will subpoena several witnesses: Monica Mason, Richard Baker, Renita Rainer, Duncan Pitts, David Moore, James

Johnston, Gregory Underwood, Marcus Davis, Morris Randell, Jabari Moore, Daniel Samson, Shaun Williams, Dr. Thomas Brown, and your client's wife as well as two CSRs from the bank. Their solid witness testimony will make the evidence in this case even more irrefutable and in turn assist your client in regaining his memory. I will also subpoena you as a witness. Please be aware that as of today, I have not served anyone to appear in court on October 7 but some of them might appear as voluntary witnesses.

You may contact me via mail or email if you have any questions.

On October 7, she came to court and terminated her services. She stated that it was a conflict of interest. My plan worked. My letter cleverly motivated her to stop playing legal games. I had better things to do. I just wanted my money. The court rescheduled the case seven days later. And once again, I responded to her actions.

Dear Ms. Blackwell:

I was truly disappointed in your actions, especially on October 7. Since the defense's last attempt (motion to continue) failed, you decided to "jump ship." You were well aware of your relationship with the agency and the defendant on the day that you accepted this case. You had several opportunities to withdraw from this case. I even mentioned the issues to you again thirty days ago. You could have withdrawn at that time. I mentioned those issues on September 6, but you waited until you got it in writing to file the motion to withdraw a few days before the trial. That was very clever, but I was really looking forward to "arguing this case" with you. Your unsuccessful attempts have only strengthened my skills and confidence. I truly expected you to "stick with this case for the long haul." I am aware that you thought that this was going to be a simple case, but you were unpleasantly surprised. I was becoming a nuisance to you and I was making your chances of winning more and more difficult. For those reasons, I have been informed that you tried to teach me a lesson. You have the law degree and I have very little experience in such matters, but one might assume that I was represented by counsel also.

The defendant attempted to "hide" behind another female for protection as he has done so many times in the past, but once again his efforts have failed. The defense's stall tactics only prolonged the inevitable. I reiterate that I will win this case. The defense is well aware that my case is strong and it was obvious that I was ready on last Thursday. I realize that I must be just a little more patient. My day in court will come soon.

You insulted my intelligence when you stated that you wanted to "work with me" and help the situation. I truly do not understand how you expected me to trust the defense. Your statements and behavior on October 7 confirmed that my instincts were correct. You were representing that which was in the best interest of your client. I am sure that you were taught during your first year in law school: "Do not trust the other side" and "Never ever, never ever underestimate your opponent."

The attorney that advised me believes that you "jumped ship" because you expected this to be a simple pro bono case. You hoped that I would give up after a few legal tactics of prolonging the court proceedings. He stated that you probably "bailed out" because the defense's strategy was not working (e.g., your client's original denial; the agreement to mediate only to disclose information; the claims of improper venue, lack of jurisdiction, statute of limitations, and bad faith litigation; filing motion after motion and your request to forward "any and all discovery documents…on or before October 6"). He also confirmed that the last letter that I sent you successfully blocked your continued attempts to frustrate me with your legal games.

This has been a very rewarding experience. I have learned a lot from this case. That's why I cross every t twice and dot every i twice. My legal advisor has given me "rave reviews" regarding how I handled this case. I showed him as well as two of his colleagues all the defense's attempts to stall and run for cover. He states that my persistence and hard work are qualities that are needed and valued in the legal profession.

My legal advisor's senior partner stated, "If this young man will go through all this time and effort for a few thousand dollars, I can only imagine how hard he will work for a serious case. And he has no legal training or education." He also stated that I have the potential to become a "fine trial attorney." The firm has decided to sponsor me in taking the Kaplan LSAT course and exam as well as the admission fees. The senior partner has also decided to write one of my letters of recommendation when I apply at Georgetown College of Law and a few other schools. I guess I am winning a lot more from this case than I had expected.

Although the proverbial war has not been won yet, thanks for the few battles. This experience has been invaluable. And my advice to you—never ever, never ever underestimate your opponent. No hard feelings; it was just business, okay. Maybe we will meet again.

Best regards

On the next court date, I finally received the opportunity to present my case. His response was that they were gifts. The judge did not buy it. Especially after I presented several bills, cancelled checks, bank statements, emails, and two money orders from him that he noted *Repayment of Loans.* The judge deliberated for ten minutes. While court was in recess, he became belligerent and rude to the officers and the clerks. The judge heard him yelling and ordered him to leave. He continued to be rude. The judge then ordered him back into the courtroom. Marcellus tried to leave until the judge yelled that he would "hold him in contempt of court" if he left. The judge lectured him regarding his attitude and his behavior and forced him to apologize. I won my case including interest and court costs: $10,836. He refused to make payment arrangements. In order to collect, I had to immediately file a FIFA, which included his bank accounts. I also garnished his payroll checks.

After I won the case, of course, I felt vindicated, but it was more than that. I defeated someone who once again underestimated me. Someone who thought I was a nuisance. Someone who tried to ignore me. She was hoping that I would just go away, a tactic often used by many attorneys. Her acts of intimidation also failed. I was sure that Ms. Blackwell would definitely remember me.

Finally, I was ready to put all of this behind me. My mind was satisfied. I did what I had to do. I felt that I had done the right thing. Now I was ready to settle my spirit. I needed peace and solitude. I usually achieved that during quality time with the LORD. I prayed and meditated for several weeks constantly asking HIM to help me. I needed HIS continued guidance. I needed HIS continued grace and mercy.

CHAPTER 11

Upward Bound

My success is not an accident. There is no doubt that I am reaping the blessings as a result of the prayers of my mother, grandmothers, great-grandmothers, and all the ancestors that I have never met. Many of their prayers have been answered. My life has been graced by the American Dream whatever that really means to a young Black man.

AFTER BEING SIDETRACKED for over two years, I needed to get back on course. I had begun to fulfill one of the hopes and dreams of those who prayed for me—my mother, my grandparents, and my great-grandmother. I was now walking on the shoulders of my ancestors, including the slaves that I never knew. All of those who fought, struggled, and died for my future. They died for the opportunity for me to succeed.

After I graduated with honors from Georgetown University, College of Law, I accepted an associate position in corporate acquisitions with a major firm in Chicago. After serving as a rising star for almost three years, I was approached with the opportunity to become a partner. But once again, my past had surfaced to hunt me. I would be the youngest partner out of twelve in the firm, one of three minorities, and the only African-American male. I was scheduled to meet with one of the senior managing partners. I had a great relationship with all the partners except Michael Garner, an arrogant middle-aged white racist who was going through an ugly divorce. His wife left him for her fitness trainer, a younger Black man.

The by-laws firm's charter specifically stated that the confirmation to nominate and confirm me as a partner required a unanimous vote from all senior partners. As I suspected, I learned two days later that it was Garner who blocked the decision.

Garner stated that the firm would not be able to place me with any of the company's clients. The mentioned incident had occurred over eight years ago. Before I was hired, I signed a waiver authorizing the firm to conduct an extensive background check. The firm was aware of the incident. Why was this an issue now?

Since then, I had successfully served as the lead chair representing some of the largest accounts acquired by the firm. I had saved our clients hundreds of millions of dollars. In addition, most of our clients that I had represented have required a level 8 security clearance and extensive and thorough background checks, a precaution taken to disclose any appearance of impropriety or conflict of interest. I have also received several professional accolades as well as various other certifications and designations, most of which required extensive background checks at the inception as well as at each periodic renewal.

After our meeting, I immediately called another close colleague from another firm, an attorney who was also a magistrate judge in Fulton County, Georgia. He advised me to acquire a complete certified copy of my criminal history report as soon as possible, and I did. No one was able to tell me why had this become an issue at the end of the three years of productivity. We reviewed the report in detail and he verified what I told Garner; I had not been convicted of any felonies. It is the substantiation of a conviction not the original charge that is pertinent. Unfortunately, the charges were not expunged from my record as previous directed by the court. The process to quickly correct that grave issue had begun on the next day.

I was well aware that a thorough explanation was not warranted, but it was extremely important and necessary that I set the record straight. So, I sent a letter addressed to the senior partners as I did several years ago when I received the demand letter from the insurance company.

Although at a first glance, the original charges in the criminal history report appear to be extremely incriminating and it was my responsibility to verify that the charges and the dispositions should have been expunged. The facts of that case were much more complicated than they appeared, as they were to the assistant DA. The case was the result of an escalated verbal altercation at the private residence of a former close friend and attorney regarding mainly a personal matter as well as numerous past due bad debts owed to me and NSF checks written to me.

The original charges: During the court hearing, it was obvious that the claimant, a corporate attorney, attempted to "manipulate and abuse" the legal system (as quoted by the judge) to cause irreparable damage to me.

The disposition: Nolo contendere (no admission of guilt but I was present at the scene of the incident). The charge of terroristic threats regarding the junior claimant was dismissed. The primary claimant supposedly felt threatened, but continued to harass me within a few weeks after the incident via several unwelcomed use of a previous personal matter and unwarranted phone calls and visits to my residence. It was disclosed in court that I did not assault the primary claimant or intentionally cause bodily harm to her. It was also discovered that she later invited me to enter. The judge "threatened" an investigation that could have led to the possible disbarment of the primary plaintiff's license regarding the "blatant abuse of power by an attorney."

During the one-year period following that unfortunate incident, I had to file three restraining orders against the junior claimant and a temporary restraining order against the primary claimant. Also, following two years after the incident the primary plaintiff was eventually sanctioned by the Georgia Bar Association. I was awarded punitive damages. I was also awarded monetary damages regarding two separate cases against the junior claimant that stemmed from the original case as well as indemnification regarding the numerous past due bad debts and NSF check fees owed to me.

Immediately after I wrote the letter, I began exploring other viable career opportunities. Then it hit me. I needed to be my own man. Since I held a license in two other states and in the District of Columbia, I decided to resign and relocate back to Atlanta. My firm immediately notified all of my clients that I was leaving the company. Little did they know that 80 percent of the national clients in my portfolio had already received anonymous calls inferring that I might be leaving the firm? I did not actively pursue them nor did I persuade them to leave. A hundred percent of my large clients and 50 percent of my smaller clients forwarded official notices terminating the services of my previous firm. Three days later, my new office manager, Patrick, received certified letters regarding exclusive right to represent from the same previous clients. I referred the rest of my clients to another local Chicago attorney.

I guess everything happens for a reason. I wanted to move back to the ATL anyway and begin the next phase of my career.

CHAPTER 12

The Body Envelope

***Tell me who you walk with and I'll tell you who
you are. It's the company you keep.***

"HEY, DEXTER, I know that you are busy, but the guys and I are
getting together this evening. It's just a small private gathering. Of
course, we want you to join us. Just wouldn't be the same without
you."

"I am not sure. I am working on a really big case."

"As usual, it's always some big case. Man, you need to balance
more."

"I love my job."

"I am not knocking that. So, what do you say, Mr. Workaholic?"

"Well, sure, I need to take a break plus I haven't seen you guys
since the funeral. It will definitely do me some good. About what
time?"

"About 8."

"Okay. Cool. I will text you the place."

"Okay, see you tonight."

Lisborn Taylor, Emerson Cartwright III, Chandler "Chance"
Jameson, Parker Dunwoody, and I have known each other for a little
over four years. Patrick and I met the guys at the five-day annual
Men of Valor Men's Conference, a national revival and Christian
retreat that was held in sunny Ft. Lauderdale. One night after the

evening program, we all ended up at a sports bar down the street from the host hotel where we were staying. Although there were over ten thousand men attending the conference, a few of us recognized each other from the first-class section of the airplane departing from Atlanta as well as from the hotel lobby during registration. Since it was so late and the sports bar was nearly empty, the hostess sat us all in the same far right corner because the other sections were closed. We received our first drink rather quickly, but the service quickly began to go downhill. The waiter apologized; stating that normally the bar closed at eleven during the week, but because of the conference, management decided to extend the hours until 2:00 a.m. Since one waiter was serving all five tables separately, Patrick went over and introduced himself to each of the other four guys. He stated that we might get better service if we all shared a table. They all agreed, and it was definitely worth it. Everyone gave a brief introduction, which included their names and where they were born. Although we quickly learned that we came from different backgrounds, we bonded rather quickly. When the waiter returned, he paused as if confused and then gave us a big smile. His facial expression showed that he definitely agreed with the new seating arrangement. After we ordered a few more drinks, the mood of the group began to relax even more. Somehow the conversation changed from the main topic of that night's sermon to an interesting rap session. We realized that we had a lot in common or at least one major experience in common.

It seemed like it was yesterday. Patrick and the guys quickly formed a much closer niche friendship shortly after the conference. Although I had known Patrick much longer, over the next few years the small clique spent much more time together than Patrick and me. But whenever we got together, we just picked up where we left off.

Later that evening we met at Chops Lobster Bar, one of the more popular upscale spots in the Buckhead Life Restaurant Group. Emerson had made reservations and specifically requested a small private dining room. Luckily, one was available. As usual after a few strong drinks, we began catching up on the latest in each other's lives; the stories began. We began to reminisce about the provocative, tumultuous, forbidden undercover relationships in their younger days. Although all of them were under the age of thirty-five, except Lisborn, who was thirty-six, each had lived quite interesting lives up until now. Although I never knew all the details or whom they dated, it was common knowledge between all of them, including Patrick, that they had been involved in long-term relationships with ministers. And not just your local neighborhood pastors of small churches. These were well-known prominent leaders of some of the largest megachurches in the country. Well, all of them accept me. Maybe that's why the five of them had a much closer bond.

I truly loved these guys, and I know that they genuinely loved me too. We shared an unbreakable bond, a serious *bromance* relationship. And our lives were inextricably linked. We shared the habits of the heart. We embraced the values that strengthen relationships— mainly nurturing the positive attitudes among each other, showing mutual and self-dependability and responsibility, being supportive of high expectations for ourselves and each other, fostering courage and support of each other's beliefs, and expressing hope for a positive future. We believed in the importance of having and promoting self-worth and self-love. Both are much needed by Black men in our culture. We deserved it. We were worth it. Unlike most Black men our age, we strongly believe that the universe wanted us to be happy.

We also shared the unmentionable, the unspeakable. We were of the life but not in the life. We were members of a secret fraternity, *The Silent Fraternity*. It had a double meaning, the life versus the lifestyle. Our secret society was a small brotherhood who shared a loyal bond, a code of silence and secrets. A brotherly love stronger than that of biological brothers. We lived behind a mask. *The false face*, an invisible mask that we wore most of the time often disguising the actual roles that we played in our personal and private relationships with men. We also mastered wearing *the body envelope;* the individual roles that we portrayed depending on who we were with—with family, with friends, at church, or at work. My boys also consciously played a large part in perpetuating one of the major controversies in the contemporary African-American Christian Church. They had been blamed for pursuing prominent ministers with clout and money. Others blamed the ministers for aggressively yet shrewdly chasing after them, the stereotypical much younger "pretty" men. To them, we were attractive, masculine, discreet, articulate, educated, hardworking professional Black men who didn't wear our sexuality or our sexual preferences on our sleeves. We were neither overtly macho nor effeminate. Most thought of us to be metrosexual, well-rounded, fashion-conscious straight men with style, good taste, and sex appeal. Actually, we received more attention and propositions from women than men. We couldn't be detected, but we weren't on the DL, or down low, either because we did not actively pursue women. And we weren't hiding, we were just private and very discreet. We were just *the "G" Men, the Gentlemen of the Silent Fraternity.*

Ironically, as progressive as our society has become over the past few decades, there was much bias against us in the face of professed Christian love and tolerance. The traditional as well as the contemporary African-American Christian Church reject us, chastise us, and try to change us. We just played our role in the church and turned the other cheek. We needed each other. So, my friends and I turned to each other for brotherly love and support.

Among various other obvious reasons, we seem to vibe together because neither of us was raised with our fathers. Neither of us consumed drugs nor were heavy drinkers. Well, when I'm stressed, I kinda indulge a little. We were extremely health-conscious. All of us had gym memberships. We were not all as strait-laced as we appeared to be, but when we did do our dirty deeds, we were very discreet. We just seemed to naturally vibe. Well, why not, only two of us were in serious committed relationships.

The most outgoing member of the group was Parker Dunwoody. He started his career as an intern at the Atlanta City Hall and is currently serving as an executive administrator in the mayor's office. The outspoken political junkie who came from humble beginnings is now considered to be one of Atlanta's most eligible bachelors under thirty-five. The slim, well-defined, six-foot suave cohort sported a polished shaved head with a neatly trimmed, perfectly outlined close-cut beard. He often cut the beard and switched it up with a neatly trimmed goatee. He looked like a model and was often mistaken for one.

Next to Parker was Chandler "Chance" Jameson. He was once the uncouth country boy who had been transformed into a sophisticated Southern gentleman. He was also the commensurate jock of the group but not the typical flashy Black superstar athlete who squandered his money on expensive grown-men toys, gaudy jewelry, strip clubs, and women. Looks were definitely deceiving when it came to Mr. Eight-Percent-Body-Fat. He had the brains to match his athletic ability. Although his slight Southern twang gave light to what part of the country he was born, he was smart, extremely articulate, and well versed on most current events, including politics.

As an NBA first-round pick who was drafted in his senior year by the Atlanta Royals, Chance received much attention wherever he went. Although he was polite to most, unlike most of the other players, he shunned from the media attention and intentionally avoided the public spotlight. He valued his privacy, and he had good reason too. He learned very early in his career that being a celebrity makes you a target.

I guess the alcohol was beginning to talk to me. Until that night, I had never really looked at him much, well, not in a sexual way that is. We were "bois." He was my homie, and homies don't look at each other like that. After my third drink, it occurred to me that he was quite fine. Although he wore plain front slacks and a starched French-cuffed fitted dress shirt, as usual, I could see the definition in his muscular biceps, broad shoulders, defined pecks, and washboard stomach. The 6'3" chiseled-framed dark-brown brutha had a body that too many women yearned for and the body most men under forty strived to achieve; as many had seen his half-naked buffed body in various sports magazines. Although many women pursued him for his money, more women chased him because it was rumored that he was quite well-endowed. Well, I knew the rumor to be true that he had a rather large piece to match his perfect physique because I saw it by accident one morning while he was getting out of the shower in the hotel gym a few years ago. The embarrassing fluke happened when we were on one of our annual group vacations. And surprisingly, unlike most basketball players, he didn't have many tattoos, only one—praying hands on the left side of his chest. And his smile was captivating, perfectly aligned white teeth behind full lips. He reminded me of a tall North African warrior prince, poised and dignified with a healthy self-confidence. It's ironic that he could be mistaken as royalty considering he was a country boy from a small town outside of Jacksonville, Florida.

And next to Chance was Emerson Cartwright III. Raised in Louisiana until his early teens, Emerson came from a long Creole lineage. Later, he moved to Richmond, Virginia, to live with his grandmother. He is now the CEO of a nonprofit full-service transitional center for inner city homeless men. Emerson is also a successful certified professional fund-raiser and a real estate broker. He was the most conservative of the group. Although the light skinned pretty boy was also the quietest of the fellows in the group, his alluring hypnotizing hazel eyes were always paying attention. When attending fund-raising events, he had a knack for spotting the large check-writing players as opposed to the perpetrators and the social status climbers. Whenever he casually entered a room, he didn't have to say or do much to get recognized. His quiet unassuming sex appeal rarely went unnoticed although he played it off by trying to ignore the obvious attention. We often teasingly accused him of using his flawless, hairless face, which was framed by a perfect fade cut and his six-foot fit body to get what he wanted without saying a word.

And lastly there was Lisborn Taylor. And speak of the devil, he just strolled in. Lisborn was a local television personality and news anchorman originally from Detroit. He was also a professionally trained pianist and accomplished gospel artist. He was the preppy one in the group. The 5'11" athletic-cut perfectionist sported a short neat Caesar cut with absolutely no facial hair. When not on camera, the medium light-brown-skinned meticulously dressed brutha often wore black-rimmed glasses. He was also known for his striking designer, retro braces and custom-made bowties.

Although I was a few years older than the other guys, I could definitely hold my own. Because I was married to my career, staying fit was definitely a challenge for me. I definitely received my fair share of unwanted and unsolicited attention from both men and women, but mainly married older men and women. They often said that I looked successful, independent, and "safe." Discretion and privacy were extremely important to them. I looked like I had just as much to lose as they did.

"Hey, fellas, sorry I'm late. I just came in from the airport. I am consulting on a class-action lawsuit out of town. My client chartered a private plane. I was waiting outside the hangar, waiting on the limo to pick me up. And you will never guess who I saw. Blew me away."

"Who?"

"Wharton. I saw him briefly coming out of a door where they house the private jets."

"He glanced in my direction then did a double take. I guess he was not sure if it was really me."

"Did he speak?"

"Not really. We just discreetly acknowledged each other with a slight nod and kept it moving. I was walking in front of him. But when I turned around, as I assumed, he was checking me out. He gave me a half-ass smile and a slight smirk. I smiled back. Although I still don't have any issues with him and I don't have any regrets leaving the way I did, I must agree that the best revenge is looking good and living well."

"I guess he will never get over the fact that you left him. No one really likes rejection, but it was the way you left him. You left so quickly, without any drama or without any attempt to work things out. You were probably one of the few people who has ever shown him that you didn't need him. He was prominent and extremely wealthy. I am sure that your quick departure completely caught him off guard, but of course, his pride wouldn't allow him to stop you. You really damaged his ego, and it seems like he never got over it."

"Who is Wharton?" Dex asked.

"Hey guys, we are talking over Dex's head."

"Dr. Jonathan P. Wharton."

"Our 'boi' is the one who Wharton let get away. And it appears as though he still regrets it."

"You mean Bishop Jonathan P. Wharton out in California? You dated him? That brutha? Damn."

While raising his left eyebrow, Lisborn just smiled in slight agreement.

"That's right. You don't know the story of Lisborn and the good Reverend Dr. Wharton."

"Dex really isn't interested in hearing about that. Are you, Dex?"

"Hell yeah, I am. I really don't know any details about any of your relationships."

"Come on, Lisborn."

"Tell Dex about your past saga with Wharton."

"Okay. Where do I start?"

"From the beginning, of course."

"Okay."

Just before Lisborn began to tell his story, he glanced down and noticed that he had received a text message.

"OMG!" Lisborn exclaimed.

"What is it?" asked Emerson.

"It's a text from Wharton. He is in town on business for a few days and he wants to do dinner."

"Well, are you going to respond?" asked Emerson.

"I'm cool but I'm not sure. And I am about to tell you why. I don't have any issues with him. I still only have dead love for him right now. Now let's change the subject. I came out to enjoy you guys. But let me start telling my story before my mood changes and I change my mind.

CHAPTER 13

Willful Blindness

Wounds may appear to have healed on the surface, but deep down they are still mending, slowly growing stronger. It takes much more time than you think.

I ALWAYS KNEW he truly wasn't in love with me. There is a big difference between *loving* someone and *being in love* with someone. But I did feel that he genuinely cared about me. Should I have expected more? He was almost twice my age. At first, I thought he was experiencing the ultimate midlife crisis. In retrospect, I now see that it was just a mutual give-and-take relationship, a relationship of convenience for the both of us. I was clearly his younger, talented, vibrant companion, a young man who could and would definitely improve his self-imagine as well as his public image, a trophy. And in turn, he would provide me with a lavish lifestyle and assist me with my career. Nevertheless, I truly cared for him and I appreciated everything that he did for me. I am not sure if I was madly in love with him either, but I eventually learned to sincerely love him. I must have cared about him a lot more than I had realized because I was truly hurt.

When I was twenty-one years old, I was awarded a full music scholarship to the Chicago Conservatory of Music. Instead of working during the summer before I began the start of a rigorous curriculum at one of the most prestigious performing arts universities in the country, I decided to spend some time enjoying myself. The fall semester would begin before I knew it. I was already three years behind schedule because I was not ready to go straight to college right after high school. I was absolutely sure that music was my passion. However, I needed some time to rest mentally and to find myself.

An unexpected trip to Los Angeles changed my life forever. I attended the week long fifteenth anniversary of the American Gospel Music Competition which was held in Los Angeles, California. At the last minute, I decided to tag along with a small group of my older friends who were in the local gospel music scene in Detroit. They participated in music workshops and entered various competitions every year for the past five years. The American Gospel Music Competition was a well-known annual conference that offered various coaching sessions as well as several category competitions for soloists, musicians, and choirs. I was persuaded to enter in three contests in three categories including male soloist, a cappella, and lead soloist leading a choir. I won first prize in all three contests. I was told that I performed quite well considering that was my first appearance in the nationally recognized competition. I guess I got my talent from my father who was a skilled musician, a lead singer in a leading male R&B group in the late '90s. Although I never really knew him because he was in and out of my life until I was three years old. Then he just disappeared completely.

The next morning after the last competition, I received an invitation to a VIP reception held before the Founder's Ball, hosted by the founder and executive director, Bishop Jonathan P. Wharton. The committee normally chose only the top winners from each of the ten categories to perform. I was asked to perform one of my award-winning songs. Because I was the youngest in the group chosen, I guess my insecurity got the best of me. I wanted to show off. So, I chose a nontraditional classical selection, "Jesus, Lover of My Soul (Jesu, Joy of Man's Desiring)." The rendition arranged by the legendary gospel artist, Richard Smallwood. I chose that one because it gave me a chance to show off my piano skills. And because it was a very difficult piece, even for a first tenor. Although he had a baby grand piano in his suite and I accompanied myself, I sang part of it a cappella. I knew that I was good and that I sang with intense passion but there were so many others that were just as talented. Well, I guess it worked, because to my surprise, I received a standing ovation. I just let it all sink in. I tried not to let it go to my head. There were too many other enlarged egos in the room.

Somehow, by the fifth day of the conference, I received the attention of the executive director. He invited a few of us to a private luncheon. The three guests and I gave a brief introduction. Of course, I mentioned my scholarship and my plans in the fall. The host seemed somewhat impressed. During the rest of the luncheon, we continued to chat about our experiences during the conference. As I was leaving the director's suite, his female assistant discreetly handed me a note. It was another invitation. But this time it was to dinner the following evening.

I wanted to make a good impression. So, to be on the safe side, I dressed in a dark suit. I arrived promptly at 7:00 p.m. This time the entire presidential suite was dimly lit. I heard soft music, but to my surprise, it was not gospel; it was jazz, Boney James. The four-course meal was delicious and the company was pleasant, but he didn't waste any time. He immediately got to the point. The four-hour dinner seemed like an in-depth interview. I was not sure why he had such overwhelming interest in me. But his increasing interest began to peak my curiosity. We had in-depth discussions about my life in Detroit, my family, about my future; mainly my education and my interest in music. But he told me very little about himself.

He finally told me the main reason for that meeting. He had heard the edited versions of the recordings of my three winning performances. He stated very bluntly that he was extremely impressed. And that was not an easy task, to impress him that is. I blushed. He noticed and just smiled. He admitted that he had been observing me all week and that he thought I was very talented. But talent was a dime a dozen in this competition. Someone with my talent needed to be coached and nurtured. I needed professional and formal training and exposure that would advance my career. Professional training? Advance my career? What was he talking about? I was going to attend one of the top three music schools in the country where I would receive excellent formal training. Intentional or not, this man was throwing a ringer in my plans. He offered me an opportunity that required that I give some serious thought, a chance to travel with him, to sing with him. I would be the principal male soloist of his traveling praise team. Along with the national exposure, I would receive an annual salary of sixty thousand dollars. He also reiterated that although I would continue to train and develop my skill, I could always go back to college at a later time. I was beaming. I could not believe it. But it was real.

I couldn't wait until I returned to Detroit to tell everyone the great news. So, I immediately called my best friend and mother about the generous job offer. My friends thought it was an opportunity of a lifetime. The decision was a no-brainer to them. But of course, my mom and family were not happy with the idea that I was even contemplating giving up my scholarship. Of course, she questioned the motives of this much older prominent man who wanted to help her young son. I explained to her that this was an opportunity of a lifetime and that I could not allow it to slip through my fingers. I assured her that I would be careful. And that I could always go back to college if things didn't work out.

After a few more days of long-distance conversations with the bishop, he sent me a first-class one-way ticket to Los Angeles, just to visit. But I would not go without my cousin Owen and my best friend, Reid. The next day I received two additional first-class round-trip tickets.

Although I had received the airline ticket, I still pondered the idea. I was not 100 percent sure if I was going to start the next phase of my life in California. For the next few days, I was still deliberating on whether or not I was planning to leave Detroit. The bishop and I had several more in-depth conversations about the future, mainly my education and my interest in music. But there was a catch. Well, there always is. If something seems too good to be true, it usually is. He wanted a "relationship." He elaborated on what that really meant. I was shocked to say the least. Yes, I felt special, but why me of all people? We really didn't know each other. I had absolutely nothing that could even closely match what he had offered me. Although he was thirty-eight years old, he looked much younger. His outer appearance exuded an understated sex appeal. However, his inner persona overshadowed the exterior. He was very sophisticated and he had much charisma. And the deep resonance in his voice only added to his sexiness. I had to give this offer some serious thought. This man could offer me the kind of life and lifestyle that I never dreamed of. He could expose me to opportunities and to people who could open doors for me. People who could advance my career beyond my wildest dreams. He chose me. Again, why me? Well, why not? I was going. My mom and family were not happy with my final decision, but I had to do what was best for me. They would get used to the idea.

When we arrived at the airport, I assumed that we would be taking Uber to the bishop's house. On the way to baggage claim at the top of the escalator, there was a middle-aged Black man in a black suit with an iPad with my full name on it, "Lisborn Taylor" printed in large black letters. He was our driver. He introduced himself as Harrison. We followed him to a black Bentley Continental Sedan with slightly tinted windows. He placed our bags in the trunk and opened and closed the back-seat door for us. Jazz music was playing; it was David Sandborn. The bishop remembered. He played the same CD during our infamous four-hour dinner at the convention. A light snack was prepared for us—a small silver plate with six shrimp hors d'oeuvres and a silver ice bucket with three blue bottles of imported sparkling water. The driver didn't say much. He asked us how was the trip and that it would take about an hour to arrive at our destination.

We finally pulled into a private driveway. About fifty yards up a hill, we approached a large wrought iron gate with a security officer on each side. As we drove through the gate, Harrison waved to the security officer standing outside a small gatehouse. As we continued another two hundred yards up another winding hill, we approached another smaller gate that opened to a large fountain accented with four large full-scale lions statues. And there it was. The largest house I had ever seen. I soon learned that the mansion, the main house, was part of a much larger estate, which I learned later was referred to as Wharton Manor.

Standing at the top of the steps waiting for us were two men. We were greeted by a distinguished-looking middle-aged Black man. He introduced himself as Benjamin, the house manager. Dressed in a heavily starched French-cuffed white shirt, black vest and tie, the bald dark-skinned slim man asked the other gentlemen standing behind him to take our bags upstairs.

Shortly after we arrived, Benjamin gave us a tour of the one-hundred-and-nine-acre estate. The four story main house had eleven bedroom suites, seventeen full baths, eleven half baths, and two elevators. Each two-room guest bedroom suite included a large bedroom with a sitting area that led to a huge private bath. Each suite also included a separate living room with a private terrace with a spectacular view of the lake. Also included were two owner's suites with a one-thousand-square-foot two-story dressing room and walk-in closet combo as well as his-and-her baths in each. In addition to the formal living room, dining room, great room, and custom gourmet kitchen, the main house also had a music room, a banquet hall, two offices, a library, butler's quarters and maid's quarters, a fully equipped workout facility with a whirlpool Jacuzzi and steam room, and a fifty-seat media room. Words could not describe the décor in that house. It was unbelievable. On top of an eight-car climate-controlled detached garage was a heliport with the initials "JPW." The estate also included a detached two-bedroom cottage, a separate recording studio, a pool with a pool house, several twenty-foot ornamental topiaries, a rose garden, and a greenhouse. It was really hard to believe that only one person lived here. My two guests walked around with their mouths open the entire time. They even made jokes that I had "struck it big," but I immediately corrected them, "Guys, don't play like that! That is not funny! None of this is mine, and I can't be bought."

After the two hour long grand tour, Benjamin showed us to our separate rooms and soon had lunch prepared for us. He later informed us that Dr. Wharton, as he referred to the bishop, would be home at six and that we should be dressed for dinner promptly at seven.

The full staff managed by Benjamin also included two butlers, a housekeeping manager, two upstairs maids, two downstairs maids, two master chefs, a team of groundskeepers, and a pool man. Harrison was also responsible for five other black exotic vehicles, a Rolls Royce, a Bentley Continental GTC Convertible, a Mercedes SLR McLaren, a Porsche Cayenne, and the Bentley Sedan that

Harrison drove to pick us up at the airport. The staff also had access to three Range Rovers. The round-the-clock security detail was managed by a separate private firm.

I soon learned that Benjamin constantly protected his personal interests as well as the welfare and the security of his job. However, his ultimate sense of loyalty was to the bishop. He had been the bishop's personal butler for ten years. I often wondered if that was the case, why he was *so* insecure about the stability of his position as the house manager? He knew too many of the bishop's secrets. If nothing else that was guaranteed job security. Besides I am sure that the bishop trusted him to the utmost. The bishop could not afford to let him go. Well, not unless he did something really stupid.

During the first week, I saw very little of the bishop, mostly at breakfast and dinner. But he made sure that we had a brief private chat every night before he turned in. We still really didn't know each other very well. My entire world had just changed forever. He knew that my move away from everything that I knew would be a huge adjustment. I was taking a really huge risk by temporarily giving up my scholarship. There were no guarantees that things would work out. He tried his best to reassure me that everything would be fine. He reiterated that he wanted me to take a few days to enjoy my cousin and best buddy while becoming acclimated to my new home. He intentionally became scarce while they were visiting. His intention was to minimize the culture shock and reduce the pressure and stress regarding putting my formal education on hold. The bishop was also concerned with my relocating so quickly and most of all beginning this special relationship with a man almost twice my age.

By the end of the first week, I had decided to stay. A few hours after Owen and Reid left, Benjamin found me by the pool. He asked me to get dressed and meet him in the library because he needed to talk with me. The bishop had requested that Benjamin take me shopping. The bishop inferred earlier that day that he wanted me to look nice and that a few new clothes would probably make me feel better. But that is not what he really meant. As soon as he left, I got the real deal. Benjamin explained how my life was about to change and that in order to play the part; I had to look the part. As of that moment,

I became a direct reflection of the bishop. I had an important role to play and there could not be no major mistakes.

Benjamin then gave me a very brief verbal course regarding the designer labels and the most current seasonal styles. Although I couldn't afford them, I had already acquired considerable knowledge regarding numerous high-end designers, the contemporary styles, and the latest trends. My new wardrobe not only included formal, casual, and business attire, but I would also be sporting new sportswear, shoes, jewelry, and accessories. We also bought a full set of Louis Vuitton luggage as well as four pieces of Gucci luggage. Each set included a matching briefcase, iPad cover, a phone cover, a wallet, driving gloves and key chains. Then we went shopping for the latest high-tech gadgets. I received a new Mac laptop, an iPad, an iPhone, and an iPhone watch that I later discovered had an active GPS that could not be deactivated. It was installed as an extra security precaution. I was cool, calm, and collected on the outside, but on the inside my heart was pounding like an electronic bass drum. He mentioned that weekly grooming would include a haircut, manicure, and pedicure as well as a biweekly massage.

When we returned from a full day of shopping, I immediately went upstairs to shower and change. But when I went to my room, all my things were gone. Grace, the housekeeping manager told me that she was instructed to move all of my things into the bishop's bedroom suite. Reality hit me in the face. I said to myself, "I am cool. I am ready. Well, I do like the man. He will continue to be patient. He has been so far. No real issues. I got this. And it will all be worth it."

The honeymoon phase continued throughout the relationship. He purchased a brand new 525 BMW for me a month after I arrived. He also gave me a Platinum American Express credit card and a $5,000 monthly cash allowance. He hired a voice coach to train me three days a week. Although the bishop and I performed at least one cardio session at least four times a week, the private trainer came to the house three days a week. He definitely didn't look his age, so that definitely was a plus. Our age difference wouldn't be so obvious in public. For a man who was almost forty, the bishop was in great shape and had a body that most twenty-year-olds would truly envy.

We definitely complimented each other. We looked like the ultimate power couple.

I learned very quickly that my lower-middle-class blue-collar Midwestern background was extremely different from the easygoing, laid-back, yet perpetrating superficial lifestyles of the Los Angeles elite. Benjamin taught me to always be aware of my surroundings, both literally and figuratively. He told me that I was only one of a very few young men who had ever held that special position and that I should always respect and continue to honor my new status. I would soon learn of the many advantages of being Dr. Wharton's special companion. Many of these privileges demanded that I uphold his well-known philanthropic, well-admired image. A stellar reputation acquired over several years. Whenever, I walked outside of Wharton Manor, I was always expected to respect his privacy, and be loyal to him. I was told that I must not take this new responsibility lightly. I would be constantly watched and scrutinized by the much envied. "But I will protect you," he said quite often. Benjamin often reminded me, "My employer has very few true friends. Most people in his circle really don't care about him. They are attracted to his wealth and his influence." I didn't understand the severity of what he meant until later. One major challenge I overcame very early was trusting other people. I had to learn from experience that most people that I would meet in my new world, in our circle, would have ulterior motives while pretending to get to know me. I listened closely to all of Benjamin's advices. I said that I would always be conscious of not abusing my role.

Before I arrived, little did I know about the bishop's little idiosyncrasies and stringent rules. But Benjamin took the time to prepare me and show me how to "handle" the bishop and how to deal with his various quirks. We ate every meal together in the formal dining room every day that we were in town together. Breakfast was at 7:00 a.m. and dinner at 7:00 p.m. sharp. My whereabouts had to be known at all times. There would be absolutely no "disappearing acts" for hours at a time. Proper etiquette was also extremely important to the bishop. So, I had to step up my game. Benjamin could help me with some things, but I desperately needed an intense accelerated advance course in how to behave in my new world. So, I found several tools to help me catch up to speed. I felt that time was of the essence. Most of my time over the next thirty days was spent with my nose to the grindstone, reading five helpful books by Letitia Baldrige: *Public Affairs, Private Relations, The Entertainers, Letitia Baldrige's Complete Guide to a Great Social Life,* and *Letitia Baldrige's New Complete Guide to Executive Manners.* I was extremely engrossed in these manuals. I lived and breathed these books because I realized that the information in these tools were essential to the success in my new role. I was determined to fit in.

The bishop continued to show extreme sensitivity to my adjusting to the culture shock. Maybe it was that he saw that I was trying so hard to get it right. He was patient and understanding. He always addressed me with kindness and respect. But there was an unspoken rule that I was personally responsible for keeping his stress level extremely low, which included, among other things, relieving him of all his sexual tension. He often gave me subtle hints and signals of what he wanted, how he wanted it, and when he wanted it. He often complimented me on my bedside manner. On many occasions, extravagant gifts would follow the next day. He was extremely "talented" as well. I truly enjoyed being with an experienced "gentle" man.

Bishop Wharton is the founder and senior pastor of the most prominent and largest Black megachurch in southern California. The first time that I attended his church, he formally introduced me to the entire congregation at both services. He referred to me as a prospective member who had recently relocated to Los Angeles from Detroit. He also mentioned that I had recently won several awards at the American Gospel Music Competition held a few months ago. I received what I thought was much unwarranted, unsolicited attention for the next few Sundays until I officially joined the church. Of course, our relationship was not public knowledge in the church or in our social circles, although I was sure that there was much speculation about our *true* association. He told me that people would definitely talk. "So be prepared, I will protect you as much as I can. People will gossip and assume the worst. So, what, they talked negatively about Jesus Christ." The bishop's huge ego as well as his pride motivated him to broadcast subliminal messages that I was off limits, as a church member, privately and socially. I officially joined the church, the first Sunday of the next month. I did not want him to give the appearance of favoritism, so I started and completed the series of twelve new members' classes, a prerequisite to serve in any leadership position in the church.

Now that I was officially a member, although I would follow the bishop's lead, I was now prepared to begin my role in the church as well as socially, thanks to the books written by Letitia Baldrige. Benjamin also continued to coach me. That evening at dinner, the bishop and I continued our conversation about my various roles. With grave humility, he asked me to refer to him as Jonathan or John while at home and at non-church or business-related functions. To avoid the appearance of impropriety and nepotism, he wanted me to call him Bishop Wharton or just Bishop while at church or during church functions. Although we had a similar conversation a few months ago, he wanted to emphasize its importance. I understood and I complied. I related his request as the friends and family of the President of the United States would not address him by his first name in public or at a state dinner. It would be inappropriate. It was always understood that one must respect his position and his title at all times, especially in public. His role was different in public. He reiterated that I was expected to play at least three special roles in the church. I was expected to attend church every Sunday and Wednesday. I would serve in an executive role on the pastor's aide committee. I would perform a solo or lead a song whenever the bishop requested. I had a reserved seat every Sunday at 8:00 a.m. and 11:30 a.m. and on Wednesday evening for the midweek service. Once a month, usually the fourth Sunday, he accepted an invitation to preach at another church. Of course, I was expected to travel with him and perform before he preached.

Every year for the next five years, I assisted him in hosting the annual American Gospel Music Workshop and Competition. I also attended several annual revivals with him. Because of his status in the community and his affiliation with various local and national organizations, we hosted numerous fund-raising events at the estate. I also escorted him to various political functions and we attended monthly parties hosted by the rich and famous in northern and southern California.

As much traveling as we did, I must say that traveling on the bishop's Bombardier G8 was the most convenient luxury that I appreciated and enjoyed. Two times a year, we took a ten-day vacation. Also, once a year, we always vacationed on one of the Caribbean islands. During the relationship, we also visited Europe, Brazil, Australia, Kenya, South Africa, and Japan. Owen and Reid came to visit once a year. And I went back home to Detroit four times a year, Mother's Day, my mother's birthday, our annual family reunion, and Thanksgiving. Christmas was always reserved for the bishop.

My life with him was great until the very end. For our fifth-year anniversary, we hosted a lavish black-tie party with over two hundred guests. The transparent fiberglass dance floor that covered the pool, the incredible thirty-member orchestra, and the six-feet butter crème cake were the topics of conversation for most of the evening.

The bishop had invited a young man to the party that we had met at the American Gospel Workshop and Competition two months before. He stayed in the pool guesthouse. I didn't ask any questions, but the bishop noticed my mood had changed a little since the party. I soon became emotionally withdrawn. He didn't like it when I internalized my feelings. He wanted to cheer me up so he surprised me with the news of my fifth-year anniversary gift. It was a new Mercedes SL 755 convertible. It was scheduled to be delivered at the party, but it wasn't ready. He had ordered a few custom upgrades, including a voice-activated system and a tracking device. It would take a few more days to arrive.

Two days after the party, our houseguest was still visiting. For the next few days, I saw very little of the bishop. And the frequency of the sex diminished. I wasn't stupid. I was loyal to him and faithful to the relationship. I cared about him very much, but I was not going to share him with another person, especially another man. I couldn't understand why he couldn't just tell me that he didn't want this anymore. He had pushed me to my limit. The life that I had lived for the past five years was about to change and there was no turning back. I was going to give it up. The day before my new car was supposed to arrive, I confided in the house manager. I told him when the Mercedes arrives, I'm leaving and going back to Detroit.

I thought Benjamin and I had formed a close relationship. He assisted me for the last five years in adjusting to my new lifestyle. And I confided in him about everything. But a new reality had set in. I now realized who received the ultimate level of loyalty. I discovered later that he was a most clever spy. Little did I know that my every move had been watched for the past five years? He reported all my activities to his employer. There was really nothing to tell. I was honest. I was completely faithful. Although over the years, Benjamin had hired a few men to test me to see if I would cheat. One of the men approached me and admitted to the scheme. Surprisingly, I was not offended. Benjamin knew that the bishop was somewhat insecure. I guess he wanted to make sure that I wasn't using him.

I had absolutely no regrets. I experienced an extremely privileged lifestyle over those past five years. I lived the life that most people envied. I was now almost twenty-six years old and I had traveled the world. I met a lot of famous and influential people. I had also trained with nationally known skilled and talented professionals.

When Benjamin told the bishop about my plan, he didn't say much. He didn't try to stop me either. He only said, "Lisborn, I truly care about you. Are you sure this is what you want to do?" I replied, "No, but I think that it's best. Why is he still here?" The bishop didn't say anything. He just turned and walked toward the bedroom door. He returned ten minutes and said in a low voice, "I am not going to stop you. You can leave. You can't be here and live your life, live this life with me, feeling the way that you do. I can't and I won't try to stop you. But just to let you know, I just cancelled the order for the Mercedes. And I cancelled your Amex card too." He turned and left the room again. Shortly after that Grace came in and helped me finish packing. We moved my things into the guest suite. I packed all my clothes, jewelry, and personal belongings. I took all the things that I had acquired as well as all the many lavish gifts given to me. I had earned an annual salary working and traveling with the bishop as well as performing at various events. However, I rarely spent much of my own money because I was given a platinum Amex card and a generous monthly allowance. I had saved most of my own money, approximately $245,000. I was also, a young talented artist with a promising career. I desperately tried to convince myself that I was going to be okay. Of course, that was no easy task.

I cried and cried most of the night. I wasn't sure if I was hurt because of the overt deception or if I was finally being confronted with the realization of how deeply I loved him. Or was it both. I was inconsolable. I felt abandoned. I had no one to talk too. I couldn't talk to my family or my cousin or even my best friend. They wouldn't understand. Knowing them, they would tell me to stay and deal with it. Their belief would probably be that the lavish lifestyle was more important than a little indiscretion. But I couldn't deal with that.

I had to get out of the house, so I took a late-night walk around the lake. When I returned, I passed his suite. Although his door was closed, I could see the light under his bedroom door. He was still awake. I turned and walked up to his door and started to knock. But to my surprise, I heard him crying. I also heard music in the background. It was "Never Meant to Hurt You" sang by Toni Braxton and Baby Face. I stood there a moment, contemplating what should I do. I finally decided to walk away. If he wanted me to stay, the ball was in his court. So I gave him some space. Although I had never seen or heard him cry, I was sure that his pride would not allow him to change his mind and ask me to stay or try to stop me from leaving.

I went to my suite to try to pull it together. My emotions were all over the place. I wanted to hate him, but I couldn't. If I ever loved him, then I couldn't be mean. I just couldn't. And I couldn't be nasty or bitter either. I couldn't strike out to hurt him or try to destroy his life. But I desperately needed to find a way to manage this pain. Until I found a way to cope, I would bury my love and the feelings I had for him. Bury them deep, where no one could find them. When I reached that moment in time in which I thought of him and I felt nothing, I would form dead love. And until I reach that moment, I had to deal with the present, my present pain. Life is pain management, but right now, I don't want to manage this type of pain. Some pain is inflicted intentionally on some people. That type of pain shouldn't be because life is hard enough. To speed up the process of reaching that moment in time, I will keep praying for GOD's sweeping grace.

I am a strong man—very strong. It might have appeared to others that my role in this relationship was emasculating and that I was the weaker of the two, but I was not. I had always spoken openly with him. And I had never tolerated being disrespected on any level, in public or in private. Although we had never had a situation or argument regarding a third person in our relationship, I had always made it clear that I wouldn't share him with another man.

The next morning, although still in much pain, I had regained my composure. I had too. I really had no choice. So, I immediately began to shut down. I slowly started to close my heart; it hurt too much. But I was too proud to let him see it. "Man, get it together! Focus! You can do this," I said to myself. I had some serious decisions to make. Later that morning, the bishop knocked on the door, came in, stared at me for a moment, and handed me an envelope. Reality was setting in. My five-year relationship was officially about to end. I opened the envelope and read the note.

> *L,*
>
> *Apparently, our season together has come to an end. This is a gesture for your new start: $500,000 for each of our annual seasons together.*
> *Be blessed.*

Also, included in the envelope was a check for 2.5 million dollars. I couldn't believe it although he was worth well over seven hundred million dollars. He owned several radio stations and a gospel recording company. He was also a successful real estate investor. So, he definitely would not miss a few million. I didn't expect that. At first, I thought it might have been a test, an attempt to persuade me to reconsider and stay. He knew that I was good *to* him and good *for* him. He knew that my feelings were genuine and that I had grown to love him. I was loyal and truly committed to that man.

I had stayed up the past few nights contemplating if I was making the right decision. My decision was final. I really didn't want to leave, but it was best. I needed to remove myself from that situation before it got ugly. Over the years, I had accepted all his idiosyncrasies and I had learned to deal with his little quirks, but I was not going to share him with another man. Although I enjoyed my life with him, that was the only stipulation in which I would not compromise. Sharing him with his prominent career, the church, and his high-profile social life was enough.

Inside the envelope was also a one-way VIP ticket on a chartered plane back to Detroit. But instead, I chose to go to Miami for two weeks. I had to get my head together and regroup before heading back to Detroit to "face the music." He changed the ticket to a one-way to Miami and another chartered plane from Miami to Detroit. He also prepaid the hotel expenses at the Ritz Carlton. He traded in my first BMW for a newer model four months ago. He had paid cash for a new custom BMW 870, but this time he registered it in my name and gave me the title. To my surprise, he did not try to prevent me from taking it. Well, maybe I was not totally correct. Maybe he loved me, but he wasn't truly in love with me. He was really good to me and for that season in my life, but seasons change. He said that I had more than earned it. He had it shipped and placed in storage the day after I left. I guess he didn't want any drama. More importantly, he didn't want a scandal. It was not in my character to try to destroy his reputation. But I could have sold my story to every talk show, entertainment news show, and magazine from the West Coast to the East Coast as well as below the Bible Belt. Not to mention the rag sheets and the bloggers. Much of the judgmental, hypocritical partisan media would have devoured that story. But that's not me. I would have never betrayed his trust even if he had asked me to leave. I left quite a lot differently from how he probably expected. I left rather quietly without an incident, with no drama.

I was ready to put all of this behind me. My mind was satisfied. I did what I had to do. Although I was still in pain, I felt that I had done the right thing. Now I was ready to settle my spirit. I needed the peace and solitude that I usually achieved during quality time with the LORD. I prayed and meditated for several weeks constantly asking HIM to help me. I needed HIS continued guidance. I needed HIS continued grace and mercy.

After I left, I soon learned that the houseguest had moved into the main house. I assumed he was my replacement. Guess I was right. A mutual friend told me that their short-lived relationship lasted only three months. I had seen the bishop a few times over the past few years. Considering the reason why I left, I was quite cordial to him, but he always avoided direct eye contact with me. It was obvious that he was intentionally distant toward me. I guess guilt will do that. I truly believe that regardless of the situation; I always try to react with class. Our breakup was no different. I don't like to burn bridges. Because when one door closes, another door could easily open. And of course, I had over 3.2 million dollars in the bank. But even with all the extravagant living and the fact that now I was starting over, I still realized a few things. The planets were still aligned in my favor. I could not allow the grass to grow around my dreams. Having it all doesn't necessarily mean having it all at once.

It was time to move on and begin the next phase of my life. After my brief stay in Miami, I immediately returned to Detroit. I reapplied to the Chicago Conservatory of Music, where I received another full scholarship. Of course, I could afford to pay for my tuition. I really didn't need a degree and I had already acquired a reputation in the gospel arena. However, I was still determined to stay focused on the opportunity that I was once given. I eventually completed my graduate work with honors and received numerous lucrative career opportunities in the Chicago area as well as in Houston, Dallas, Washington, DC, and Miami. But with much contemplation, I decided to begin the next phase of my life in Atlanta as a local weekend anchor. Within two years, I was hosting *Straight Talk*, a daily cable talk show. Now as you know I am the coanchor on *The AM Atlanta Morning News*.

CHAPTER 14

Under The Radar

Stay under the radar, or else you will become the target.

CHANCE STARTED TO tell his amazing saga next. Ironically, before he began to give an account of the details of the relationship with his minister "friend," he started to reveal the details of two life-changing experiences.

Although Chance had a multimillion-dollar contract and he was somewhat of a local celebrity, he was unlike most basketball players in the NBA. Before he became involved with his current minister "friend," he had more than his share of casual sex with women, mainly one-night stands and short-lived flings. It was rumored that the word had gotten out regarding the size of his piece and his exotic bedside manner. Young, single and middle-age married women and especially young white women were constantly trying to "try him on for size." And some even attempted to seduce him for another reason, financial security. But Chance wasn't having it. He was much smarter than that.

During the period that Chance frequently had sex with women, one of his major self-created rules was that he would never ever allow himself to fall asleep right after sex. She was also never allowed to spend the night. The second major rule was that if it was a one-night stand, which it was in most cases, he always made sure that he personally disposed of or flushed the condoms. He swore that he would never become a baby's daddy. That's also why he always wore two condoms. Even the XLs were a little snug, but he dealt with it. On one occasion, he almost became a victim of one night of wild and passionate sex. It could have resulted in a potentially very expensive mistake. A mistake that would have affected him for at least eighteen years in the future.

One night after a wild team party and then sex with a random girl, he accidentally fell asleep. When he woke up in a panic, he realized that he had not disposed of the condoms. Not to alarm the female who appeared to be still asleep, he casually went to the bathroom to "take a leak" and to wash up. He distinctly remembered that he had not taken off the condoms and flushed them down the toilet. At first, he thought maybe she had taken them off and threw them in the garbage. Still frantic, he looked for them and could not find them. Then he remembered the rumors of a premeditated plan used by some women who aggressively pursued sports stars and entertainers. He opened the ice bucket. He saw something. And there they were, tied in a knot, enclosed in a small plastic sandwich bag in the bottom of the bucket. He couldn't believe it. But as usual, he stayed calm and did not overreact. Chance's instincts were correct. He never said anything to her about what he saw. She woke up a few minutes later and went to take a shower. When she went into the bathroom, she saw something that she was not expecting. She immediately noticed the empty sandwich bag in the sink. Realizing that he knew what she had done, she skipped the shower. He saw the guilt on her face when she came out of the bathroom. Not saying a word, she quickly got dressed and left.

The sinister plot was to steal the semen-filled condoms and keep them chilled until she left. And as soon as possible, she would immediately take it to a doctor who would begin the process to prepare it for immediate artificial insemination. Depending on the quality and the amount of the specimen, and if the doctor was able, some women would even share the same semen with a close female friend. Sometimes it worked. Sometimes it didn't. It was luck of the draw. This was also a big moneymaking scheme for a few well-respected yet secretly unscrupulous physicians throughout the country. The doctors knew exactly what the women were doing, but they didn't ask any questions. It was just business.

Chance breathed a big sigh of relief. Reality had set in. That was a close call. Unlike several others, he has known in the league, he had dodged the proverbial bullet—in his case, a potentially multimil-lion-dollar bullet. He curtailed his reckless behavior several months before he met his current minister "friend." He transformed from being a rambunctious self-indulgent, self-pleasing country boy to a mature Southern gentleman, one who was committed to his present discreet and private relationship.

Before the guys had a chance to let that tale marinate a little, Chance continued to tell another unique personal experience that seriously impacted his life. A few years ago, several months before he met his current friend, his team, the Atlanta Eagles, had one of its regular season games in Miami. This game would determine if they would be going to the playoffs. The team had a great year so far, but they were still under a lot of pressure. The Eagles had been in the same predicament, leading as the front runner several times in the past. They had a history of coming so close, and then at the very end; lose it all. He began.

One of my usual rituals that I often practiced to reduce my stress level, the day before a big game, was to rent a convertible and go for a drive. A long late-night drive usually cleared my head. In retrospect, I should have rented a car that was a little less conspicuous.

I really wasn't aware of where I was going; I just drove. Besides, I knew that the GPS would get me back to the hotel if I got lost. But unfortunately, I accidentally ended up in an area in which I should not have been.

Appearances can be very deceiving and being in the wrong place at the wrong time can definitely give the impression of wrongdoing. A Black man driving a convertible Bentley in an area of town locally known for being a haven for drugs and male prostitutes caused much suspicion, especially at 2:00 a.m. When it was discovered that it was a professional ball player, it added more cause for alarm. That could be even more incriminating.

I was stopped by a policeman. He said that I changed lanes without signaling, which was a lie. But of course, I was not going to argue with him. He asked me the usual questions until he looked at my driver's license and realized who I was. Then he asked me what I was doing in that type of area at that late hour. I didn't answer. He just gave me a verbal warning, and I drove off. To this day, I believe I was a victim of racial profiling, although I couldn't prove it. I didn't want any negative media attention, and I did not want to cause a scene. However, the news of the incident quickly spread. "Chandler Jameson, NBA basketball player was stopped at 2:00 a.m. by the Miami Police in an area known for drugs, cruising and male hustlers." Now I can imagine what the well-known Black Hollywood comedian/actor as well as the former Atlanta baseball player went through several years ago. But I wasn't looking for anything, and I didn't know where I was. Fortunately, my teammates, my local fans via social media, the town, and the league didn't treat me any differently. That's mainly because I tried to quickly defuse the story. Besides several of my teammates had recently gone through much worse scandals, mainly with drugs and fights in the clubs.

I never allowed the media to control me or affect my image or my career in a negative way. It was not that difficult because I was not a reckless, egotistical hothead with a big mouth. Yes, I suspected that it would more than likely go viral, but I had to try to stop the bleeding by immediately taking action and aggressively applying damage control. I had learned much very early on in my college career from the mistakes of other high-profile celebrities and athletes. It is simply best to just shut down a potential damaging story as quickly as possible before it goes viral by making a very clever one-line public comment and then changing the subject by pitching a positive story. And I did just that. I simply commented, "I am not going to comment regarding such ridiculous rumors. I know who I am and I know what I am. Now if you want to ask me an important question like, is it true that I might be a free agent next year and if so, do I plan to stay in Atlanta. Then I might give you a hint."

Eventually my mother was confronted with the rumors. Wondering minds can be very dangerous. That is why even the slightest of innuendoes must be snuffed out quickly. I had to speak to her before the busybodies started whispering and putting crazy ideas in her head. I responded as soon as I heard, but I pretended to call her one day out of the blue. My instincts were correct because I could tell that something was wrong. I had to shut it down and shut it down with the quickness. The brief discussion must have worked because her mood and the tone in her voice quickly changed. The upbeat conversation seemed to calm her nerves. But to make sure, a few days later, I wrote her two letters, one unequivocally denying the rumors and the other was a half-truth, which I considered to be a well-crafted lie. But the most difficult decision was deciding which one to mail.

Letter #1:

Dearest Mama,

Behind every rumor there is some truth. And this is no exception. But I wanted to write you this letter because it would allow me to present it in a way to divulge how I felt without falling apart.

I am a Black man with a preference. That preference depends on who I am with, if with anyone at all. I do not like to label myself as gay or as bisexual or as a homosexual. I might have strong sexual desires for men, but my preference would be to be with a woman. But I will say that I do not and will not live the typical gay lifestyle. By that I mean that I don't go to the gay bars, clubs, or parties. And I do not live in the small isolated world in which the large majority of my friends and associates are gay. Nor do I not live the life of having very little or having nothing to do with the heterosexual world except going to church and to work. On the other hand, I do not and will not accept any label that society chooses to put on me. I am not ashamed, although

158

I consciously and intentionally hide my sexuality. I am who I am! I am of the life but not in the life. The bisexual lifestyle, that is. Why does it matter who I love, whether it is a man or a woman, as long as I'm not hurting anyone.

No matter what you think of me, I'm no effeminate, reckless, or sexually irresponsible man! I am the man you raised me to be. This feeling, this tendency, whatever you want to call it is such a small part of who I have become. Look at me and all that I have achieved. I have accomplished a lot in my life. I have earned your respect. And I want and need your continued respect. Also, I really need you to understand. You never would have known about this, as most other people don't know. My desire for another man isn't going away because I think I might be in love with some woman or just because I might get married someday. I know because I live that lie, that life every day.

I love you with all my heart. I never intentionally meant to hurt you. It hurts me that my celebrity status exposes you to such ugliness. You were and still are the best, most loving and caring mother that anyone could ever have. I would not change anything about you. Please don't blame yourself for anything that you think you might have done or for anything that you feel like you didn't do. I hope and pray that one day you will understand.

I love you,
Chance

Letter #2:

Dearest Mama,
The haters are just hating on me. Again, all lies.

I'm not that way! I am the man you raised me to be. Look at me, and all that I have achieved. Women chase me all day, every day. I am admired and well respected. I am well liked by millions. I have accomplished a lot in my life. I have earned your respect. And I want and need your continued respect. That is so important to me.

I love you with all my heart. It hurts me that my celebrity status exposes you to such ugliness. I never intentionally meant to hurt you. You were and still are the best, most loving and caring mother that anyone could ever have. I would not change anything about you. Please don't blame yourself for anything that you think you might have done or for anything that you feel like you didn't do. I hope and pray that one day you will understand.

See you soon!

Love ya,
Chance

It wasn't an easy decision. With much hesitation, I sent the second letter. I had to lie to my mother. I love her too much. As much as I wanted too, I just couldn't tell her the truth. The truth would have broken her heart. She would've blamed herself. I did it to preserve our relationship and the image that she had of me. I could not tarnish the image that she had of her golden boy. My mother lived her dreams through me. I could not and would not destroy that. Maybe deep down she knows or she always knew. They say mothers always know. But she never brought up the subject or even gave me a hint that she ever suspected anything. I was not going to confirm it. Besides I truly believe that people believe what they want to believe. I was also protecting myself. I would deny it to my grave.

She responded with a heartfelt "I am thinking about you" card. It began with this:

My Dearest Son Chandler,

I love you with all my heart and soul. I am so happy that you have turned out to be the type of man that any mother would be proud to have as a son. I am so blessed that I was the one; the one that GOD chose me to nurture and raise. Even if some of those rumors were true, they would not change the love that I have for you. You will always be an inevitable part of me.

I pray that GOD continues to watch over my son.

I love you,

Mama

We never mentioned that subject again, and it never became an issue again. I finally had to face reality. Balancing my celebrity status and my private life was not going to be easy. It was probably going to be a lifetime, long-term chore, not to mention the fact that I was involved with a high-profile minister. Those two potentially earth-shattering incidents could have cost me my future. Yes, they were caused by my actions. Yes, I was responsible. But they were also partially due to my being a celebrity. If I was not somewhat famous, I would not have been such a target. And both of them involved women.

I am definitely a prime example of someone who quickly learns from his mistakes. Those two potentially detrimental incidents definitely shaped me to be who I am right now. Well, I guess I had to learn from my mistakes the hard way, but I am a better man for it. Lessons learned. The key is to try to stay below the radar. Although I was never drawn to the spotlight, I proactively put forth much more effort to avoid unnecessary attention. The change was necessary, but the adjustment wasn't difficult at all. Actually, constantly trying to be inconspicuous was quite easy. It was a major part of our being a well-kept secret. Thus staying under the radar was vital.

Those two situations also helped me realize that GOD was trying to get my attention. Well, HE definitely did. HIS allowing me to go through those experiences; taught me that if I spent more quality time with HIM, I might be able to avoid similar situations in the future. HE was protecting me from myself. In doing so, I developed a daily personal ritual of praying and meditating. Each day I asked HIM to help me. I asked GOD to help me think clearly, to help me weigh my options, and to make the best decisions. I realized that I desperately needed the guidance of the Holy Spirit on a daily basis. I also discovered that I needed HIS continued favor, mercy, and grace.

CHAPTER 15

The Need Is Greater Than The Vow

Words I used to live by: Never to allow my head
to rule my heart. Like most men, in some cases
that applies to both "heads."

MY RELATIONSHIP IS just a little more complicated than Lisborn's situation. I am feeling, what I am feeling. And I like it. I like it a lot. But it took a long while to get here.

I played high school basketball, then college ball and now I am in the starting lineup in the NBA for the Atlanta Eagles. I can definitely vouch that there is an entire underground world of Black male professional men, celebrities, and star athletes who are homosexual or bisexual. This is nothing new. There have been several recent scandals and several tell-all books written exposing their dirty secrets. They know who they are and other homosexual and bisexual men know who they are. But because many are married or have girlfriends or exaggerate their "macho-ism," they are not easily detected by the mainstream. Although over the past two decades, a few Black authors have made a slight attempt to educate Black women regarding their alternative lifestyles, the general public still equates "macho-ism" with being straight. In addition, their involvement with naive white women usually makes it easier to perpetuate the cover-up. The façade is easily perpetrated because most white women are not familiar with our history, and they don't know our culture. Most of my fellow bruthas, especially those in the basketball and football leagues must protect their images at all costs. Most of our taboo dirty little secrets seem to be hidden from the mainstream, although recently two athletes, one football draftee, and a former Atlanta basketball player came out of the closet. Because our fame overshadows our personal lives and the fact that people put us on a pedestal, many people don't pick up on it while others just don't care. And from personal experience, we all know that there is also another high-profile select group of professional homosexual and bisexual Black men whose image is protected. It is protected by the sacred cloth. I have been involved with one for several years.

After that eye-opening, life-changing experience with that female several years ago, I was forced to curtail my risky behavior. I needed a break. So, I tried to be celibate.

I never slept with men and women during the same period of time. That was a major self-created moral rule. I have always had homosexual tendencies, but I rarely acted upon them. Although I dabbled every blue moon, for the most part, I tried to bury those urges. Besides, I rarely found a discreet but secure, well-rounded easygoing laid-back brutha that I was attracted too. And I definitely had no intentions of playing around with another high-profile athlete. Although the hyperactive "friend" in my pants often wanted to come outside and play, I was quite successful in keeping him on lockdown. We usually played together one-on-one once or twice a day. I felt that was a good compromise. My new life of celibacy with both men and women lasted a good ten months. I thought I was handling it pretty well. That is, until I met him.

I met Maxwell in my massage therapist's office. I had just finished one of my weekly deep-tissue massage sessions. I was standing at the receptionist's desk waiting to schedule my next appointment. He was sitting, waiting to be seen. As I was leaving, we gave each other a friendly nod.

The second time I saw him, we crossed paths the following week at the elevator. I was leaving, and I assumed he was coming for his appointment. Again, we acknowledged each other with cordial nods and a hello.

Two weeks later, we found ourselves sitting across from each other in the waiting area. I was busy texting, making plans for the weekend. I glanced upward for a second and noticed that he was staring. I continued to text. As I glanced up again, my eyes met his. I quickly looked away. I thought, was it my imagination or was this guy checking me out? I wasn't quite sure because it was a different type of gaze. I just thought it was a good thing that we were the only two in the waiting area because he didn't try to hide it. Those dark piercing eyes seemed to be looking right through me.

Then his phone rang and he answered. The deep resonance of his voice captured my attention. After the call, he leaned forward and said, "Hello." I guess that I didn't hear him the first time. He greeted me again. I was so engrossed in my texting that I still didn't hear him. After he snapped his fingers a few times to get my attention, suddenly, I snapped out of the trance.

I looked up.

"Are you intentionally ignoring me?"

"Excuse me?"

"I spoke to you twice."

"Sorry. It was not intentional."

He said, "This is the third time we have seen each other, and I don't even know your name."

I thought that was a rather forward comment, considering where we were. But I didn't overreact. If my senses were correct, this man was flirting. Naw, he couldn't be.

He introduced himself, but I didn't catch the name. From his reaction when I introduced myself, he didn't know who I was either. We stood up and shook hands. The firm grip of this hand-to-hand contact sent a mild electric shock throughout my body. From his reaction, he obviously felt a gentle spark between us too. I sat back down and continued to text. Then I suddenly stopped for a moment. What was wrong with me? With a slight chuckle, I said to myself,

"Boy, why are you trippin'." Now that he had my attention, I was beginning to pay a little more attention to him. But of course, he didn't notice.

The very attractive, well-kempt man looked like he might be in his early thirties although I learned later that he was much older. I was off by almost ten years. His shiny shaved head only drew more attention to his jet-black eyebrows and his dark-brown eyes. His cleaned shaven strong facial features alluded that he might be a professional model, or maybe a kept man. Time must have been good to him. Or maybe it was just good clean living.

It was quite evident that he was quite fashion-conscious, always staying abreast of the latest styles. He wore a tailored European-style taupe suit with cognac-colored slip-ons with a matching belt. His French-cuffed shirt with diamond cuff links added a distinct personal touch to his ensemble. His well-manicured hands were accented with a platinum diamond bracelet on his right wrist, a platinum Rolex watch and a platinum wedding band with two rows of diamonds on the left hand. The ring gave insight that more than likely, he might be married. Although a lot of guys in Atlanta wear wedding rings for professional reasons while others wear them to throw women off their scent.

I have been accused of having a healthy self-confidence, but this guy took it to the next level but with subtlety. His posture and mannerisms exuded sex appeal. He wore a suave unobtrusive sexy "swagga" that was impossible to ignore. If he was trying to captivate my attention, he succeeded. But I still played it cool. I didn't want to be too obvious.

Just before I was about to enter for my session, he handed me a ticket. He said it was for a men's shelter charity function. I asked him to slide it in my portfolio that I left on my seat. When I finished my session, he was gone. I grabbed my portfolio and left. Later that evening, I remembered the ticket. I wanted to read the details and put it in a safe place just in case I decided to attend. When I opened the portfolio and picked up the ticket, I noticed that a handwritten note was attached. I assumed it was from him. It read,

> *Hello,*
>   *I will be at Veni Vidi Vici Atlanta on Friday at 8:00 p.m. I would like you to join me if you are free.*
>
>   *Max*

The note included his cell number too. I smiled and chuckled. This man was too bold. And surprisingly, I was actually intrigued, but was I reading too much into it. His brief note left me thinking about him the rest of the week. I really didn't know what to think. I didn't want to assume the worst. Maybe he wanted to talk about the charity. I had three days to make a decision.

The level of curiosity grew. I didn't call or text to give notice that I was coming. I just showed up. I guess he left word with the restaurant maître d that I might be joining him. When I arrived, I was escorted directly to his table. He didn't look too surprised when I approached him. Or maybe it was hidden behind the big smile.

He stood up. We shook hands. He ordered wine and I ordered a Jack Daniels on ice. I knew I was in training. One drink wouldn't hurt. I figured I would work it off tomorrow.

I didn't know what to expect but I actually had a great time. No one really dominated the conversation. He talked about his charities and I mentioned a little bit about my background as well as a few charities for which I volunteered. We continued to chat about things in general, nothing too serious. But I still didn't know if he had an ulterior motive or a hidden agenda. The evening ended on a good note. As we were leaving, I mentioned that I would contact him at the end of next week to confirm if I would be able to attend the charity event. Actually, I had to go out of town for a few games, but of course, I didn't tell him that. When I returned, we had dinner two more times in the same week. I really enjoyed his company. We really seemed to vibe. And it felt good. I could just be myself.

The first evening that we had dinner, he told me that he was a counselor and an advisor. I kinda alluded to what my true profession was also. After our second meeting, he told me that he was a minister. Of course, he avoided disclosing his true identity. He failed to mention that he was the pastor of one of the megachurches in Atlanta. I really didn't put two and two together until several days after our third outing together. In retrospect, it was a good thing. I probably would have treated him differently.

During that third get-together, the conversation took an unexpected turn. He began to reveal a little more.

Out of nowhere he said to me. "I like the time we spend together."

"Okay. So, do I."

"And, I like you."

"Okay. You are cool. I like you too."

"Look at me. I am serious. I really like you."

"What do you mean, you like me?"

"I am growing rather fond of you. And I think I want more."

"You want more?"

"Yes."

"More what?"

"For starters, more quality time."

"So what are you saying?"

"Being with you, takes me to a special place. I am totally relaxed when we get together. I feel free to just be myself. And if I am reading your signals correctly, you are kinda feeling me too. I think we could be good together."

I just smiled.

"Is that a yes? Am I right?"

"Well, to be honest, I have been wondering why so much interest in me. I was kinda waiting for your sales pitch or the line you were going to try to sell me. I figured if I waited long enough, you would reveal your true motive."

"Well, I had to make sure. And I think you were feeling me out too."

"I don't like drama. Aren't you married?"

"Yes, but it's complicated. Well, it's actually more complex than complicated. We have an understanding."

"An understanding?"

"Yes, an understanding. I will explain everything a little later. But I want to make it clear. I am not trying to play you. I won't try to take you for granted and I won't lie to you."

"Okay. But I am going to be honest with you. Yes, I am young. Yes, I have been known to break many hearts. I have had my share of sexy women, Black and White, young and old, and married and single. No real commitments, mainly casual sex. And I have also dealt with a few men too but nothing serious.

"That is all in the past. And for now, although I don't like labels, I am leaning toward my preference to be with a man. I just feel more comfortable with men. But at this point in my life, I won't take any BS from anyone, man or woman, Black or White, young or old, married or single. With me, what you see is what you get. But when I truly care, I am loyal and committed. When I love, I love hard and deep."

Whenever, Maxwell looked at me with those piercing dark-brown eyes, they seem to be penetrating me, as though he was looking for something. He seemed to touch my soul. No one had ever affected me like that. He did something to me. I felt so hot inside. And I don't mean from the waist down either.

I was not afraid to admit that I had serious trust issues with men. They stemmed from short-lived superficial dating situations with unscrupulous cheaters. They underestimated me and assumed that I was stupid and naive. I only gave them one strike then I cut them loose quickly. I also had issues with people accepting me, for me. I had internal conflicts regarding believing that people truly wanted to be with me and not my money or sex. Most turned out to be leeches who pretended to care while others just wanted a freak session. Maxwell understood what I had experienced because he had the same issues with a few men. However, his past experiences were not as severe. Although he could appreciate the finer things in life, he also treasured the simple things. That was one of his most attractive qualities. He was a refined gentleman, not a typical pretentious mitch (male bitch) with a constant attitude, like many successful Black men in Atlanta. That negative self-projection is one of my biggest turn-offs. And most of all, he didn't treat me like an uncouth dumb jock just because I was a professional athlete. When we were on dates, he always tried to grab the check first, which was a nice change. Actually, he paid most of the time. Something I was not used too. We begin to spend more quality time together, mostly dinner and in-depth conversation. After the fourth week of getting together, we began to hang out a few days a week, even on some Sunday evenings. It proved that people make time and do what they want to do.

Although it was obvious that there was a strong mutual attraction, no one made the first move. At the time, I didn't really know what I wanted with him. All I knew was that I was just enjoying the present. One evening, it seemed like the time was right, so I brought up the subject.

"I could have sex every day if I wanted to, but I have outgrown that. I wanted something much more meaningful. I like you and we seem to vibe well. But I have to be real with you.

"If I thought I might be interested in another brutha, I would have to take it slow. Sex can really complicate things. Whether we plan it or not, feelings can evolve. Believe it or not, I have been celibate for almost a year. I have attempted to practice the ninety-day rule before sex, but unfortunately, it only happened once. Twenty-one days was the longest."

He didn't have much of a reaction to my little spiel regarding my current views about sex. He only replied that he didn't have any expectations. He just wanted to take things day by day and just go with the flow.

Feeling very relieved, I agreed.

Soon after, the next few weeks of spending more quality time together, most of my suspicions became void. I enjoyed the time we spent together, and I was pretty sure that he did too. Just talking and sharing about our lives. As I rambled on and on, he seemed tuned in to every word. His eyes told me that he was really interested in what I had to say. He seemed to genuinely care.

I began to realize just how much I depended on Maxwell as a sounding board. I was sure that my issues were minuscule compared to his. When I was with him, problems were suddenly solvable. It seemed as though I did not have a care in the world. My problems seem to just work themselves out and fly out the window.

And in the beginning, I think he enjoyed the novelty of our newly found situation mainly because I didn't treat him like the almighty bishop of a megachurch. He used to say, "I like you because you like me just for me. Not because of my status or my money. Well, at least you make me feel that way. You don't seem to have ulterior motives." But it was not easy at first. I still had some issues, so many defensive walls up. And things were about to be tested. Our situation was about to take a drastic change.

CHAPTER 16

Human Nature

Heal the brokenhearted, and bind up their wounds.

"MAN, I COULD tell you a story that would blow your mind, but your puritanical virgin ears couldn't handle it," said Chance.

"Dude, I am a grown-ass man. Don't let the pretty-boy face fool you. I am not as innocent and naive as you might think," said Dexter.

Chance asked, "Are you sure you want to hear this? I don't think you can handle the graphic details of what really happened, the way that it happened. So, I will give you the clean abbreviated version."

Dexter's excitement to hear grew even more. He reiterated. "I said I can handle it! Come on, bring it! And I want you to give the version that you would tell the guys if I was not here."

"Dude, you got me curious too," said Lisborn.

"Come on, playa, you know I'm interested," said Emerson.

"Okay, but stop me if it becomes too much," said Chance.

So, Chance begins.

Well, things were progressing well between us, so I decided to do something a little different. I wanted to do something special for Max, something that I had never done before. I had been only drafted my second year when we met. My team had a great season and we were a shoe-in to dominate the top three positions in the playoffs. But once again, our fate took a turn for the worse. I

172

still wanted to attend the championship finals. The next three games would be played in Miami, Florida. So, I rented a house for the week, a private beachfront property in Fort Lauderdale. I wanted to find a secluded quiet place right on the beach less than an hour north of the city, far away from South Beach. Although the odds were pretty even as to who would win the next five games, I preferred to arrive a few days prior to the game just to relax. I also wanted to stay a few extra days to rest after the crowds had left town. I also didn't want to deal with the hustle and bustle of all the crowds in a rush to leave. I just didn't feel like coping with all that drama, this year. But mainly it was because, I valued my privacy. This year I had even more reason for additional privacy.

Although Max was not an avid basketball fan, I invited him down for a four-day weekend getaway to a somewhat exotic place that would make him feel a little out of his comfort zone. We had been getting to know each other for almost three months. I thought that the finals weekend would be a great way for just the two of us to get away and spend some quality time together outside of the city. But although we had been spending time together longer than twenty-one days, it definitely wasn't going to be *that* type of party. I liked him. I liked him a lot, but I still had trust issues.

Max arrived the day before the first next big game. Shortly after he unpacked and settled into his room, we went on a two-hour private dinner cruise up the Gold Coast. After dinner, we returned to the house. Since both of us had experienced a rather long day, we decided to chill during the rest of the evening. He went to his bedroom to make a few calls and to check emails. Although I was kinda tired, I convinced myself that I needed to burn off some of that late-night seafood dinner. Just as I had finished three sessions from my P90X video collection, he walked in. I always traveled with it just in case I did not have access to a decent gym. I sat on the floor in position to start the last part of my daily regime of two hundred crunches. And just as I had finish and was about to sit up, he came over and sat next to me.

He smirked and said, "You have great technique. I really need to burn some stress and a good workout would really help, but I am not really in the mood. Yeah, I know, my life seems so great, but I am under a lot of pressure. I just need something to help relieve some of my stress. You know what would help?"

Not responding, I lean back slightly and just stared at him, waiting for him to answer.

"I want to feel you. Come here." He placed his hand on my knee. "I'm pretty sure that you can help me to relax. I guarantee that it will feel good to you too."

Surprised and confused, I ignored that remark. This came out of nowhere. Until this moment, he never made a pass.

Then he slid his hand up and rubbed between my legs.

I pushed his hand away. "Hey! Don't do that. I'm not ready. I didn't invite you here for that. If you came here for sex, then you might want to reconsider staying and either go to a hotel or head back to Atlanta."

He jerked his other hand away, stood up, rushed into his bedroom, and closed the door. From the expression on his face, I could tell that he was mad. His ego was probably a little hurt too. From the short time that I had known him, I had learned that no one rarely said no to him. It was also obvious that he was not used to rejection.

I felt a little uncomfortable, so I left the house. I needed some fresh air, so I decided to partake in one of my favorite rituals when I vacationed in a tropical place with a coastline. I really enjoyed a peaceful midnight walk on a serene beach. I valued the much-needed quality time alone because it was one of the rare moments that I truly had to myself, my time for soul-searching and self-reflection.

I returned an hour later, but the house was completely dark. I wondered if he had actually taken heed to what I had said and left. For a few moments, I thought I was right. Then I turned on one light, just enough to make my way to the rear balcony which overlooked the pool. The sound of splashing water gave me the answer. I also heard music—light instrumental jazz. I made my way down to the terrace level and walked over and looked down. I saw him swimming. He did not hear me when I approached because he was underwater. I stood on the side as he swam a few laps, periodically coming up for air. The underwater lamps highlighted his toned body. He was butt-ass naked. Max was sexy in his clothes, but his conservative yet fashionable clothes did not do him justice. This brutha's body was extremely toned, especially for a forty-year-old man with such a hectic schedule. They say forty is the new twenty. Well, Max is definitely living proof of that. I was in great shape because I worked-out daily. It was part of my job as an athlete. I was pleasantly surprised to say the least; he was almost as ripped as I was.

Finally, after several more laps, his head emerged from the water. Wiping the water from his face, he paused as he saw me standing there. His brief puzzled look and overt hesitation confirmed that I had startled him. Obviously, he was not expecting me to be there, standing directly above him. As he slowly climbed out, sparkling drops of liquid light clung to his hairless light-mocha-colored flesh. Not saying a word, he slowly strutted passed me, wearing nothing but a half smile. His light-brown smooth wet body glistened as the light from the cast iron torches reflected off his skin. It quickly became obvious that I was staring, and I didn't try to hide it. Once I caught myself falling into a slight hypnotic state, I snapped out of it. I tried very hard to stay focused on his face as he walked by. That was the first time that I had actually seen him naked. He subtly looked in my direction and noticed that I was still gawking. Still wearing only a faint smile, he walked toward the direction of a table to get a towel to dry off. He took his time drying off, all the while casually turning his back to me. The sly smirk on his face and the direction of his slight stare told me that he knew what he was doing. I looked down as I felt my piece swell, pushing against the fabric of my khaki walking shorts. It was obvious that I was sexually aroused, and he saw it. It seemed as though all the blood in my body had rerouted to my crotch. With my skull constantly pounding, it fell into the same rhythmic beat as my throbbing piece of manhood. I'd had hard-ons before, but nothing like this. Up to that point, no man had ever made my body respond that way. I was in a trance. I have seen many naked bruthas in the locker room, but I did not see them that way. Most men cannot get a rise out of me. There must be a strong attraction and a connection. I must be really interested, for that to happen.

Surprisingly, the night was hot, but a soft ocean breeze helped ease the humidity. Still partially wet, he allowed the evening air's gentle caress to dry the rest of his body. Casually walking over to a chaise lounge at the opposite end of the pool, he put on a thigh length robe tying it slightly below the waist, intentionally exposing his sculptured chest and fully developed six-pack. He leaned over to spread the two towels on the chair. As he laid down on his stomach with his head turned in the opposite direction, I continued to stare at the smooth curve of his partially exposed ass peeking from underneath the short robe. Then he peeled back the robe exposing his arms and lower back. I wondered what he would do to entice me even more.

Completely unaware at first, I soon realized that I had stuck my hand down my shorts slowly rubbing my piece through my underwear. I don't know why I did it but suddenly I was unbuttoning my shirt and taking off my shorts and shoes. I slowly walked over to him, not sure how he would respond, considering how I had treated him earlier. I stood over him, my shaft pulsating in the bulging pocket of my black semisheer low-rise boxer briefs. When I kneeled beside him and stroked his back, he tensed and quickly turned his head toward me. I told him I was sorry about the things I had said.

"You didn't deserve that," I whispered as my hand glided over warm, wet flesh.

He rolled over on his back and looked up at me. My eyes were drawn to his chest and worked their way down his hard-rock abs. The towel covered his piece, but I could tell that it was hard. The rich essence of his natural scent and his warm flesh ignited my senses.

As I kneeled over him, his eyes were locked to the massive, throbbing bulge in my briefs. He could see it pounding against the soft silk fabric, and with a sly knowing smile creased his lips. "I want to help you," he whispered. "Lie down, I will be right back."

He grabbed another towel and went inside. Although he said that he would be back in only a few minutes, I just couldn't lay still. I was in heat. I desperately needed to cool off and quickly. Still only wearing my briefs, I dove in. Several laps in the cool water quenched my heaving body. When I got out of the pool, I took off the wet underwear, squeezed out the excess water, put them back on, and wrapped a large towel around my waste. I walked over and sat back down on a lounge chair. I laid-back and closed my eyes. A few minutes later, I heard the French doors open again. My eyes were still closed, still enjoying the music. I heard him walk toward me. He asked me if I was okay. I nodded. Then I heard him put something down on the table next to me. He grabbed my hand and said, "Try this." He had brought drinks outside. I took a sip. It was my favorite, Bacardi 151 with a splash of Sprite and lime juice.

Eyes still closed; I took another sip. I heard him sit in the chair next to me. Nothing was said for a while. After the third sip, the liquor began to do its job, I was beginning to really relax. I just laid there as he did, continuing to bask in the mood and enjoy the music. Several minutes had passed. By this time, I was really feeling the effects of my favorite libation. Then I suddenly heard him get up. From the sound of the direction of the footsteps, I could tell he was walking toward the other side of me. Although my eyes were closed, I could see his shadow partially over me. He asked me again if I was okay. I just smiled as I slowly exhaled. He got the message as he whispered, "Yeah, that's it, just relax."

Then all of the sudden he straddled me. He caught me off guard. I twitched a little, but I didn't overreact this time. I was still not sure if I was ready for this, but this time I played it cool. Eyes still closed, I played along. He began to massage my chest and nipples. Initially unaware of what he was doing, he soon noticed that he had found the most erotic spot on my body, besides my now rock-hard stick.

He whispered, "I am not trying to pressure you. Listen to your body. Trust your body. When your body says run, run. When your body says let go, then let go. What is your body saying, now?"

I didn't respond. He could tell that I was enjoying it and that I didn't want him to stop, this time.

While completely stretched out in the lounge chair, he leaned over and kissed me on the neck. My entire body trembled, and my rod felt as if it would burst through the towel. It pulsed and pumped wildly. I was on fire. Then he kissed me on the lips. His tongue began swirling around in my mouth, fanning the flames that were already roaring through my body. No man had ever made me feel that way, not to mention the numerous women from my past.

He turned up the flame as his lips and tongue glided over my chest and left a wet track across my stomach. Hot breath caressed my skin as he lightly raced his fingers up and down my thighs. My rod was beating like a drum and every muscle in my body was stretched tight. Suddenly my entire shaft was engulfed in moist heat. Max was sucking and tonguing me through the fabric of the towel. It was the most incredible sensation I had ever felt. My head rolled from side to side and loud moans exploded from my throat. Each time his tongue stroked my shaft, I felt as though my stick grew yet another inch.

Then in one swift motion, Max shifted his body so his knees straddled my head and his rod was exposed to my eager mouth. Steaming wet fluid spilled from him and I licked every drop. He leaned back slightly and slowly peeled my wet shorts to my knees. My stick sprang free, like a young wild, untamed purebred stallion breaking out of the gate of a corral. He watched it throb in sync to my wildly beating heart as he eased his hardness in my mouth.

My lips sucked on his mushroom tip and my tongue slid down and stabbed in his wet hole. I felt him quiver. Suddenly my shaft was surrounded by the silky wetness of his mouth. I rolled my hips upward, forcing my rod into his mouth and throat. Moaning, he pushed his stiff stick down into my face. His head rose then fell in a slow, continuous motion. His lips locked, slowly slurping around my shaft, his tongue swirling at the head.

The intensity of the passion I felt slowly increased. The heightened erotic pleasure continued. It began with a tingly pins-and-needles sensation down deep in my balls. He poured a silky liquid on my mushroom head which I assumed was a lubricant. It smelled of strawberries. Then he turned slightly and wiped a little bit on my lips. I was right, the essence of strawberries. The tingling aphrodisiac only heightened the sensation. As our mouths ravaged those secret places, Max's tempo picked up. I stayed with him, slamming my hips up into his mouth as his lips slid downward on my stick. At the same time, my tongue worked feverishly at his huge swollen shaft of manhood. He bucked and rocked madly as we both soared toward an explosive volcanic peak.

He reversed the 69 position and leaned back and started massaging my stick, alternating slow, long strokes with fast jerking strokes. I continued to lay back and just went with the flow. As my shaft reached its peak, standing straight up, I opened my eyes slightly without him seeing me. I couldn't believe it. Somehow, he had slid two condoms down on me without my being aware of it. I closed my eyes, laid my head back down, and smiled. I was truly in the zone.

Then he grabbed my hardness and rubbed it against his lubricated hole. He slowly slid down on it. "Uuuuggghhhh!" He gasped, immediately reacting to the shock of the initial penetration from the girth and length of my piece. On the third attempt and after two more big gulps of whatever he was drinking, I could tell that he was beginning to relax. His grunts gradually turned into moans.

Lying completely still, eyes still closed and hands behind my head, I continued to relax. I allowed him to do his thing. When I opened my eyes for a moment, he was looking at me with those ever so piercing eyes. Then he leaned over and kissed me again and whispered in my ear.

"Don't say anything. Just relax and enjoy it. I got you."

So, I closed my eyes again. I took a big deep breath and exhaled. He continued to slowly slide up and down. I couldn't hold back any longer.

"Oh my God! Damn, man, it's so tight but it feels so good."

"I know," he replied. "Give me a minute. Just relax."

Then he was beginning to loosen up. The exotic moans and groans said it all. I could tell he was enjoying it too. Once he got a rhythm going, to my surprise he began riding me with ease. He actual took a little more the half of my rock-hard piece. Sliding up and down, alternating slow long strokes with short choppy ones. I was definitely impressed, especially it being the first time with me. I was well aware that was no easy task.

The mind-blowing riding session went on for just a few minutes. I know how I can get carried away sometimes, so I pulled out and peeled off the two condoms. Still straddling me, he slid back a little as I began to stroke myself. I felt my juice boiling in my loins. My shaft felt as if it was about to explode. And then suddenly it did, juice pumping feverishly. The force of the volcanic burst of my orgasm was so strong that I actually shot in my own face. I was spouting like a runaway oil well. I continued to stroke until every drop had oozed out. Head spinning, gasping heavily, and trying to catch my breath, I felt total euphoria. After a few moments, my breathing slowly began to stabilize. All the while Max never missed a stroke. He continued to jack his stick until he exploded. He came twice, the second even more powerful than the first. His warm liquid spewed from him on his chest and down his leg. I lay there for a moment, head still spinning a little, allowing myself to float back to earth.

Imagine my surprise when he asked me why I was crying. I wiped my hand across my cheek. Sure enough, my face was wet with tears. He said it happened when he was riding me just before I pulled out. He thought at first that I was shouting out with pleasure and then realized that I was crying. It was true. Not only had I allowed this man to take me to that special place of ecstasy, but he had used the only weapon strong enough to smash through that hard-callous wall that I had built within regarding my relationships with both men and women. The weapon was love—sex with intense, heart-pounding passion. Although my feelings were growing toward him, that night, it was hard physical love that would wipe away all the pain that I felt inside. With his passionate and satisfying gift, all the tears I had held back over the years burst through.

Later, he told me that he had decided that the only way he could convince me to allow myself to let go and begin to care about him or anyone else was to seduce me. I had to admit to myself that he was right. All the love and affection that I had bottled up for so long came pouring out in that single intimate moment.

He gave me a lingering kiss, jumped up, went inside, and took a shower. After my head finally stopped spinning, I followed a few minutes later. Still in a slight daze, I stumbled inside and hopped in the shower. When I got out, he was in bed. I contemplated whether or not I should sleep with him or in the other bedroom. After what had just happened, it wasn't a difficult decision. I climbed in bed with him, snuggled up behind him, and placed my arm around his waist. He gently reached for my hand, and we dosed off to sleep.

The next morning, I woke up to the smell of bacon. As I sat up, reality quickly set in. It hit me what had happened the night before, but I was okay. I got out of bed, stretched my muscles, brushed my teeth, and then strolled into the kitchen. There he was just standing there wearing nothing but black silk pajama bottoms and a smile. Sporting only a black and red striped pair of my favorite name brand fitted boxer briefs. I said, "Good morning."

Standing at the stove making waffles, he looked up, turned in my direction, smiled, and said, "It surely is. I hope you slept well. I surely did. Breakfast in ten minutes."

I replied, "Yeah, like a baby." Then I turned and went to take a shower.

After breakfast, I apologized again and told him how I really felt about him, about relationships, and about what I thought I wanted. Shortly after our moment of sharing our feelings, we went to the game. He commented more than once that he had a great time.

I casually said, "We really looked good together today."

Both of us seemed extremely comfortable and relaxed in public. Was it that we didn't care what others thought? Although we always seemed to get attention whether alone or together, I think it was more so that we didn't have to try so hard to be inconspicuous anymore. We were just two attractive clean-cut men having a good time at a game.

He smiled in agreement. Then he responded, "I agree and I feel really comfortable with you in public. I don't like unnecessary attention in public, and I noticed that you shy away from the spotlight too. I definitely like that about you. I can definitely see myself spending a lot more quality time with you without being subconscious and concerned about what others think."

I replied, "So are you trying to say that we would make a great team?"

He replied, "Definitely! In time, if we found each other more compatible and decided to make a go at it, I know we could." He also said that if I nurtured him and took care of his needs, "I would take you on an unforgettable journey that you would never want to end."

"Are you referring to the unforgettable ride you gave me last night?"

"Well, no. I mean a lot more than that."

"Okay, where do I buy a ticket?"

"You don't need a ticket. You already have a carte blanche VIP pass."

We spent the next two days sightseeing and shopping. After the early evening games, the late evenings were filled with more erotic bedside activities, much like the previous passionate night by the pool but this time they were in the bed.

The quality time we spent together that weekend brought me much closer to him. I began to understand the magnitude and the importance of his profession as the minister of a large church. It was a lot of responsibility, a lot of pressure. Sometimes they needed an outlet, a way to relieve the stress. But the vice that they use causes much internal spiritual conflict. In his case, the needs of some ministers to have sex with men is much greater than the vow. The vow they took to be celibate or loyal to the church and committed to their marriages. It is an extremely difficult job to be constantly burdened with the stigma and pressure of always living by example, always being watched, always trying to be perfect.

The weekend was also the start of a new beginning, an unchartered emotional journey. I allowed the shadows of my past to be lifted. And it really wasn't the actual sex. It was how he handled the situation after I initially pulled away from him. Instead of blowing off the handle and accusing me of teasing him and playing games, he let me have my space and allowed me to come to him when I was ready. We shared an intimate encounter that turned into a most pivotal moment for me, a moment that persuaded me to give it a chance and pursue a relationship with him.

The unplanned chain of events was the catalyst that sparked my willingness to temper my many hang-ups regarding trust. My issues continued to fade. Never in a million years did I ever expect to find this in a man, especially in a much older man, and never a minister.

Naw. But it happened. As I slowly began to release the fears that guarded my heart, it became much clearer what I really wanted. I just wanted someone to love me for me. And I thought I could have possibly found it in him. He saw the true essence of who I was. The defenses toward him were gone, and thanks to him, I learned to let go and we continued to grow. Because of him, I have a healthy attitude regarding sex and a happy healthier appetite for it. And he gave me something more. He gave me back my emotions and the ability to love freely and openly. I kinda consider it to be a gift. It's a gift I'll cherish forever.

Chance said while smiling, "Guys, I told you it was going to be explicit. I felt that it was necessary for me to describe the graphic details the way that I did. I didn't want it to sound pornographic. It was the only way to help you to truly understand the effect it had on me. And it wasn't just the sex. It was the intense passion that I experienced and the 'mind job' that he did on me. I didn't think I wanted it, but I was lured into it. And in the end, it was exactly what I needed."

"Man, if I were a smoker, I would have lit up two cigarettes after that one," said Parker.

Emerson cosigned by stating, "I'm speechless. Dude, I didn't know Mr. Preacher Man had it going on like that. Damn."

"Dude, now I see why you have been together for six years. You better keep him," said Lisborn.

Chance shook his head. "Sho ya right, he is definitely a keeper."

CHAPTER 17

Marriage Confidential

*For rich or richer, for good health and health-
ier, for promoting the façade, for keeping up
the image and for keeping the big secret even
after death do us part...we do promise.*

STILL OBVIOUSLY EXTREMELY curious about Chance's relationship, Dexter commented, "I am just fascinated. You are a celebrity. How has it worked with a married prominent local minister
in the same city? And for so many years. And you seem somewhat
happy."

Chance replied, "Dude, I am happy, very happy. But more
importantly, I am content. I am not out there still searching. But
believe me when I tell you, that it has definitely been a process to get
to this point."

Chance continued to tell his story about his relationship with
Maxwell. Chance stated that Maxwell was forthcoming from the very
beginning. He stated that he was married, but it was a very different
type of marriage. He explained the complex details of the unconven-
tional relationship with his wife shortly after we met. He stated that
his marriage was the result of a well-planned business arrangement.
It would be a marriage of convenience.

"She needed me," said Maxwell. "She was an up-and-coming
leader in the evangelical world, and she desperately wanted to take her
career to the next level. In order to do that she needed to marry. Single
women in the ministerial African-American Christian circles are not
as highly regarded as much as married, settled women. In the Black
Church, married couples are viewed differently than single people.
For some reason, they are considered more stable, more responsible,

and more likely to promote the same morals and values as those of the staunch religious hierarchy as well as actively practice their stringent religious beliefs. Single people, especially those who acquire fame and fortune, are more likely to stray away and sin and follow the ways of those of the secular world. There were also unconfirmed rumors that she had been involved in several short-lived lesbian relationships. Until that point, she had been quite successful in containing the potential career damaging scandal. Although the gossip was not widespread and the media had never gotten wind of it, she admitted that a few years before she had met him that she had experimented in a few sexual encounters with women as well as a few affairs with married men.

"It was not only strongly recommended that she find a suitable husband, but she needed to marry into a well-respected Christian family, a family approved by the senior leaders of the upper echelon in the traditional as well as the contemporary African-American Christian Church. I was a perfect choice. So, she chose me. She pursued me. I was from a highly respectable family with a long Christian lineage. My father was a minister as was both of my grandfathers. My brother, two of my uncles and four cousins were also ordained ministers. I was single, never been married, no children, and most of all, I had never been involved in a scandal.

"We married after only six months of courtship. The agreement also included no children. It was mutual. She didn't have time for children, and I didn't want them either. The arrangement worked for her and it worked for me."

Then Maxwell continued, "Yes, I love her and she loves me in her own way. But I am not passionately in love with her. And she is okay with that. Again, it is a marriage of convenience. She simply does not complete me. She does not fulfill all my desires or all my sexual needs. And she understands that too. It's also about business and the image that she and I have chosen to portray. We discussed it in grave detail, and we decided that it was in the best interest of the both of us that we should operate on a 'don't ask, don't tell' policy. As long as I was discreet and respected her position in this arrangement, it worked for us. It was a win-win for the both of us. And this could be a win-win-win for all of us."

"What do you mean?" I asked.

He continued. "I know that all this is probably hard to believe, but it is true. Let's just take things day by day. Over time, if things progress between us, you will discover that what I am saying is the truth."

"Will I be the only one, and I mean the only one outside of your marriage?"

"Is that what you want?"

"If things develop between us then maybe, yeah. Yes, that is what I would like, but I am not sure if that is possible. If things progress and we develop strong feelings for each other, sharing you with other men will not be an option. If I am willing to give all of me, then you must do the same, given the currently known parameters, boundaries, and restrictions. I can try to deal with your current marriage situation. I still have a lot of questions, but I think it's best that I not overanalyze it right now."

"I agreed. 'And that goes both ways. As long as, I am the only guy in your life, it can work. And I must be the only guy that you have sex with, if we ever reach that stage of a relationship. Until then I will try to just go with the flow.'"

Maxwell continued, "I am extremely private and discreet. I have never disclosed the details or the arrangement regarding my marriage to anyone, but to a few extremely close people in my immediate circle. Very few people know about my alternative sexual preference. My family does not even know, and I have no intentions of ever telling them, and I mean never. I will never go public. My business is my business. I used to sleep around with women before I got married, but I don't anymore. It's too complicated. Now, I prefer a long-term one-on-one situation with someone I can trust, someone who makes me feel secure. I want a person who can fulfill my needs and desires, and yes, that includes my sexual appetite. I want to be monogamous. But more importantly, I want someone who is just as private and discreet as I am. One of the main reasons that I don't socialize with many in the clergy is because most ministers gossip. And not to mention the unspoken competitive rivalry between the pastors' wives who may or may not be the co-pastor of his church. They appear to be prim and proper in public but some of these women can be downright vicious behind the scenes."

Chance continued to elaborate, "Once we set certain parameters and agreed upon full disclosure, the relationship began to grow and develop. Part of our original agreement, more so a request on my part, was to keep our potential relationship completely separate from his marriage and his church. I had never seen his wife. I didn't even know her name and didn't want to know either. And there was to be absolutely no comingling. I never attended his church, nor did I ever watch his televised sermons. I didn't preview his church website, nor did we discuss his church business. But if he needed to vent, I listened attentively. On the other hand, I did attend several of the out-of-town men conferences in which he was the main speaker. Usually when I registered and it was discovered that I was attending, I was treated as a VIP guest, but of course, I was inconspicuous. Although I had never seen them, he and his wife were on two billboards. Each located in high-traffic areas of town. He also submitted to my request to replace the two billboards of the two of them with a single billboard of him alone and the other featured several of the outreach ministries. Well, my philosophy is that if you don't ask, then you don't get. I was not sure how he explained that one to her or to the church, and I didn't ask."

Then Dexter asked, "Does his wife know about you? Doesn't she know who you are? It's kinda hard to believe if she doesn't know. Well, you are a local celebrity."

Chance replied, "Well, actually that kinda makes it easier for us, in that it's not as conspicuous as it might appear."

Dexter continued with the questions, "You have been in a long-term intimate committed relationship with her husband for over six years. You mean to tell me that she has no idea that you exist. You mean that no one has told her. I have a really hard time believing that if this woman is so shrewd to have orchestrated such a clever *façade* of a marriage and it has survived for so long, but she doesn't know. That doesn't make sense to me. I just refuse to believe it."

Chance replied, "Well, for the first two and a half years she didn't know about me. Later, Max admitted that she had suspected that there was someone. She used to tell me, 'I seem so much happier than I had been in years. I don't seem to be as stressed and uptight all the time.' Her thought process was that if there was someone of interest or someone special, as long as she was not confronted with the situation then she could deal with it. She had an odd internal philosophical thought process regarding the carnal things in life. What she did not see, hear, or touch, really did not exist although a woman's intuition, the little voice inside told her differently. She just learned to tune out those periodic moments of short-lived suspicions. That was her reality. As long as he continued to be very discreet and that he promised that the situation would not become public, she was okay. She could not handle such a scandal."

After over ten years of marriage, she finally had reason to confront him although he kept his end of the agreement. Normally she was not nosey. She did not touch his two cell phones, his iPad, or his laptop. Nor did she open his personal or business mail or his emails. She did not eavesdrop on his personal calls. And there was never a cause to check the GPS on any of the vehicles that he drove. All their personal as well as their business finances were managed separately. In addition, both of their assistants were given strict instructions not to repeat or divulge anything that they had seen or heard relating to the other, no matter how damaging. Everything was fine until she stumbled across something that motivated her to ask questions. While looking for some photos, she stumbled upon a small box filled with several recent VIP passes to all of my home games and several away games. It also included private box tickets to two of the championship games in which I had played in since we met. She knew he was not a sports fan, not to mention an avid basketball fan. So, she asked, not really expecting the answer that she got. He reminded her of their unofficial "don't ask, don't tell" policy regarding their personal lives. She asked again; this time without a smile and with a serious tone. He was somewhat surprised. *Where was this coming from?* he thought. Standing there with her arms folded, she waited for an answer. He felt that if she had the nerve to finally ask him about his outside involvements, and this time with a slight attitude, he was obligated to give her what she wanted. He bluntly told her about me, and to add fuel to the fire, he also admitted that he loved me and that we had been involved for over two years. She asked, so he told her. He reinforced his admission by stating that it was probably best that he told her rather than finding out from someone else. Although I truly doubt that would've happened in a hundred years, if such a slip of the tongue did happen, hopefully she would be better prepared. Of course, she was not happy that she was forced to acknowledge the reality of their marriage. After a few days of serious thought, she finally came to the conclusion that he was probably right. But was it over? Not quite.

A week later, Max and I attended a charity fund-raiser that would provide scholarships to inner city kids. We attended several such functions throughout the year. We usually came together, and we left together, but we rarely sat together. The event organizers usually wanted me to sit and interact with the corporate executive sponsors. It motivated them to give more.

During the cocktail hour of the evening, while I was standing, talking to another guest, all of a sudden someone tapped me on my shoulder. I thought it was another fan, but was I ever wrong. I turned and saw a very attractive, well-dressed older lady. She asked to speak with me privately. She stated that it would not take very long.

Oh no, I thought. *Not another woman coming on to me again.* This was not the time or the place. But I obliged and followed her. We stepped into a private room next to the banquet hall.

"Hello, young man, do you know who I am?"

"Ma'am, I apologize but I don't. I don't mean to be rude, but what is this about."

"This will not take very long." She introduced herself. "My name is Willameana Moss-Graham. But most people know me by my professional name, Evangelist Mena Moss."

With an obvious puzzled expression on my face, I didn't respond. I still did not know who she was. Her professional name kinda sounded familiar, but I couldn't remember.

I asked her, "Ma'am, what was the reason for such privacy? I am confused."

She didn't answer. Then she gave me a piercing stare from head to toe. Why was she looking at me that way? I still didn't know what she wanted. My mind was racing. She obviously knew me. Did I sleep with or briefly date her daughter years ago? How did this woman know me? And why was there a need for such privacy? I really didn't know who this woman was.

"Ma'am, I must excuse myself and get back to the party." As I turned and took two steps toward the door, she reintroduced herself again.

"Well, maybe you will recognize me by my married name. Young man, I am Mrs. Maxwell P. Graham IV. Does that name sound familiar?"

I literally stopped in my tracks. I was floored, dumbfounded. I couldn't say anything. I slowly turned and looked at her. But before I could even try to respond, the door opened. Max must have seen us leave the banquet hall because he opened the door to the secluded room as soon as she acknowledged who she really was. Time had frozen for a moment. Max and I just stood there, noticeably worried about her next move. Within their ten years of marriage, no such drama had ever happened between the two of them. But surprisingly, she did not cause a big scene, nor did he. Both of them were well aware that one's image was very important in this city and people love dirt and scandal, especially the naysayers and the busybodies and those who were extremely critical of the contemporary Christian megachurches.

Considering she was confronting a man for the first time, a much younger man who was deeply involved with her husband, she was rather calm and quite polite at first. I could see that she was playing this thing really smart. She knew that whatever she was planning would be more effective if she was calm and civil and not hysterical. But I was not stupid. And I was not going to let my guard down.

Her outer persona showed subtle signs that she was thinking; her mind was ticking a mile a minute. Although she put up a really good front, I could tell that she was nervous, probably even more nervous than the two of us. As an athlete, I have learned the art of reading my opponents. And she was reading me as well, trying to figure out who I was and what type of person I was. Was I a danger to her and all that she had built? And what were my intentions? Could I, or more importantly would I, attempt to bring down her house of cards?

After a few moments, her body language drastically changed again. She gave me another a loathing glance, a moment that seemed like an eternity. I was quite sure that I looked like a deer with his eyes caught in headlights. Then she slowly turned and looked at her husband with much disdain. But because I was her main focus, she immediately redirected her energies back to me again. She did all the talking. At first, that is. Her tone also changed from being somewhat civil to overtly condescending.

"Don't be so surprised because I'm not. I don't know what my husband has told you about me, but I am not going to cause a scene. I am also not even surprised that you are a man and not a woman." She gave Max another scathing look. "But I must say that there is definitely one thing that I am extremely surprised about—your age."

Then she asked me, "Well, do you have anything to say?"

I did not respond. After the initial shock wore off, I composed myself slightly altering my stance, a defensive posture preparing for possible verbal attacks. Of course, I wasn't afraid of that woman, and I didn't regret being in a relationship with her husband. It's just that I just never thought it would happen in a setting like this. And it was becoming obvious that she was not going to play the role of the innocent victim. But little did she know that I was not going to take the blame either; I was not her nemesis.

Then she continued. Surprisingly, she was very frank about many details regarding their marriage. She corroborated Max's story that he had told me when we first met regarding his matrimonial business relationship. Also, to my surprise, she actually told me that they had stopped having sex shortly after the fifth year of marriage. And they had lived separate private lives ever since.

She stated, "Young man let me explain a few things to you. A marriage is more than about love and procreation. It is a partnership and, in our case, a complex business relationship. It is a union between two people with common goals and common values. They make plans and share hopes of building a life together. But it also includes allowing each person to grow individually. I have my own individual interests, and now I see that he has his, as 'midlife-crisis-like' as one of them may be."

Then her tone slightly changed even further, again elevating to angry condescension. I wasn't sure if she was testing me to see if there was something that he had not told me or if she was just trying to get some type of reaction from me. She told me right in front of him, "Young man, I am not sure what you want out of this, but I truly hope that you don't expect to be number one. If you are, you are truly delusional. The relationship and the life that you think you have with my husband is not a romance novel."

Then she stated emphatically, "And I hope that you do not have any crazy ideas, because I am not leaving my marriage. Young man, divorce is not an option. I have built a great life over the years before and during my marriage. I have worked too damn hard and I am not going to give it all up for anyone. I am not going to disrupt my life—the life and the lifestyle in which I have grown accustomed. I am not going to be foolish like a lot of women, especially because of some young boy."

Then she boasted that she had a reputation too. She reiterated that if the relationship became public that Max would have just as much to lose as she did. His reputation as well as his family's reputation would be damaged beyond repair. Then she looked at me again. "And as for you, young man, we are not even going to mention your perpetrating reputation in this city. You definitely don't want your teammates and your sponsors to find out about this so-called relationship with a married man and especially with a prominent mega-minister."

It took everything in me to keep my cool. I truly believe that regardless of the situation, one should always try to react with class. Considering the place and the circumstances and although her attacks kinda made it extremely difficult, overall, I think I held it together rather well. But I had to respond. I folded my arms and took a step in a more defensive stance. I gave her a stern look, a stare that said I wasn't afraid and that it was her time to listen. I had something to say.

"Now are you finished? Once you told me who you were and considering where we are, I was hoping that you were going to keep this civil. But it's kinda obvious that this impromptu meeting is slowly escalating to a level that it definitely shouldn't. I strongly advise you to slow your roll. First of all, I am not your enemy."

She didn't respond.

"Lady, no disrespect, but you don't know a damn thing about me except the fact that I play basketball. I don't do drama, and I won't be a part of your little bitch hunt. That little speech that you just made was not even necessary. I actually think that you did it to make yourself feel better. I never understood why is it that the angry, bitter wife always has the tendency to come after the other person and not her husband? You should be addressing him. I am not your problem. You are lucky and you don't even realize it. You are lucky that Max found someone like me. He could have chosen someone with a bigmouth, a disillusioned, naive younger guy who could've tried to persuade him to leave. Or someone who could've used sex and manipulation to control an older man. But he didn't.

"Actually, if I really wanted to and if I really tried hard enough, I could have any one of 80 percent of the women in this city. I could even have you if I really wanted too. I am considered one of the sexiest and most eligible bachelors in this city although I don't consider myself as single because I am with him. I have a lot of money and I'm not stingy with it either."

Then I crossed the line. Although I didn't look at Max directly, I glanced in his direction with a slight smirk on my face.

"Not to mention the fact that I have a big stick and I know how to use it very well. And of course, both of us are well aware that Max has mad skills when it comes to sex."

Yeah, I crossed the line, but she deserved it. She opened up Pandora's box. Now she deserves whatever comes out. I continued.

"And just for the record, Max chose me. He aggressively pursued me. Yes, I admit that it was difficult at first. I didn't chase after him as I'm sure that you might have assumed. Again, I have my own money. It's Max decision. And it needs to be made perfectly clear that I am not leaving either. Lady, you are no competition to me. But you shouldn't feel threatened by me either. This arrangement that you call a marriage definitely can't compete with what we have built over the past two and a half years. You have him in name and in name only, but I have everything else, including a piece of his heart and much quality time. I don't want his name. I don't need his name. This façade of a marriage does not bother me. I see you two as two halves in a marriage of convenience, a marriage that is not truly fulfilling either of you. Regarding healthy relationships, two halves don't make a whole, two whole partners make a stronger bond. Together, we are that stronger bond.

"But I want to make something else very clear. Although I love him and this relationship has changed my life for the better, I won't fight over a man or anybody else for that matter. He is free to leave whenever he pleases. But I don't think he will anytime in the near future. Again, you can't compete with me. And deep down, you know you can't."

She didn't respond.

"Well, cat got your tongue now? I'm not sure what you expected. It looks like your supposed well-planned setup backfired. You started it. But I finished it."

Then I addressed Max.

"Max, you are slipping. How did you let this happen? How did she find out about me, huh? I told you from the beginning that keeping me completely separate from that part of your life and keeping me anonymous were two very important factors that would determine the success of our situation. You really need to handle this. And I mean with the quickness. I am outta here."

He grabbed my arm.

"Babe, I did not want this to happen like this. But it probably needed to or would have happened eventually."

Then he asked her, "How did you find out?"

"I hired a private investigator to find out who he was. It was difficult at first because you two seem to cover your tracks well. Anyway, this was the first time that I ever did this. You know that I don't eavesdrop or snoop, but my curiosity got the best of me. But I stumbled on the ticket stubs and VIP passes. I won't apologize, so don't even ask. And I don't regret it. If I had to do it all over again, I probably would. I needed to know. I could not live with the wondering."

Then she turned and headed for the door.

"Mena, wait! Don't leave yet. I have something to say."

She turned around and slapped him. "What! What could you possibly have to say to me right now? And you just stood there and allowed this little boy to talk to me the way that he did." Then she took a step back, folded her arms, and gave him another scathing stare.

"Well, I guess I might have deserved that. But just listen. I really do have something to say. Chance, I have not lied to you. And, Mena, I have not lied to you either. When I felt comfortable with Chance, I disclosed most of the details of our marriage. I had to. But he did not know who you were. I had to be real with him, honest with him. After a few months, he decided that he was comfortable with the arrangement. I want both of you to hear this. Mena, you know why you married me. I don't have any regrets marrying you. I care about you. You know that I love you. But it's different. I will stay in this marriage and continue as we have. I also want to continue my relationship with Chance. I will continue to keep these two relationships completely separate. I will continue to be very discreet as I have been. I know you are not happy with the result of your findings. And it's obvious that this discovery is uncomfortable for you. And I don't like the way that you found out either. Again, I am not leaving you or my marriage. But let's be clear. My relationship with him is not going to change. So, deal with it!"

Neither of us responded.

"Chance, I did not plan for this to happen this way. I want to make it very clear that this is not just an affair either. Some people believe that having affairs or sex outside of the marriage just happens. I say that is a cop-out. Nothing just happens. Even if the explanation is not immediately known, it can be explained later. This was just the season in my life for something like this to happen. It happened because I wanted it to happen. I strongly believe that you can prevent certain things from happening by not allowing yourself to get caught in certain uncompromising situations. It minimizes the urges so that you will not become tempted to act on those desires."

Max felt sorry about the turn of events that evening not for what happened but how it happened. He did not apologize either, but he was a little remorseful. He did not admit any personal wrongdoing. He admitted that he loved both of us but in different ways. He also reiterated that he was in love with me and he wanted to be with me.

After that awkward one-sided tête-à-tête, I gained a better understanding of their complex matrimonial relationship. And I got the impression that after she met me, she felt a lot more comfortable that her secret was safe. They are still together, and we are still together too.

Chance said with a slight mischievous smile. "A good man is hard to find. And a hard man is good to find. I have found both—both in one man. We recently celebrated our six-year anniversary two months ago."

"Wow," said Dexter in amazement.

"Wow is right. Hey, look, this is my anniversary gift, this Rolex. You know I can afford my own, but it was the thought that meant so much. I bought him a Cartier diamond and platinum bracelet with two pair of matching cuff links. We take a trip every year for our anniversary. Last year for our fifth, he bought me a new Range Rover, the one that I drove to the funeral."

"Okay that is enough. Man, I need a drink, a strong one. I can't take anymore right now. That sounded like a story line in one of the top shows on Netflix, Starz or in the Thursday night prime time line up."

After a few drinks, Dexter began to turn his attention to Emerson.

"Okay, Emerson, what about you. What is your story?"

"Well, I know that I definitely can't top that last story. My situation definitely had much less drama."

CHAPTER 18

His Calling, His Career, And His Curse

Listen to your heart. Your heart has a voice.
It speaks to you with the rhythm of each beat.
It protects you. Shielding you from the same
things you can't see or those things you lack the
courage to face. Your heart knows who you are
and who you will turn out to be in the future.

I'M NOT THE person I used to be. I used to be too emotionally honest. I had a strong need for freedom and travel. Any restrictions made me feel claustrophobic and panicky. I valued collecting information and people to amuse and entertain me. They were my hobbies. Working on relationships was too difficult for me, and I hated to commit. I was always looking for the next challenge or the next short-term affair. My emotional weaknesses prevented me from balancing work and play. I was unaccepting of others whose values were much different from mine. I also had a strong need to deny myself nothing. Although I was the maestro of efficiency, I was also my own and everybody else's worst critic. I desired perfection and detested shabbiness. I had an overwhelming tendency to get lost in my overly adventurous vision of the future. I was a bit of a self-established activist. My major strengths were being committed to heartfelt causes and loyal to family and friends; being a true realist and being responsible. I still possess many of those qualities, but I had to curtail some of them because someone special dropped out of the sky; into my life and changed me. To my surprise, I allowed our meeting to change me. I became a better person. My strengths flourished. My weaknesses became shortcomings, character traits that I am constantly improving.

I had just completed my second year at Virginia Tech. Although my major was business administration, I wanted to focus on incorporating business organizations and developing nonprofit organizations. After I received my undergrad degree, the plan was to wait a year or two to gain some much needed and valuable experience in the workforce. The next step would be to continue my top-notch education, a feather in my cap that would advance the opportunity for me to make really big money. My first graduate school choice was to aggressive attack the rigorous MBA program at Wharton Business School. But a turn of unexpected events changed my plans.

During the fall semester of my junior year, I had to temporarily relocate to Atlanta, the Black mecca of the South. I was awarded a paid internship position as an admin assistant in the executive office at one of the most well-known civil rights nonprofit organizations in the country, The King Center. In late September, only a few weeks after I had arrived, the senior admin staff began planning the annual Christmas party, the New Year's Eve party, and the annual King Week Celebration. Although the main purpose of the Christmas celebration was to express the organization's appreciation toward the employees and volunteers, the underlining agenda was to invite other supporters, especially the major benefactors. This was a great opportunity to network and to acquire valuable experience, but I really wasn't in the mood for socializing. I was exhausted from working and perfecting last-minute details but, of course, I didn't complain. All interns had been strongly advised to attend. And since I was on the committee, my attendance was not an option—it was mandatory. Besides I didn't have anything else to do on a Friday night. Because the internship required that I work long hours, I didn't have time to meet many people socially. Actually, I didn't mind. I preferred to keep it that way. On the other hand, since my internship was only for nine months and it would be ending in May, time was of the essence. I needed to begin networking as soon as possible because I had hoped to temporarily relocate to Atlanta after graduation.

Everything went off with a hitch at the Ritz Carlton. Everyone must have really liked the live band because the dance floor was packed. The servers were quite consistent in replenishing the large variety of exotic hors d'oeuvres and gourmet desserts. And from the view of the steady line at the open bar, I assumed that the bartenders were definitely earning their tips that night.

Whenever I had a free moment, I was at the buffet table as usual; this time getting my third plate of Mardis Gras wings. When I reached back for my drink, I mistakenly touched another man's hand.

"Oh, excuse me. I wasn't paying attention. I thought I was reaching for my drink."

"No, my mistake. I thought it was my drink."

And there he was. I smiled and walked away.

When the party ended at 2:00 a.m., there were still at least one hundred guests present. At 2:15 p.m., the lights were finally turned on and the announcement was finally made, thanking everyone for coming. Each guest was also given a party favor on the way out. I had to stay an extra hour to wrap up the loose ends, to make sure that no one had left any personal items, and more importantly to verify that all necessary parties were paid in full.

One down now two more to go. Although The King Center was closed until January 5th, I had to work throughout the holiday break. I was also serving on the committee to host the New Year's Eve Party. This was to be a much smaller intimate black-tie soiree. It included only the board members, the executive team, their staff, their spouses and dates, and several special guests.

As usual, I was standing all alone as the last ten seconds of the countdown began. I looked up and there he was again, the same guy from the Christmas party. He was standing twenty yards away, near the band. He held his champagne flute as to toast to someone. I turned around to see who he was referring to. I read his lips: "Happy New Year." I looked around again. I pointed to myself. He shook his head signifying, yes. I smiled and I gave a toast back to Mr. Mystery Man.

During weeklong Dr. Martin Luther King Jr. Day celebration, which was only three weeks later, the organization hosted its annual Salute to Excellence Awards Gala. This corporate sponsored awards dinner also served as the most important fund-raiser of the year, presenting various honored recipients with a prestigious award based on their accomplishments and contributions in their respective fields.

I guess the third time was a charm. When I was making my usual rounds checking in with the banquet manager, the bartenders, and the music director to see if there were issues that I needed to be aware of, guess who I saw stroll in? Mr. Mystery Man. I was somewhat surprised to see him. Although I had been working there for a little over four months, I had met most of the special guests and major donors on various previous occasions.

Once again, I caught him staring. I tried to play it off by staying busy and socializing with the other guests. But he didn't make it easy. Who was he? And why was he giving me so much attention. I could just hear him thinking; thinking about me. Whenever we were close enough, I would give a polite half smile and a nod and keep it moving. I couldn't completely evade him all evening. He was a guest and apparently someone important. Besides, he was very attractive. Actually, I found it kinda sexy that he was trying to be a little mysterious. But I still played it cool. But when I saw him out of my peripheral vision coming toward me, to avoid contact, I made a quick detour to the bar. I needed something to calm my nerves. After two big gulps of my drink, I wasn't nervous anymore, but I was still rather curious.

I continued to work the crowd, making sure everyone was having a good time. I didn't see him for a while, so I assumed that he had left. Then I got this eerie feeling that someone was watching me but when I looked around, I didn't notice any one staring. I continued to check on the support staff and mingle with the guests. As I was talking to a guest, he suddenly appeared behind me, our backs almost touching. I knew it was him because I distinctly remember his extremely expensive cologne—*Creed Aventus*. Now with his back now slightly touching mine, I got a more intense whiff of his hypnotic men's fragrance. The tantalizing erotic scent caused me to lose focus. I froze. Still not completely turned around I was even more curious. What was this man up too? Why was he giving me so much attention? What did he want from me?

Still trying to be inconspicuous in a room full of people, he turned slightly and leaned even a little closer.

"Everyone that I meet I meet for a reason. I don't believe in accidents or luck or coincidence or happenstance. We needed to meet in this particular season in my life. This was supposed to happen. I have learned over the years that life is a journey of life experiences with others."

He paused a moment then added, "Yes, I know that what I am saying is kinda deep, but I had to get your attention."

Okay, now I began to see where this was going. He was obviously and deliberately trying to initiate a response from me. So, I responded accordingly and gave him one but probably not the one he expected.

"Whatever you are selling, I'm not buying. Well, I'm not buying this evening." Then I walked away.

I guess he did not get the message. Eventually he boldly cornered me again while I was at the bar waiting for another drink.

"We gotta stop meeting like this."

I turned quickly. "Excuse me?"

And there he was again.

"Oh, okay. I remember. The toast at the New Year's Eve party."

"Yes."

"And before that, the mix-up at the buffet table at the Christmas party."

"Good memory."

"I am Emerson Cartwright III. I am an intern in the executive office. And I am kinda on the clock. Excuse me."

He smiled and then replied, "I know who you are?" I paused. "I saw you staring from across the room earlier. Do you recognize me from somewhere?"

"No, we have never met, well, not officially. And yes, I am well aware that I was being quite rude, but I couldn't stop staring. Maybe I went a little overboard but that was my intent. I wanted you to notice me staring. But don't worry. No one else saw me. It's something about you. You are a very handsome young man. And you are very mature. I have been watching you and how you were micromanaging the two previous events as well as this one. And you know what? That is sexy. Maturity and ambition are very sexy characteristics in a young man. And you know what else? Those hazel eyes are hypnotizing. You make me dizzy. And I like it."

"I make you dizzy?" It took everything in me to keep from laughing. Was that the corniest come-on or what?

"Oh, okay. So you were trying to get my attention. But I see you played it safe by waiting to see how I would react."

"Yes. Something like that. Or was there more that you wanted other than to simply get my attention."

"What if it was?"

I was not sure of my next response.

Then he stepped a little closer, leaned forward, and whispered, "But before you answer that, be careful. Be very careful of your thoughts. They may become words at any moment. Words that you can't take back. And remember you are an intern and I am a guest, a very important guest."

I responded, "So it was not my imagination. You were flirting. At first, I thought naw, he couldn't be. This distinguished, debonair fine-as-hell older man couldn't possibly be overtly making a pass at me. Not me! And especially not at this type of event. Not in front of all these people. But here we are again."

"I admit it was a daring move. I took a risk. And so far, it's paying off. We are chatting and you are smiling. Looks like I might be breaking through a wall."

"So who are you? Are you someone famous? Apparently, you are."

He just smiled. But he didn't respond. He politely turned and reached for the drink that I had just ordered and walked away. I wasn't sure if I had embarrassed him or hurt his feelings. I didn't see him the rest of the evening.

After I returned from lunch on the following Tuesday, because Monday was the official holiday, the security guard in the lobby stopped me. He stated that a courier had delivered an envelope addressed to me, and it was stamped confidential. I went to the conference room to open it. Inside was a note card.

> *Hello, Mr. Intern,*
>
> *Just to let you know, I was a little out of character a few nights ago. I was not stalking you. I should have respected the fact that you were working. I hope I didn't make you too uncomfortable. Let me make it up to you. Meet me tonight for a late dinner.*
>
> *Signed,*
> *G. S. G. (a.k.a. I Stole Your Drink)*

On the back of the card was a number to RSVP. Kinda nervous at first, I didn't know what to do. I just smiled. I was intrigued. The smile slowly turned into a slight smirk. I knew as soon as I read it that the answer was yes. But I played it cool. I waited until six o'clock to respond.

The envelope also contained a smaller envelope with another card in it. It was one of those musical greeting cards. When I opened it, it played a few verses and the main chorus of the song "Can I Take You Out Tonight" by Luther Vandross. It was a good thing that I was in the conference room because I couldn't stop laughing. It was so corny, but I kinda liked it. I was pretty sure by now that he knew that he really had my attention. But it still left me wondering, why me. What was this man really up too? We were in Atlanta of all places. I was sure that there were thousands of women and probably just as many men who he could have chosen. Many who would have anxiously jumped at the opportunity to be with a man like him. He had a certain sex appeal that was hard to ignore, a quiet confidence. He carried himself in the way that most men and no women in his or her right mind could not resist. Again, why me? I really hoped that guy didn't think I was some young innocent boy toy who was easy. If so, he was sadly mistaken. He was definitely going to be disappointed.

Although he was much older, after a few more getting-to-know-you sessions over dinner, we quickly learned that we had similar interests and many things in common. The age difference didn't seem to matter. I really didn't notice it. He definitely didn't look his age. I didn't act like the typical guy my age, and most of our conversations were not generational. The first time we went out, I was pleasantly surprised that we shared many of our favorite things and interests, especially regarding entertainment. A few of our favorite movies included *The Pursuit of Happiness*, *The Count of Monte Christo*, *Idlewood*, *Hitch*, *The Taken* trilogy, and *The Temptations* as well as any movie starring Steven Segal. Our favorite top television shows were *Blue Bloods*, *Scandal*, *How to Get Away with Murder*, *The Closer*, *The Catch*, and the first two seasons of *Empire*. Morgan Freeman, Samuel L. Jackson, Alfree Woodard, Viola Davis, and Lynn Whitfield were our favorite actors and actresses. The late Bernie Mac was our funny man. Favorite songs included "Human Nature" by Michael Jackson, "No Rhyme, No Reason" by George Duke, "Where Whenever Whatever" by Maxwell, and "It Doesn't Matter" by Lauren Hill and D'Angelo. Both of us enjoyed Prince, Kenny Lattimore, Anthony Hamilton, Neo, and Big Luther as well as most contemporary jazz instrumentalists. Favorite gospel artists included Richard Smallwood, Smoky Norful, Tasha Cobbs, and Jason Nelson. Although we rarely attended concerts, it was unanimous that we would pay big money to see Janet Jackson, Oleta Adams, Lauren Hill, Toni Braxton, Jenifer Hudson, Goapele, and most of all the late Whitney Houston. He was really surprised that I used to have a really huge crush on the opera star Kathleen Battle. Although we were very health conscious, he much more than me, we admitted that we occasionally over indulged with a few of our favorites—shrimp, pasta, Popeye's spicy chicken, and most spicy foods. We could eat Louisiana hot sauce on anything except maybe cereal and ice cream.

He thought it was funny that one of my favorite movie lines was "Success is nothing without someone to share it with." Billy Dee Williams said it with heartfelt passion to Diana Ross in the movie *Mahogany.* I guess I understood the humor considering the movie was released almost over two decades before I was even born; and the fact that it must have been an extremely odd choice for a young Black man. But soon after I mentioned that it was one of my most important personal mantras, I noticed that the tone of the conversation kinda changed. He seemed to look at me a little differently, more seriously. He seemed more inquisitive about who I really was. He wanted to know more about my hopes and dreams and short-term and long-term goals.

He eventually told me that he was divorced with no children. They were still amicable. But he was still kinda mysterious about what he did for a living. Whenever I mentioned it, he quickly but shrewdly changed the subject. I did not press the issue much. I just thought he was a very private person. Two months after we met the big secret was finally revealed. He was being honored by the local city government with an award, and he wanted me to attend as one of his special VIP guests.

"The attire will be black tie so you will need a tux. But don't be concerned, I made an appointment for you with my fashion consultant at Saks. I will text you her number later. She will take very good care of you."

A few days later when I arrived, I was greeted by a very attractive Japanese lady.

"Hello, I'm Emerson. I have an appointment with—I am not sure how to pronounce it, but her first name is Naki."

"Hello, Mr. Cartwright. I am Naki Sakimoto, and I have been expecting you. Please follow me. Would you like something to drink?

We are going to be here for a while so I want you to be comfortable. We will begin by taking your measurements."

After trying on at least twelve to fifteen different designer tuxedos in various cuts and shades of black, we finally chose a black six-button, double-breasted Giorgio Armani tux with silk piping on the lapel and on each side pant leg. I also chose a single button, Tom Ford tux as a back-up. Naki was extremely patient. I had never experienced anything like that. She even helped me pick out all the accessories, including three French-cuffed shirts, two bowties, one black and one white. I also chose a set of Gucci cuff links with matching button covers. I also picked out a pair of Ferragamo slip-ons. She stressed more than once that I should not only choose items that I liked but also pick items that fit my personality. She mentioned that if I took good care of it, depending on the style and quality, a tux could last for fifteen to twenty years. Even if the styles slightly changed, classic looks could always be updated with minor alterations and a few accessories. She made sure I felt comfortable with all the choices. When we finally wrapped it up, she suggested that I come back tomorrow for a final fitting. That was hard work for me. I needed a big meal and a long nap.

The day had finally arrived. Although we had spoken a few times that day, he asked me to text him two hours before I was to leave. A few minutes after I did as he requested, I received a call. To my surprise, he had reserved a limo to pick me up. They called to get my address. Promptly at 7:30 p.m., a black town car pulled up. That was the first time that I had seen a Black female limo driver. And of course, she was sexy and fine as hell.

When I arrived at The Biltmore Hotel, I was directed to a reception hall. As I presented my invitation to the attendant at the door, another attendant escorted me to my table. Since most of the guests were still mingling, I didn't want to feel awkward by sitting alone, so I went to the bar for a soda. As soon as the bartender placed the drink on the bar, someone tapped me on the shoulder. I turned and it was him. He flashed that grand piano; I call a smile. It lights me up.

He whispered, "We gotta stop meeting like this."

Beaming from ear to ear, I shook his hand. "Thank you for inviting me."

"Thank you for coming. You look very handsome."

"Thank you. Ms. Sakimoto took very good care of me."

"She mentioned that you were one of her best first-time clients. She also stated that you have very good taste and that you made her job easy. It was just time-consuming because it was your first time, and she needed a moment to learn your style. But, I see that it was all worth it."

"Although, I am sure that she was just doing her job, but she made me feel really special. Thank you again."

"I'm glad that you enjoyed it. Well, I have to go now. I just wanted to personally greet you before the program got started. Enjoy yourself. I will chat with you later after the reception. Do not leave until you hear from me."

"Okay."

"See you later. I am so glad that you came."

He was being honored as Man of the Year by the Fulton County Board of Commission for his humanitarian work to combat inner city poverty. At first, I still didn't understand the big secret. But when they announced his name Bishop G. Solomon Grant, founder and senior pastor of Word of Life International Christian Church and when they read all his accolades over the last ten years, it all became clear. I assumed that he wanted me to get to know him without being impressed by his status and his image. I'm sure that he also wanted to make sure that he could trust me not to expose the details of his private life.

Immediately after the event, he sent me a text. It read, "Meet me in the lobby at the Ritz Carlton, Buckhead, at midnight, the same driver who brought you here is waiting for you."

I replied, "Okay."

"Text me when you arrive. See you soon."

"Hey, I'm glad you could make it." As he shook my hand, he discreetly gave me an envelope. "Inside is a key card for the private elevator that goes to the thirty-ninth floor. Then go to PH-3. Ring the doorbell, then use the key card and then come in."

"Hey. How are you?"

"I am fine."

"Great!"

"Well, now you know who I am."

"Yes. I do. But that does not change things. Well, not for me."

"I need to explain my hesitation to share certain things with you. Over the years, I have had to learn a lot about discretion and protocol when in public. A high-profile person's image is extremely important. It must be guarded and sometimes handled with grave caution."

"I understand."

"I am so relieved that you understand. I wanted you to accept me for me, the real me and not the image I portray. I also wanted to see if you could fit in my life. Then I wanted to gradually see how you would react if I exposed you to some things in my life and my lifestyle. You did not appear to show any serious signs of culture shock, so I felt very comfortable. Well, to be honest, it was also a test. One of a series of tests given beginning the first time we had dinner. And you have passed all of them with flying colors. I hope you are not too offended, but I had to be sure."

"Naw, I am okay. I am not naive as I look. I was well aware that I was being drilled and grilled."

"Remember that time when you jokingly asked me if I was someone famous and I just looked at you and smiled. I said to myself, 'He really doesn't know who I am.' Wow, that's great! Well, now you know why I hesitated."

"Yes."

"Now let's sit for a moment. I want to talk to you."

"Okay."

"So, did you have a good time tonight?"

"Actually, I did."

"Would you like a drink? You are twenty-one, right?"

"Yes, I am. And only if you are having one."

"Yes, I could use one, a stiff one."

"So, what did you want to talk about? It sounds serious."

He handed me my drink. "I know we haven't known each other long and there is a lot to learn about each other, but I like you."

"I like you too."

"I really like you. And I want you to be with me."

"You are kidding, right? You can't be serious."

"Do you see me smiling? Yes, I am very serious."

"I have enjoyed the time that we have been spending together but I was going with the flow."

"So is that a no?"

"No, I am not saying that. I just didn't expect this. And so soon."

"I know what I want."

"Oh. Oh. Okay, I understand, but why me? You are what, forty? I am a twenty-one-year-old college student. And I have nothing to offer you. Well, there is one thing I can offer you. But that isn't going to happen; well not in the near future anyway."

"I can find sex anywhere with a man or a woman. I am choosing you. I like the way we vibe. This new relationship paradigm could be a beneficial situation for the both of us. A very interesting dynamic. A win-win for the both of us."

With a sarcastic grin on my face, I replied, "Oh, okay. I'm sure."

He obviously didn't like my answer or the shift in my body language.

"Emerson, let's make it clear, I am not an older man looking for a young attractive boy toy. And I am not going through a midlife crisis. I really wasn't looking for you. Especially someone your age. I admit that when I saw you the first few times, I was very attracted to you. You didn't know who I was and that made me even more interested in you. I knew that if we got to know each other, you would see the real me and not the image that most people see. When I first approached you, I was intrigued by the chemistry. I want you to understand that I have given this a lot of serious thought and I don't take this decision lightly.

"I am very attracted to your maturity. The little bit that I have learned about you tells me that you are spiritual, stable, compassionate, passionate, and somewhat nurturing. You are strong-willed, reliable, persistent, solid, practical, warmhearted, trustworthy, and laid-back. And of course, you are also younger and very sexy. You are the full package.

"My job will be to be here for you, to help you, to take care of you in the ways I know how. And I don't just mean just sexually or financially, although they are extremely important. Yes, I am a grown man first. A grown man with grown man needs, but I am also very realistic. I am mature enough to know that sex and money won't make a solid relationship. Well, probably not a meaningful one anyway.

"I can help you financially and socially and provide you with the love and care that you have probably never had. Although there is an age difference, I will respect you at all times. I want to make it very clear that this relationship or situation would not be a sex for money and gifts situation. This is not a boy toy or sugar daddy relationship. This is not a game for me, Emerson.

"Emerson, I have a great life, and I want for nothing. And you seem to be doing okay. Remember your favorite movie line about sharing and success. I want to share my life with someone, someone special. When I met you for the first time or even the third time, you didn't know who I was. And when you realized that I was a person of means, you still did not try to impress me. You met the real me. I do not have to play a role with you. I want someone who accepts me for me and not because of my status or my money. I need someone near me who does not allow material things to affect him. I need someone who is well rounded, someone who can blend in while we are together in various social situations."

"Okay, and what do I give you in return?"

"Well, just for now I want only quality time. Quality time with you relaxes me. You provide me with a safe haven. When I am with you, I do not have to think about the problems and stresses of everyday life. When I am with you, I am in a special place of solitude and peace.

"Yes, on a superficial level, you will make me look good. But more importantly, your presence will enhance my life in so many ways. I think we can grow spiritually, emotionally, socially, and psychologically. And I truly believe you can offer me some of the things I just mentioned from a different perspective.

"Whether it is a personal relationship or an intimate relationship, I have developed my own set of *secrets to a long-lasting committed relationship*. They are Christ, chemistry, commonality, communication, consistency, covenant, compromise, clarity, and comedy. I called them *the nine Cs*. If I have a combination of all of those qualities in a relationship, it is bound to succeed.

"In addition to *the nine Cs*, the other things, I demand that you make me a priority. Also, giving me the ultimate respect at all times, expressing your love for me and showing me that you genuinely care are also a few of my expectations. I also demand the utmost level of privacy and discretion. And hear me when I say that I won't ask or demand anything from you that I can't or won't give in return. I am being completely honest with you."

"Okay, speaking of honesty. I have a question. And this question that is kinda off the subject. But I want to know."

"Okay."

"I noticed something about you."

"Yes, what is it?"

'Why do you surround yourself with mostly women? All your assistants and consultants are females."

"How do you know that?"

"Well, because that is what I see. It seems that all of the people that you have introduced me too as well as those who have relayed messages from you have been women."

"Why do you ask?"

"I am just curious."

"It seems more than just curiosity. Do you have a problem with that?"

"Well, no, I don't have a problem with it. It just seems kinda odd that you would surround yourself with all women, but you want to be involved with me."

"Well, if you must know. Call it my personal and professional method of image protection. Through trial and error, I have developed a small group of extremely loyal and dependable assistants and associates who have learned to adapt to my discriminating tastes. They go through grave efforts to protect my image and prevent any disclosure of my professional business as well as guard any details of my personal affairs. Yes, it is not by accident that all are women.

"Unconsciously I have made considerable conscious efforts to avoid the appearance of impropriety. This somewhat misleading image resulting in such harmless false impressions has prevented much idle gossip in my sphere of influence as well as in my churches. In my case, a single prominent pastor who is only surrounded by men attracts hungry and desperate women as well as breeds gossip. My personal and professional images are extremely important to me and I must be aware of both of them at all times.

"I am also a perfectionist. I like my personal matters and business handled a certain way. And they understand that. Besides I feel more comfortable with women working for me. And believe it or not, they respect me and my privacy, they mind their own business, and they don't give me any drama. And just for the record, I want to make it clear to you that all the relationships with my female assistants and business associates are strictly professional. Another underlining caveat is that it sends subliminal messages to everyone. As a result, it will deter suspicions regarding the true nature of the situation between you and me."

"Okay. I guess I understand your rationalization. You seemed to have thought it through."

"I know that this is a lot to comprehend right now, considering we have not known each other for long. And I understand that these are heavy demands. Serious demands."

"Well, I definitely didn't expect any of this when I came here for the internship."

"I know that this is a big decision, and I know that there are several things that you must consider. If you need to think about it, take some time. Take as much time as you need. One last thing, just so you won't be wondering, I am here. I know that you are very independent, but I am here to help you even when you don't really need me."

"Okay, I will. I will give it some serious thought. I will call you in a few days. Good night."

I reached out to shake his hand. Instead he grabbed me. With a tenacious heartfelt squeeze, he reiterated.

"Look at me? I mean, really look at me. I wasn't actively looking for anything when I first saw you, but meeting you made me realize that I wanted something more, someone who genuinely cares about me. But that is no easy task. To love me is to truly get to know me and more importantly understand me. You don't have to accept all my little idiosyncrasies or even like them. But if you try to understand them, we can deal with it and accept it and move on. So far, we understand each other. I think we are going to make it. No, I know we are going to make it. Man, I really meant everything that I said. This is not a game. I really hope you think about how good we can be together."

Wow, I didn't expect that. But I realized that this guy was really serious.

Although I was only twenty-one, I was quite mature for my age. I think that was one of the things that he was attracted too. Until then I had always been so focused on my education and my career goals. I was kinda excited and a little scared at the same time. I had some serious soul searching to do and life-changing decisions to make because I was not going to take his proposition lightly.

I prayed and prayed the first night. I asked the LORD to help me think clearly, to help me weigh my options, and to make the best decision regarding a long-term solution. Then of course, the carnal side of me took over. For the next few days, the pros and cons were busy battling, busy struggling back and forth, back and forth.

During that stressful nerve-racking period, I began to realize just how much I depended on Solomon. Although we had not known each other for very long, when I was with him, my problems were suddenly solvable. It seemed as though I did not have a care in the world. My problems seem to just work themselves out and fly out the window. I called him five days later and left a message that

I wanted to meet him that evening. In short, I accepted his offer. I really liked him, and I wanted to give it a try.

The very next day our situation gained more momentum. The frequency of our getting-to-know-you sessions increased. We discovered that both of us loved to travel. Although he was much too busy and I really couldn't afford it, we enjoyed leisurely two and three-day weekend getaways every other month. I soon realized that he really paid close attention to our conversations because the following two weeks after the award celebration, he began with another series of special surprises. He took me on a few romantic getaways, one in particular that I would never forget.

The weekly mysteries began on each Thursday after lunch. I received a balloon with a card and an envelope was also attached. Although he never gave away the secret weekend plans, he always gave a clue, so I could prepare. But for an obvious reason, we always had to return late Saturday night. It was that he had to be at church early the next morning.

The very first envelope that I received was labeled "I always wanted to be a Boy Scout." I assumed that it had something to do with camping. My guess was sorta in the ballpark. It included an overnight stay at Big Canoe, a private cabin resort and community village an hour north of Atlanta. Just before the journey began, he stated that he didn't want to talk. At first, I thought that was odd. Then he mentioned that he had asked his assistant to download fifteen or so songs recorded by his favorite R&B and jazz artists on his iPod. The songs were to be arranged in a particular order—a sequence that told a story, a story of how he felt and what he wanted from our developing situation. Although he had previously expressed his growing interest shortly after we met, he thought it would add more meaning if I heard it again in songs.

Before he started the playlist, he paused and looked at me with a serious stare.

"Before I start this, I want to say something, and I hope that you don't take it the wrong way. The songs tell a story about where my head is right now. I want you to relax and listen. Some of the songs are instrumental jazz, and some are performed by a man. But the man is singing to or about a woman. He might use the word woman, girl, or lady. Please don't take offense to that. I am not trying to emasculate you. I am not comparing you to a woman, and I am not asking you to play a role. I guess I could have had the songs professionally redigitized, deleting inferences to a woman." The first song was "Best of Me" sang by Anthony Hamilton. The third song was "I [Who Have Nothing]" sang by Luther Vandross.

The songs were all over the place, various performers and different genres over several decades. But I liked it. I liked it a lot. The ole charm definitely worked.

We arrived just in time to watch the sunset over the North Georgia Mountains. Waiting on the elevated decorated deck was a bottle of wine and light hors d'oeuvres. While relaxing on the lounge chairs and continuing to listen to his custom array of soulful ballads, he turned and asked me out of the blue, "Tell me your dreams." Then he asked, "If you had five wishes, what would they be?" I didn't answer. I just smiled. He took considerable interest in my plans for my future. I assumed he wanted to know so he could see where he might fit in.

An attendant arrived an hour later with a catered gourmet dinner. After the attendant returned with dessert, we showered and changed into the designer silk lounging sleepwear that he had bought for us. We soon returned to the deck to talk.

It was almost midnight, when he suggested that we turn in. The cabin had three bedrooms. And although he never pressured me for sex, I knew that he wanted it. Not only was this man was good *to* me, but he was good *for* me. He never really asked much of me, only that I respect him, express my true feelings, and continue to be honest with him. By the end of the evening, I felt that I was ready to give him much more. He was always full of surprises. Well, that night, I flipped the script. He was quite surprised when I followed him to his bedroom. He turned, paused, and smiled. I did not feel that he had planned this special weekend just for sex. But if he did, and because he had worked so hard for it, he was going to get his wish. That night I was going to give him one of the most erotic surprises of his life. The next morning when I woke up, I found him lying next to me just staring. I guess he had been watching me sleep.

"Good morning."

He didn't respond. He just smiled.

"Are you okay?" I asked.

He didn't reply. He just continued smiling. A few moments later, the doorbell rang. It was the attendant again with another gourmet meal. Shortly after we ate, we went back to bed for another session of some of that long-awaited good stuff. After a brief nap, we got up and spent the rest of the day playing tennis and relaxing by the pool. Later, we had an early dinner in the village and then drove back to Atlanta that night. On the way home, he plugged in his iPod again. I reclined the seat all the way back, grabbed his hand, and just reveled in the moment. I thought to myself, whether it was a ten-day cruise in the Mediterranean or a weekend in Savannah, when most people head back home, they often say, "Well, back to the real world." But in our case, we were looking forward to returning to the city. It was the start of a new and exciting beginning.

The following week the envelope that I chose was labeled "A Progressive Evening." The evening included events at four different locations in the downtown area including cocktails, dinner, a show at the Fox Theater, and later a light dessert.

The surprise romantic dates continued for the next three months but with a different twist. Every Thursday we met for an early dinner. Near the end of each evening, he would hand me three envelopes labeled #1, #2, and #3, but I could open only one. Each envelope included a hint about the plans for the weekend. On the back of each card read, "Please prepare for this date."

The out-of-town romantic escapades continued for several more months. However, because of our hectic schedules, the frequency of the trips decreased to once a month. Other envelopes included several short trips including overnight excursions to Florida. He preferred relaxing in a few of the cozy communities like West Palm Beach, Delray Beach, and Destin.

One evening, he casually asked me what exotic place had I always wanted to visit. Three weeks before my birthday I learned why. I received a couriered envelope from him. It was a first-class ticket to Bermuda. It also included an Amex gift card for $2,500. The note attached instructed me to buy clothes and anything else I wanted for the trip. We stayed at a five-star resort for five days.

Solomon made it very clear that he was not trying to buy my affection. He constantly reminded me how he valued our quality time together. Because of his hectic schedule, he felt that he would be able to give me his undivided attention out of town. We would be able to focus on each other without thinking of the pressures of work.

That was six and a half years ago, and we are still together. I love what we have. It works for the both of us. I call him the Eagle. He always protects me, and he soars above all pettiness. And I am his Sparrow. His focus is always on me. His eye is on the Sparrow.

After my internship, I transferred to Georgia Tech. After I graduated, I acquired my real estate license. I also worked part time at The King Center. Twice a week, I volunteered at a men's shelter and a men's transitional home. Two years later, I went back to Georgia Tech, where I receive my MBA. As a reward for my diligence and hard work, he surprised me with a new custom Limited Edition BMW 870 Sedan.

From the start of our relationship, he listened attentively to my dreams. That was one of the major qualities that attracted me to him. He knew that my ultimate dream was to create and develop my own nonprofit full-service transitional center for inner city homeless men, specifically for the mentally ill and homeless veterans as well as those who were living with HIV/AIDS. Not just a shelter or a food kitchen but a full-service agency that housed the services and tools necessary to help them become integrated back into our society as productive and proud citizens. The proposed high-rise facility would include office space for the Social Security administration, the Veterans administration, a full-service clinic, continuing education programs with several local area schools and a full-service cafeteria. The center also included intensive offsite thirty-day, sixty-day, and ninety-day drug treatment programs before qualified candidates could be accepted into the program. He knew someone who was managing such a facility. So of course, I volunteered in each department for three months to learn more details about the day-to-day operations of the business. With his assistance, I formed a nonprofit, rented a building, and formed partnerships with the county hospital to develop a clinic, the Veteran's Administration, the Social Security Administration, and various social services organizations. And with the funding of a federal grant, I was able to completely furnish the building including a state-of-the-art security system. I purchased all of the supplies and hired an executive director and a small staff. And within a year, the full-service transitional home was in operation. And as you know, I serve as the CEO. He stills serves as my chief advisor on the board.

"Now you guys know me well so you know I am not a 'yes boy.' I am my own man and I have my own mind. But I rarely say no to him whether it's regarding planned quality time or sex or just any time of the day that he wants to see me. He is my top priority. Well, excluding my business."

The other three fellows nodded in agreement.

Dexter was just staring in space.

"What's wrong Dex? Are you all right?"

"Yeah, I am fine. I guess I never really understood the intensity of your relationships. I just thought that they were superficial sexual relationships and that you all were 'kept' men. I understand everything much better now. I see things much clearer now. Well, guys, I have a really big announcement to make next week. A public announcement."

"What is it?"

"Can't say yet."

"Is it big?"

"It is huge. I will be contacting you early next week because I want to meet with you to discuss some of the details regarding the announcement. Okay, guys, it is getting late. I gotta go. See you next week."

Dexter gave each guy a hug and then he left.

CHAPTER 19

The Lesser Of Two Evils

What looks good or feels good is not always good to you or good for you.
Eyes that don't see; a heart that doesn't feel.
What's done in the dark will eventually come to light!
That is why I never allow my heart to rule my head.

"WELL, I GUESS it's my turn to share," said Parker. "Similar to Lisborn's run-in from the past, I received an ominous email a few months ago from the man who broke my heart."

"And who was that?" asked Dexter.

"Bishop Morgan G. Reid, replied Parker."

I have been reminiscing ever since I received the three-page letter. Reading it really conjures up a lot of memories, really good memories, and some really bad ones also. I had the world in the palm of my hands. Several years ago, I began the start of a bright future in Atlanta. It may seem that I have it all together right now, but it took some time to get here. It took a few traumatic experiences to get here. I don't regret any of the mistakes that I made because everything that happened, happened for a reason. That period of drama and trauma only lasted for a season. I'm just grateful that the ramifications didn't last for a lifetime. Who would have thought? How did I get myself in that predicament? That experience taught me to be more careful about asking for certain things. I learned to watch what you wish for because you just might get it. I had it bad, and I mean really bad. This relationship almost destroyed me. I actually thought I was going to die. GOD had to heal my heart, so I slowly learned how to laugh again, trust again, and eventually learned how to start to love again.

I met him when I was twenty-two years old while living in Birmingham. He was a regular customer in the men's clothing store in which I worked. As he began to visit the store more often, we began casual conversation. He mentioned that he was a minister of a large church in Atlanta. I mentioned that I had applied at several colleges in the Atlanta area and that I might be moving there in the fall.

He gave me his business card and asked me to give him a call if I were ever in the area and if I needed anything. No one really means that of course. But I took it anyway. Eventually, when I visited Atlanta, I gave him a call and to my surprise, he invited me to his church. A man of his word. I wasn't sure what to expect, but I was pleasantly surprised. The Spirit was definitely in the air that Sunday morning. During the service when they recognized the first-time visitors and asked them to stand, he acknowledged me by smiling at me and nodding. After the service, he invited me to brunch. To be a well-known prominent minister of a large church in Atlanta, I was a little puzzled. Why such an overwhelming interest in my future and my goals. But of course, I just went with the flow. I accepted his kindness and generosity for what it was and nothing more. We talked in more detail about my attending college in Atlanta. I mentioned more than once that my number one preference was to attend Morehouse College. I desperately wanted to become a Morehouse Man. And I wanted all the perks and privileges that came with it. I had not been admitted yet, although I qualified for the Oprah scholarship. Because I was an out-of-state applicant, it would be more of a challenge to be accepted, not to mention with a full scholarship. After dinner, he drove me back to my cousin's house.

He visited Birmingham again a few weeks later and of course, he stopped by the store. But this time the tone of the conversation was somewhat different. He wanted to know more about my personal life—my parents, my siblings, and if I was dating someone. Of course, I wasn't stupid. I kinda knew where this was going, but again, I just went with the flow.

Later that evening at dinner, I felt that he wanted to ask me something, so I asked him point blank, "Why are you so interested in me?"

He replied, "Why do you think I am interested?"

"I don't know and I don't want to assume. That is why I am asking."

"I would like to help you."

"And what do you get in return. What do you expect of me? I have nothing to offer you."

He replied, "I admire you. You remind me of myself when I was much younger. I wish I had someone to help me when I needed it, when I was trying to further my education."

A week later, he called me and invited me to a men's retreat in Washington, DC. He paid for all the expenses including a private hotel suite. He also gave me spending money. He stated that he wanted me to be exposed to a different type of life. He hoped that this trip would motivate me to continue my journey of pursuing my education. It was a reward for all the hard work of working part-time while trying to prepare for a better future. During the weeklong retreat, I attended several activities and classes. The last night of the conference included a formal awards dinner. I sat at his table. I felt important. This was the first time that I felt that another adult male, specifically a Black man genuinely cared about me. It felt different. I felt wanted. I felt loved.

After dinner, I went back to my room. The light on the phone indicated that I had a message. It was him. Then he texted me asking if I had made it back safely and that he wanted me to stop by his suite. When I arrived, the room was dimly lit. Contemporary instrumental jazz was playing, and I also noticed that his assistant and his small entourage were not present. He wanted to hear about my experience during the conference. I told him that I was a little overwhelmed by the experience, but I was having a great time. Then he wanted to know more about the status of my getting accepted into

Morehouse. I mentioned that it was a lot of paperwork and that I was trying to schedule a final in-person interview in two weeks.

"As I stated before, I want to help you," he replied. "I will have my assistant call you on next week. Give him the details of your situation about what I can do to help."

The next day when I returned to Atlanta, I received a call from Birmingham. I had a family emergency. So, I had to rush back to Birmingham for a few weeks. Once again, I had to put my plans on hold. Two months later, I finally returned to Atlanta. However, I didn't have the nerve to call him. My pride wouldn't let me. I was supposed to call his assistant a few days after I left Washington, DC. I felt that he wouldn't think I was serious. I felt ashamed. I still had not received my acceptance letter from Morehouse. But I was still determined to pursue my dream. I relocated anyway and got a job in retail sales at Macy's in Lenox Mall. I also worked part-time as a server at an upscale restaurant in Buckhead. Although I spent most of my time working and trying to save for a down payment for a car, I was barely making enough to pay my rent and other bills. I didn't want a roommate to split my expenses, so I made due. I hadn't made any close friends and I didn't have any family in town, except one female cousin. And my pride wouldn't allow me to call home for help.

A fellow server mentioned during a drink after work one night that he was a student at Emory University. Of course, I drilled him regarding how he financed his education, whether through scholarships, grants, student loans, or financial aid. He mentioned that he was a model and a male escort. But he quickly clarified that he was not a prostitute. He mentioned that he had been watching me at a distance over the past few weeks. He also stated that if I was interested, he would give me a reference. I was definitely intrigued. I pondered over the idea a few more days and finally called for an appointment for an initial interview. The office was in a high-rise building, walking distance from Lenox Mall. The agency only dealt with high-end clients. It seemed legit. But I still had my doubts. I still suspected that it was a front for male prostitution.

As soon as I walked in and signed in, I was asked to read and sign the last page of a strict client confidentiality and nondisclosure policy. The rigorous interviewing process took three full days. The first day included completing a detailed application. I also had to watch several short company videos that consisted of company policies and protocols as well as videos regarding an overview of the type of clients. Day one also included an aptitude test and a series of personality tests. The second day involved a series of three interviews and a final panel Q&A. I assumed they were interested because before I left, I had to sign several disclosures authorizing detailed credit and criminal background checks as well as professional and personal references. Then three days later, I received another call to come in for a photo shoot and a sixty-second video. I sure was glad that the coordinator stated that I shouldn't worry about bringing any clothes with me. They would have all that I needed and a stylist to assist me. This was nothing like I expected.

After several days of anxiously waiting, I finally received a call to come in and sign a contract for hire. I was officially hired as a model and an escort. When I saw the starting pay, I almost choked. It was no joke.

My first assignment was to attend a private party at a mansion. The client was a senior vice president of a company. He wanted to impress a major prospective client, so he needed fillers. Fillers are very attractive, articulate, somewhat intelligent models who blend in the crowd and mingle with the other guests. Fillers are also always required to be prepared to discuss most trending topics. However, we are also strongly advised to avoid serious discussions regarding politics and religion, for obvious reasons. Our only client that evening was the host. There was to be no "extracurricular activities" during or after the party with any of the other guests.

My next assignment changed my life forever. It was with a much older male client. I was to meet him on the twenty-ninth floor of the Atlantic, a luxury condo high-rise building not far from downtown

Atlanta. The concierge had to escort me in a separate private elevator that required a key card. When the client opened the door and I saw who it was, I was floored. I couldn't believe who it was. I didn't know what to say. It was Bishop Reid.

He just smiled and said, "It's okay. Everything happens for a reason."

He invited me inside and motioned that I have a seat. I immediately excused myself and went to the bathroom. I didn't really have to go, but I was extremely nervous. I couldn't leave because I didn't want to lose my job. I just needed a moment to compose myself. As soon as I returned and sat down, he walked over and handed me a glass of white wine. I guess I gulped it down quickly because he immediately refilled my glass without my asking. As I began to relax, the awkward chatter turned into a more pleasant conversation. I soon told him what happened immediately after I returned from the men's retreat in Washington, DC. Although he said that he was initially disappointed, he understood. He was sympathetic; he wished that I had called him to let him know why I had seemed to disappear.

I asked him if he knew it was me who was coming tonight because each exclusive client receives a login ID and password so they can log in to see a photo and brief bio of who was coming. He stated that a colleague had setup everything so he never saw my picture.

He walked over to the bar to fix himself another drink and gave me another glass of wine. I needed that. I wasn't much of a drinker, but the wine was definitely doing its job. I was now completely relaxed. He sat close to me and placed one hand on my knee. I didn't say anything. Then he placed his hand on my other knee. Still, I didn't say anything.

"The past is the past. We can't do anything about that. This is now. Let's live in the moment. You know what? There is something I have wanted to say to you ever since the first time I saw you. I really like you."

"But you are a minister."

"I am a man. And I have needs. I am not perfect."

"So, what are you saying?"

"Let me show you."

Then he walked out of the room and into the bedroom and closed the door. Part of me wanted to leave and part of me wanted to stay. Of course, I was curious. I wanted to experience whatever he had planned. A few minutes later, he came out of the bedroom room with wearing silk boxers and a wife beater T-shirt. He just stood there saying nothing. I was very tone, but this man was only thirty-eight, but he had the body of a twenty-five-year-old—smooth, ripped, and rock-solid. This man could probably have any woman that he wanted. Why did he want me? Then he took a few steps toward me. He took my hand and led me to the bedroom. Yes, I was breaking company policy but I wanted what I wanted. And he definitely was not going to tell anyone. I logged-in the company app on my phone and noted all went well and notated the time. Then I turned off my phone and took out the battery. I am glad that I stayed. He was gentle, passionate, and caring. I had never felt like that before.

The next morning, he told me his story. I began to understand his need to balance. It was a lot of pressure running a large church. Not to mention the overwhelming pressure of living up to the image of the title and high expectations of the parishioners. And most of all the pressure from his colleagues, mainly his upper-echelon clergy. He stated that he had a connection with me and that I wanted nothing from him. I didn't care about his status or his money. I accepted him for who he was and not what he could do for me. He discussed that he would like to have a special discreet relationship with me. He was very blunt about what he wanted. He wanted to share special moments with a mature younger, attractive man. A hard worker who was ambitious and hungry to succeed.

"So, what are you saying?" I asked. "Do you want me to be your pay-for-play guy? Well, that ain't gonna happen. Yeah, I admit that I am in need, but I am not a hoe. Yeah, I might be escorting for a while, but I am not having sex with any of the clients.

I make them feel special just by talking. Yes, believe it or not we just talk. It's mostly lonely older men who want someone to spend a few hours with someone outside their business and social circles. Or older women whose husbands are too busy to spend quality time with them. It is true that time is money."

He stood up, gave a stern stare, and interrupted me. He said that I had jumped to the wrong conclusions. Then he began to explain about more of what he really wanted.

As he promised, on the following Monday, his assistant called me. I told him the details of the status of my getting into Morehouse as well as the financial struggle I recently had trying to relocate Atlanta. A few days later, he bought me a car. He signed a lease for an apartment and paid one year in advance. He gave me a debit card with a monthly $2,000 allowance. He called in a favor from one of his colleagues who *was* also a Morehouse administrator. Three days later, I received the call. I had been formally admitted with a full scholarship. I would be receiving the official admission packet email the next day. I soon joined his church and became very active in the men's ministry, the pastoral aid committee, and the youth education department. I eventually graduated with honors and received an internship in the mayor's office that led to a permanent position. I was looking forward to a bright future. And surprisingly, for the first time in my life, I was content and genuinely happy.

We continued our secret affair for almost five years. No one suspected anything and I didn't even tell any of my closest friends. However, my best friend knew that there was someone but never knew who he was. After I got settled in at Morehouse and settled into a regular routine, we saw each other an average of three times a week.

Things were going quite well between us. Two years into the relationship, he gave me a great surprise. He called me two days before Christmas.

"Hey, how are you?"

"Okay."

"Are you going home for Christmas?"

"No, I will be here."

"Do you have any plans for this week?"

"No, not really."

"Okay, I want to drop by for a minute. Is that okay?"

"Sure."

"What is this about?"

"Before I get there, I want you to pack a few things. Not much, just your wallet and your passport. If you don't have a passport, just bring your birth certificate. You can bring your cell phone, but you won't need it."

"Are we going somewhere?"

"It's a surprise."

"Just get those things ready and I'll be there in an hour."

When he arrived at my door, he didn't come inside.

"Hey. Good to see you. Are you ready?"

"Yes."

"Let's go."

When we walked outside, I didn't see his car.

"Where is your car?"

He didn't say anything. He just motioned me to follow him. We walked toward a black limo.

"Where are we going?"

"To the airport."

"What? But where are we going?"

We spent four days in Cancun. I was so glad that I had a current passport.

A few days after we returned, my best buddy, Blair and I celebrated New Year's Eve together. We went to dinner and then to a club. Of course, we had one too many drinks. Since Blair lived closer to where we were, we took Uber back to his place. A few hours later I woke up disoriented to something I really had a hard time believing that was happening. I thought I was still dreaming. I was completely naked. My piece was hard as a rock, and someone was giving me oral sex. Still groggy I didn't remember where I was or how I had gotten there. For a moment, I thought it was with Morgan. But when I looked up, then I remembered where I was. To my surprise, it was Blair. I jumped up and told him to stop, but he wouldn't so I pushed his hand away. He said just relax and enjoy it. After the initial shock wore off and his obvious disappointed subsided, we talked. I asked him how he could do that to me. He knew how I felt about Morgan. I asked him if I led him on. Did I do something to entice him to do that? Blair admitted that he had romantic feelings for me and that he wanted to be with me. He said that the feelings had been growing for a while. He said that we had such a great time that night. And when he was watching me sleep, I started squirming and moaning. He said that I started talking in my sleep. So he interpreted that it was what I wanted.

I was completely shocked. I had no idea. Of course, I replied that I was flattered and I cared for him too but just as a friend. I told him that I loved my friend and that I was happy with him. Soon after, I got dressed and left. I decided to put some distance between us because I could not risk anything to disrupt my relationship. Blair didn't take the rejection very well, to say the least. He became even more possessive and demanding of my time. Later, I found out that he followed me one night, a special evening that ended at the Ritz Carlton in Buckhead. Coincidentally, it was on Blair's birthday. For the past few years, I had spent the entire day with Blair celebrating—a full day at a spa, shopping, a movie, dinner, and a show or concert, ending with a few drinks at a nightclub. I didn't forget that year and I had a similar day planned, but I just didn't want to give him the wrong impression. So, I cancelled the plans.

The next day Blair sent me a text: "You really don't know how bad you hurt me. You just can't see everything, but, one day you will. One day soon you will."

I finally became fed up with the drama. It was not worth it anymore. The few bad times outweighed the many years of great memories. We needed some space. The last time I saw him was the night of the incident. I later realized that ignoring him was a huge mistake. Although he had expressed his hidden feelings for me, I also thought it was a simple case of best friend envy. I soon learned that my best friend was even more jealous than I had assumed. I guess I should have listened to my best girl, Deidra. Deidra warned me a few months ago, but again I didn't listen. She told me to be careful.

Coincidentally, a few days after his birthday, she told me, "Blair is trying to set you up. You just don't know how much that boy loves you. He feels that things are changing between you two. He feels rejected and that you don't make time for him anymore."

Over the next few days, Blair tried to reach me. He called and texted me numerous times, however, I did not respond. Apparently, there was an incident that happened two days before his birthday and he really needed to vent. Ignoring his calls for several days initiated a devious plan that resulted in the destruction of a big part of my life as well as Morgan's life. He became more demanding of my time and eventually borderline obsessive. And when he didn't get what he wanted, he went behind my back and eventually exposed the relationship. He didn't get what he wanted so he got even.

"How did Blair find out who he was?" asked Chance.

"I told Blair many of the details of my relationship over the years, but I never disclosed Morgan's identity. At the time, I didn't see the harm. He was my best friend, my closest confidant. He never seemed envious or jealous of me or my relationship. Until that point, he never caused me any harm. I trusted him more than anyone. But he eventually betrayed me in the worst way. How could he have done that, to me of all people? I never thought in a thousand years that he would use my personal and private business against me. It was ultimately my fought for trusting him. But in retrospect, I never thought he knew the identity of Morgan. I tried to be extremely careful."

"So how did he actually find out about him?" asked Dexter.

Two months after the incident, I called Blair. I wanted to celebrate my birthday with him because Morgan was out of town. Although Blair and I weren't in the best space, I wanted to be with my best friend. We ended up celebrating my birthday at my favorite restaurant. We were having our usual festive time. When I briefly went to the men's room, I left my phone on the table. When I returned, Blair immediately mentioned that my phone rang. Completely unaware, he saw the code name and number on my phone, but of course, he didn't answer it. I casually glanced at my phone and noticed that I had a missed call from Morgan. I didn't return the call until he texted me twice within ten minutes. That was odd. It must have been important, so when we left the restaurant a few minutes later, while we were waiting for the valet to return my car, I returned the call. I tried to talk in the usual code to let him know that I was not alone. I had reminded him that I had told him earlier in the week about my birthday plans. He mentioned that he had forgotten. Anyway, I didn't think that Blair picked up on who I was talking to. But I noticed that his mood kinda changed while driving to the club. He became quiet. But when we arrived, and after a few drinks, he seemed to loosen up and the party continued. Everything seemed cool. We continued to have a great time.

When I fell asleep at his house after our night of partying, I forgot to lock my phone. How could I have been so stupid, so careless. But again, he was my best friend. But apparently, curiosity got the best of him. He searched the recent call log in my phone and found the number. He called the number and got Morgan's voicemail. His voicemail message includes his title and name. When Blair Googled his name, he discovered who he was, and he immediately began his devious plan.

A few days later, all hell broke loose. My best friend set up a formal meeting to meet with the elders of Morgan's church. It was also the church in which I was an active member. The meeting included a fourteen-page typed letter, screenshots of text messages, photos from my phone, a list of gifts, and dates of vacations, conferences, and out-of-town trips.

The next day at the 8:00 a.m. service after the morning invocation, Elder Randolph Willingham approached the podium. He didn't say a word for at least sixty seconds. He just gazed at the congregation, not staring at anyone in particular. Then he closed his eyes as though he was in prayer. He finally looked up and began.

"Good morning, church family. GOD is good all the time!"

The congregation responded, "All the time GOD is good!"

"Yes, yes, and amen"

Again, the congregation responded with "Hallelujah" and "Amen."

"GOD is still a good GOD."

"Amen!"

"But the rocks are about to cry out, in this place this morning."

He had a very serious look on his face, a strange grimace. He immediately dismissed all the children under the age of eighteen and then he apologized to all the visitors for what they were about to hear. Then he began.

"The board held a very important meeting on yesterday, an impromptu formal meeting that would affect the future of this church. I am about to read a letter to the congregation. This letter is extremely disturbing. The details are mind-boggling. All will be very surprised. There will be a wide range of reactions. Feelings ranging from anger and great sadness to feelings of overwhelming disbelief."

He paused a moment. Everyone could see the pain on his face. He continued.

"It truly hurts my heart to tell you what I am about to tell you. Although this particular format of presenting this type of news to you all is extremely unorthodox, the board unanimously agreed that it should be handled in this manner. I am about to tell you a story, a story about a minister, a supposedly devoted man of GOD. But when I finish this letter, although we are not supposed to, many of you will judge him regarding his character and that title. Most of us hold him in the highest regard and some of you actually worship him. However, after I share some details with you, many of you will probably feel that he might not deserve the honor or the right to continue to perform such a role; the sacred title that had been bestowed upon him."

Elder Willingham began to read, deliberately omitting various details that were not appropriate for a Sunday morning service. Some parts were just too graphic. At first, there was complete silence. You could hear a pin drop. Then he continued to read more details relating to sex, extravagant gifts, and exotic trips, and gasps, mumbling, and whispering could be heard throughout the congregation.

He paused a moment. Then he slowly looked up. He took off his glasses and wiped the tears that streamed down his face.

"We were just as surprised," he continued.

After about fifteen minutes into the letter, suddenly my special friend, the bishop, walked in the pulpit and sat in his chair. Once again complete silence covered the sanctuary. It was obvious to the bishop that something was terribly wrong. He seemed very confused. What was going on, I'm sure that he wondered. Usually the remote monitor was turned on in his private office so he could hear the praise and worship team while he was preparing for each service. I learned later that it was intentionally disconnected. The online live feed was also cancelled. It was part of the board's plan, an element of surprise. His confusion slowly turned into slight irritation.

"Why was the elder reading such a letter without informing me first?" he whispered to the assistant pastor sitting next to him. But he received no response.

Since he didn't hear the beginning of the letter, he was racking his brain trying to decipher who he was talking about. At first, he thought the elder was testifying about something he had done until he saw him reading. Then he thought the letter was about one of the associate ministers. The elder continued. Then he realized, "Oh my GOD, it's about me."

When the elder finished, he stated, "The reason that I read the letter in this morning's service was because, this church has always believed in transparency. The board wanted to resolve this issue publicly and as quickly as possible because secrets, cover-ups, and lingering gossip would not be tolerated among this congregation."

He paused again. Everyone could tell that this was extremely difficult for him.

"Because we don't like scandal, the board decided to resolve this issue with expediency."

Then the elder turned and looked at the bishop. Then he turned and addressed the congregation again.

"We have a serpent in the pulpit, and not just any ole slithering snake. We discovered yesterday that we have been in the midst of an extremely sly and cunning entertaining charmer. His treacherous actions have hypnotized this congregation for at least five years, possibly longer."

He paused and sighed again.

"All that I have, all that I own, I would give not to be here today to tell you what I am about to say."

He turned to the bishop again.

"The person in the letter is our very own leader, the leader of this church."

A roar of "ah's," "wow's," and "oh my god's" covered the sanctuary. The outbursts of screams, cries, and shouts of disdain and disbelief continued for several minutes.

"Please, please stay calm. I feel your pain. I ask all of you to pray and ask GOD to provide this church family with the strength to get through this. We will get through this together. The board has decided that there is no way to redeem an evil, sneaky, and conniving snake in the grass who has poisoned this church. So, it was unanimous. We decided that the quickest and most efficient way to kill a snake is to chop off the head."

Then he turned and looked at the bishop and signaled him to stand. He turned again addressing the congregation.

He stated, "This pulpit has been used as his personal 'serpentarium.' But no longer. There is absolutely no room for discussion. Our decision is final. So as of this moment, this pulpit is vacant. Bishop Morgan Reid, you are fired. Your services are no longer needed in this church."

In a very stern voice, he continued, "Security, please escort Mr. Reid out of the building. And I want to emphasize *Mister*. In addition, we will send a full report along with a copy of the entire letter that was presented to us on yesterday to the state board and to the Secretary of State's Office. We are still contemplating whether or not we will pursue criminal and civil actions, citing 'misappropriating and comingling' of church funds."

But he wasn't finished. Then he said, "Would Clinton Jones and Anita Ward please stand."

They were the bishop's armor bearer and executive assistant.

"The board suspects that the two of you knew about this relationship. If by some slight chance that you weren't aware of his secret life, then you should have known because you worked so closely with him. Consider your dismissal as collateral damage. Security, please escort them as well," said Elder Willingham.

"Church family, I feel your pain. The board feels your pain. Because many of us place religious leaders on pedestals, when we are disappointed by their actions, the depth of our pain is magnified tenfold. A wide range of negative emotions will continue to overcome many of you for many, many weeks. So, before your anger begins to take root and eat away at your soul, all because of the actions of another man, be still. You must pause a moment and think. You must realize that fact, that he is just that, a man. Each of us will have to cope in our own way. Each of us must find a way to accept what has happened and try to move on. So, my advice to you is to find yourself a quiet place and spend some serious time in that special place. And don't allow anyone or anything in that space. Then begin to pray, then pray some more. And if that doesn't seem to work, then pray some more. And of course, try to stay busy. I ask GOD to have mercy on us and help us to heal."

He read the letter at the 11:00 a.m. service and disclosed that the bishop was the person described in the letter. Even more remorseful this time, he announced again that the bishop was no longer the leader of the church.

Morgan Reid directly blamed me for what happened to his life and his career. Initially, I understood and I did not fight his decision to end the relationship. But that feeling quickly changed. I truly believed that regardless of the situation, I try to always react with class. I was not going to cause a scene, but I wanted to fight for my relationship. I truly thought that we could work through this together. I must have called him over fifty times within a three-week period. I sent him several emails and I constantly texted him. I didn't think I was being obsessive. I had been in a relationship with this man for five years. I couldn't just walk away. I still loved him. And I felt that he needed me, especially now. He was completely alone. I gave him something that no one else could. But after the relationship was exposed, he never returned my calls. He wouldn't respond to my emails and text messages either. Of course, I was devastated. I was completely heartbroken. I experienced a deep, deep depression. Of course, I didn't like him shutting me out. But what could I do? So, I gave him his space. We never spoke again. I eventually got over it and moved on.

Within twenty-four hours, the details of the scandal went viral. He lost his church and most of his close circle of friends in the clergy. He also lost the moral support of most of the upper echelon local and national clergy associates. They ostracized him and eventually abandoned him in fear of association and the backlash of the scandal. The church eventually sued him for misappropriation and comingling of funds. The humiliation as well as the pressure and the stress were too much to bear. I heard that he became highly depressed; to the point that he had to be hospitalized. He was diagnosed as being borderline suicidal. After a ten-day mandatory suicide watch, the doctor discharged him. But the severity of bouts of depression continued. A month later after being released, he had a mental breakdown. He voluntarily checked himself into a private clinic in Colorado. After he was deemed competent, he was again released. But he did not return to Atlanta; he moved to Dallas. He immediately realized that it was too soon to rejoin the ministry. He was not welcome. The circle of clergymen which was once considered to be a group of his closest associates and biggest supporters continued to shun him. He had grave difficulty adapting. So, he relocated again and tried adjusting to New Orleans. He had been offered a few positions in small-country churches in rural areas, but his ego would not allow him to consider such a demotion. I heard that a year later he began to regroup.

He started a nondenominational church, a storefront in a strip mall in St. Louis. His current congregation is about a hundred members.

I hated how much I loved him. I needed some quiet time, some quiet time with just me and the LORD. So, I focused on my career. A little over a year ago, I received a letter from him. From the tone of the letter, it seemed as though he was beginning to heal. And the email that he sent me a few months ago, which I mentioned earlier when I initially began to tell my story, conjured up the entire spectrum of emotions. But I am okay. I have moved on, and I can't live in the past.

CHAPTER 20

Secrets Behind The Cloth

Shining the light on a on a dark taboo secret is never easy but always necessary when it hurts so many.

"EXCUSE ME FOR the brief interuption, Mr. Cavanaugh, but I just received an anonymous call from a man suggesting that you should immediately turn on the TV to WNNN. There is a special report that will definitely interest you."

"You said an anonymous call?"

"Yes. The person did not want to identify himself and he called from a private number."

"Hummm, interesting. I also received a call from a friend who is one of the station's producers. He said that I might get a kick out of the headline news story at the top of the hour. He also strongly suggested that I watch."

Lisborn Taylor, the lead anchor for the afternoon news, began.

> First, there was the infamous over-the-top, drama-filled Jimmy Bakker sex scandal almost three decades ago. Then a few years later came the fall of Jimmy Swaggart as a result of his widely known implication in a sex scandal involving a prostitute. And of course, over the past few years was the most recent and controversial Catholic priests' child molestation scandal, which is still unfolding. Another church sex scandal is about to hit the media stratosphere. But this time, it comes from a culture not known for airing its

dirty laundry for all to see. A major controversial money and sex or sex and money story has been brewing for several weeks now, but this one is in the African-American Christian world.

Within the past three weeks, three separate civil lawsuits have been filed in Los Angeles, Dallas, and Washington, DC, against three African-American megachurch leaders. I have reviewed the three lawsuits filed in superior court in the respective local municipalities. Several young men have filed sexual misconduct lawsuits against the leaders and the churches, accusing them of using scripture and church money to sexually seduce them. All claimants were at least eighteen years old, so we assume that criminal molestation charges will not be filed.

The claims cite "inappropriate long-term sexual relationships" with three different young men from Faith United Christian Church in Los Angeles, three young men from St. Paul Christian Cathedral in Dallas, Texas, and two young men from Grace Temple Christian Center in Washington, DC. Specifically, the claims accuse the three well-known international spiritual religious leaders of each megachurch of using their "charisma," their "spiritual authority," their "influence," and their "wealth" to "coerce and entice" several targeted young male parishioners into engaging in long-term sexual relationships disguised as long-term mentorship relationships. In exchange, the young men received lavish gifts.

The scandals have rocked the contemporary African-American Christian community, sending a massive wave of inquiring minds to Google with searches of all three ministers, their respective churches, and the accusers. In addition, all their

Facebook accounts have been temporarily shut down. And since the first case was filed in Dallas, over a million have tweeted voicing a wide spectrum of opinions ranging from anger and outrage to overwhelming sadness. And of course, the bloggers and the naysayers are having a field day. Once again, social media has proven that it can be your best friend or your worst enemy. Once the genie is out of the bottle, we all know that you can't put him back in. Whether true or not is one issue. But just as important is that the simple allegations against these wealthy and prominent ministers' entanglements in money and sex scandals will surely cost them their reputations and possibly the fall of their religious empires. I will continue to follow this story as more details develop.

This is Lisborn Taylor reporting, National Network News, WNNN, Atlanta.

"Wow! I really didn't expect this! Hmmm, well, I definitely have to speed up the process of filing my cases. Marissa!"

"Yes, Mr. Cavanaugh."

"Please notify the team immediately. I need to schedule a last-minute high-priority mandatory meeting. We need to meet in the boardroom in exactly fifteen minutes. And tell them not to be late."

"Thank you for attending this meeting on such short notice, but time is of the essence. Just in case you have not heard, there was a breaking story on WNNN about twenty minutes ago. I recorded it, and I will play it again for you all. So, pay close attention."

Cavanaugh played the news story. His support team watched in awe. Most seemed shocked while others only smirked.

"Well, team, as you can see, this is a very serious story. And from the expressions on some of your faces, you were surprised to say the least. Well, I am not! I also sensed some of you were saying, 'So what?' I am sure you are wondering what this story has to do with us. Well, Marissa and I have been meeting privately offsite for the last six weeks. We have been meeting with five individual clients regarding a very sensitive and confidential case. Also, we have been meeting with private investigators and expert researchers who have spent countless hours verifying the information given by the clients. The case is similar to the story just seen; only it's here in Atlanta."

"Wow's," "ah's," and "oh my god's" filled the room.

"Oh, okay! Settle down everyone. Calm down. I was planning to make this announcement a few weeks from now but this recent headline story has prompted me to speed up the process. The firm is representing five young men in similar cases as the one just seen on video."

Another brief moment of wow's and ah's filled the boardroom again. Then of course as expected, someone asked, "Who is it? Who is the minister?"

Cavanaugh replied, "Not yet, not quite yet. But in due time, very soon."

Then he continued. "This will be one of the most important and most controversial cases of my career. I can't blow this one. I won't blow it. I can't afford to make any mistakes. This firm and I will become a serious target for taking this case. I am sure that I will lose a few high-profile clients and maybe a few friends. I might even be asked to resign from one of my corporate board of director's seats. But that is a risk I am willing to take. I will press on.

"Now, I just want to make it clear. You all are extremely familiar with our 'no comment' policy regarding all cases. This case is no exception. I cannot emphasize how the utmost level of confidentiality will be strictly enforced. If word gets out before I am ready to officially file charges or give my first press conference, that person or those persons will be terminated immediately. Need I remind you of the three associates terminated during the Colby case? You are not to discuss the details of this meeting with anyone, including spouses or mates. No exceptions."

Cavanaugh stood up and gave each team member a stern stare.

"Ladies and gentlemen, I must stress no mistakes, absolutely none. This is the one I have been waiting for my entire career."

Several minutes after the meeting adjourned, Marissa returned to the boardroom. Cavanaugh was on the phone. He excused himself from the call.

"Excuse me, Mr. Cavanaugh, your five clients are here. I quickly escorted them in your office so that they would not cause any unnecessary attention. They have been patiently waiting for fifteen minutes. I gave them refreshments because I didn't know how long you were going to be."

"Thank you. I will be there in two minutes. Please continue to wait with them in my office."

"Hello, gentlemen, thank you for coming. We have a lot of work to do. This will be the first of several such group meetings over the next several months, although I will schedule additional private individual meetings with each of you. Please, Marissa, have a seat. Although the meetings will be recorded, please take detail notes.

"Gentlemen, let's get started. I want to reiterate again as I have said numerous times over the past several weeks that confidentiality and nondisclosure are extremely important in any legal case but especially cases like these. I cannot stress the importance of not discussing a single word regarding the details of these cases. Do not talk to anyone. This includes church administrators and members, the defense attorney, and especially the media. This also includes close friends or family members. Not even your mothers. Until this case is settled, do not log onto Facebook, and do not blog or tweet either. And Instagram can be your worst enemy right now. Please be very careful about responding to emails and texts.

"I will defend you to the best of my ability. Just to let you know, I take personal interest in this case. But if I am willing to give you all at least 200 percent of my unyielding hard work, then I need 100 percent cooperation from each of you. You are the clients, but I am the boss. I am the professional expert. I know what I am doing. It is not my intention to be harsh with you. So, if my tone or my direction seems harsh, please don't take it personal."

"What if he contacts us?"

"Don't answer the call. Let it go to voicemail and make sure you save the message."

"He has called me six times within the past three days but I didn't answer. See, the missed calls, they are still in my phone, and I saved the messages."

"Great! He is playing right into our hands. It was smart that you saved them. How long can you save each message? I will have my assistant make a copy on tape."

"He called me several times too but I wouldn't answer either. So, he came to my job. I wouldn't talk to him, and I asked him to leave. Of course, he would not dare make a scene in public so he left. But I could tell that he was pissed. He got so mad at me one time that he took my car keys for two weeks because I drove to Ft. Lauderdale for spring break with a few friends. He wanted me to go on a business trip with him, but I was already gone and I didn't tell him that I was leaving."

"Yeah, he has taken my car from me too on more than one occasion over the past three years."

"Are you kidding me? I really can't believe this man."

"He is controlling, possessive, domineering, and very jealous and he doesn't like being told no."

"Controlling and jealous, I agree. I can't even have close female friends. He says they just want to drive my car, spend my money, and have sex with me."

"He had access to my Yahoo and Gmail accounts as well as the passwords to my Facebook and Twitter accounts."

"Okay, guys. All of this is useful information. But that is not the reason for this meeting. Let's stay focused. Over the next few weeks, the process will begin to move rather quickly. If any of you can't follow my exact directions over the next several months, then leave now. I won't take it personal."

No one stood up or left the room.

"Great! Now let's continue. Did all of you bring back all the items that I requested, your laptops, iPads, and cell phones? Have any of you found any more saved texts and emails? What about photos and receipts? Where are your passports? I need a copy of each lease that he signed and the auto registrations, do you have those items? What about bank statements?"

All but one nodded and answered yes.

"Perfect!"

Then the other replied, "Yes, I have almost everything. I will get you everything you requested, in a few days."

"Okay, fine. Let's continue."

"Marissa, did you get all of this?"

"Yes, and I can't believe this. This case is going to be groundbreaking. It's unprecedented. Nothing like this has ever happened in the Black community."

"That is an understatement. Let's get the final paper work started. But until we file the case, I need to review all of the viable evidence. It will make this case irrefutable. Until then Marissa, and I must keep all of the pertinent evidence regarding this case. No need for concern. All evidence will be kept in a safe place, under lock and key. The potential defendant has a lot of clout in this town, and we can't risk having some of the evidence mysteriously disappearing.

"I know that your emotions are still involved and whether you realize it or not, you all are still extremely vulnerable. This case will be extremely difficult for all of you, but again I must emphasize that we will focus on the facts. As I stated before, the major claims will include sexual misconduct and inappropriate sexual relationships. It will also accuse him of utilizing his spiritual authority to coerce certain young male members into engaging in sexual acts and relationships. The case will include accusing him of using scripture and church money to sexually seduce all of you."

Cavanaugh paused a moment. Before he continued, he gave each young man a seriously long stare. His intention was to infer that this was not a game.

"Now I need each of you to listen and listen very carefully. The next several minutes might seem like I will be rambling but I am not. I am prepping you. So again, please pay close attention.

"In a high-profile case, in which rich, powerful people with influence are accused of a serious crime, they operate in a different world than poor people. Those with bigger-than-life egos believe that the legal system is different for them. They are above the law. They are special and they should be treated as such. They 'work,' or manipulate, the legal system for their best interests. They are well-known for overwhelmingly scrutinizing the prosecution's tactics and the supposed evidence. And if the prosecution makes a minor mistake or technical error in the investigation, they usually try to find a way to have the case dismissed or the evidence suppressed, or they usually try to have the witness discredited or disqualified. They have enough money to hire a legal dream team that will give them and their case the individual attention needed. They acquire the best professional investigators and the best expert witnesses that money can buy. When they are involved in a crime, many of them call their attorneys before they call the police, the fire department, or an ambulance. They feel that it is more important to protect their public images and reputations. They must save their careers, and more importantly, they would rather preserve their wealth than to do what is right. Just watch to news on any given day. Major crimes or minor indiscretions committed by entertainers, professional athletes, politicians, and the super wealthy are prime examples.

"In their worlds, Lady Justice is not blind or deaf. She can see and hear very clearly. And the scales of justice are not balanced or equal. Money, influence and a great defense team usually always tilt the scale. Usually when a person is accused of a crime, public opinion says you are presumed guilty, and you have to prove you are innocent. Also, being not guilty and being innocent are two entirely different things. There are three major issues in proving the guilt or innocence in every legal court case. Is the accused innocent? Is the accused guilty? And can you prove that he did it? The mind-set of the rich and powerful is such that 'You can't touch me. I can't go to jail. Too many people depend on me. And as much good as I have done and continue to do for this community and this country, I don't deserve this.' Some narcissists believe that 'my legal dream team will get me off.' O. J. Simpson, need I say more?

"Many high-profile cases are tried in the media. And this one will be no different. So, over the next few weeks I will continue to coach you and prepare you, regarding how to handle the pressure. You will have to be strong, very strong. Be prepared. Be prepared to have your character scrutinized under a microscope. People who you thought were your friends will soon chastise you and ostracize you. This case as well as your lives will be discussed in the media every day for a least a few months. Half-truths and full-blown lies will be reported and printed online, flooding social media. People who know you as well as others who don't know you will be interviewed to make money as well as get their fifteen minutes of fame. You will be the target of malicious and scandalous stories. You will be labeled as opportunists, gold diggers, backstabbers, traders, and hustlers. And don't be surprised if you are called "dirty, manipulative little faggots" who may have seduced the defendant. I know that hurts. It will get worse.

"Now let's switch gears for a moment. Let's talk about the legal system versus the court of public opinion. The opposition, their supporters, and of course the media might try to paint a negative opinion of you in the court of public opinion. The court of public opinion is extremely powerful and it has a tendency to spread like an aggressive nasty virus. And of course, in most cases, the public does not have all the facts and details. In some cases, they have none of the facts. When someone is accused of a crime and the media implodes the story, it is very difficult to put the genie back into the bottle. The media loves to report scandal, drama, and high-profile cases, especially when it involves money and sex. And this one involves the third most controversial issue in our society, religion. All three make the deadliest combination. The more scandalous the more the media salivates. And with the various forms of social media, news travels faster than the speed of light. I know that you think Facebook, Yahoo, Gmail, Twitter, and Instagram accounts are your best friends, but now they may soon become your worst enemies. Multimedia, in the era of the easy accessibility to social media can destroy a case. Case in point, just think about much of the evidence we have in our favor from social media, emails, iPhones, and iPads.

"We have a lot of evidence corroborating the claims in the case, evidence that is indisputable. But I must also emphasize one very important issue. Perception is everything in this case. How will he be able to logically explain his actions and the hundreds of thousands of dollars spent on all of you over the past several years? So don't worry.

"This case will be won by winning several large and small battles and eventually the war. Does it become a battle of the most favorable perception in the media and likeability in the courtroom? Or is it who wins the war by presenting the best delivery of the facts in the case? Good questions. Time will tell. But I am absolutely confident that we will win."

Cavanaugh gave the client's a list of the questions that he had planned to ask them in court. The young men skimmed over the list.

"As you review the list, you will notice that most of them look familiar. I am well aware that I have previously asked each of you most of these questions. It is part of our strategic mission to present a fierce defense. Do not discuss the questions or your answers with anyone including each other."

He continued. "These questions are very personal and they will be rather embarrassing. Some will be difficult to answer. That's why I am giving you the questions now. I will meet with each of you again individually to discuss each question. I will ask you all of these questions in open court. And just to let you know, your answers might become public record."

Cavanaugh reiterated, "Does anyone have a change of heart? I will completely understand if any of you feel that you cannot go through with this."

No one responded.

Then Cavanaugh read the list out loud:

Do you feel like you are innocent of the events surrounding this case?

How old were you when you officially met the defendant?

How old were you when you officially became a spiritual son?

Here is a list of gifts that you supplied as evidence before these proceedings. Attached is a signed affidavit that you stated that the mentioned items were given to you by the defendant. Does this list look familiar? Is it accurate?

Have you ever taken an out of state trip with the defendant? And if so when and where?

Have you ever taken a trip out of the country with the defendant? And if so when and where?

"Now the next group of questions are going to be rather sensitive and sexually explicit. So just take a deep breath and take your time when answering."

Have you ever had sexual contact with Mr. Short?
How many times?

How many times did Mr. Short initiate sexual contact?

Did you ever initiate sexual contact?

When and where and please be specific?

How many times?

Why did you continue to have sexual contact with Mr. Short?

Were there any witnesses?

Did you ever tell anyone?

Why did you not tell anyone?

And three last questions. Please take your time in answering them.

Do you feel like you were coerced into having sex?

Do you feel like you were forced into having sex?

Do you feel like you were raped?

"Any questions?" No one responded. "Come on, gentlemen."

Brandon stood up. "Well, I have a few questions but they might be pertaining only to my situation."

"That is fine. We will speak privately as I will with each of you. I am not trying to scare you. But I don't want you to be caught off guard either. I am trying to prepare you for what could happen. It may have seemed like I have been lecturing you for the last hour or so but you will understand later why it was necessary. Preparation is key—another important key factor in winning this case. I just hope that this meeting has placed all of you in the right frame of mind. Many aspects of this case will affect you for the rest of your lives."

CHAPTER 21

Unleashed

Don't call my bluff when I have the smoking gun in my hand. Big, big mistake.

"MR. CAVANAUGH, THIS is Adrian Stitt. It is my understanding that you visited my client, Bishop William H. Short, on yesterday afternoon."

"Yes, that is true."

"I think we need to meet today. Where are you? Are you free now?"

"No, not really. I am just leaving court. And I have another appointment in forty-five minutes."

"I need you to cancel the rest of your appointments for the next few hours. Where are you? I will come to you."

"Sorry, but I don't cancel meetings. You can call my office for an appointment."

"Mr. Cavanaugh, this is important!"

"And so is my next appointment. Mr. Stitt, I am headed back to my office to prep for my meeting. I have to go."

"Okay, I will meet you there."

"Okay. I will be there in fifteen minutes. If you catch me while I am there, I might be able to see you for a few minutes."

"Great, I am on my way. I am not far from your office. I have your address. You left your card with my client."

"Okay."

Stitt arrives fifteen minutes later. He formally introduces himself. But he did not come alone. "And this is my cocounsel."

"No introduction needed. Vivian Blackwell. We meet again. What a small world."

"Vivian, you know Mr. Cavanaugh?"

Her eyes almost popped out of her head. "Yes," she said in a scathing tone. "Our paths crossed several years ago regarding a case against my best friend's husband."

"Come, on Vivian, we both know that it was more than that. Mr. Stitt, her best friend is also a corporate attorney. I filed a complaint that motivated the Georgia Bar to sanction her best friend's license for a year. And I was awarded punitive damages for her deliberate and malicious abuse of power as an officer of the court. And a year before that and several years before I became an attorney, I also represented myself regarding another case against her best friend's husband. Ms. Blackwell represented her husband. Frustrated with Ms. Blackwell's constant and blatant stall tactics, I initiated a strategy that forced her to eventually withdraw from the case. Of course, I still won. And ironically, Ms. Blackwell was one of the main persons who motivated me to continue to pursue my interest in law soon after.

"Well. enough about that, you can give me the details of that case at another time. Now back to the business at hand."

"Mr. Stitt, did your client inform you of the details of my visit."

"Yes, he did. That is why we are here. Of course, I want to avoid a scandal. In doing so, my first priority is to separate the Honorable Bishop William H. Short, the devoted community leader, from the demagoguery of being labeled as an accused hypocritical narcissistic, bisexual false prophet. That is, before the media gets wind of this."

"Well, good luck. From the conversation that I had with your client, you definitely have a serious challenge. And unfortunately, I can't and won't wait on you to convince your client to do whatever. I plan to file five civil cases against your client regarding the mentioned allegations. And we both know that when civil cases like these cases go to trial, the jury will base the evidence on the preponderance of the evidence rather than absolute certainty. Are you and your client ready to take that chance? Mr. Stitt, you don't know me or my reputation in the courtroom, but mark my words, this is not a bluff. The mounds of evidence that I have are overwhelmingly incriminating.

"Mr. Stitt, when your cocounsel and I met several years ago, although I was young and inexperienced, I was extremely determined to win those two cases even as small as they were. Now I am a seasoned and skilled gladiator. As a fearless soldier, when I defend my client, I not only become determined to win each battle, but I am determined to win the war. I am not sure if you are aware of my reputation, but I will tell you that I possess a particular set of skills, a nonyielding, relentless diligence that allows me to win my cases. Either way, I defend my clients to the best of my ability. I give them everything that I have.

"Now, regarding your client, sometimes one must avoid the appearance of impropriety—the appearance of wrongdoing and the appearance of guilt. Apparently, your client doesn't understand that. In this case, your client has made several serious errors in judgment. The flesh is weak. And I'm sure that he is well aware of that. Most pastors preach on that subject many times a year. And of course, your client's continued arrogance will only make it much easier in assisting me in winning my cases. In preparing my cases, there are two major issues that will be my main focus. Did he do it and can I prove he did it. I have no doubt that I can. And I will.

"Let's just take a moment to consider the type of jury that will be chosen. A jury of his peers? We both know that perception can have its own reality. Especially when people don't like you. Especially when people are jealous of your lavish lifestyle, a private plane, a mansion and vacation homes, exotic cars, and expensive jewelry. Many feel that people like your client lives this lavish lifestyle while hiding behind the cloth. Not paying taxes while people in the congregation struggle financially. Although this is his career and the lifestyle that he lives may symbolize his success, it makes him a target. And in this case, that is not a positive thing.

"Yes, he is the CEO of one of the largest African-American Christian nonprofit corporations in the southeast. Yes, he is the leader of a twenty-thousand-member congregation. Yes, he does a lot of good in the local community. That's all well and good. But that does not change the facts of these civil cases. These allegations have been substantiated. The facts and the evidence in this case are irrefutable. My goal is to seek the truth and to fight for justice. Bishop Short is not above the law. And someone needs to prove to him that he can't walk on water. The narcissistic attitude displayed during my meeting with him convinces me that he thinks he can.

"Well, I have to cut this meeting short. I have to prepare for my next meeting. Please contact my office when you are ready and available for a formal meeting. And if not, I guess I will see you all in court."

From the expression on his face, I guess the meeting didn't go as smoothly as he expected. What did he expect? Apparently, he does not know my reputation, especially regarding high-profile cases. And if not, I'm sure that he will Google me and make a few calls by the time we meet again. And of course, I'm sure Ms. Blackwell will give him an earful.

The next day Cavanaugh met with each client individually. He discussed the meetings with Mr. Stitt. He prepared each petition in advance and reviewed each document with each client. He reiterated that once the document is filed in court that it would become public knowledge. The media will have immediate access to the filing. This story would be in headline news every day for the next several months. And the story will become viral via social media.

"Are you prepared for the negative attention and the criticism?" he asked each client. "You will be targeted and you will be betrayed as opportunists." He reiterated to each client that, "Although you are the plaintiff, you will be attacked also." The next day, Cavanaugh filed the charges in superior court.

CHAPTER 22

Going Rogue
(The Clap Back)

In the American justice system, when you are accused of a crime, especially if you are a Black man, an educated Black man, an educated Black man with power and influence, in many cases you are guilty until proven innocent.

"BREAKING NEWS, THIS is Lisborn Taylor reporting for WNNN NEWS in downtown Atlanta. Atlanta is added to the list of cities included in the scandal of megachurch leaders accused of sexual misconduct. Five separate civil lawsuits have been filed in Superior Court in Fulton County in Atlanta, Georgia, against Bishop William H. Short, founder and senior pastor of the Cathedral of Grace Christian Church, one of the largest African-American megachurches in the southeast. The attorney and the pastor are about to make a statement regarding the charges."

"Good afternoon. I am Adrian Stitt, legal counsel representing Bishop William H. Short, founder and senior pastor of the Cathedral of Grace Christian Church. And this is my cocounsel, Vivian Blackwell. I will make a brief statement and then my client will make a brief statement. There will be no questions taken at this time.

"My client and I formally answered the allegations in court on yesterday. He has been unfairly judged in the media since the day after the claims were originally filed. Once again, the news media has been extremely irresponsible. And social media has been ruthless and downright vicious. We waited until we thought it was appropriate to make a public statement. This recent public lynching is a prime

255

example of how the court of public opinion loves to support and root for the underdog or in this case the supposed victims. But who is really the victim here? It is easy to attack the powerful, the elite, and the rich. The various headline news stories and social media are prematurely ready and willing to convict my client without hearing all the facts. But no one has heard our side of these cases. That simply is not fair. Fake news. Fake news. And I will say it again. This is a prime example of fake news. I see that many of you in the audience are giving us funny stares. You know it and I know it. So, don't be surprised when I call you out. That is not how our justice system is supposed to work. Yes, we agree that these accusations are very serious. They are defamatory and emphatically untrue. And we plan to fight this with everything we have. The main reasons for the delay in making a public statement were that after we reviewed the claims in detail, my client wanted to wait until he personally consulted with his family and officially addressed his congregation.

"When my client was first introduced to the accusers in these claims, they were underprivileged, unsaved, wayward young men from broken homes headed down a road of self-destruction. They were the product of low-income dysfunctional families. They were raising themselves in the streets of the projects while their single or divorced mothers were struggling trying to support the other siblings. These accusers had no father figures in their lives. No male role models. My client mentored these young men. He wanted to keep them on the right track and keep them busy and focused on the right path so that they could eventually break the cycle of poverty. His main focus was to give them the spiritual, emotional, and financial tools required to become successful, productive Christians as well as expose them to some of the finer things in life. The close mentorship would continue until they reached the age of twenty-one.

"In exchange, they would become active members of the church. Each would maintain a 3.0 grade point average while enrolled in the Christian Academy. Each would apply and enroll in a marketable program at an accredited college or university. Each would also apply for scholarships and financial aid and my client would pay for the balance and miscellaneous living expenses.

"They did not hold up their end of the agreement. Each lost focus and violated the agreement. For some reason they stopped attending church or church activities on a regular basis. They did not perform as well as they should have in school. Again, each lost focus and violated the agreement. Each had reached the age of twenty-one and neither had applied or enrolled in a college. Apparently, they wanted to continue partying, smoking marijuana and wasting their lives away. So, my client terminated their monthly allowance, and he cut off all other financial support. Now it's obvious that they considered his support and financial assistance as a free ride. In retrospect, we see that it's obvious that they were trying to milk this situation for everything they could. They took my client's kindness for weakness. The free ride is over. My client gave each of them several opportunities to straighten up. They threw away the bright future that my client had been preparing for them over the past few years. These accusers are being assisted by unknown conspirators who are hiding in the shadows. This is overt coercion. It appears as though these opportunists have created a plan to secure their future and to continue the privileged and lavish lifestyles in which they were accustomed.

"My client will make a short statement but again, there will be no questions after the brief statement."

A reporter yelled out, "Mr. Stitt. Why are you or your client not going to respond to any specifics regarding the incriminating allegations?"

"Allegations are just that, allegations. Allegations are allegations, not facts or evidence."

"Yes. That is true, but once the genie is allowed out of the bottle, it's almost impossible to put him back in."

As Mr. Stitt was leaving the podium, and before Short began to speak, another reporter interrupted.

"Mr. Stitt, but the original charges were filed in court exactly twenty-three days ago. Why so long to respond? You gave a reason at the beginning of your statement, but what is the real reason? We can understand your waiting to respond in two days, but twenty-three days? We have been trying to get a statement from you and your client for almost three weeks. As an attorney, you must be aware that the perception of 'no comment' or hiding from the media gives the impression of a person's guilt. When a high-profile person is accused of a serious crime or if accusations are made that affect a person's reputation, it is strongly advised by most PR experts that a brief comment or press release regarding serious allegations should be given within a few hours and a more detail response should be given, at the latest, within twenty-four hours. A statement after forty-eight hours requires serious damage control. As his advisor and counselor aren't you partially responsible for the backlash and this media circus. This story could be bigger than the Jimmy and Tammy Faye Bakker scandal."

Mr. Stitt ignored the question and gave the reporter a very stern stare. Leaned over and reiterated, "Again, no questions will be taken at this time."

Then Short approached the podium. "I am here to set the record straight. There is a reason that this is happening right now. The enemy is always busy. Satan's job is to attack the righteous. Wolves in sheep's clothing are targeting me and my church. There is a reason I am targeted with such demagoguery. A *swarm* of rabid ravens mixed in with a flock of hungry vultures have been hovering for some time just waiting for something like this to happen. But they picked the wrong target. I am not weak prey for anyone. And I will not be devoured.

"This is a difficult time for handling difficult situations. I must find a remedy to deal with the reality of such a painful situation. Personally, I can handle the pain. But it hurts me tenfold to see how it hurts my family and my church. I have the ultimate level of faith. I believe that we will be delivered from this painful situation."

With his head down, he paused a moment. He looked up and scanned the audience again. Then he continued.

"I am a man of GOD. Like Solomon, like David, like Noah and like Abraham. I am a man of GOD. They were not perfect men. I am not perfect either, and I have never claimed to be perfect. Solomon was the wisest and wealthiest of men. And he had three hundred wives. But he was not perfect, and he also had seven hundred hoochies, or as the young people say, THOTs. And yes, I said hoochies and THOTs.

"And David was after GOD'S own heart. But he was not perfect; he was a thief and a murderer. He stole a man's wife and had her husband killed.

"Noah built the ark. But he was not perfect. He was a drunk. And if you are a drunk, you can't or shouldn't have a drink on the job or drink and drive.

"Abraham was the father of nations. But he was not perfect. He was a liar. He told a lie about his wife and said that she was his sister.

"Like these men, I am not perfect. I am not a perfect man by far. I ask GOD to forgive me of all the wrong I have done. Forgive me for all whom I have done wrong. And that is why I am here to confess. I must confess that I am guilty. Yes, I am guilty."

An immediate loud roar of ah's and whoa's swarmed across the room. Mr. Stitt quickly stepped forward and covered the microphone with his hand.

"What are you doing! This was not part of the original statement that you showed me. Why are you going off script?"

"I know what I am doing. This is what I do. I do some of my best work in front of skeptical audiences. I know how to 'work' an audience. In order to control the media, I have to go rogue. They are not expecting what I am about to do. I have to flip the script. I can't change the topic, but I can definitely change their perspective and their main focus of attack."

Then he gave Stitt a very serious stare. "I got this. The entire African-American Christian world is watching. My peers are watching. My church is watching. My family is watching. Now step back. And smile a big smile." He turned and continued.

"Now, as I was saying, I am here to confess. I must confess that I am guilty. Yes, I am guilty. I should have been a little more cautious regarding my behavior. I regret so much that I cannot change the past. I am guilty of so many things. Many, many things."

The roar of ah's and whoa's across the room became louder. All the while, Stitt stood behind him, looking dumbfounded. He was obviously caught off guard. His client was going rogue and he couldn't stop it.

"I am guilty of trying to fill a much-needed void in the lives of others. I am guilty of helping mentoring young men without fathers or father figures in their lives. I am guilty of sharing my blessings with the less fortunate. I am guilty of caring too much. I am guilty of letting people get too close."

Then he turned and looked at his attorney. Stitt nodded with a smirk on his face. Although Stitt still didn't agree, he understood Short's strategy. His plan was to manipulate the biased media by changing the focus and the overall tone of how he was being portrayed in the court of public opinion. Stitt took a step forward and leaned over and whispered, "I just wish you had told me your plan. But I know why you didn't. Because I definitely would have tried to talk you out of it. But I get it. Now, man, do your thing."

Then Short continued. "Yes! Yes! I am guilty! I am guilty of showing the vulnerable side of who I really am. I am guilty of not recognizing that I am a target and not protecting my image as I should have. I have my faults, but I am not guilty of the things in which I am accused. I am not the man portrayed in the media. I am not this man that some of you think I am.

"I am a GOD-fearing Christian leader who tries to live a Christian life. GOD chose me to be a shepherd, to lead my church. And I will not allow anyone to destroy all that I have built. The fight is on. I will fight vigorously against these vicious claims. The truth will be disclosed. The real truth will set me free. Victory will be mine. Justice will be served in my favor. I will prevail. Yes, I'm clapping back.

"I forgive those who have accused me of these alleged wrongdoings. For they know not what they do. And may GOD have mercy on the souls of my enemies, those who are behind this conspiracy. I would like to thank my family for your love and support. To my friends, colleagues, and parishioners, thank you for your support. Please continue to keep me and my family in your prayers."

Bishop Short stepped back and they walked away from the podium.

"I will follow the story as it unfolds. This is Lisborn Taylor reporting for WNNN News in downtown Atlanta."

The following day the much-anticipated news story continued.

"This is Lisborn Taylor bringing you an update from WNNN News in downtown Atlanta on Bishop Short, founder and senior pastor of the Cathedral of Grace Christian Church and the sexual misconduct civil case.

"As I reported earlier, the official claims accuse the well-known international spiritual and religious leader of using his "charisma," his "authority," his "influence," and his "wealth" to entice young, impressionable men into long-term sexual relationships.

"Now more damaging evidence has been released. Several pictures, incriminating pictures have been released are floating on the internet that feature Bishop Short and several other young men. The photos show Bishop Short with two young men at what appears to be a party. Sources also confirmed that some of the photos include pictures taken at Short's recent forty-fifth birthday party in Miami. Short is on the beach surrounded by three young men. But sources did not confirm if any of the young men in the photos were any of the accusers.

"The accusers' attorney Dexter Cavanaugh is responding to the press conference made by the accused pastor and his attorney on yesterday."

"I am not going to respond to the alleged photos. And regarding the press conference on yesterday, that's just it. That was not a press conference. Technically, there should have been a Q&A after a formal statement is made. I hope that they realize what they did on yesterday. Once again, they just pissed off the local media even more. Not a good thing. Not good at all. The defense filed a motion and the court has ordered a strict gag order regarding any specifics of the cases. So, I will just indirectly comment on the inference and tone of the message that Mr. Stitt and his client presented. I strongly advise that someone other than an attorney should be responsible for providing public statements regarding defending high-profile cases. Maybe I should not say this publicly, but Mr. Stitt needs to convince his client that they need to hire a PR firm with a real good spin master. Controlling the media and coaching defendants on how to respond or react in public are extremely important factors in a legal defense. Attorneys are not public relations experts although many portray that role. When someone is accused of something, especially a high-profile person, damage control and spin-mastering are two of the most important skills that must be executed with finesse and controlled aggression. What to say? What not to say? How to say it? When to say it? Where to say it? And why you say, what you say? Prepping and coaching a client on delivery are extremely important. Whether in a televised press conference, a written statement from the attorney, or a press release from the PR department, style and finesse are extremely crucial to the case. And even one minor mistake can be disastrous."

"Now that they have officially made public statements, it appears that the battle has officially begun for all to see. Thank you for your comments on all of our social media accounts. I will follow the story as it unfolds. This is Lisborn Taylor reporting for WNNN News in downtown Atlanta."

CHAPTER 23

False Face

There are two of me. Two little mini mes, one on each shoulder. When making difficult decisions, the right side usually tells me one thing while the left side tells me something else. Both are spiritual beings with different views on the same subject. Sometimes one has good intentions, while the other is extremely self-serving. They help express and vocalize that which is in my subconscious. What I want to do; what I should do and what is best for everyone involved. All of those things should be the same thing, and if not, then there is chaos. Consequently, sometimes when I make a decision, I must choose the lesser of two evils. Sometimes I feel that heaven is going to have to wait.

"HEY, GUYS, THANKS again for sharing the other night. I really appreciate it. And I know it wasn't easy for Lisborn and Parker to tell the last part of their stories."

"It was okay," replied Lisborn.

"I'm cool," said Parker.

"I have never experienced anything like what you all have. I definitely understand you guys a lot better now. In so many ways, I kinda envy you guys. For so many years, I have been a workaholic with my nose to the grindstone. Regarding my personal life, I have had acute tunnel vision ever since I left my humble beginnings in the projects. Of course, I am not ashamed of where I came from and don't regret it, but all you guys have experienced unbelievable adventures, journeys that most people dream of. And not to mention, all of you were young men at the time. And look how you turned out. The average brutha at that age would not have been able to bounce back, adapt, and progress so easily, so quickly. I guess you guys didn't have time for pity parties, long bouts of depression, drugs, and promiscuity."

"You are right. We didn't," said Parker.

The others nodded in agreement.

"Uhm, Dex. Do my eyes deceive me or do you have an admirer?" asked Chance.

"I wish, man. Naw, that is my temporary security detail," responded Dexter.

"Damn, dude is fine. Wish he could guard my body," replied Parker.

"It's not even that type of party. I received several threats from a few loyal fanatics supporting the defendant in a big case that I am working on. I'm not really worried but better be safe than sorry."

"Does it have anything to do with the story that has been all over the news since this afternoon?"

"I plead the fifth."

"Very interesting, to say the least."

"I smell a big scandal. And I mean huge."

"I have been getting text messages and emails all day regarding that story."

"I'm sure."

"But, Dex, why didn't you tell us? Why did we have to find out on the news?"

"Well, Lisborn knew because I am giving him the first exclusive before I make my rounds to the other network stations. But you guys are my boys and I truly trust you all. But I don't think you know how huge this case is. This is the first time in the history of the contemporary African-American Church that a story like this has become public. Yeah, there have been scandals but nothing like this. This story is getting national attention. Even the major three networks as well as Fox and CNN are following this story. I am representing five young Black men all under the age of twenty-five. All of them feel like they are alone in this. I had to protect their best interests. I also instructed them not to discuss the claims in this case with anyone including their families. Privacy, secrecy, discretion, and timing are everything regarding cases like these."

"Yeah, that's true."

"I understand. You had to do what you had to do."

"I guess these guys have their reasons for doing this. I really can't take sides right now, but I am sure that all four of us agree that our situations were much different from the young men mentioned in this recent scandal."

"Different? How so?"

"We were not their *spiritual sons* as your clients call themselves. None of us were members of our "friends'" churches. Well, none of us except Lisborn and even his situation was different. Lisborn was not being mentored. Parker's situation was different also. And we were not used or abused or manipulated or controlled. We knew what we were doing. These young men were approached by the senior pastor of the church in which they were members. We were not. In the beginning of their 'relationships,' they probably thought that they were being mentored. And technically the accused clergyman was their spiritual leader. So legally, the religious leader was accountable for his actions. These young men might have been manipulated at first, but I'm sure that they eventually became used to the perks as well as the extracurricular activities in which they were engaged. And let's not get on the subject of sex. Well, I think that these guys knew hat they were getting themselves into. These guys were eighteen years old and older. It's not like they were victims like many of the young little boys molested in the Catholic priests' scandal. I refuse to believe that these guys were innocent, naive, sheltered little boys who had no common sense. Growing up in the hood or the ghetto, which is where they came from, one acquires street smarts very quickly. Street smarts are required to survive. They were not stupid. All these guys had some type of street smarts. I am sure that they became very well accustomed to the special treatment of being one of the privileged few. Not to mention the lavish trips and expensive gifts. And I would bet you that they would have continued to accept money and even more gifts if things had not changed."

"There is another major difference that must be strongly considered in distinguishing your clients' involvement with that minister and our relationships. Those guys have committed the ultimate betrayal. They have broken the code. They have exposed themselves to the world. They have exposed their secret lives for all to judge. That is something that we would have never done. Until recently, mainstream society had no idea of this closely guarded taboo issue and how it has divided our subculture. This destructive uncompromising judgmental virus has plagued the African-American community for several decades. Although we were and still are one of the best-kept secrets in the Black Church, we don't hide in the shadows. We were kept right under everyone's noses. Although we are in plain view, most really don't know who we are. The true essence of our relationships is so obvious, but most people just don't want to see it. If they only knew. Well, I am sure a few busybodies as well as the haters probably had suspicions, but fortunately, they only gossip about us among themselves. And of course, they wouldn't dare confront us directly."

"In my opinion, both sides are guilty. The minister is a narcissistic hypocrite and he should be stripped of his license. And the church should fire him immediately based on his conduct. If the church board or the members truly feel that they were truly harmed, then they should sue him in civil court for his past salary during the time period of the inappropriate relationships. But in most cases, that wouldn't happen because in most cases, the leaders of most non-denominational megachurches are the founders as well as the chief executive officers, the chief operating officers, and presidents of their respective nonprofit religious corporations. This means that they possess the majority of the voting power, and they have total control regarding all major decisions."

"Well, what about Parker's friend? He was publicly outed and immediately ousted."

"Again, his situation was different. If a man murders someone, he will be judged according to the specific circumstances. It depends on why he did it. Did he murder someone by accident, a car crash, or in self-defense, a robbery or home invasion or was it premeditated? It matters. Murder is murder, but motive and intentions determine guilt."

"Point taken."

"But do you really think these five guys were the first with whom he had such relationships? I think not. I would bet you my year's salary that this minister has been doing this for years. We all know that many Black ministers have been living this type of hypocritical lifestyle for several decades. So why is it that these guys are doing this now?"

"I am sure that most of the young guys in the past enjoyed the same privileges for a few years, then they probably took advantage of the minister's kindness by allowing the minister to pay for their higher education. Both sexual and nonsexual relationships. It was a win-win situation. Both benefited from the relationships."

"Personally, I think that the guys you are representing are spoiled and lazy. Now, they need to grow up. They should accept the fact that the free ride is over and move on. They need to get a job or enroll in college. If they had handled this situation differently, it could have continued to be a win-win situation for all of them too."

"I agree. I can definitely vouch that this was not the first time that this has happen. He has been doing this for years. Also, I personally know other ministers who have been involved in similar situations for many years as well. They preach one view while standing in the pulpit, but they have sex with men young enough to be their sons. But one major factor in protecting their secret is that they are usually very selective with whom they choose. The minister mentioned in this scandal should have been more selective. Like Chance just said, relationships like these are normally a win-win situation. Usually the young guys usually play the game according to the rules, but obviously, your clients didn't. They should have gotten all they could have gotten, while the getting was good, until they couldn't get anymore. Then they should have allowed him to pay for their education and then started the next phase of their lives. Apparently, something changed. Maybe they didn't follow the plan or broke the rules. And because they broke the rules, he cut them off. So it looks like these guys have decided to get revenge and violate the code of silence."

"You are so right, Chance. There are probably many more guys out there that were involved in similar relationships. They probably played the game and followed the rules and eventually allowed the minister to assist them in the next phase of their lives. But those same guys are now in undergrad or grad school or in med school or law school. Others may have already graduated and have begun their careers. Some maybe living the bachelor life while others have girl friends or fiancées on the side. Some may have even settled down and have started families. But neither of them would dare go public. They would have too much to lose."

"Well. of course, I can't discuss the cases so if y'all don't mind let's kinda change the subject. I know that I have fried your brains, but I have more questions for you guys. How do you all label your relationships?"

Why do we have to place a label on them? That is one of the major problems within our culture—the Black heterosexual culture, that is."

"I am just trying to understand. I mean, is he your boyfriend or your soul mate or what?"

"He calls me his public secret. What an oxymoron, huh?" said Chance.

"And I am his discreet companion," said Emerson.

"Wharton called me his special friend," said Lisborn.

"But none of us hide in the dark. Well at least we didn't think we were hiding. And not being members of their churches ironically makes it easier too. It's like coming on someone's job all the time. And I definitely don't want him to come by my job often. When he is at work, he should be working and not focused on me and vice versa."

"I love you guys like brothers, but I just didn't know how complex these relationships really were. I had no idea. Patrick often tried to tell me certain details, but I really didn't pay much attention to it. I didn't want to hear it. But I am beginning to see that this is serious stuff. I truly wish I had listened to my buddy when he tried to share things with me. I truly regret it sometimes.

"You say that you are his public secret. So how does he introduce you in public or how do you introduce him to others? Do his close colleagues know about you and the extent of your relationship?"

"What do you think? Of course not. Full public disclosure is not an option. They respect each other and they operate under the code of 'don't ask, don't tell.' His close colleagues are not stupid. They see us. But to some it may seem like we hide; hide in plain view. Actually, we don't think we hide. We are visible yet inconspicuous."

"But I still say that these ministers seem to be bold risk takers. A lot is at stake regarding their decisions to pursue an affair because an affair can leave a person in their position being open to blackmail by you or someone who finds out about the relationship."

"First of all, dude, I have to correct you on your thinking, once again. Dude, it's not an affair. And secondly, we are in a committed monogamous long-term relationship. And as for someone finding out, we are not worried about that. He definitely has that covered. That's why I am his public secret."

"Well, I operate with the primus that our business is our business. Major personal disasters happen, and relationships decline and eventually dissolve when people, especially well-known people allow others to have the inside scoop regarding their personal business. And on top of that, the haters will always try to make you the focus of so much negative attention. And as a result, the pressure will usually affect the relationship in a detrimental way."

"The less people know, there is less likelihood of you becoming a target."

"I definitely agree. Prime example—a lot of people in the spotlight definitely learned from Oprah's and Steadman's constant attacks for almost thirty years." And they definitely weren't hurting anyone.

"Why do people with so much to lose risk it all for sex?" Dexter asked with a raised eyebrow.

"Not truly understanding Dexter's naiveté, his inquisitiveness was quickly mistaken as an attack. The guys immediately jumped into a defensive mode."

"Whow! Bruh, don't get it twisted," said Chance. "There you go, like so many others with that typical judgmental perspective."

"Wait a minute, Dex. You got it wrong," said Emerson.

"That's where you are wrong, totally mistaken," said Lisborn.

"Now, maybe the guys that you are representing were in a superficial sex for money and gifts situation, but again our situations were completely different," said Parker.

Dexter responded, "Well, what about you, Parker. They kicked Bishop Reid out of the church because of a risky relationship and you were partially responsible."

"I am sure that I can speak for all of us. We spend more quality time outside the bedroom than in bed. It is not all about the sex. We are not naive. Yes, sex is a big part of it. We are young, but we are grown. We are grown men with grown men needs. Men are very sensual, sexual beings. The four of us are discreet, educated, professional, mature younger men who respect their positions as well as accept, with much pleasure, our roles in their lives. We are successful in our own right. And they are all successful, vibrant, sexy older men who have chosen discreet, committed relationships. These are prominent, rich men who just so happen to be ministers. We can find sex anywhere with a man or a woman, older or younger. As well as they could choose to have a series of anonymous sexual escapades. We freely chose to be exclusive with them. And they obviously chose to be with us for a reason. We are special, and we consider them to be special also."

"Okay, guys, you don't have to get hostile. I just asked a simple question. You made your point. I understand the relationships a little better now. So, we are cool, right?"

"Yeah, we are cool."

"Just wanted to set the record straight."

"Yeah, we are straight. No pun intended."

The guys looked at Dexter and smiled.

Dexter continued.

"So many women as well as a lot of men pursue the ministers that you are or were involved with. How can you be sure if he is faithful? We are talking about male-to-male relationships. How can you be so sure that they are monogamous? Ministers are the masters of manipulation, making others believe what they want them to believe. They constantly sell their religious beliefs and their religious values. They are constantly deceiving others regarding the extent of their relationships with you. They are also masters of domination, alienation, and isolation. In so many ways, they kinda control the relationship. They kinda keep you in a box and the relationship is somewhat separated from so many parts of his world. They could be deceiving you too."

"Okay, Dex! Damn! What is your point?" asked Parker.

"Monogamy is often an extremely lofty ideal," said Dexter.

"Not in my world. Sharing is not an option," said Lisborn.

"I second that. I made that very clear. I will be the only one," added Chance.

"And you guys know me. I will not compromise. That is a major stipulation," agreed Parker.

"I definitely agree. That's why I left," said Lisborn.

"That is one of the main reasons, my relationship works for us. He dictates a lot in our situation, but there are certain things that I will not tolerate. And that is the main one," said Emerson.

"Honestly, I think that they like it when we push back regarding certain issues. Probably because no one says no to them," said Chance.

Emerson jumped back in adding, "On the other hand, regarding sex and quality time, I never say no to him and vice versa. He constantly says that I am his priority. Dex, we clearly understand the special roles that we play, and I don't mean just in bed. Both of us have very busy schedules. It is a major priority for the both of us to balance work and play; most importantly play together."

Chance nodded in agreement.

Emerson continued. "Man, nothing is absolute. You could think the same thing about our men. The relationships are not absolute. But to answer your question. Yes, I think he is. I made it very clear after he decided that he really wanted me and that if he wanted me exclusively, that I required that I was to be number one outside of his calling and his career. And of course, I must be the only one. That is the one thing that I would not compromise on. He knows that if he wants someone else or if he strays away or if I suspect that he is stepping out on me, I am gone and I won't look back. I won't share. I can't share."

Then Chance continued, "Man, I have come hell of a long way. My attitude about relationships, especially a situation with a guy is completely different now. I used to be reckless. I am not promiscuous anymore. No, I am not perfect. I never claim to be. And I don't try to be. But I do try my damn hardest to be the best person and best-committed partner that I can be. I am totally monogamous with Max. He affected me the first time I saw him although I really wasn't sure what that feeling was at first. He takes me to a special place, a special place in which I feel safe. He allows me to be myself. He doesn't judge me. He accepts me for who I am. One time in my life, I suffered from the male version of the *Madonna-Whore complex*. Basically, it is never dating people you consider your own equal. No matter whom they are. Some men are that way. Protecting themselves from getting hurt. There is almost no chance of ever falling in love. They pose a threat. They can steal your heart."

"Why does it matter who I love, whether it is a man or a woman? As long as I'm not hurting anyone," said Emerson.

Then Chance said in a jokingly manner, "There is an unproven theory that men who sleep with men make better lovers with women? Even many women who have had relationships with bisexual men that they have tried to change have acknowledged a big difference. They say that those men seem to feel more connected, and they focus on pleasing the women instead of just focusing on themselves. And from experience, I can definitely vouch that there is some truth to that myth. I truly enjoyed sex with women, but I often wondered if I had been too methodical in my lovemaking. And why I couldn't allow myself to totally let go as I had done so many times before with my male partners. I wondered sometimes if making love to a woman was more work versus pure passionate enjoyment for me. With women was it just physical, just meaningless sex. With men, although there was no real emotional long-term attachment either, it was just different. With my friend, there is definite real love and intense passion. I also realized that there was a big difference in how I feel after the actual sex between male and female lovers. There were times after reaching an orgasm with a woman that I did not want to be touched anywhere. But with some men, it was nice to just caress and hold each other for a while. And if it was a hot and steamy sex session, both of us would just turn over and fall into a deep coma. Or we might just get dressed and leave. And we all know that it's exhilarating when two men reach an orgasm simultaneously. Of course, I'm down playing it with a woman. Because, damn, it feels good when we explode together too. But emotionally, it's just different experiencing an orgasm with a man.

"Of course, the women that I have been with have no idea of my secret life mainly because their focus was on my appearance, my money, the fame, the sometimes-rough sex, and my sexual prowess.

Of all things, my male prowess may have been my most prized attribute. Prowess is potency. My confidence in mastering, dominating, and fulfilling the vital sexually urges of whichever partner only continued to invigorate every aspect of my sex life.

"Although it doesn't hurt to have money, being well endowed plus knowing how to use it is a more treasured commodity with men and women. Many women say that size does not matter. It is not the size of the ship but the motion of the ocean. But experience has told me that most men and women would rather ride on a luxury cruise liner than on a tugboat. And my dude definitely likes it," He said with a big smile. Chance's smile grew bigger and bigger. Because from his personal experience with both men and women, he knew it all to be true.

CHAPTER 24

A Cross To Bear

I don't want normal and easy and simple. But I also don't want drama, confusion, and constant headaches either. And I definitely don't want to be walking around with knots in my stomach and always wondering if he is faithful to me. On the other hand, when I play by the rules, I miss all the fun. I want exciting, life-changing love with someone who compliments me. Someone with whom I can really feel comfortable.

THE GUYS GOT together again the following Friday night at Chance's place. He owned a two-bedroom condo on the forty-fourth floor in Park Place, a luxury condo building in Buckhead, behind Phipps Plaza. Everyone met at eight.

Soon after Chance fixed everyone a drink, he motioned his guests to make their way outside. The million-dollar view from the wraparound balcony was even more spectacular than the interior custom designed décor. The panoramic scene featured a breathtaking view of the midtown and downtown skylines as well as a distant view of Stone Mountain and the airport. Whenever he had a party, the balcony was the most sought after meeting place.

The guys began catching up on the latest news.

"Dex? How is your social life?"

"It's aight."

"When are you going to meet someone and settle down? You know what they say about all work and no play."

"What?"

"Before you know it, you will be in your late forties and the only way to get your piece hard is with extra strength Viagra."

"Man, I do okay. But I am definitely not worried about that."

"Dude, you are too damn fine not to be with someone special or at least with two or three special friends with benefits. Or at least until you find that serious someone special like I have."

"Well, it's kinda ironic that you said that. Because during my last checkup, the doctor mentioned that my testosterone level was extremely high. He asked if I had a girlfriend. I said no. He replied, 'Well, it definitely wouldn't hurt to find one or two or three friends. You are a young man who loves his job. I am a workaholic too. And I am well aware that you work out regularly. But the physical contact during sex has a much different effect on the mind than working out and masturbating. Sex a few times a week can also reduce stress levels and decrease blood pressure in different ways much differently than exercising and jacking off. I'm just saying that it definitely would not hurt. Just always remember to use condoms.' I couldn't believe I was having that conversation with my doctor. He was actually advising me to go out get laid, and often. Well, I confess. It would be nice."

Dexter rarely shared the details of his experiences with his buddies. For the first time he opened up and expressed his view regarding a major stumbling block.

"Well, I must admit that one of my main issues is that I have major trust issues. I am so sick and tired of being sick and tired. I am so tired of worrying if someone can really be faithful to me. I want true love, not just lust. I believe the best romantic relationship is one that is solidly based on friendship and an overwhelming amount of mutual respect. I have always had strong desires for men, but I have just learned to suppress them because I can't trust them.

"Sometimes I feel like searching for safe love, if there is such a thing. I want someone who can love me more than I love myself. I want someone who will love me for me. Love the true essence of who I am.

"Guys, just follow me for a minute. My journey of finding love is like driving along the circular local outer perimeter, Interstate 285, in search of a great restaurant. You know you don't want anything too extravagant. On the other hand, you don't want to settle for anything too bland either. You want something that looks good on the outside, but we all know that looks can be deceiving. More importantly, I focus on the atmosphere on the inside. You also want something reasonably priced that fits your expectations and standards. You would like to think that investing in quality, with or without a lot of fancy frills, would satisfy your insatiable appetite. It just might be what you need but there are no guarantees. Sometimes you just can't put your finger on what you want, but you know when you see it. So, in the meantime you continue to just drive and drive then eventually settle for greasy Waffle House or fattening McDonald's, neither good for you, or good to you.

"I am hungry as hell and I'm tired of fast food. Damn it," Dexter said, laughing. "I want a seven-course delicious meal that satisfies my insatiable appetite. And I want to take the leftovers home with me. I want to save it and enjoy it because we all get late night urges for something really good. I want the full monte. I need some excitement like you guys. You get what I'm saying."

All the guys laughed.

"Whew. Man, you were really out there with that one. But I hear you."

"Yeah, I think so."

"Yeah, I am with you."

"Dex, maybe you are concentrating too hard on what you think you want. Or you hesitate to stop at some places because of fear that you might not be completely satisfied with the service or the meal. On the other hand, if you don't find it when you get off a particular exit, you can get back on and drive until you exit another one. Your urges and hunger might increase, but you will eventually get what you want."

"Yeah, you were lucky."

"What do you mean lucky?"

"Well, one of the major differences with us was that we were not looking for these men. They found us. They were pursuing us. Sometimes the best things are found when you are not looking."

"I guess I should take my mind off trying to find someone and stop looking so hard. Until then, I will continue to focus on my career. Who knows maybe when I least expect it, I might find that special someone?"

Dexter also never told them about his secret, about that tumultuous, toxic love triangle that could have ended in a situation that could have destroyed his life and his livelihood.

Well, the light chitchat didn't last very long. After Dexter drank his second stiff cocktail, he started with the questions again.

"Dang, dude, why do I feel like I am being interviewed? But it's cool. Dex, let us help you, man. If we can shed some light and help you understand the true essence of who we really are as well as how we manage these seemingly complicated relationships with the men who we are involved with, then it's all worth it. It kinda sounds like you want a relationship, but you have conflicting views."

"Yes, I do. Sometimes I yearn for a meaningful relationship like the ones you two currently have and you two had."

"Well, dude. That's cool. Now that you are finally admitting what you want, then maybe you will find it. I definitely understand where your head is now."

"One of the main internal issues that I struggle with daily is the fact that my feelings contradict the things I was taught in church."

"I understand. I have been there."

Then Chance added, "Why does it matter who you love as long as you are not hurting anyone. I didn't plan this. Love is an involuntary reflex. I love this man. I can't help it. I can't help how I feel. And just like Emerson said earlier, he affected me the first time I saw him. He takes me to a special place; a special place in which I feel safe. He allows me to be myself. He doesn't judge me. He accepts me for who I am. And those are just a few of the main reasons that our relationship has worked for the both of us."

Chance continued, "And I understand him. And believe me, that is a lot of responsibility, a lot of pressure. Sometimes he needs an outlet, a way to relieve the stress. Prayer helps. Exercise helps. Bimonthly vacations help too. But his need, his desire to have a caring monogamous relationship and to have sex, sex with me, a younger man, is much greater than his calling. His unyielding yearning over-shadows the devout commitment he took to be celibate or loyal and committed to his marriage as well as to the church. It is a curse that he deals with daily, constantly being burdened with the stigma and pressure of always living by example. Always being watched. Always trying to be perfect. Masquerading behind a *false face* and wearing the full armor of *the body envelope*."

Emerson continued, "Although, Solomon introduced me to the 9 Cs and we actually make a conscious effort to practice them daily, that vital ritual has definitely kept our relationship solid and strong. Not to mention, filled with passion. But actually, I do have a secret. My secret is to treat him like I am a male 'mistress.' Let's be clear. I am not a 'side-piece' and I am not treated as such. And I don't mean just the sex although the sex is great and I have this man climbing the walls. I have a huge responsibility and I don't take it lightly. It is a major part of my job in this relationship to take him away from all his problems, at least for a while. I never get too comfortable in the relationship. I always focus on keeping it exciting. I make a conscious effort to stay focused. I gotta stay on my toes. And most importantly, I am always aware how my actions might affect his career and his image. In doing so, regardless of the situation, I always try to act and react with class."

"That makes since and I understand that. But with a minister?"

"Culture, in particular Black culture, has been bias on various issues for generations. And unfortunately, Black culture has taken an even harder stance on some social, cultural, and religious issues than the main stream culture."

"I understand. Let me explain something to you. Over the years, I have evolved. I realize that there is a major difference between religion and having a spiritual connection with GOD. I consider myself to be more spiritual than religious. A spiritual relationship means that you have an unconditional love relationship with GOD the Father, His Son, and The Holy Spirit. Because Jesus died for our sins, you can ask HIM to come into your life to help you, to protect you and to guide you. In turn, HE gives you grace and mercy."

"I second that. Now as for his being a minister, his profession only stresses the importance of defining and clarifying this issue. I can't stress it enough that people really do need to understand that there is a huge difference between religion and spirituality. Religion is man's interpretation of the Bible and the Holy Spirit. In so many cases, religion is steeped in man-made tradition rituals, man's version of the Bible based on his personal opinions and in many cases man's personal agenda. Just look at the doctrines and specific beliefs by which the various Christian denominations operate. Just to name a few, the Baptists, which are a different fraction from the Southern Baptists; the Methodists; the Lutherans; the Apostolics; the Pentecostals; the Church of God; the Church of Christ; the Church of God in Christ; the African Methodist Episcopal Church; and the Jehovah's Witnesses as well as the numerous nondenominational churches. And not to mention many of the non-Christian religions and other fractions of religions.

"Another main factor is that currently many Christians read and study various translations of the same Bible. In the original Bible, the Old Testament, was written mostly in Hebrew, with a few short passages in Aramaic. The New Testament was written in Greek. I truly believe that the Bible is the Word of God, and it is considered GOD's written revelation of HIS will for man. Our current most widely used English version of the Bible, the King James Version, is only one of many translations from these languages. And since then the King James Version has been rewritten in over a hundred translations in English and those various versions have been reinterpreted and modified. A few others include the New King James Version, the English Standard Version, the New International Version, the New International Reader's Version, the Abridged Version, and the New Age Version. A few others also include the New American Standard Bible, the Christian Standard Bible, the Amplified Bible, and the New Living Translation. When the original version is translated into various other 'easier to read' modern-language versions, whether unintentional or not, there is a propensity to slightly alter wording of the original version. This may be due to the fact that the meanings of numerous words and phrases have changed over the years.

As a result, these revisions often and ultimately change the original intended message of the scripture.

"In the beginning of our relationship, this issue was widely discussed. We had numerous serious conversations about this very subject. He explained it to me like this: 'My profession is my lifetime; long-term career and I love it. I can't imagine myself doing anything else. My career is also my calling. I was called to do what I do and I am passionate about what I do. This is my destiny to help others reach their destiny. But sometimes I feel that the feelings I have for men is also my curse. I am not promiscuous, never have been. That's not me. I might be many other things but definitely not that.'"

Dexter listened very attentively as Emerson continued.

> If a man thinks he is, then so is he.
>
> I am an African-American. I am a Black man. Man is a noun. Black is an adjective. It describes only one aspect of my persona. But there are many other aspects of who I am.
>
> I am also articulate.
>
> I am also educated and intelligent. Note that there is a difference between the two.
>
> I am a happy man.
>
> I am a thinking man.
>
> I am an analytical man.
>
> I am a realistic man.
>
> I am an optimistic man.
>
> I am artistic, creative, and aggressive.
>
> I am a son, brother, lover, working professional, and a GOD-fearing Christian.
>
> Don't limit me to one aspect of who I am. I am still a MAN!
>
> Don't try to lock me into one aspect of my being.

Then his toned changed. At first, I was not sure if he was trying to convince himself or me. Then Emerson continued, "'If there is such a thing as a real man, I am he! Real men drink life! Whatever life brings my way, I deal with it. I devour it! But I had to learn the hard way that having it all doesn't necessarily mean having it all at once. I had to wait so many years until I found the right person for me—YOU.' He looked at me with an intense expression on his face. 'When I met you, it didn't take me very long to realize what I wanted. I knew that I wanted you in my life.'

"Then all of a sudden, Solomon went scripture on me: 'In 2 Corinthians 12:7–10, the Apostle Paul is speaking about a thorn in his flesh: "A thorn in the flesh was given to me, a messenger of Satan to buffet me, lest I be exalted above measure. Concerning this thing I pleated with the LORD three times that it might depart from me. And HE said to me, MY grace is sufficient for you, for MY strength is made perfect in weakness."' Then Paul gladly 'glorified in the infirmities,' also referred to as weaknesses 'that the power of Christ may rest upon me. Therefore, I take pleasure in my infirmities; in my faults, shame, and blame; in my needs; in my persecutions; in my distresses; for Christ's sake. For when I am weak, then I am strong.'

"Of course, I had heard that scripture many times before. But then he broke it down in plain English, so I could understand it even better: 'Paul had been dealing with his issue for many years. Just think, he had not even mentioned it for fourteen years. Three times he pleaded with the LORD that the "thorn" be removed, but GOD had a better plan. Like Paul, this strong feeling that I have had for men many years is my proverbial thorn in my flesh. Of course, for many years I did not have the level of faith that Paul had. I still wanted my "thorn" removed.'

"He continued, 'Like Paul, I had acquired a strong need for prayer. I needed some quiet time, some quiet time with just me and the LORD. I had spent many years in deep prayer thinking that I could pray it away, but HIS grace was sufficient. I spent many more years struggling with that issue before I began to act on it. So, I began to just deal with my feelings while accepting and believing that HIS grace really was more than enough.'

"Although I was quite familiar with the story, I had never heard that passage interpreted that way. I continued to listen attentively. This time it was much more personal. I could relate to it.

"He continued, 'I manage those strong urges daily. I must also continue to temper my behavior and bear it. Sometimes I can't control how I feel about something or someone but I can always determine how I react to a person or a situation. One way is that I don't allow my little head to rule my big head. If you know what I mean. Again, I am not promiscuous. I have never been, nor will I ever be. But I do want someone with whom I can share my life. That includes emotionally, spiritually and financially. And let's be realistic, sexually too.'

"He spoke with such overwhelming passion. And I really don't think that he was making excuses for his behavior, or twisting the meaning of Paul's story to rationalize his behavior. It's just how he deals with it."

"That makes sense."

"Yeah, I hear you."

After a few moments of silence, Dexter started again. He continued with another controversial issue that has caused another minor uproar in the new age of the megachurch.

"What about the lavish lifestyle; his career versus his calling? We all know that big church is big business. In nondenominational contemporary Christian Churches, the senior pastor, who in many cases is the founder, is usually considered the CEO of the nontaxable, supposedly nonprofit religious organization. The superfluous cash cow operates as a legal tax shelter, which allows him many benefits and perks not to mention large sums of cash, numerous extravagant gifts, and exotic vacations given by the numerous church ministries; various church leaders, and countless individual members during his annual pastoral anniversary celebration. He, or in a few cases, she, also receives an undisclosed weekly 'love offering' versus a salary and some cases both. In addition, whether solicited or given as a token of appreciation, they are often given monetary honorariums while preaching at other churches and conferences. And of course, their literary and personal branding money machine, which proactively markets their books and other marketing material is managed under a separate but interrelated separate side business, sometimes bearing his or her name. The megachurch clique is treated like rich and famous religious celebrities. I attended a service and they collected money five times during one service; the usual missionary offering, a donation for the TV and outreach ministry, the regular tithes and offering, a collection for the pastor's anniversary, and a special offering for the guest speaker. When I briefly served as an administrator on the pastor's aide committee, one of my major responsibilities was to review the contracts and agreements submitted by prospective guest pastors. Numerous senior upper-echelon ministers were widely known for submitting ten to fifteen-page advanced copies of detailed contracts, which included four first-class plane tickets for him and his entourage, accommodations at an all-inclusive five-star hotel with daily spa treatments, a private limousine and an administrative assistant. And it was also normal to include an elaborate booth to be set up in the vestibule to display and sell his or her marketing material."

"Wow! But it's true. And just to think, Mother Teresa had over seventy charities and she even gave her Nobel Peace prize monetary award to charity. She lived as a pauper in her hometown of Bangladesh until her death. I was told that she didn't even like to be driven in limos. And I just wonder what would Jesus do? Would HE fly around in a custom G-10 with HIS name on the tail or a private helicopter with 'JC' on the side? I think not. Especially in a bleak economy in which many of the parishioners are financially destitute. I know for a fact that many are pressured to give what they don't have. But they must show appearances. I never understood how a person could be a cheerful giver when he has only a hundred dollars in his checking account to pay a past due electric bill that is three hundred dollars. Of course, I believe in obedience as well as sacrifice, but I'm sorry but I just think that the LORD would banish a person to hell for not paying ten percent of one-hundred dollars or supposed ten-dollar 'tithe.' I just don't."

Emerson continued, "I am not making excuses for my friend, and I am not defending him because he is my friend. But he is different. Yes, he is extremely image conscious. Yes, he definitely appreciates the finer things in life. Yes, he exposes me to a lifestyle that most people dream of. But he is not a superficial, materialistic egotistical minister who expects privileges or one who insists on preferential treatment. I believe that GOD gave us more than five senses. HE also gave us, well most of us, a sixth sense, common sense. But who I am to judge? I refer to it as *his career versus his calling.*"

CHAPTER 25

Far From Heaven

The crisis of today is the joke of tomorrow, but there are always exceptions, especially when going public.

THE NEXT DAY Dexter Cavanaugh made his first public statement in an interview on WNNN NEWS.

"Continuing the breaking national headline news from last week, a taboo subject has erupted in the media that exposes the "underground" lifestyle and relationships between several upper-echelon clergy in Los Angeles, Dallas, and Washington, DC, and targeted young impressionable men in various African-American Christian Churches. Well, now we can add Atlanta, Georgia, to the list. Pandora's box definitely has been opened once again, revealing the many perilous secrets and the private lives between several bishops, ministers, and young male parishioners. According to sources, the lifestyles and behavior of many in the Catholic priests' scandal have no comparison to the narcissistic behavior of these high-profile African-American ministers, leaders of the mentioned Christian megachurches. But two main issues are quite different in these recent cases. The young men were of legal age when the relationships started. And the relationships were mutual. Therefore, sexual abuse and molestation are not issues.

"Whether labeled as victims by some and ridiculed as opportunists by others, the young men definitely appeared to be reaping the benefits of being chosen and "nurtured" as one of a few privileged "spiritual sons," as the five Atlanta young men are commonly known. At first glance, the young men appear to be the innocent victims by some. But as the story unfolds, they reveal that they are neither innocent nor naive. Rumor has it that each relationship recently changed. It is reported that over time various problems ensued in each relationship. The five young men claim that they began to feel neglected, rejected, and ostracized. In addition, the financial support as well as the lavish gifts ceased. Scornful, revengeful, and possibly coerced, it appears as though they have created a plan to secure their future and to continue the lifestyle in which they were accustomed.

"The clergy's self-incriminating actions, their blatant hypocrisy, and their abuse of their authority and misuse of their professional license, gave the young men the ammunition and proof needed to prompt several civil lawsuits. But why did these young men really file lawsuits? Was it necessary? Was it their last resort? And on what basis did they think a lawsuit was warranted? Don't they realize they will be exposing themselves to ridicule and constant gossip? Who really put them up to this? They alone were not smart enough, not intuitive enough, to wage war against these powerful, egotistical men of GOD. And not to mention intentionally attacking the most powerful institution in the African-American community.

"The five young men in Atlanta have hired Dexter Cavanaugh III, a locally known attorney known for winning high-profile controversial civil cases. Welcome, Mr. Cavanaugh, thank you for joining us today. Mr. Cavanaugh, can you begin with a little background about this sensitive issue in the contemporary African-American Christian Church and why this case has received so much national attention? The media, especially social media, is eating this up. The church's website had to be taken offline because it crashed. Its Facebook, Instagram, and Twitter accounts as well as the minister's social media accounts also have been closed. People are tweeting about it all day every day, and of course, the bloggers are having a field day with this story."

"Hello, Lisborn, and thank you for inviting me. From personal experience, I am well aware of this unspoken social and religious issue that has been brewing in the African-American community for many years. Unfortunately, most victims would not come forward—well, not until recently. My main strategic approach will be to try to relate to the jury through uncomplicated rhetoric. However, my relatable yet unique no-nonsense style will be relentless. My ultimate goal is to continue to use this highly effective style to win these cases and to make an example of the accused minister. I am determined to stop the perpetuation of this overwhelming amount of negative behavior. The frank and open conversations during several intense interviews and the evidence provided by the young men led to a collaboration of verified facts that prompted an in-depth internal investigation by my team. As this larger than life scandal continues to grow, the public will soon learn that there really are three sides to every story. My clients' side, the minister's side, and the case presented to the judge and jury. And in this case, of course, the media will create a fourth perspective.

"The unmentionable brings to public light, a hush-hush and forbidden subject in the African-American Christian Church. This extremely sensitive issue forces or provokes the previously quiet and intentionally ignored eight-hundred-pound gorilla to beat his chest. Finally, a bright light is shed on the big pink elephant in the room, or should we say, in the main sanctuary.

"Let's start by shedding a little light on a grave taboo subject in the African-American Church. This extremely sensitive issue has divided Black culture for several decades. Actually, this case is more than about the Black Church. It's about the Black culture. Many of us grew up believing that the church, the Black Church, was the ultimate safe haven, the safest place on earth. A refuge for peace, solace, and solitude. It was once the foundation of our community. A place of moral support, total acceptance, and unconditional love. But unfortunately, not in many Black Christian Churches. Especially not in many of the contemporary Black megachurches. Many of these huge commercialized religious organizations operate like huge moneymaking businesses where the leaders live like wealthy celebrities. Others function almost cult-like with an undying loyalty to their spiritual leader, a leader who can do no wrong. And when the leader or his reputation is attacked by anyone including the media, they rush to his defense and try to rescue him. The loyal parishioners surround him and protect him closer than the president's secret service. They proclaim that any derogatory accusation is Satan's way of attacking a righteous, spiritual man. They are blinded by the sixth sense that GOD gave us, the sense of reason and common sense, and discernment and wisdom.

"Imagine this. On any given Sunday, the pastor of a large mega-church having the power to snap his finger and a large part of the congregation disappears for ten minutes. This includes all men who are either homosexual or bisexual or men still in the closet or on the DL. It also includes those men, who are confronting and struggling with their sexuality, to the many men pressured by the Black Christian Church to 'be straight' or 'act straight.' And it also includes engaged or married men who have suppressed such emotional feelings and have never acted on them. Not to mention the women who have the same tendencies. More than half of the pews would be empty. Just imagine. How many associate ministers in the pulpit, administrators, elders, deacons, youth mentors, praise team leaders, ushers, greeters, security officers, and general members of the congregation would disappear? Not to mention the choir directors and choir members. How many of them would disappear? And lastly, in many cases, there is a strong possibility that the pastor himself could disappear.

"It is not only unethical and hypocritical for a male minister to have continuous sex with a young male parishioner in his church, but sodomy is also illegal in some states. Not to mention the more serious issue of a licensed professional operating in bad faith. As many are well aware, there are several professions that require that someone is licensed to practice a particular profession. A licensed ordained minister is such a professional. They are required to take an oath to uphold a certain level of ethical behavior. They must not abuse their authority or inappropriately misuse their authority. This includes intentionally or unintentionally manipulating a layperson under his care. Also, they must not use their position or their power to coerce someone to do something that is inappropriate. This is such the case, serious and numerous ethics violations.

"The minister in this case as well as others have disguised their relationships by mentoring, counseling or befriending the impressionable young men of their congregations. Young men who have no father figures in their lives. Young men who have never really received special attention from a potential role model, especially an influential man. Extremely close relationships between an underprivileged young man and his rich, older spiritual leader who can shower him with gifts in exchange for a sexual relationship is definitely inappropriate. It is misplaced love. Plain and simple. In most cases, this is the type of relationship that doesn't cause too much attention or suspicion. It appears to be the perfect cover-up. It is their belief that sometimes the best way to get away with something is to do it under someone's nose. They use charisma and authority to influence and manipulate the young men by gaining their confidence. More common than not, the close bond eventually evolves into a sexual relationship. Some have long-term relationships with one young man while others have several spiritual sons simultaneously. And in many instances, the spiritual sons think that they are the only special chosen one, all the while they are one of many."

"Well, Mr. Cavanaugh, thank you for sharing your in-depth and thorough incites to quite an interesting drama. Of course, we will follow the story as it unfolds. This is Lisborn Taylor reporting on WNNN NEWS."

Later, that day I had been bombarded with requests for interviews from the other local news affiliates and cable networks. I received numerous calls from fellow colleagues and a few national senior clergymen. I even received a call from a local superior court judge. He said that he wanted to invite me a private meeting regarding the future of my professional career. What timing! And on top of that, I even received a call from one of the board members from the congressional Black caucus of the state legislature. Hmmm, they were pulling out the big guns.

Several other local senior clergymen had also called me on my private phone line asking to meet with the local chapter of the United Concerned Black Bishops and Ministers of America, the Organization of Regional Concerned African-American Clergy, and the National Ministerial Alliance Organization.

I don't cave in to pressure, especially when it comes to Black on Black civil or criminal cases. And of course, I had to decline all future interviews until next week.

CHAPTER 26

The Smoking Gun

There is a time and place for everything. Now is the time. Let the holier-than-thou judge be judged.

THE JUDGE ORDERED pretrial mediation. Cavanaugh and his clients had no objection. Although it was quite a struggle, Mr. Stitt finally convinced Mr. Short that it was in their best interest to at least attempt to settle the cases out of court. His main convincing argument was that the mediation process would give the both of them a chance to examine Cavanaugh's evidence. They would also gain some insight regarding his strategy and approach. And lastly, they would be able to study Cavanaugh's courtroom style and delivery. It would also allow Stitt to learn more about the young men. Stitt was well aware that the best defense was a good offense. Which meant in this case, attack the supposed victims, their character, and their reputations. But he also knew that this strategy could backfire.

The defense immediately filed a motion for another more stringent gag order. The judge granted the request with a few limitations. Only the attorneys were permitted to make a formal statement to the media and one formal interview with the media. The defendant was permitted to make only one public statement along with his attorney. The five young plaintiffs unanimously decided not to speak publicly. Both sides were also ordered not to discuss the case with friends, family, other parishioners, or the media. The plaintiffs and the defendant were also banded from discussing the case via any social media.

Six weeks after Cavanaugh originally filed the claims, the long-awaited big day had arrived. To Cavanaugh's surprise, Mrs. Short attended the first day of mediation. When he saw her, he immediately approached Mr. Stitt?

"What is Mrs. Short doing here, Mr. Stitt? I strongly suggest she not attend this session. Bad idea, very bad idea. This is the first session. There will be a lot of incriminating evidence presented as well as extremely explicit testimony given. And I'm not sure how much she knows. When you filed your motion for discovery, I'm sure that you recall that I only responded with a list of items and witnesses. You and your client are not even aware of the specific details of all the damaging evidence that I will present today. And I really don't think this woman should be exposed to this. Not for the first time and not in public. So whatever your strategy is today, it's not going to work. Between you and me, I'm just letting you know that I am not holding back."

Cavanaugh couldn't believe that Short would expose his wife to be publicly humiliated. And that was exactly what was going to happen. Maybe he thought that Cavanaugh would respect her by going easy on him. Or maybe he thought that Cavanaugh would plead his case wearing soft gloves—big mistake, very big mistake. Whether she knew anything or not, that was not Cavanaugh's main concern. He said he was not going to hold back and he definitely meant it.

The first day of mediation definitely set the tone for the rest of the proceedings. The court appointed mediator began by making a rather lengthy statement regarding the stringent guidelines and the rules of the proceedings. There were to be no interruptions or objections. Unlike an official jury or bench trial, this mediation process would be used to allow all parties to disclose potential evidence, make statements, and informally testify. Based on the outcome, the mediator would make recommendations as well as advise if a possible settlement should be made by both parties or if both parties should proceed to trial. All parties were sworn in. Then Cavanaugh began.

"We can make these mediation proceedings relatively brief and less painful for all parties involved. Or if the defense chooses, we can play several legal tennis matches tossing stall tactics back and forth as well as cleverly attempt other calculated strategic moves. I am fine with either way. But we all know that the media is out for blood.

They are thirsty and extremely anxious to continue to put their own spin on this case. And when they find out, and we know they will, that the defense might settle in lieu of an exploitative trial that will make their already-biased version of the story even more one-sided, the media frenzy as well as social media will erupt to an all-time high. Again, that's fine with me.

"Another point that the defendant should consider is that the longer these cases are open and active and the media is reporting on them daily, the greater the chances of other young men will come forward. Let's be real—we know it's possible. And of course, I will be ready to defend them too.

"Sometimes good excuses make great confessions. The defendant's reasoning for his actions could be disguised as simply excuses with plausible explanations that are being misinterpreted by the accusers and possibly a jury of his peers. Or by some chance, a miracle could happen and he discovers that the only way out of this serious dilemma would be by true confessions. He could admit his wrongdoings and ask for forgiveness and then just pay up. But we know that is not going to happen. Both strategies are rather shrewd and both have the potential to minimize the damages. But in this case, as clever as these legal maneuvers might be, I guarantee that most won't buy it. The evidence and the witnesses first account testimony are irrefutable."

Mr. Stitt interrupted, "Really, Mr. Cavanaugh! Really! We don't need a lecture from you. Can we get started?"

"Yes, Mr. Cavanaugh. Let's get started shall we!" exclaimed the mediator.

"Okay, as you wish."

He began again, "My clients used to believe that the safest place on earth was the church. The African-American Christian Church was supposed to be their place of refuge, a safe haven. Church leaders are men of grave influence, a large majority of them are undisputedly the most influential force in the Black community. My clients, these young men presented today, trusted their spiritual leader. Their trust was violated. Yes, they came from dysfunctional broken homes, but that is not the main issue in this case. My clients experienced a wave of domination tactics, manipulation tactics, and alienation tactics all intentionally used to control them. The defendant, Bishop William H. Short, founder and senior pastor of the Cathedral of Grace Christian Church, one of the largest African-American megachurches in the southeast, was at the helm, all the while controlling the powerful forces that tempted my clients. The well-known international spiritual and religious leader used his charisma, his authority, his influence, and his wealth to entice young, impressionable men into long-term sexual relationships. When he speaks, everyone listens."

Each of Cavanaugh's clients came in one by one, not being allowed to hear each other's statements. Then Cavanaugh continued by allowing each plaintiff to give a detailed fifteen-minute verbal statement outlining each entire relationship with Bishop Short. Cavanaugh had already carefully prepared his clients to be calm and to give short or one-word answers. If they did not understand the question, they were instructed to ask whomever to restate or rephrase the question.

"My name is Ethan Griffin. I thought I was special. I thought I was the only one. The special one. The chosen one. Then I learned that there were others; and many others before me. Yes, I'm angry and disappointed and hurt but that is not the point. I feel that I was used and manipulated. My trust was taken for granted. He used his authority and position to justify his actions and our 'relationship.' He was my mentor and father figure. He called me his spiritual son.

"I truly loved him and actually I still do. But I also hate him. I guess it's true what they say there is a thin line between love and hate. I really don't know if I am reacting because I am emotional distraught or if I just want to expose the relationship and his actions. Either way, I still feel like a fool."

"Well, I understand. Mr. Griffin, tell us what happened," said Cavanaugh.

"Well, where should I start?"

"Start from the beginning leading to the last details."

Ethan Griffin began to tell his story, then Cavanaugh interrupted. "Before we continue, I would like the record to show that the majority of the testimony can be and will be corroborated if necessary. I will start by asking each plaintiff a series of brief questions pertaining to the physical evidence to be presented in this mediation process. The mentioned supporting evidence will include proof gathered from laptops, iPads, and iPhones, just a few of the expensive gifts given to my clients by the defendant. Corroborating evidence will also include photos, saved texts and emails, bank statements and receipts, passports, copies of rental leases signed by the defendant, and five bills of sale along with five auto registrations.

"Okay, Mr. Griffin. Let's continue. Do you feel that the defendant used his charisma, his authority, his influence, and his wealth to entice you while under his mentorship into sexual acts?"

"Well."

"Answer the question, yes or no? You just made inference to such in your brief statement. And remember you are under oath. You swore to tell the truth, the whole truth and nothing but the truth so help you GOD."

"Yes."

"Did you ever initiate sex?"

"Never in the beginning. At first, it was difficult to perform, but as he continued to counsel me, he convinced me that it was the right thing to do. He reiterated that it was my duty to try to please my spiritual leader. He quoted scripture supporting his stance regarding servicing our leader in various ways, one way being sexual. He was under a lot of pressure. He needed something to take his mind off the stresses of the day—the church, his family, his ministries, and the constant hectic schedule. He often said, 'Being with you in this way takes me to a safe place, a place that I can get away for a few hours and not worry or be concerned about anything. Just relax and we will make each other feel really good.' It was uncomfortable mentally and physically at first, but as he continued to coach me, I learned to tolerate it. As he continued to reiterate that it was my duty to serve him, I soon began to believe it. After much coaching, I eventually began to believe that it actually was part of my duty. And I eventually began to enjoy it too. This was the first time that a man, a father figure that ever showed any real interest in me. He took the time to care for me and nurture me. I loved him. And I still do.

"But after the second year, yes, I must agree that I began to realize that something might not be right. Yes, deep, deep down I kind of knew it was not right, but he was the pastor. He took care of me in so many ways—spiritually, emotionally, and financially. He was my confidant and counselor. I felt that he understood me too.

"Later, probably after the third year, things began to change. I didn't want to have sex any more. But I did it anyway. If I didn't, he would show subtle signs of anger and he would withdraw. I felt that I was betraying him and that I was not serving my duty as a loyal servant and member. I began to internalize my feelings. As a result, my behavior drastically changed. I was no longer interested in spending quality time with him. I also did not want to participate in any of the church activities and I didn't want to go to college. As I withdrew, he responded accordingly. He withdrew further and eventually confiscated most of the electronics and the other major gifts, but I got most of them back except the car."

"How did you get them back?"

He did not respond. Cavanaugh had prepared his clients earlier not to answer that specific question; in lieu of incriminating themselves. His intention was to throw out that issue as bate for the defense. Then Cavanaugh continued as he began to initiate his key strategy of showing a pattern in the defendant's behavior. He questioned the second plaintiff who also gave a detail account of how their "relationship" began. He told a very similar account as did the first plaintiff, but of course, his gifts as well as trips, the type of cars and amounts of cash were quite different. As each of the others testified about their gifts, Cavanaugh intentionally asked again the question regarding how they recently regained possession of their gifts. Again, each client did not respond. As the line of questioning continued, the third, fourth, and fifth plaintiff gave very specific and similar details of how the relationship changed from just a strictly mentoring relationship to a cleverly disguised, mentoring relationship, which included the cash, a weekly allowance, expensive gifts, and trips.

Mrs. Short sat quietly in a chair behind her husband. Her body language said that she kinda knew that something had been going on. But because of her position in the church and in the community, she ignored it and looked the other way. Many prominent public high-profile wives do that. She was suffering from The *Jackie O Complex*, when a wife is in the ultimate state of denial about her husband's infidelity and in turn redirects her energy toward the children and her other pet projects. If the direct evidence is not presented in front of her, it doesn't exist.

As uncomfortable as it was for his clients, Cavanaugh continued the line of questioning.

Do you feel like you are innocent of the events surrounding this case?

How old were you when you officially met the defendant?

How old were you when you officially became a spiritual son?

Here is a list of gifts that you supplied as evidence before these proceedings. Attached is a signed affidavit that you stated that the mentioned items were given to you by the defendant.

Have you ever taken an out of state trip with the defendant? And if so when and where?

Have you ever taken a trip out of the country with the defendant? And if so when and where?

Now the next group of questions are going to be rather sensitive and sexually explicit. So just take a big deep breath and take your time when answering.

Have you ever had sexual contact with Mr. Short?

How many times?

How many times did Mr. Short initiate sexual contact?

Did you ever initiate sexual contact?

When and where and please be specific?

How many times?

Why did you continue to have sexual con-
tact with Mr. Short?
Were there any witnesses?
Did you ever tell anyone?
Why did you not tell anyone?

"And three last questions. Please take your time in answering them."

Do you feel like you were coerced into having sex?"
Do you feel like you were forced into having sex?"
Do you feel like you were raped?"

From the expressions on Mrs. Short's face, it was obvious that she did not know the depth of each relationship or any of the gory details. After the third hour, as my third client began to present his opening brief statement, she began to cry.

Cavanaugh turned and looked at her and paused for a moment. But realized that he had to do what was in the best interest of his clients. He continued the same direct and uncut line of questioning.

The defendant's attorney did not cross-examine any of the five plaintiffs. From the expression on his face, he was definitely surprised at the graphic inflammatory details of each relationship. Apparently, his client had not been completely forthcoming. It was now time for Cavanaugh to place Short in the hot seat.

After the fifth plaintiff testified, the mediator called a twenty-minute recess. When the process resumed, Cavanaugh directed the inquisition toward Short. During the questioning process, he presented each piece of evidence first to the mediator then to Stitt and Short.

Mrs. Short continued to cry.

"Mr. Stitt, are you sure you want your client's wife to continue to stay? She is obviously upset." He didn't say anything. Cavanaugh continued. "Okay. I guess that is a yes. Mr. Short, what type of relationship did you have with Mr. Ethan Griffin?"

"I plead the fifth on the grounds it may incriminate me."

"Was it ever sexual in nature?"

"I plead the fifth on the grounds it may incriminate me."

"Mr. Short, what type of relationship did you have with Mr. Colan Richardson?"

"I plead the fifth on the grounds it may incriminate me."

"Was it ever sexual in nature?"

"I plead the fifth on the grounds it may incriminate me."

"Mr. Short, what type of relationship did you have with Mr. Brandon Cooper?"

"I plead the fifth on the grounds it may incriminate me."

"Was it ever sexual in nature?"

"I plead the fifth on the grounds it may incriminate me."

"Mr. Short, what type of relationship did you have with Mr. Nicholas Devereaux?"

"I plead the fifth on the grounds it may incriminate me."

"Was it ever sexual in nature?"

"I plead the fifth on the grounds it may incriminate me."

"Mr. Short, what type of relationship did you have with Mr. Jonathan Devereaux?"

"I plead the fifth on the grounds it may incriminate me."

"Was it ever sexual in nature?"

"I plead the fifth on the grounds it may incriminate me."

Cavanaugh continued, "Has Mr. Ethan Griffin ever seen you naked including your penis and genitalia?"

"I plead the fifth on the grounds it may incriminate me."

"Has Mr. Colan Richardson ever seen you naked including your penis and genitalia?"

"I plead the fifth on the grounds it may incriminate me."

"Has Mr. Brandon Cooper ever seen you naked including your penis and genitalia?"

"I plead the fifth on the grounds it may incriminate me."

"Has Mr. Nicholas Devereaux ever seen you naked including your penis and genitalia?"

"I plead the fifth on the grounds it may incriminate me."

"Has Mr. Jonathan Devereaux ever seen you naked including your penis and genitalia?"

"I plead the fifth on the grounds it may incriminate me."

"Okay, I see where this is going. So is this how you plan to cooperate going forward. Okay, it's on you."

Then Cavanaugh gave several photos to Mr. Stitt and to the mediator for review.

"Mr. Cavanaugh is this really necessary! These are nude photos!" Stitt gasped.

"Of course," Cavanaugh continued. He could have ignored Stitt's comment but had to respond. "Mr. Stitt, just how well do you know your client? How forthcoming has he been regarding the details of the relationships with each of the young men. This is evidence. Believe me, if you think these photos are bad, just wait until you see some of the other evidence. Apparently, your cocounsel didn't school you about my relentless diligence to prove a case. Big mistake, very big mistake.

"Let me put some of my cards on the table. I am going to be frank as I only know how to be. As I stated earlier, I have in my possession iPads, iPhones, and passports belonging to my clients. I have over one hundred incriminating photos, pages and pages of emails, text messages, and numerous voicemail messages. I have copies of the case medical files and depositions from various psychiatrists who are currently treating each plaintiff. I have enough evidence that would prolong my case for ten entire weeks not including witnesses and subpoenaed documents."

Then he handed the pictures to the defendant. He refused to take them. So, Cavanaugh placed them on the table in front of him. He glanced at the pictures then quickly turned his head.

"What's wrong, Mr. Short? I thought you were going to fight these accusations with everything that you have. I told you I wasn't bluffing."

"You son of a bitch! How could you?" shouted Mrs. Short. She jumped up and stormed out. Short ran after her.

"I knew this would happen," said Cavanaugh.

The mediator called for a fifteen-minute recess.

"Liz, wait!"

"Get your damn hands off me! William, how could you allow me to walk into something like that? I feel like the worst type of fool. I asked you time after time after time, were any of these stories true? And you looked me in my face and said no. I stood next to you during the press conference, supporting you, holding your hand! Now I see! I was your perfect cover-up for all these years! Our marriage was a front for all of your dirty, scandalous deeds! The lies! The secrets! And the worst part of it all is the betrayal. And with men, of all things. And not just one but five. And there are probably others who just haven't come forward yet. I might have been able to understand if you were accused by young women. But with young men! Not much older than our sons. And you have been doing this for years. Years, William! And what about our boys? Oh my GOD!"

"I'm sorry. Please just don't leave me. I will get counseling."

"Huh, you need a lot more than counseling!"

"Liz, please. Please don't leave me. Please just don't leave me. We can work this out. We have been attacked before. Many times before. And you know that."

"Is that all you are worried about, my leaving you? If I leave you, then you will look even more guilty. That is the one thing that you don't have to worry about. Well, at least not right now. I have invested just as much as you have in this marriage and in building our church. Besides, if I left you right now, I would easily take half of everything you own and probably half of the church would follow me. You better be glad that I am not an irrational vindictive woman.

"First, you need to resolve this mess you have gotten us into. And I strongly advise you to take heed and listen to Mr. Cavanaugh. You need to settle this fiasco quickly. William, you could lose everything we have built. You have done so many great things over the years and you have been risking it all. Please don't let your bullish pride and your big ego prevent you from thinking rationally. Think about your children. Settle this mess quickly.

"We can continue this charade of a marriage because I have worked too damn hard to build this life to throw it all away. I'm not going to give up my current lifestyle just because of your indiscretions with those young boys. I have a reputation too. But for right now, I have to get the hell out of here. You know I am not a drinking woman, but I really need a strong one right now and that is exactly where I am headed before I do something really stupid."

"Let me explain."

"Explain what, William! What's to explain? Are you denying the things that I heard? What about the pictures!"

"I love you! Baby, please let me explain!"

"Shut up! You had your chance. I gave you too many opportunities to explain and tell me the truth. Or at least prepare me for what I might have heard today."

"But, baby!"

"Shut the hell up! Lies! More lies! William, how could you! How could you! You are poison! I have been a fool all these years."

She slapped him. She slapped him again. "You brought snakes into our garden. I can't wait until you meet your maker. And don't give me that sorry-ass line that the devil made me do it. Damn you, William. You are the devil. You have been using me all these years."

He grabbed her arm. "Wait, Liz! Please wait! Damn it, listen to me!"

"Get your goddamn hands off me! GOD knows that I am not a hateful, vengeful woman. But right now, I actually hate you. I hate you with every fiber of my being."

"But, baby, wait!"

Walking toward the elevator, with her back to him, she threw her hand up in a motion signifying that she was through with him. She had had enough. She didn't want to hear anymore. "Don't talk to me. Get away from me. And you need to find a place to stay for a few days. Well, at least until I wrap my mind around what I just heard and saw."

She stepped into the elevator, slowly turned around, and looked him in the eye with a cold and piercing stare. "You should be scared, very scared. I don't even know if the Almighty GOD HIMSELF can save you from this. Then again, why should HE. Maybe losing everything including your reputation is what you deserve."

As the elevator door closed, a single tear ran down her face.

Short returned but there was no sign of Mrs. Short. The mediation proceeded. Cavanaugh began again with more questions.

"Let's continue. So, Mr. Short, have you ever seen these photos."

"I plead the fifth on the grounds it may incriminate me."

"Is that you in these photos?"

"I plead the fifth on the grounds it may incriminate me."

"Have you ever seen a tattoo similar to the one in the photo?"

"I plead the fifth on the grounds it may incriminate me."

"Is it not true that you have a tattoo just like this in this photo?"

"I plead the fifth on the grounds it may incriminate me."

"Over the course of two years, did you take nude pictures and email or text them to Ethan Griffin, Colan Richardson, Brandon Cooper, Nicholas Devereaux, or Jonathan Devereaux?"

"I plead the fifth on the grounds it may incriminate me."

"Have you ever kissed, had oral sex, or had intercourse with Ethan Griffin?"

"I plead the fifth on the grounds it may incriminate me."

"Have you ever kissed, had oral sex, or had intercourse with Colan Richardson?"

"I plead the fifth on the grounds it may incriminate me."

"Have you ever kissed, had oral sex, or had intercourse with Brandon Cooper?"

"I plead the fifth on the grounds it may incriminate me."

"Have you ever kissed, had oral sex, or had intercourse with Nicholas Devereaux?"

"I plead the fifth on the grounds it may incriminate me."

"Have you ever kissed, had oral sex, or had intercourse with Jonathan Devereaux?"

"I plead the fifth on the grounds it may incriminate me."

Cavanaugh continued his questioning for over an hour. He drilled him about the extravagant gifts, the cars, the jewelry, iPhones, iPads, and the apartments, as well as the monetary gifts. He also drilled Short about each exotic trip disguised as a business trip or a church related conference. He asked Short was the church aware of these mentoring relationships. He also asked were these expenses paid from his personal account or from church funds. But Short stood his ground. He refused to answer the questions. His reply was the same: "I plead the fifth on the grounds it may incriminate me."

After Cavanaugh completed his questioning, the mediator adjourned the meeting for twenty minutes.

Short immediately left the room. Cavanaugh walked over to Stitt.

"Mr. Stitt, you and you client seemed very prepared several weeks ago when the two of you gave that award-winning performances at your press conference. You two stated that 'we plan to fight this with everything we have.' What happened?"

Stitt replied, "I knew that this case would be a challenge. For now, all I can say is that I will try to convince my client to settle."

"Yeah, right. Good luck but I don't see any success in that. His denial of any wrongdoing and his arrogance are only making my job easier," said Cavanaugh.

After the brief recess, the mediator addressed Cavanaugh regarding an offer.

"So, Mr. Cavanaugh, what do your clients want?"

Cavanaugh handed the mediator a document addressed to the court. It read,

> *Settlement Offer:*
>
> *As shown from the facts and evidence presented and contained herein, Plaintiffs have suffered immediate and long-term emotional and psychological injury.*
>
> *Plaintiffs pray for the following:*
>
> 1. *One million five hundred thousand dollars (five hundred thousand dollars each) in actual damages to be paid by Defendant.*
> 2. *Three years of weekly mandatory psychiatric counseling sessions for each Claimant.*
> 3. *All tuition, expenses, and fees to be paid associated with a four-year curriculum at a college or university to be chosen by Claimants. This is to be paid by Defendant.*

4. *Twenty-five million dollars (five million dollars each) in punitive damages to be paid by Defendant.*

5. *Plaintiffs' attorney fees and expenses to be paid by Defendant.*

Wherefore, in addition, Plaintiffs prays for the following:

That a temporary restraining order is hereby issued to Defendant enjoining him and restraining him from:

- *Harassing Plaintiffs.*
- *Having any physical contact with Plaintiffs.*
- *Speaking to Plaintiffs either by telephone, email, social media, text messaging, or in person at any place or at any time.*
- *Corresponding with Plaintiffs via mail, parcel post, or any other package.*
- *Corresponding with Plaintiffs via any other person.*

GIVEN UNDER MY HAND this _____ day of _____, 20___, at _____ o'clock, _____A.M./P.M.

_____

JUDGE,
FULTON COUNTY SUPERIOR COURT

Then Cavanaugh gave copies to Mr. Stitt and to Mr. Short. They didn't respond of course. But from the obvious facial expressions, they were shocked to say the least.

"Mr. Mediator, I request a few days to confer with my client to discuss this settlement offer," stated Mr. Stitt.

"I'm sure you do. Meeting adjourned."

As Cavanaugh walked down the hallway toward the men's room, he overheard Stitt and Short talking by the elevators. Stitt was actually yelling at his client. To avoid being seen, Cavanaugh quickly stepped back around the corner in an attempt to hear the conversation. Cavanaugh knew that eavesdropping on an attorney-client private conversation was unethical, but he didn't care. He just couldn't resist.

"Why the hell did you allow me to walk into a situation like that? I was completely blind-sided; completely unprepared. Will, how could you put me in that predicament? Man, I am well aware that I am your legal counsel and that I have been representing you for several years, but I also thought I was your friend. You have absolutely no respect for my profession as your legal counsel and that fact that my job is to protect you and your interests. But how in hell can I protect you when you are not forthcoming and when you blatantly lie to me. You made me look like a damn fool in there. Not to mention during the press conference. It's not just your reputation at stake here. I have asked you on numerous occasions. Do we have anything to worry about? From the first day that Cavanaugh came to your office, I have asked you over and over and over again, 'Will, I need to know if these boys really have anything on you.' Man, you know I don't like surprises.

"I should quit, but I am not. Considering all that I have heard today and all the evidence that I have seen, I will continue as your legal counsel. No one can minimize the damages as well as I can. Besides, there are not that many really good attorneys who will deal with your BS. No matter how much you pay them. As I always have, I will continue to represent you to the best of my ability, protect you and your interests, and negotiate the best deal. But for now, I need a few strong drinks. I will meet you at your condo at eight o'clock. And be ready because I need to know everything. And I mean everything! No more surprises, okay."

There was silence for a moment.

"I know I was rather harsh, but you really need to know how serious this is. So, are we cool? So, do you have anything to say? And what about Liz? I just hope that I don't have to refer you to a good divorce attorney because it looks like you might need someone way above my pay grade."

Short didn't respond. He just slowly turned and stepped into the elevator. As the elevator door closed, Cavanaugh stepped from around the corner and passed Stitt on the way back to the conference room. Stitt turned in his direction. Cavanaugh just smiled. He didn't say a word; he didn't have to. He thought to himself, *My job was done for the day.*

The mediator adjourned the next session for three days. Short's blatant denial and refusal to answer questions continued for the next three sessions. After several weeks of the defense team's delays, requests for a continuance and numerous failed negotiations, Cavanaugh petitioned the court to go to trial. The judge ordered continued negotiations until they could reach a reasonably mutual agreement.

CHAPTER 27

Kindred Spirits

The whispers in my life... GOD talking to me... I must listen...

TOMORROW IS THE big day, judgement day. But I still have so much to do.

After every major high-profile case that required working extremely long days and late nights, Cavanaugh usually needed to get away for a few days. His mind, body, and spirit required that he allowed himself to relax, relate, and reenergize himself. And this case was not much different; he was mentally and physically exhausted, completely drained. A four-day weekend of self-relating and soul searching was well deserved. He chose to vacation in the Turks and Caicos Islands in the Caribbean.

But because this case was so high profile, Cavanaugh had decided to quietly sneak out of town a few hours after the settlement proceedings. He intentionally wanted to avoid the media circus. He wanted to address them when he was ready. He had also instructed his clients to disappear until he returned.

The night before Cavanaugh was about to leave, he was alone in his bedroom sitting at his desk, preparing several to-do lists and delegating duties for his team during his brief vacation. Suddenly he felt a slight chill. He got up and walked into the sitting room and glanced at the French doors, but noticed that they were not open. *Hmmm,* he thought. After returning to his desk and completing the lists, he then began proofreading the closing arguments for another important civil case. He wanted to be prepared to hit the ground running as soon as he returned to town. As he continued to make slight adjustments to his legal brief, he paused for a moment. He thought he heard something. *Hmmm*, he thought again. *I really need some rest.* He continued to read again. This time he heard a distinct voice. "I know I am not hearing things."

"Dex?"

As Dexter turned around and looked up. He screamed, "Oh my GOD! Patrick! Man, is that you? It can't be!"

"Hey, buddy. Don't be afraid."

He dropped the papers and stumbled backward knocking over the desk lamp.

"Am I dreaming? Yes, that's it. I must be dreaming."

"No, you are not dreaming."

"Are you a ghost? I must be working too hard."

"No, I am not a ghost. There are no such things as ghosts."

"How is this possible? I don't understand? Are you real?"

"Dex! I need you to calm down and focus. Focus, man, focus! I need you to really focus. Do you understand?"

"No, not really. I don't understand. But I'm calm now," Dexter said with tears in his eyes, tears of sadness and joy.

"Man, I really didn't mean to scare you. I am here for a reason. So, I need you to pay close attention and listen carefully. I have transitioned, but my presence is here with you. Let me explain.

"I used to exist as a mind, body, and spirit, a trichotomy. When I transitioned, the three separated. My body was just a shell that housed my spirit. Now I exist only in the spirit form and I only appear to you as you remembered me.

"My presence will always be with those who loved me and well as with those who I loved. Do you remember how your great-grandmother used to visit in your dreams after she transitioned? It's the same thing. Well, kinda. Everyone leaves a part of themselves, a part of their hearts."

"Yes. I remember. She still comes to me when I am really going through difficult times. It is her way of telling me not to worry or stress. That everything was going to be okay. I usually wake up rejuvenated. And in many instances, I would wake up with answers. And I am usually at peace. Sometimes I wouldn't have to do anything. The problem would work itself out. I had to just be patient and wait.

I also realized that in most cases, I was worrying for no reason. The problem was not as detrimental as it seemed.

"My dreams of her were always happy dreams. Dreams of how she was when I was a child. Happy times. Before she became ill. When she was vibrant and full of life."

"Yes. That is GOD's way of sending you a message and HIS way of allowing you to deal with some of the problems in your life. Sometimes that is the only way, the only time HE has your undivided attention. That is when you are asleep. I see that you still get it. Most people don't. You are right. She comes to you indirectly to distract you and prevent you from thinking about problems. She is there to tell you that everything is going to be okay. Don't worry. Just continue to pray, even when you don't feel like praying. And never lose faith. As long as you continue to work hard and continue to trust in GOD and HIS Word, HE will do HIS part. And shortly after you had the dream, you found the answer to your problem or the problem was resolved. It was GOD blessing you, answering your prayer. But you had to pay attention and receive it. You allowed HIM to give you the blessing, as long as the blessing was in HIS will."

"But my great-grandmother never came to me directly. She never spoke to me directly. I only saw her in my happy dreams. But this is much different. You seem so real. And we are conversing."

"There are infinite ways to communicate—speech, sign language and hand gestures, and body language. But unfortunately, most people only use one, and that is speech. And you are also aware that there are different levels of spirituality, various levels of consciousness. You talked about this often."

"Yes, I remember."

"You always said how GOD sometimes speaks to us indirectly although we would prefer to hear a voice from the sky. HE communicates with us in many ways. Most of the time, HE communicates with us on a level of spirituality that most people don't pay attention too. HE sends us signs through visions and dreams, through incidents we refer to as coincidence and luck and through feelings like a mother's intuition. Others call it a six sense or the little voice inside each of us, the voice that we should listen to most of the time, but unfortunately, we don't. HE sends people to us to help us figure out things. Sometimes those people are there for just a moment, a brief season. Just for a particular reason. So that is why we must always be in-tuned with the levels of spirituality.

"Whether for a few moments, a few days, weeks, months, or several years; everyone you meet, you will meet them for a reason, a season or a lifetime. We rarely know which one. It is part of GOD's plan. Again, it is just another way that HE communicates with us. Sometimes we don't realize which one it is until it's too late. So, we must be alert and always pay attention because once in a while that reason may not be realized. And the very small window of opportunity might just slip through your fingers or before you know it that person is gone. Is any of this making any sense to you?"

Dexter shakes his head in agreement.

"Good. Again, pay attention. Life is a journey of planned and unplanned moments, experiences, and lessons. If we pay attention, the Holy Spirit will teach us things and GOD will communicate with us through these moments, experiences, and lessons. We must learn from these things so we can evolve and grow, thus become better people. We might need to learn a lesson or simply reach our goals or receive a blessing. No matter how short the time period of the interaction or the meeting with this person, the lessons have meaning that will affect you for the rest of your life. It is very important.

"How many times have you thought of someone you haven't seen in months or years and then that person calls you or sends you a text message or hit you up on social media? Or you run into the person in the grocery store and you say, 'Wow, I can't believe it, I was just thinking about you. You have been on my mind all day.' Or 'I saw so-and-so the other day, and we mentioned you. We were wondering how you were doing.'

"Things just don't happen. In such cases, elderly people say that the souls or spirits are getting together, something is about to happen. But most people call those occurrences luck, chance, or coincidence, but actually, they are unforeseen, unplanned events that happen at just the right moment. Messages in dreams and a mother's intuition are prime examples of spirits communicating. When a mother has an impromptu feeling that something is wrong with one of her children or if one of her children is in pain and she senses it, her subconscious spirit is communicating with her child's spirit. Although you didn't completely understand it, your intuition was correct on that day that your heart felt heavy and you couldn't stop crying but you didn't know why. That's why you were crying so much that day before you heard that my condition had worsened. Our spirits were connecting while I was transitioning."

Dexter interrupted, "How did you know that I was crying all that day? And that my heart was so heavy."

"Dexter, man, I know you. We are kindred spirits."

"Was I right?"

"Well, yeah."

"Well then."

Dexter continued, "The same thing happened when my great-grandmother, both grandmothers and my grandfather transitioned. The three of them died unexpectedly without much warning. On each occasion, I was out of town. All of a sudden, my heart felt heavy. I started crying and I couldn't stop, but I didn't know why. Later, I learned that each had just passed away. That's when I later realized that during those moments before I received the heartbreaking news that their spirits and my spirit were connecting with theirs as they were transitioning."

"Yes. You are correct. As I mentioned earlier that when such events happen in which spirits connect, the souls are getting together, something is about to happen. So pay attention to such events."

"Okay, I understand. But why have you come back."

"Do you remember when you came to my hospital room those four days before I transitioned? Of course you do."

"You knew I was there? I loved you so much. And I wondered if you ever really knew how much I cared and how important you were to me. I never truly told you enough."

"Yes, man. I heard every word. And to correct you, you told me in so many other different ways. And your intuition was correct. I was responding to you when I was kicking my foot. And just to let you know, it was not a mere muscle spasm or a reflex action when you saw me rise up although I was hooked up to all those monitors and the life support systems. I was letting you know that I heard you and that I loved you too.

"I will always be with you. It's just that GOD will allow you and I to communicate on a different level in a different way going forward. So, expect me to come when you least expect it. Listen for me to come. Hear my voice. Pay attention to unexpected things that remind you of me. Things like songs on the radio, television commercials, and movies and places that remind you of me. Pay attention to dreams that you might have about me. Pay very close attention. Sometimes these moments will be signs that I am here. My spirit is here.

"I am here because you need me. Sometimes GOD will communicate with you by allowing my presence to visit you. HE knows that I was one of the few people who would be totally honest with you. I would tell you the truth, whether it's the good, the bad, or the ugly. I would tell you what you needed to know not just what you wanted to hear. I was brutally honest with you, well, about 95 percent of the time. Going forward, you will need to hear the truth more than ever.

"Your life is going to change soon. You are about to be truly tested regarding a subject that is dear to your heart."

Dexter asked, "But is this personal or work-related? And will it affect other people, and if so, who?"

"You must do what you know is right as you always have. The Dexter B. Cavanaugh III that I knew follows his passion. Dex, you are being watched by many and you will be tested time and time again. Even by many in your inner circle. So, continue to focus on your passion and not your emotions; they are distinctly different. And listen to the Spirit in you. Again, it is the little voice inside you, the little voice that most people don't pay attention too. And because they ignore that little voice, they don't receive the blessings or the answers they are looking for. Pay attention to the subtle 'whispers' in your life. GOD is talking to you. You must listen."

"Yes. I will."

"And, Dex, one last thing, you haven't seen your best days yet. The best is yet to come."

"What do you mean?"

"You will see. Just pay attention."

"I just finished a really big case and lately I have had brief moments in which I question myself. This major case that I just won was personal. I really wanted to expose him. I put everything that I had in this case. Was I wrong?"

"Naw, you were not wrong, but let's be real. It was more than just exposing him. You wanted revenge against Stephanie Richardson, the coordinator of the homosexual deliverance ministry, for the way she made you feel. She partially blamed you for the issues between Marcellus and his wife. In addition, Bishop Short publicly condoned her actions. And deep down in your spirit you really know why you did it with such vengeance; you did it for me. You wanted to get even."

"How did you know?"

Patrick just smiled.

"You did the right thing. You will soon discover that this case is just the beginning. This case will cause the rocks to cry out, exposing others for their blatant judgmental hypocritical attitudes. Hopefully, things will eventually change in the African-American community as a result of your continued determination. And that's a good thing. And regarding the fall of Bishop Short, please don't blame yourself. You have no reason to feel guilty although those cases were the result of personal vendettas against him. It was his arrogance and narcissism and, most of all, his hypocrisy that caused his demise.

"Man, you did well! Very well! And, Dex, do me a favor. Try to relax, relate, and release. You must learn to be happy. Man, you really deserve it. You are a very special man. You have a lot to offer. And not just money. I know you. You have a lot of love to give too. My dear buddy, let love find you."

Dexter turned and reached for a tissue box on his desk. He wiped his face and looked up. The image was gone.

CHAPTER 28

Judgement Day

Confessions don't always heal the soul. Sometimes they make you face the consequences of your new reality. And if vengeance is mine, then payback will be a mutha!

THE JUDGE MANDATED continued mediation for an additional two weeks. With no agreement insight, Cavanaugh finally terminated the failed attempts to negotiate. The court set a date to begin trial for four weeks later. That must have really gotten Short's attention. Two days before the jury selection process was to begin, Stitt hand delivered a settlement offer to Cavanaugh. It took four months and thirteen days of delays and court ordered mediation to reach an agreement. An equitable settlement had finally been reached as a result of an extremely determined attorney, Dexter B. Cavanaugh III.

Although the plaintiffs' cases were similar and there was only one defendant, Cavanaugh thought it was in the best interest of his clients to file the cases separately instead of a class-action suit. Because of the complexity of the five cases and because of the fact that those cases might set precedence for future cases, the judge wanted to review all aspects of the mediation proceedings and the mediation records. He ordered that the final settlement proceedings be presented in his closed court. The media tried with grave effort to label this as a sex case, but it was not. This civil case was the result of "the abuse of power and reckless authority caused by a licensed professional in addition to numerous other ethics violations." Initially the judge tried to minimize the public spectacle surrounding this case by ordering a gag order by all parties, but the relentless media still found ways to sensationalize the case. To avoid another potential media circus, the judge mandated that all parties would be given only a one-hour notice to appear. His intent was that all the court proceedings would be concluded and all parties would have enough time to go into seclusion; if that was their preference.

Before the court officially reviewed and authorized the tentative settlement agreement that was accepted by the plaintiffs and their attorney, the judge allowed all parties to make a statement. Each plaintiff was given the option to address his statement to the court or directly to the defendant. Although unlikely, the defendant was also given an option to address the court or the plaintiffs. Conversely, each plaintiff had prepared a letter address to the defendant.

Cavanaugh intentionally prepared his clients for the mediation questioning and answering sessions. However, he had not prepared his clients regarding what to say in their personal statements. He only advised them to respect the court and to speak from the heart. He also advised each of them to address the defendant by his official title. He suggested that each letter begin as "Dear Bishop." Cavanaugh's past experience and his professional intuition said that at this point in the game, it was best to switch back and focus on their professional relationships with the defendant and his leadership title rather than their personal connection. Although he was sure that each letter would have an emotional touch.

First, Ethan Griffin walked in the courtroom and took the stand. Before he read his letter, he turned and addressed to the judge.

"Your Honor, this is not easy for me. I just want to personally thank the court for allowing me to make one last statement."

Then he took a deep breath and began.

> *Dear Bishop,*
> *Why did you do what you did, when you did, what you did to me? I will never understand.*
> *I put you first, first in every way. I turned away so many people that you did not approve of. Most were people who genuinely cared about me. Now that the scandal has become public, I have*

received letters, texts, and emails from a few of them confirming what they already suspected. Some of them said that they were not surprised at all because they already knew about us. Others even told me details regarding similar relationships in your past. Now I see that your history of developing these types of relationship has been a pattern of yours for many years. It was so difficult to read that you did some of the same things with so many other men my age. I don't feel special anymore. I feel dirty.

Now that reality is setting in, I have nothing. I have no one. But you have definitely taught me something. Something that I never wanted to learn. Something that will affect me for the rest of my life. And something that I will never be able to give someone else, ever. That is trust. I will never ever, never ever trust anyone again. I don't even trust myself anymore.

You pretended with me for the last three years. Three years that you stole from me. Stolen moments from which I don't think I will ever recover.

I truly feel that if you had told me the truth from the beginning, I would have been able to make the decision to walk into this situation with open eyes or to walk away. I would have been better pre-pared to handle my role in your life. I guess that you were not willing to risk my saying no.

It wasn't all bad, but right now, I can only focus on the ongoing deception and manipulation throughout our relationship. I am damaged goods. And now the entire world knows that I was being played. I thought I was in a special relationship with you. I was the chosen one. I allowed you to control every aspect of my life, my mind, and my body.

Now I see things much clearly. My plans for my future and your plans for my future were com-

pletely different. You used to tell me that everyone that I meet, I meet for a reason, a season or a lifetime so pay attention and focus on each meeting. It may last five seconds, five minutes, five years, or fifty years. You might meet this person because you have a need and they can help fulfill it. Sometimes it is as simple as that person saying something to you which gives you hope. Or he or she may be there to give you information that you might need at that time. Or vice versa. You might be the person they need for a moment. Everything that has happened between us has happened for a reason and a season. But it is obvious to me that your season together was much shorter than mine. I thought our season together would have lasted closer to a lifetime. Nevertheless, the effects of our relationship will affect me forever.

Then it was Colan Richardson turn to speak.

Dear Bishop,

You made me love you—the gifts, the money, the car, and the sex. I sold my soul for you, to be with you. I love you and I always probably will. But I also hate you. I feel so much heart-wrenching pain right now. It started when I found out about the others, and we began to share stories. I trusted you. I believed in you. I believed in us. I thought I was special. I thought that the things that we did; the intimate things were just between us. You said that I fulfilled a need that no one did.

I am not ashamed to admit that my present situation is not totally your fault. Once I discovered some things about you, I was still willing to continue the relationship. I took a risk and lost big time. Now I feel left out in the cold. You have something to fall back on. I don't. I have to start completely over.

That's going to be so very hard to do, getting to know someone and allowing feelings to develop. I have so much baggage going to my next relationship, but I will survive. One of the most difficult issues that I am still dealing with besides the obvious lies, manipulation, and deception is the fact that I gave up my two best friends to be with you. You felt that they hindered my growth. One died not truly knowing how much I cared for him. And the other wanted and waited patiently for another chance. Again, I have nothing to fall back on. I guess I have a lot of self-repairing to do.

Over the past two years, a few people tried to get close to me and warn me about you. Most just couldn't place their finger on it. Some said that there was something about our relationship that didn't seem right. Others hinted that I was not the only one. I thought they were "just hating". Now I see that they were right. So many people told me not to put all of my trust in you because it wouldn't last. They told me that I would get hurt in the end. But I didn't listen. Those who really knew me just couldn't believe I was behaving that way. I was acting out of character. Because I have so much time on my hands now, I can only think of all the "I told you so's".

That's another thing that I dread the most; all the humiliation. Everyone knows now. Everyone knows that for three and a half years; I was having a sexual affair with my pastor, a man old enough to be my father. Since this case was filed, there have been several moments in which I have just wanted to die. I know that this devastating pain will be with me for a while. It's going to be very hard, but eventually, it will subside. I have learned that although it will take some considerable time, I will get over you. I will survive. I have too.

> *I really don't understand how I got myself into this mess. Hopefully distance and time will allow me to begin to heal. As I have for months, I will continue to ask the LORD to take the pain away and replace it with something else as soon as possible.*

After a ten-minute recess, the next person slowly walked in and sat on the witness stand.

Cavanaugh approached him.

"Mr. Nicholas Devereaux, are you ready to make your statement?"

Still looking down at the letter in his hand, his client didn't say anything.

"It's okay, Mr. Devereaux, just try to relax and just take your time."

Cavanaugh handed his client a glass of water. He takes a sip.

"Now let's try again."

He took a deep breath and paused again. He unfolded the letter and attempted to read it. Just staring at the words and barely moving his lips but nothing came out. He looked up at Cavanaugh then he looked at Short. Then he turned to the judge.

"Your Honor, I really need help. I'm sorry but I can't do this right now. At this time, I must decline. I can't read it. I thought I was prepared to face him today. I spent several days writing this letter. I thought I was ready to put this behind me, but I just can't do this right now."

Then he looks at Short again.

"I am extremely depressed and ashamed to admit that I still want you back. I still love you, and I wish I could continue our special relationship. But I know that is not going to happen. I must be really messed up."

Then he looks at Cavanaugh again.

"I'm sorry, Mr. Cavanaugh."

Cavanaugh approached his client.

"It's okay."

Suddenly Nicholas refolded the letter, stood up, and gave it to Cavanaugh. Cavanaugh turned and gave it to the judge.

"Your Honor, I request that the letter is read at a later time," said Cavanaugh.

The judge stated that after all the other parties had read their statements, he would take a brief recess and read it in his chambers with the presence of both attorneys.

Nicholas stepped down and quickly rushed out of the courtroom.

Cavanaugh apologized to the court, sat down, and waited for his next client.

As each man read his statement, Short just sat there, motionless, showing absolutely no emotion. To everyone's surprise, he expressed none of his usual arrogant antics. He appeared to be in a trance.

The court clerk motioned the bailiff to ask the next plaintiff to come in. Brandon Cooper took the stand and read his letter.

> *Dear Bishop,*
>
> *You used your charisma, your wealth, and your status to entice me. I was naïve and impressionable in the beginning. I fell for you. I fell hard. When I began to figure out what you were doing, I didn't care because I was in too deep. But things are much different now.*
>
> *I am angry. Naw, scratch that. I am more that angry.* I am mad! *And I want you to feel the pain that I feel. I wish you could feel the mental anguish, the disappointment, and the self-loathing that I feel right now. My heart is truly broken. I wouldn't wish the pain I am feeling right now on my worst enemy—well, excluding you. I need some relief right now.*
>
> *Everyone calls me the victim. I might be a victim right now, but hopefully, one day soon you will reap what you have sowed. I hope that one day you will experience what I feel—emptiness—because I*

learned that I have been used and abused without even knowing it for over three years.

I wish I could tell all who would listen, who you really are. Everywhere I go, people look and stare, with looks of shame and pity. Others look at me with disdain and hatred, blaming me for trying to destroy your church and for hurting the first lady. Even the treatment I receive from those close to me is different. Although they say that they understand, I see the truth in their eyes. I will probably have to leave town; leave my family and my friends.

And lastly, I really don't understand why you are still in denial. Your press conference was unbelievable. Better be glad that you came to your senses and decided to settle because I was prepared to tell everything. And I really mean every detail. And why not? I have nothing else to lose now.

Well, today, it looks like the judge is being judged. Again, I truly hope you reap everything that you have sowed.

And finally, Jonathan Devereaux took the stand.

Dear Bishop,

I was in love with a narcissist. I couldn't help it. I still love you, but I also hate you. I think much of the hurt that I feel is based on the fact that I thought I was the only one. The chosen one to serve you in special ways that no one else could. You chose me. I felt special because I was the chosen one.

But the most disappointing thing is that the things you were doing to me, you were doing to my brother. You were having sex with my brother too. My twin brother. My other half. My better half. I guess you told him the same story too. Both of us fell for the lies. Both of us were manipulated.

*This has dramatically changed our relation-
ship forever. We were so close. The trust between us
is gone. I lost my best friend. I feel like a part of me
has died.*

When Jonathan Devereaux left the courtroom, Cavanaugh addressed the court.

"Your Honor, all plaintiffs have made their statements."

Then the judge addressed the defense attorney. Mr. Stitt replied that no statements would be made on behalf of the defense.

The judge asked all attorneys to join him in his chambers to read the letter from Brandon Cooper. The judge read the letter silently, then he gave it to Cavanaugh to read aloud.

Dear Bishop,

*It's obvious that I really need help because
I still want you. I still love you. I would give the
money back. I feel inconsolable. I feel abandoned.
I have no one now. I wish I could just walk away
from all of this. If we could turn back the clock and
go back to the way things used to be; the way we
used to be. I am not really handling this as well as it
may appear. I am really angry and disappointed at
myself for allowing this to happen.*

*The pain is too deep right now. When someone
influences your emotions directly or indirectly, that
means that they control you. So, I guess that you still
have much influence over me because I can't forgive
or forget. Well, maybe in time but not right now.*

*Some say that if you douse enough money on a
problem, the problem will go away. All the money in
the world can't fix my heart right now, but hopefully
with this settlement, I will drown myself in things
that will start the process of my healing.*

*What's done is done. I can't turn back. The
damage is done. After all I have been through, who*

can I turn too? Not even my brother. And my mom even looks at us differently. Actually, I really don't want to be around anyone. I need to be alone. The only thing that can help me is prayer. My need for prayer will get me through this. I need some quiet time—some quiet time with just me and the LORD.

"Thank you, Your Honor. I might not be qualified to say so, but this is not normal. The letters that we heard were extremely unusual. My clients need help. It is obvious that they are still suffering. Although I am not a psychiatrist, my experience tells me that they need continued long-term serious counseling, treatment that might include medication."

All parties returned to the courtroom. The judge made a brief statement to both parties, mostly legal jargon.

Suddenly the proceedings were interrupted. A man sitting on the back row stood up.

"Excuse me, Your Honor. I truly apologize to the court, but I have something to say."

One of the bailiffs rushed toward the back of the courtroom to restrain the stranger and escort him out.

"Bailiff, wait! What is this about?" the judge said as he motioned the man to come forward.

"Objection, Your Honor!" exclaimed Stitt.

"Sit down, Mr. Stitt."

To everyone's surprise, anxiously walking down the aisle was the mourner from Patrick's funeral.

"Stop there!" He ordered him to stop a few feet behind the attorneys' tables.

"My name is the Reverend Dr. Trenton D. Woodrow."

"Yes, I know who you are. And that is the only reason I stopped the bailiff and that you are not being held in contempt of court. Now you have sixty seconds, and it better be good. Court recorder, please stop recording."

"Again, I truly apologize to the court. I have something to say, and it indirectly relates to this case. Your Honor, may I approach."

"No! Absolutely not! Sir, my courtroom is not a circus. Minister or no minister, your theatrics are not amusing."

The man did not respond. The judge paused a moment. He glanced at Cavanaugh, then Stitt and then at Short, then back to Cavanaugh, then Stitt and then at Short again. Then he stared at the minister. The judge noticed the pain and anguish on the minister's face. The judge's grimace turned to slight concern. This man was serious. He actually appeared to have something relevant and important to say. To everyone's surprise, the judge stood up with gavel in hand.

"This court will take a twenty-minute recess. Both attorneys, the defendant and you, pointing to the minister, follow me. Oh, and also, court recorder, and, Mr. Bailiff, I need you also."

All followed the judge to his chambers as instructed. He ordered everyone to sit except the minister.

"Now say what you have to say."

"I was a very special friend of Patrick McIntyre. Mr. McIntyre passed away earlier this year from complications of an apparent accidental overdose of prescription drugs. He was prescribed drugs for depression as a result of his being stripped of all his administrative responsibilities in the defendant's church. Mr. McIntyre was an executive administrator and dedicated leader of the defendant's church for over seven years. He was one of the two primary visionary architects directly responsible for the current growth and financial success of the defendant's megachurch.

"Your Honor, Mr. McIntyre was homosexual. His private life was completely separate from the church, and it did not affect his professional roles and responsibilities in the ministry. Actually, very few people even knew he was homosexual—well, not until the witch-hunt began.

"During an official board meeting officiated by the defendant, Mr. McIntyre was ordered to participate and successfully complete all twelve sessions facilitated by the homosexual deliverance ministry, an outreach ministry in the defendant's church. The main goal of this ministry was to supposedly 'cast out the demonic spirit' and cure him of his homosexual tendencies. Mr. McIntyre rejected the ultimatum and in return, he was terminated. When knowledge of his personal business quickly spread throughout the church, he became ostracized by most of the senior clergy. As a result, the stress of being an outcast motivated him to leave the church. He felt that it wasn't fair. And it wasn't. That church and his role in that ministry was his life. He was consumed. He gave his blood, sweat, and tears to help build the membership as well as the financial stability to where it is today—well, before the scandal. That drastic change caused the onset of deep depression and stress. He was very successful in masking a lot of things, one in particular. But as hard as he tried, he simply couldn't mask the pain, the pain that resulted from the wrongful termination and from the unjustified blatant rejection. Soon after, he was diagnosed as manic-depressive and was prescribed several drugs to stabilize his volatile mood swings and severe bouts with depression. Before the defendant started his campaign to become a bishop, Mr. McIntyre's personal life had never been an issue. The church unofficially practiced a 'don't ask, don't tell' policy. And because he performed one of the most high-profile and pivotal roles in the administration and because he was successful in exceeding his goals, it was never addressed. It only became a problem when the defendant implemented his mission and began his campaign to 'clean house' referencing a certain group of men. All the while, he was practicing homosexuality with several of his young parishioners as well as committing the other egregious acts in which he has been accused. If that was not the most blatant display of hypocrisy, I don't know what is.

"Your Honor, of course the defendant did not force those pills down his throat. However, I feel that the defendant's overt actions and blatant hypocrisy were indirectly responsible for the death of Mr. McIntyre. He directed the church board to fire Mr. McIntyre. His deliberate self-serving actions served as the catalyst that sparked the chain of events that eventually led to the accidental death of my special friend. Your Honor, I am a minister, and yes, I admit that I am passing judgment on him. But in this case, it is warranted. The defendant needed to be taught a lesson, so I initiated these cases against him. There had been much speculation in the Black clergy for many years regarding the defendant's unmitigated gall regarding his hypocritical actions. So shortly after Mr. McIntyre's untimely death,

I became aware of the special relationships that the defendant had with these specific young men. So I implemented the chain of events that brought us here today. Not only did he need to be taught a valuable lesson, but along with that, he needed to be punished severely. And one way was to expose his behavior over the last twenty years."

Then the minister turned and sneered at Short.

"Someone needed to finally judge this holier-than-thou judge himself. So I motivated these young men to file suit. All that they have said is true. He needs to pay, and pay dearly. And from what I have been told, he is still claiming his innocence."

He glanced at Short again with another stare of contempt.

"It appears that he still has no remorse for his actions. And since he still admits to no wrongdoing, then maybe he will have to pay millions. And when the details of this scandal become even more public, maybe there will be a slight chance that he will humble himself, show at least an inkling of remorse and drastically curtail his behavior."

"So why are you here? What do you want?" asked the judge.

"Your Honor, I know that my remarks today will not be included in the court records of this case and that a settlement has already been made. I just wanted the defendant to hear from me that I was the one responsible for starting this. This was personal. I also wanted him to know as well as the court to understand how many lives he has destroyed. Mr. McIntyre's public out-casting was only one of many experienced by many young men who were members of the defendant's church. This was retribution. So, if any of my comments today will influence the court to add a stiffer punishment than the out of court agreement, then my job will be done. I will feel vindicated. And Mr. McIntyre's untimely death would not be in vain. His memory would no longer be tarnished. And lastly, hopefully my friend would finally be able to rest in peace."

After another brief recess, the proceedings readjourned and the judge read the final settlement details. Stitt nor his client wanted to make a statement. Short never admitted any wrongdoing. He fought diligently to give the plaintiffs absolutely nothing. When most people say that it's not about the money but it's about the principle, and usually it is about the money. Cavanaugh and his clients wanted to make a statement, and apparently, they did. But off the record, Cavanaugh always knew that his clients were only thinking about their financial security although he never disclosed his true thoughts. He also always knew that his clients were not completely innocent. They definitely played an important role. They grew up in the streets. They grew up around hustlers. They knew the game. It was about the money. They knew what they were doing when they became involved with Bishop Short. Fame and fortune was their goal. They wanted a shortcut to greatness. Well, in a way, now they finally have it. They definitely got what they wanted—financial security.

The total settlement included four hundred and fifty thousand each in actual damages and nineteen million eight hundred thousand in combined punitive damages, which was to be placed in five separate trust annuity accounts. The court ordered that a few specific guidelines be placed on the allocations of the settlement. Each claimant was assigned a court appointed a trust administrator to manage each account. Monthly payments would be dispersed to each claimant over a ten-year period. Other stipulations included twelve months of biweekly mandatory psychiatric counseling sessions for each claimant to be paid by the defendant. Each was also ordered to enroll in a college or university within the next three months, the costs to be paid from the settlement. The defendant was ordered to disband his mentoring programs affiliated with his church. The defendant agreed to three years of mandatory psychiatric counseling. Quarterly psychiatric progress reports for all parties would be forwarded to the court.

And of course, Cavanaugh and his firm received the standard fee of the award plus expenses. Strict confidentiality agreements were signed between all parties. But after all legal fees and expenses were subtracted, each plaintiff actually received between two million three hundred thousand and three million forty-nine thousand. The settlement also specified that all parties, including the attorneys, could not disclose any details of the cases. Tell-all books were also banned. No interviews were to be given via any media outlets. This included all forms of social media. If anyone violated any part of the agreement, he would forfeit future disbursements of the award.

At the end of the mediation proceedings and after the courtroom had cleared, Cavanaugh had begun to pack his files.

"What a day, what a day," Cavanaugh said to himself.

Feeling a little stressed and exhilarated at the same time, he suddenly began to question himself again. He wasn't sure what to think. The day he had been waiting for had finally arrived. He should have been jumping for joy. He had absolutely no doubt that he would win, but for some reason, he did not feel like celebrating. But this case was unprecedented, especially in the African-American community, not to mention the Black Church. Winning this case would force this issue to be seriously discussed, possibly causing change, change for the better.

"Was it all worth it? Was it really worth it? Exposing this taboo issue for all mainstream America to see; exposing this man of his hypocritical secrets and while destroying his empire. Or was it strictly a disguised subliminal act of simple revenge?"

Cavanaugh achieved the intended outcome. He got what he wanted. But he wasn't sure how to feel. Suddenly he snapped out of his temporary moment of insanity. Then he slapped himself and smiled.

"What the hell is wrong with me! Hell, yes! And I would do it all over again if I had the opportunity."

As soon as he turned on his phone, he started receiving numerous text messages. But he ignored them. He casually glanced at the time and noticed the date. He had been so busy that he did not realize what day it was. That date had a much deeper meaning, than most had realized. He just smiled; today was Patrick's birthday. What irony. He paused for a moment, then he looked up and turned to leave. Suddenly he stopped in his tracks. And there he was; Patrick sitting in the far-left corner of the courtroom. With his arms folded, Patrick smiled and nodded in approval. Cavanaugh smiled back at him. His phone rang. He glanced at the number then sent the call to voicemail. When he looked up again, his best buddy was gone.

Short and his wife stayed together. She convinced herself that she could not divorce him. She was not going to give up her position in the church and her position in the community. Acquiring the role as the first lady of one of the largest megachurches in Atlanta was a position that she could not and would not give up easily. She was not going to allow her social status to change. She was not giving up her life, a lifestyle that she had been accustomed to for over twenty years. It was also rumored that he paid her to stay. There was a possibility that the magnitude of the ongoing backlash would be minimized a little if she was at his side. They continued to perpetrate the façade of a marriage. They only made formal public appearances together regarding the church and formal social parties as well as activities involving the children. But behind closed doors were a different story. They continued to live separate personal lives, separate bedrooms, and separate vacations. She stated that a marriage is more than about love. It was now just a business.

When Short made his first public appearance denying the scandalous charges, his church congregation rallied around him with overwhelming support. He continued to campaign that Satan and evil spirits were once again determined to tear down and destroy what he had spent so many years trying to build, a worship center, a family center and a community training center. But when the members found out that the case was in mediation, many questioned his actions and they quickly began to change their tone. Eventually the number of members slowly dwindled from over twenty thousand to less than five thousand. Several members stated that they did not understand why he would consider settling. And why would he want to avoid his day in court to prove his innocence. He had told them that the accusations were all lies and that he was ready to fight with everything he had. He was looking forward to his day in court. Short eventually stepped down as the leader and senior pastor for one year. The following year he retired and became the bishop emeritus. He also lost all his corporate and collegiate board memberships as well as his official positions in the elite cliques of the upper echelon of national ministers.

Cavanaugh's groundbreaking victory spawned numerous other similar cases throughout the country. The constant negative multimedia exposure and local gossip eventually resulted in the fall from grace of several charismatic, prominent false prophets. Their inspiring, holier-than-thou public images and stellar reputations were drastically diminished. Their level of respect, popularity, and success in the Christian world would be changed forever. Publicly and painfully imploded, these scandalous shake-ups also prompted the beginning of the spiraling decline in the continued unprecedented growth of several of the largest ministerial empires in the African-American communities.

CHAPTER 29

The Silent Fraternity

TIME HAD FINALLY come again to close another one of life's chapters and to begin a new one for *The Silent Fraternity*. A combination of soul searching, reminiscing, and renewing commitments of brotherhood brought the close friends together to reflect, to grow spiritually, and to celebrate life. Lisborn, Emerson, Chance, Parker, and Dexter decided to meet in Bora Bora, a luxury resort destination island in the South Pacific for New Year's. They had a ritual of planning a lavish group vacation getaway every year for the last four years. But this year, the rendezvous would be a little different because Patrick would not be there. The last day of the trip, Dexter planned a surprise, a special night for everyone at the beach; a tribute in honor and remembrance of their best buddy.

Instead of having five days filled with sightseeing, scheduled tours, shopping, and clubbing at night, the fellows focused on just the opposite. The men experienced valuable quality time filled with moments of relaxation and rejuvenation over the past several days. But their cheerful dispositions slowly turned into seemingly endless moments of silence and far off gazing. Once again, reality was setting in. The once joyful peace was replaced with acute melancholy. But the meticulously well-planned intimate soirée on the last evening culminated into which was to be a memory that would give much solace to the small group of close comrades.

The men met to watch the final sunset. The blinding bright orange sun slowly cascaded down over the horizon. The crisp evening air carried gentle cool vapors lightly spraying the faces of those nearby. They soon retired to their private bungalows to rest. An hour later, wearing all white linen and barefoot with their pant legs slightly rolled up to avoid getting wet, the men met in front of Dexter's cottage. He suggested that they take a casual stroll several yards down the beach.

Lisborn noticed a glowing white structure in the distance.

"What is that?"

"Gentlemen, welcome to A Night of Ten Thousand Lights," said Dexter. "You know I could not let this week end without planning something very special for my boys."

As the men came closer to the illuminating white vision, they recognized what it was, a white gazebo draped with shear white curtains. It was also covered with numerous loosely hung stringed lights. The faint contemporary instrumental jazz soon became distinct. It was Boney James, David Sandborn, and Winton Marcellus on the sax, all their favorites. As they stepped into the elevated structure, an ornate silver and crystal candelabra centered on a large round white linen table cloth dominated the platform. The tastefully decorated table was adorned with five formal place settings which included Wedgwood china and Waterford Crystal stemware. The elaborate décor was accented with white roses and candles as well as silver and marquisate ornaments.

Three attendants wearing white tuxedos greeted them in unison, "Good evening, gentlemen, and welcome."

"Dude, you really outdid yourself."

"Man, I'm speechless."

"Hey, dude, this is really nice."

Dexter just smiled. Then he replied, "Sit. Eat. Drink. And enjoy."

Dexter did not miss a single detail in his planning. His extreme attention to detail was seen everywhere. Everyone sat in his assigned seat.

The bright full moon glistened over the calm ocean forming an endless silver street, providing a most whimsical natural backdrop. As soon as they seated, suddenly the contemporary instrumental jazz was replaced by a string quartet, only adding to the ambience of an anticipated private special evening. The men enjoyed a catered five-course gourmet seafood dinner and several bottles of wine. Later, Dexter initiated a casual midnight stroll under the stars. The men talked and laughed for hours, reminiscing about the past year and their fondest memories of their friend Patrick.

Dexter said, "I was thinking about not coming this year. But I definitely would have regretted it. I didn't think I could handle Patrick not being here. So that's why I planned this special evening in remembrance of him. I had a great week. This trip ranks in my top three ever. Well, considering. Being here with you guys and the moral support you all have given me this past year has definitely reinforced my relationship with each of you. I feel even much closer to all of you than ever before. Although our close buddy is no longer with us, we must continue these annual getaways. I really need this. I need all of you too."

Parker and Emerson nodded in agreement.

"Yes, I definitely agree too."

"I love all of you. You guys are my closest friends, my best buddies, my confidants, my ace boon coons, the brothers I never had. We possess a bond that most people, most Black men, would die for."

Sharing special moments just before the beginning on another new year, inspired a re-commitment of their unconditional love, the fellows were once again back at the gazebo. The attendants approached the table with a silver tray with five long stem crystal glasses filled with champagne and a plump strawberry dancing at the bottom. It was now one minute until midnight on the last night of the year, the ending of a year of great sadness, redemption, and triumphs. It would soon be the start of endless possibilities for all. Dexter stood.

"Fellas, let us stand and toast to our brother, Patrick. May he rest in peace? May his light continue to shine through us? May we continue to smile when we think of him? May our memories of him fill our hearts with love for our fellow man? Life is short. May we continue to live life to the fullest as he always did?" They all smiled and raised their glasses and drank.

"And may we continue this celebration every year for the next fifty years?"

The guys chuckled.

"Well, it could happen, GOD willing."

They all laughed and nodded in agreement.

After dinner, they strolled several yards along the beach, close enough to the low tide to allow their feet to be covered with cool receding white foam.

The three attendants approached again and handed each man a white Chinese paper and bamboo lantern. Each man lit the candle inside the lantern and in unison threw it in the air. As the light ocean breeze carried the glowing opaque symbols higher and higher, one could only hear the sound of the roaring waves of the receding tide.

As the lanterns disappeared far off in the distance, the men stood there a few moments, admiring the magnificent view and sound of the thrusting waves against the naturally sculptured rocks. A scene resembling dancing waves accompanied by frequent alternating currents mimicking a seemingly harmonic tune.

Then they turned, holding hands in a circle. As a tribute to their friend Patrick, they recited a new *Silent Fraternity Mantra*.

> *GOD loves me and I love myself.*
> *I deserve the best of everything.*
> *I will continue to strive to be the best that I can be.*
> *Inside—my heart, my mind, and my spirit—and*
> *Outside—my health, my body, my finances and lifestyle.*
> *I will not allow anything or anyone to stop me.*
> *I am worthy of the best!*
> *I deserve the best!*
> *As long as I work hard, give my all and keep the faith; I can have it all.*
> *I want it, and I am going to get it.*
> *Nothing but death can keep me from it.*
> *Every morning as I wake,*
> *I will continue to take a moment to retreat to that quiet place*
> *Within the pit of my soul and*

Unleash my right to decide what is best for me.
My commitment as a "G" Man.
We are The "G" Men, The Gentlemen until
the day we die.

EPILOGUE

Silent Anguish
Confessions

Confessions really do cleanse the soul, even if no one hears them but GOD.

October 24
9:11 p.m.

Dear GOD,

I have a confession. And this is Major; a Big One. I know that YOU already know, but I really need to tell YOU anyway. YOU are the only one I can turn to. The only one I can talk to. The only one who knows the excruciating pain I have been enduring over the past three months. All hell is breaking loose in my life; all because of something that I have done. I behaved as a willfully participant. And the only reason that I am telling YOU in the form of this letter is that hopefully this letter will be the first step in my recovery. I need to release this and hopefully it will set me free.

Well…I was involved in a personal and sexual relationship with Reverend Dr. Trenton D. Woodrow. Trent, as he originally introduced himself. I didn't plan it; it just happened. It lasted for three years, five months, and eight days.

Of course, when he approached me, I did not know who he was. Completely unaware and unprepared for what was about to happen, the events during the rest of that day seemed to be a nebulous blur. Apparently, my obvious naïveté and my initial curiosity prompted me to accept his invitation to give him a massage in a hotel only within a few hours after our initial brief introduction. The massage led to an intimate encounter. This weekly and sometimes biweekly routine of seduction continued for several months in various hotels.

When he finally disclosed who he was and that he was married and that he had a family, I still treated him as Trent, my special friend, not Reverend Dr. Trenton D. Woodrow, senior pastor of one of the largest churches in Atlanta. A strong bond quickly developed into what he often referred to as a deep-rooted spiritual connection between the two of us. The romantic relationship was solidly based on friendship and an overwhelming amount of what I thought was mutual respect. I saw him as just a man; not as a minister and I did not acknowledge all the other professional titles that he had acquired. The relationship filled a void in his life as well as provided him access to an emotional place of solitude, an outlet to retreat and get away from all of the pressures of life. When I used to say that everyone that I meet, I meet for a reason, a season or a lifetime, he would reiterate by saying that our season could be for twenty years. I now know that the effects of our relationship will affect me for a lifetime.

Although we were very discreet, I learned later that he loved me so much that he was willing to risk including me in every aspect of his life including his ministry and his business. Initially I shunned the idea. He also wanted to include me in his family life. Initially I consciously avoided any contact with his personal life. I was still reluctant. However, he convinced me to reconsider. That was a decision that turned into a major gift for him because several months later, the relationship became much more complicated. But for me, the issues soon began.

I was exclusive. When he called, when I was available, I usually dropped everything and came running as soon as I could. But when he called me from out of town while attending a funeral in Chicago last November of the previous year, an argument ensued. I had heard rumors that I was not the only man. And when I asked him about it, his response was that he was not going to answer that question. And that it was none of my business. And that I should just focus on us and not him and anyone else. Boy, what a reality check. I guess I couldn't see through those rose-colored glasses. He was right. He really wasn't mine. I was in love with a narcissist. I was in deep. Real deep. I couldn't help it. Unfortunately, I still love him, but I also hate him sometimes. Well, I think I just hate the way he makes me feel sometimes. Actually, it's the way in which I allow him to treat me and those negative feelings are internalized. But the hate does not last for long. I think much of the hurt that I feel is based on the fact that I thought I was the only one. The chosen one to serve him in special ways that no one else could. He chose me. I felt special because I was the Chosen One. But that was the final straw. I refused to share him with another man. As a highly educated, professional man, I was extremely unrealistic and foolish. What was I thinking? He cheated on his wife. Why should I expect him to be faithful to me? And I know that I was not his first male affair; he told me so.

I was done. Of course, it wasn't easy. So, I walked away from the situation as I called it, that day, mainly because of my insecurities and my trust issues. I cared about him very much, but I was not going to compromise by sharing him with another man. He had pushed me to my limit. The life that I had was about to change and there was no turning back. I was going to give it up. My ending all contact was a difficult decision, but I was okay. I was fine.

While he was still out of town, he called me several times a day as well as sent numerous text messages. I guess he didn't take me seriously. When he returned, I continued to ignore all of his calls. I was ready to put all of this behind me. My mind was satisfied. I did what I had to do. I felt that I had done the right thing. Now I was ready to settle my spirit. I needed the peace and solitude that I usually achieved during quality time with YOU, LORD. I prayed and meditated for several weeks constantly asking YOU to help me. I needed YOUR continued guidance. I needed YOUR continued grace and mercy. I needed YOU to heal my heart. I begged YOU so many nights when I was alone. That was the first time that I actually told YOU that I would do anything, if YOU would take away all the love I had for that man and replace it with more love for YOU. And I meant ANYTHING!

Then in January of the following year, he appeared at my door. It wasn't easy, but I didn't answer. He continued to call several times daily and he left numerous cards and gifts at my doorstep. Suddenly, a few weeks passed without any calls. Then on a Sunday, shortly after church, the calls started again. I ignored the first few calls. Then I finally made a decision that I still regret. I answered his call.

There were many great memories. I accompanied him on various business trips and we attended several concerts together. The Anita Baker concert at Chastain Park was my favorite. A few weeks later, we celebrated his birthday in Antigua and Barbuda, a small island country in the Caribbean. We also continued to have secret hotel rendezvouses and intimate massages at my home as well as numerous outings and meals together. The most recent on this past Sunday night after the LORD'S Supper at the church that I currently attend.

I took a really big risk and allowed him back into my life. I wasn't ready. Things were much different. He reiterated that I didn't appreciate what we had. He said that I had disappointed him and hurt him too much. He said I even made him cry several times, one time while in Antigua and Barbuda. No man ever made him cry, not even his father. He still often says that he cared too much. The last time was last night.

Now the tables are turned. Now I am miserable. I desperately need to get out of this situation and move on. We are not good for each other. This situation is not the safe haven that it used to be. My insecurities sometimes get the best of me. In turn, he accuses me of trying to control him or handle him as he calls it.

On this past Sunday night, I was attending the monthly LORD'S Supper service at the church that I attend. Suddenly he walked in thirty minutes late and sat close to the front. I lost focused. I desperately wanted to leave, but I stayed. Besides he would have noticed. And as soon as the service was over, I left. But before I could even make it to my car, he texted me. After a brief conversation, we met for dinner, but I couldn't eat. It was extremely difficult for me to say no to him.

Over the past several months, I tried to deal with this situation the best way that I could. Including therapy and attending at least four different church services a week. And of course, prayer and more prayer. I would make progress for several weeks then something happen and I would have a setback. I should have never answered his call during this past January. This man has a hold on me that I can't break. LORD, I know that the flesh is weak. And that this is spiritual warfare. I am not making excuses. I played a grave part in this. I simply can't get this man out of my head. As a result, I have serious bouts of depression. Prayer is helping. Therapy is helping but this situation is extremely toxic for me. And I realize it is my fault.

It sounds stupid when I say it but he made me love him. I am learning more and more about him every day. I truly underestimated his abilities to manipulate. He is not a stupid man. Not stupid by far. His charisma and laid-back, easy-going persona only masked his shrewd and cunning ability to persuade others to do what he wants; the way he wants it. He knew what he was doing; doing to me. I sold my soul for him; to be with him. I love him and I probably always will. But as l stated before I also hate him. I feel so much heart wrenching pain right now. It started when I found out about the others. I trusted him. I believed in him. I believed in us. I thought I was special. I thought that the things that we did; the intimate things were just between us. He said that I fulfilled a need that no one did.

I am not ashamed to admit that my present situation is not totally his fault. Again, I played a huge part. Once I discovered some things about him, I was still willing to continue the relationship. I took a risk and lost "big time." Now I feel left out in the cold. He has someone and something to fall back on. I don't. I have to start completely over.

LORD, I know that hating someone is not good, but I can't help it. Holding on to this hatred means that he still has control over me. I have enough evidence to destroy this man's life; his stellar personal and professional reputation in the community and in upper echelon of Black clergymen, his ministry, his teaching career, his family and probably his marriage, BUT I CAN'T. I want to just walk away and never look back as I did almost a year ago. A grave compromise would be to try to just love him at a distance as I have others. As soon as I think I am strong enough to move on, I am pulled back in this situation, but with a stronger grip.

GOD you know that I ask YOU daily to rid me of these emotions. Erase my memory. I would give everything that I own to turn the clock back. The wide spectrum of emotions that I deal with weekly is partially the result of this situation. I attend biweekly therapy sessions. I also attend intense daily spiritual study sessions.

LORD, no one knows the personal hell that I have been going through the past several months but YOU. I am a prime example that outer appearances can be very deceiving. It appears as though my life is great. I am so stressed. I am so sick and tired of being sick and tired.

It was wrong on so many levels. I am truly sorry to those who will be affected by this heart-wrenching confession. It was never my intention to hurt our families as well as any other innocent party, but I have no choice. A true confession seems to be the only viable option. I have tried everything else to try to get this man out of my head. All other attempts have failed. As hard as it is for me to ask, LORD, please forgive me for all that I have done and what I am about to do. I know I have no right to ask for YOUR mercy because I don't deserve it.

I have proactively and overtly guarded our secret as well as aggressively protected his reputation and his family. My first thought is to close my heart but it hurts too much. I am determined to LIVE, LOVE and LAUGH again. I should not be experiencing this emotional turmoil during this point in my life.

I have asked myself a thousand times, "What good will come out of this confession." I often reference the statement, "The only way to quickly kill a snake is to chop off his head." My open confession will destroy this relationship and there will be, no turning back.

GOD, please have mercy on my soul and for all involved.

Again, I come to YOU because of who YOU are and how YOU are. YOU are still called Wonderful Counselor. YOU hear my heart. YOU understand me. YOU love me unconditionally. YOU will not forsake me. YOU will forgive me.

I come to YOU because I am determined not to give Satan any credence over my emotions regarding what I have done. He is the master manipulator.

I must remember YOUR WORD. I am established in the righteousness of GOD. The sacrifice that YOUR SON made gives me that right. Depression, guilt, and fear shall no longer overwhelm me. I am fearless in grace.

Let it be written, let it be done. Amen and amen.

Love,
Patrick

THE AUTHOR'S THOUGHTS

I AM SO grateful that I did not allow fear of criticism and rejection as well as the worry of backlash and personal confusion to prevent me from starting and completing this rewarding project. I truly believe that this body of work continues a much-needed discussion of a serious taboo subject, not just in the Black Church and in the Black community but also in mainstream America. Although mainstream America briefly became aware of this major unspoken issue in the Black community several years ago, this serious widespread issue still needs much more in-depth dialogue. It is my hope that this novel will initiate many more conversations that will at least motivate others to respect the diversity of others. It is also my greatest hope that effective communication will begin to change the minds of others and eventually change the behavior of others.

I wanted to write about a subject dear to my heart. Too many have died thinking that no one truly loved them, especially the Black Christian Church.

So, I decided to write a "tough love letter" to the Black Christian Church, specifically to the conservative staunch non-wavering Black clergy. I also wanted to include the devoted judgmental Christians and the holier-than-thou loyal parishioners of the contemporary megachurch who have appointed themselves as judge and jury.

Although this body of work is fiction, I also wanted to get the attention of the numerous young Black men who have experienced similar life experiences and lifestyles changes mentioned in this novel. However, my intent was not to target only young male African-Americans but to focus on men in general. Whether homosexual, bi-sexual or men still in the closet or on the "DL (down low)." To those men who are confronting and struggling with their sexuality. And to the many men pressured by the Black Christian Church to "be straight" or "act straight." Men who are single, engaged, or married as well as those who are thinking about marriage with children in their future.

And lastly, in writing this novel, I wanted this book to have a broad appeal, but I did not want to be vague. I did not want to skirt around the main subject and issues. Of course, I don't have any issues with male-on-male relationships or relationships between older men and much younger men or even committed relationships between clergymen and other men. My intention was to make sure I was completely clear in discussing the issue of the hypocrisy in the contemporary African-American Christian Church regarding those who preach one thing all the while practicing something else. I purposely intended to stir up every emotion possible experienced by ostracized and criticized young men, including sadness, frustration, anger, confusion, denial, narcissism, revenge, self-defiance, self-confidence, self-assurance, self-determination, self-acceptance, and lastly a little joy and happiness.

DEAR READER,

THE LATE GREAT civil rights icon and US Congressman John R. Lewis often said, "When you see something that is not right, not fair, that is not just, you have a moral obligation to do something or at lease say something."

While the world is watching, watching a series of major issues in the African-American community, issues that have plagued America for over four hundred years, it is finally receiving its just attention. These issues include overt prejudice, systemic and institutional racism, and now televised police brutality against Blacks, specifically Black men (as well as some young Black women).

Well, another major issue within the African-American community has also caused another internal social plague for too many decades. This issue has also invoked violence within the community, destroyed families and relationships, resulted in alcoholism and drug abuse, has indirectly caused suicides, and has invoked many other destructive behaviors. Too many men, young Black men (as well as many young Black women), have been mistreated, disowned, and have been literally "thrown away" as a result of this widespread cultural epidemic. Too much unwarranted direct and indirect pain and suffering has been deliberately inflicted upon them—at the place that was once considered the primary refuge for spiritual comfort for Black people, a place of healing for the broken-hearted and spiritually injured. Many considered it to be the safest place on earth—a place of peace and solitude. However, a specific group of young Black men (and many young Black women) have been constantly chastised, ostracized, degraded, and subjected to much unfair treatment. Such harm has caused, in many cases, irreputable emotional and psychological damage.

A little over ten years ago, a major scandal rocked the contemporary African-American Christian Church community in Atlanta. For the first time, this scandal, which involved a small yet very important sector of the Black community, received much attention from mainstream America. Social media interest peaked by record numbers. The major national networks, including ABC, CBS, NBC and CNN, headlined this scandal for almost a year. However, this scandal never uncovered the deep-rooted cultural virus that developed many unhealed wounds of so many targeted and hunted young Black men (as well as many young Black women). This unavoidable yet curable virus has plagued a great number of young Black men (and many young Black women) for decades. More serious attention needs to be placed on a cure for this other major cultural disease. Because only one layer of this issue was covered by the media, I was inspired to write about a deeper layer, a more fragile layer of wounds that will never begin to heal without the start of viable discussions.

I am well aware that the subject matter of this body of work is extremely controversial. Self-consciousness of many will be realized. Self-reflection of many will be difficult to face. Those who have judged others unfairly might feel as though they, in turn, are being judged unfairly. Fragile egos will be rattled, and in some cases some overinflated egos will be shattered. However, I am well prepared for the potential backlash. That's what "good trouble" is all about.

Instead of the continued toxic patterns of fight, flight, or freeze that most experience as a result of conflict, my hope is that this novel will create a safe space for at least the start of a mutually civil, respectful discussion—a discussion that will one day lead to change. Broken silence. Let the dialogue begin.

Broken Silence

Silence refers to not hearing.
Not hearing refers to not being told.
They were not told the truth.
Not being told the truth refers to not knowing.
They did not know.
They needed to know
The truth;
The whole truth and nothing but the truth.

The silence was deafening.
The silence was killing me.
Killing my spirit.
At last, the silence is broken.
So now that it has been written,
So, let it be done.

Let the discussions begin.

ABOUT THE AUTHOR

 TRISTEN A. TAYLOR'S riveting tale of the *unmentionable* is told in Dexter Cavanaugh's brutally honest, uncompromising, antagonistic, defensive, dead-on voice, which brings to public light a hush-hush and forbidden subject in the African-American Christian Church. *The Silent Fraternity* provokes the previously quiet and intentionally ignored eight-hundred-pound gorilla to beat his chest. Finally, a bright light is shed on the big pink elephant in the room, or should we say, in the main sanctuary. Taylor stirs up every emotion and behavior, including sadness, frustration, anger, denial, narcissism, revenge, self-defiance, self-confidence, self-assurance, self-acceptance, and lastly a little joy and happiness.

Tristen A. Taylor is an author based in Atlanta, Georgia. For many years, he has also served as a certified and licensed senior consultant. Until recently, Taylor kept his passion for writing a life secret, not even telling his family and closest friends. The silence finally has been broken. His passion finally has become a reality. He is currently continuing his lifetime passion of writing novels about serious thought-provoking issues as he is working on the second novel of *The Silent* trilogy.

CPSIA information can be obtained
at www.ICGtesting.com
Printed in the USA
LVHW040019290123
738154LV00010B/81/J